YOU WERE NEVER HERE

Other books by
KATHLEEN PEACOCK:

Hemlock
Thornhill
Willowgrove

YOU
WERE
NEVER
HERE

KATHLEEN PEACOCK

HARPER TEEN
An Imprint of HarperCollinsPublishers

HarperTeen is an imprint of HarperCollins Publishers.

Library of Congress Cataloging-in-Publication Data

Names: Peacock, Kathleen, author.
Title: You were never here / Kathleen Peacock.
Description: First edition. | New York, NY : HarperTeen, [2020] | Audience: Ages 13 up. | Audience: Grades 10-12. | Summary: "Cat sets out to discover what happened to her childhood friend when she discovers that he's been missing for months"— Provided by publisher.
Identifiers: LCCN 2020000850 | ISBN 9780063002517 (hardcover)
Subjects: CYAC: Missing persons—Fiction. | Friendship—Fiction. | Psychic ability—Fiction. | Canada—Fiction. | Mystery and detective stories.
Classification: LCC PZ7.P31172 You 2020 | DDC [Fic]—dc23
LC record available at https://lccn.loc.gov/2020000850

Typography by Chris Kwon
20 21 22 23 24 PC/LSCH 10 9 8 7 6 5 4 3 2 1
❖
First Edition

To Judy and Bill and long summers filled with books

PROLOGUE

FOR WEEKS AFTER THE DAY RILEY FRASER DISAPPEARED—A cold Saturday in March that seemed ordinary in every other way—people thought he would come back.

It's not that bad things never happened in Montgomery Falls. There was the schoolteacher who poisoned her husband with arsenic in 1919 and the textile mill fire of '44—the one that killed thirteen men. There was the man who died on the old rail bridge and the university student who went for a walk five years ago and never came back—the one a group of kids found near the spot where chimney swifts nest in the thousands.

But those things were few and far between, spread far enough apart that they didn't threaten the town's reputation as good and safe.

When bad things did happen, they certainly didn't happen to boys like Riley; they didn't happen to boys who shone so bright the whole town waited to see what their futures held.

And so Montgomery Falls rallied.

There were search parties and flyers.

Announcements and pleas for information.

There were public meetings and Facebook groups and vigils as Riley's father flew in from Toronto and offered a reward so large that Riley's face was on the national news.

But as the days stretched out, as the river rose with snowmelt and swelled up past its banks, the rumors started.

What if Riley Fraser wasn't as perfect as he seemed?

Maybe he had gotten a girl into trouble. In fact, hadn't something happened just before he disappeared—some sort of incident at a party?

Maybe he was still upset about his parents' divorce—a split so contentious that it had been the talk of Montgomery Falls for over a year. Everyone knew Riley went a little wild after his father left. Everybody said that the divorce was proof that no matter how much money you had—and some people claimed the Frasers could buy and sell half the town if they wanted to—there were some things you couldn't fix.

Wasn't Riley one of the kids who found that university student up by the mill a few years ago? Riley and his brother and that Montgomery girl from New York. What if something like that changed you? Wormed its way in and hollowed you out.

And if all of that wasn't enough, plenty of people remembered what Riley had been like when his family first moved to town. Quiet and skinny and just a bit odd. A far cry from the charismatic, popular boy who went for a walk in the woods one day and didn't come back.

It didn't take Riley's mother long to stop leaving the house. It took even less time for his father to fly back to his new life in Toronto, leaving Riley's brother—two years older and as dark as Riley was golden—to drop out of college and move home.

More than 900 miles away, I knew none of this.

I hadn't spoken to Riley Fraser since the summer I turned twelve. Not since the day he kissed me—a first kiss that tasted like lucky pennies and grape bubble gum—on the old swing on my aunt's front porch. Not since the day he figured out what I really am.

I didn't know Riley was missing or that his photo was on posters from the border of Maine to the edge of the Atlantic Ocean.

Even if I had known, there wouldn't have been anything I could have done.

More than 900 miles away, my own world was crumbling.

Now, of course, it's different.

Ask me where I was when Riley Fraser disappeared.

I can't tell you.

I don't know where I was.

Or what I was doing.

Or who I was with.

But ask me what happened to Riley Fraser—ask me that, and I'll tell you everything.

ONE

BAD GIRLS GO TO NEW YORK. I SAW THAT ON A T-SHIRT once. I had been wandering around a street fair with Lacey when she spotted it on a vendor's cart. She reached past me, careful not to let her arm brush mine, lifted the shirt, and then held it up to her chest. The guy behind the table tried to convince her that purple was her color, that the shirt looked so great against her skin that he'd practically give it away—as long as she took his number at the same time.

Things like that are always happening to Lacey.

"Aren't you the one who's usually giving it away?" I asked, rolling my eyes skyward as I tried to bring her down a peg or two.

"Jealous?" she retorted.

"Not even a little."

It was fine if she saw through the lie. For someone who seems to have everything and has always been able to tell people exactly what she wants, Lacey may be the most insecure person I've ever met. My jealousy reminds her that she's doing okay, that things are on track, that people want to be her even if she desperately wants to be someone else.

If Lacey's life were a movie, I'd be the plucky sidekick. The short, fat redhead who provides comic relief and moral support without ever stealing the scenes. The one always standing just a little bit behind her in Instagram pics.

And that suits me just fine.

At least it had. Back when it seemed like there was safety in Lacey's shadow, when being near someone with a personality that big allowed me to be part of things without ever drawing too much attention to myself.

Before it had all backfired and my entire life blew up.

From where I'm sitting right now—eight rows back on a bus that smells like week-old pizza and dirty socks—that T-shirt had gotten it wrong: Bad girls don't go to New York. Bad girls get put on a Greyhound back to a place they'd rather forget.

The bus slows and pulls into a gas station with peeling paint and a hand-lettered sign advertising live bait. *Stop forty-three*, I think as a trickle of people climb aboard and search for spots.

Up until now, I've been lucky: I scored a pair of seats at the start and somehow—possibly through a combination of guarded posture, prayer, and the sound of the Violent Femmes blaring from my earbuds—have managed to hold them for the first ten hours of the trip.

But luck deserts me as a plump woman with gray hair stops in the middle of the aisle and shoots me a friendly smile. The scent of vanilla wafts from her like perfume as she glances from my face to the backpack on the empty seat next to me.

When I don't immediately make room, the friendly smile slips a notch. It doesn't disappear completely, though, and she doesn't keep walking.

I hesitate a second longer before pulling my bag onto my lap. As the woman lowers herself next to me, I tug the sleeves of my shirt down as far as they'll go and then hunch in on myself, trying to make my body as small as possible. Lacey calls it my "subway slump." Also good for crowded shopping malls, the hallway between classes, and apparently, the bus from New York to Canada.

But there's only so much you can do when you're big. You can twist and contort all you want, but volume is volume, and with both of us fat—"overweight," my dad always corrects, as if that somehow sounds better—a trickle of sweat forms where our hips press against each other.

Before long, my shoulders start to ache from the effort of holding my torso as still as a statue, and eventually, the distance between New York and where I am now—not to mention all of the hours and weeks it took to get to this point—catches up with me. I slip a little farther down in my seat, and as the bus makes its way across Maine, my eyelids get heavy and then heavier.

Eventually, I close my eyes. I close my eyes and pull in a deep breath and—

Water rushes up my nose and down my throat, filling my lungs.

My eyes fly open as pressure rips through my chest. I gasp and struggle as someone tries to hold me under. Fingers dig into my arms. Whoever it is, they're stronger than I am. I manage to break free just long enough to glimpse a wide face and gray hair and catch a handful of words—"I'll show you. You're not laughing now"—before I'm forced back down.

I'm forced back down and I can't breathe and I can't break free. I can't break free and . . .

Everything shatters, and I'm left struggling for air in an unfamiliar place.

The bus, I realize as I press a hand to my chest. *I'm on the bus.* Even though the sensation of being unable to breathe was only in my mind, my lungs ache and my heart races.

"Are you all right?" The woman in the seat next to me has a hand on my shoulder. Her fingers must have skimmed the exposed skin at the collar of my shirt; they are, in fact, perilously close to touching skin right now. "We're almost at the border. I thought I should wake you."

Outside, the rushing landscape slows and then spins as we make the turn for the border crossing.

The woman's face knots with concern as she removes her hand. She glances toward the front of the bus, wondering, maybe, if she should call out to the driver.

Other people twist in their seats to see if anything interesting is happening, but they barely register. I stare at the woman, trying to reconcile the concern on her face with the sensation of being held underwater. I force myself to nod, to tell her I'm fine, to play the whole thing off as a nightmare as the bus comes to a stop.

She doesn't look convinced, but she gathers up her things and disembarks with everyone else. Determined to put as much distance between us as possible, I linger for a few minutes before stepping off the air-conditioned bus and into the summer heat. Shouldering my bag, I head to the small customs building at the edge of the parking lot.

A faint but steady ache begins to chip at my temples as I slip through the door and take my place at the end of the line.

As people inch forward, I can't help but think that what just happened is some sort of omen and that maybe it's not too late to sabotage my father's plans and head home.

It wouldn't even be that hard.

All I would have to do is step out of the line. Head to the bathroom and shred the documents Dad's lawyer drew up. Flush the pieces down the toilet like contraband. They can't let me cross without those papers—no matter what destination is printed on my ticket. They won't let me cross, and I'll use half of the money in my bag to get myself home.

Between problems with his publisher and his upcoming trip to California, Dad might not even realize I'm back. Not right away.

Of course, it's not like my father is the only one in New York I have to worry about. As much as this trip feels like a punishment, there might be a tiny part of me that's almost relieved to have an escape.

A very, very tiny part, but a part of me nonetheless.

And so I stay in line until I reach the front and then hand the letter and my passport over to a customs agent whose open, friendly expression practically screams, *Welcome to Canada!* He asks to see my bus ticket. "Mary Catherine Montgomery on her way to Montgomery Falls? A girl who has a whole town named after her."

I force myself to smile. It feels tight around the edges. "Coincidence," I lie.

"New York," he says, still scanning the ticket. "Hell of a bus trip. You know you can fly into Bangor or Saint John and then just take the bus from there?"

"Yeah," I say dryly, "I've heard that." My father claimed the bus would be an adventure. Like being Jack Kerouac or Paul Simon. I didn't bother telling him that I had only the faintest idea who he was talking about. Personally, I think his choice was motivated less by the romanticism of traveling America by road and more by the idea of saving a few hundred bucks on the ticket. Dad's last two books were critical and commercial flops, and he hasn't sold a screenplay in years. Things have been tight for a while—not that we ever directly talk about it.

The agent hands everything back. "Someone meeting you at the station?"

"My aunt." It's all in the letter, but he nods as though me saying those two words makes some sort of difference and tells me to enjoy Canada.

I buy a bottle of Coke in the duty-free shop and then wander back toward the bus, pausing in front of a bulletin board to take a drink. The headache is still dancing around my skull, but it's not nearly bad enough for me to reach for the pills in my backpack. On the scale of one-to-awful, it's a four at most.

My eyes trail idly over the brightly colored flyers on the board next to me. A hardware store on the US side that will hold parcels for Canadians. Reminders that plants aren't supposed to be taken across the border. Ads for whale-watching tours along the coast and antique sales up and down the valley. Ordinary, forgettable stuff. But in among the other notices, partly covered by a plea for the return of a lost engagement ring, is a missing poster.

The word "missing" by itself wouldn't be enough to hold my attention. Not really. It's the name underneath that wraps itself around me and pins me to the spot.

Riley Fraser.

It has to be a coincidence, I think. *There have to be about a thousand Riley Frasers in the world.* But I still find myself reaching out and peeling away the flyer for the lost ring to reveal a black-and-white yearbook photo.

The boy in the picture is handsome. Chiseled jaw and wavy hair kind of handsome. The kind of handsome that gets crowned prom king or maybe class president. Even though the smile on the boy's face looks forced around the edges, it's wide enough to bring out the dimple in his left cheek.

A dimple isn't proof, but there are other hints. Planes and angles around the eyes and the mouth. Echoes of a boy I used to know. The boy I've spent years trying not to think about.

There are a thousand Riley Frasers in the world, and the boy on the poster is mine.

TWO

THERE'S A MOMENT, WHEN THE BUS CROSSES THAT IMAGI-
nary line between the US and Canada, that I catch myself
listening for the second something changes. It's a thing Dad used
to do on our infrequent trips back to his mother country. "Do you
hear it?" he'd ask as the car rolled toward the place where America ended and something else began. He swore there was a sound
when you crossed, one you could hear if you really tried.

According to my father, hearing that sound was about a thousand times better than any lucky penny you could find. Hear that
sound and you'd better make a wish.

For someone who doesn't believe in magic, he talks a good
game.

At six, I had tried so hard I gave myself a headache and threw
up thirty paces over the border. At nine, I had been suspicious,
but unwilling to completely discount the idea. Now, at seventeen,

I know it's bullshit, but I still find myself closing my eyes and holding my breath.

Because even though it was only ever just one of my father's stories, I could use a wish or two.

But as hard as I listen, I can't hear that moment any more now than I could when I was six, and when I close my eyes, I see the missing poster—Riley's missing poster—and my head fills with questions. The date on the poster—the date Riley vanished—was March 19. Three months ago.

I rest my forehead against the window as the bus slows for the turnoff into Montgomery Falls. I can see my reflection in the glass—chubby cheeks, frizzy red hair, a nose that turns up just a little at the end—but this close, my face becomes just a collection of shapes and colors.

I tell myself that anything could have happened in three months. Three months ago, my life was completely different, and it's definitely more than enough time for Riley to have turned up. He's probably fine. If he wasn't, Aunt Jet would have called. It doesn't matter how strained things are between her and Dad or how scattered she can be. It doesn't even matter that it's been years since Riley's name has crossed my lips. If Riley had been missing for any real amount of time, Jet would have called.

People put up posters and forget about them all the time. It's just an old, forgotten poster.

The bus passes a strip mall and a succession of fast-food places and then rumbles across the river—a wide blue ribbon that winds through the lowland between two ridges of rolling green hills.

The whole thing looks like a postcard. Even the rusting, abandoned train bridge and the ruins of the old textile mill—a jumble of bricks just visible in the distance—look picturesque. If you don't know any better.

Two red lights and three turns later, we pull into the bus station—although calling anything so tiny a "station" might be giving it too much credit. Three other people disembark and are quickly scooped up by waiting friends and family. There are hugs and greetings. Suitcases tossed into the backs of waiting cars.

The driver pulls my duffel bag out from the luggage compartment and hands it over. I take it as I scan the parking lot. No rust-pimpled Buick and no Aunt Jet. I linger next to the bus for a moment, uncertain, and then head for a patch of shade next to the station.

I know Dad called Jet two nights ago to remind her—among other things—what time the bus would get in, but I overhear a passerby say that it's 5:45 p.m. The bus isn't early; it's fifteen minutes late.

If Dad hadn't confiscated my phone, I could call Jet, but my phone—at least what's left of it—along with my laptop, is currently locked in the bottom drawer of the filing cabinet in his study. Right where they've been for the past two weeks.

Supposedly, this is not a punishment.

Supposedly, this is for my own good.

Supposedly, ignorance is bliss and a little space will be healthy. That's what my father claimed the night I'd gotten upset enough to throw my iPhone across the room—something that would have gone completely unnoticed if my aim had been just a little bit better. Pro tip: If you're going to throw an iPhone, make sure you don't accidentally throw it at your closed bedroom window. And if you are stupid enough to throw it at your closed bedroom window, don't tell your father the reason.

A woman with a too-tight perm and thick glasses appears in the station doorway. "You waiting for someone, sweetheart?"

"My aunt."

"Have you tried calling her?"

I shrug. "Can't find my phone."

"Do you want to call her? There's a pay phone inside, but you can use the phone in the office." As she speaks, I notice a missing poster taped next to the door—identical to the one I had seen at the border.

My stomach twists. Sure, a poster at the border could easily be forgotten, but if Riley had been found, wouldn't they have taken down the posters around town?

I open my mouth to ask, but the woman is summoned back inside before I get the chance.

Ten minutes later—ten long minutes of trying not to stare at the poster, of trying not to think of what it might mean while reminding myself that Riley Fraser isn't someone I'm supposed to care about—I have to accept that Aunt Jet isn't coming.

I could take the woman up on her offer of the phone, but it's not like my bags are that heavy, and the house isn't all that far.

I adjust my backpack and my grip on my duffel bag and start walking.

It's been five years since my last visit to Montgomery Falls, and as I make my way through the small downtown core, I try to catalog the differences between present and past. There are more empty storefronts than I remember, but the art store is still here, as are the town's two bookstores—one Catholic and one not. The record store is dark and has a For Rent sign in its window. That hurts: the record store was one of the few things I was actually looking forward to. Lacey claims I'm a nostalgia nerd, and maybe she's right because I love old things. Especially if they're music related. Bands, posters, records—my room is filled with flea market and thrift store finds. Once, Lacey caught me smelling one of her father's albums—he has a seriously impressive collection—and called me a "vinyl sniffer," like it was something perverse.

I guess there won't be any vinyl sniffing in my near future. It's like I've literally gone to the place where music died.

At least the movie theater is still open—though it has just two screens. One is playing a horror flick, the other a romantic comedy. A girl sits in the glass booth at the front of the building, chin resting in her hands.

My steps falter in front of another missing poster. Rain and wind have torn the paper and left Riley's face smudged, but it's a word scrawled in red marker that makes me stop.

Cocksucker.

The letter *s* snakes around a rough drawing of something that is clearly supposed to be a part of the male anatomy.

I spot another poster, yards off. Even at a distance, I can make out strokes of red.

Something takes hold, and before I completely realize what I'm doing, I reach out and yank the first poster down. Maybe it's lingering childhood loyalty—a few last dregs that haven't, for some inexplicable reason, completely faded. Maybe it's just that I hate the way the word is scrawled: ugly red letters that make it clear that whoever wrote it was stupid enough to think it was something bad. Maybe it's simply that I've had so many insults of every kind thrown my way over the past few months. Whatever the reason, I crumple up the poster and shove it into my bag.

When I glance up, the girl in the ticket booth is staring at me. I walk away, cheeks burning.

I know I don't owe Riley Fraser anything—not after the last things he said to me—but I still rip down the other poster.

"Wait!"

I keep walking.

"Hey!" A hand falls on my shoulder, forcing me to turn.

I'm short, but the girl from the theater is pint-sized. Up close, she looks like she stepped out of some gothy comic book. Her long dark hair is pulled into two pigtails, black liner sweeps over her eyelids in wings, and a thin velvet ribbon has been looped around her neck and tied into a sloppy bow. Her pink uniform is adorned with buttons that look innocuous on first glance but say things like *M Is for Monster* or have pictures of Bela Lugosi or creepy girls climbing out of wells.

Loser, says a voice in the back of my head—a voice that sounds a lot like Lacey. Or, at least, the way Lacey has started to sound over the past year.

Having successfully stopped me, the girl seems weirdly at a loss for words. She rocks back on her heels and swallows before finally saying, "They'll just do it again. The poster in your bag? The one in your hand? More will go up, and someone else will come along and write on them."

More will go up.

Even though I was already sure that Riley must still be missing, I find myself gripping the crumpled poster a little more tightly. "They?"

The girl stares at me, blankly.

"You said 'They'll just do it again.' Who? Who's they?" I guess those dregs of loyalty really do exist because there's a harsh edge to my voice that I can't otherwise explain.

"Just . . . people. People from school."

"So they what? Go around trashing someone who's missing and everyone's fine with that?"

"Someone who's . . . ?" Confusion fills her eyes and then shifts to something else as a blush creeps across her cheeks. "You thought they were saying Riley was . . . that he . . ." She shakes her head. "They write on the posters around the movie theater because I work there. So that I'll see them. They mean the word for me."

She stands in front of me, small and dark, and as her blush bleeds away, she raises her chin a tiny fraction of an inch.

There's something in that tiny fraction that I almost envy. She doesn't apologize for the word or what other people say. She stands there, chin raised, like it doesn't matter what they—or I—think.

And it doesn't. Or at least it shouldn't.

17

Whether it's true or not, that word—and what it represents—shouldn't be an insult.

A deep male shout comes from the direction of the theater, breaking the moment. "Skylar—there are customers!"

When she doesn't immediately move, the voice booms out, again. "Skylar! Customers!"

She turns and runs, pigtails bouncing, and I'm left alone, holding a ruined poster.

THREE

AUNT JET CATCHES UP WITH ME A FEW STREETS LATER. BY
that time, I've counted eleven other posters, none of them defaced.
Some have ribbons or homemade cards pinned beneath them. One
sits above a small stuffed lion—the local high school's mascot. I'm
standing there, staring at that silly lion, when Aunt Jet pulls her
whale of a car up to the curb.

She leans across the passenger seat and pushes open the door.
"I'm so sorry, Mary Catherine," she says. "I told them I had to
leave at five, but they're so short-staffed, and I just couldn't . . ."
She cuts herself off and shakes her head as she looks at me, eyes
wide. "Wow. You look so much older. So grown up."

Between social media and the occasional video chat on birth-
days and holidays, my appearance really shouldn't be that much
of a surprise, but maybe there are some things that pictures and
video can't capture, because as I stand there on the curb, I can't
help but notice how much older Aunt Jet looks herself. She and

Dad are twins—born thirteen minutes and three seconds apart—but you'd never guess it. Dad looks young for his age. In fact, few people realize he's old enough to be my father. Aunt Jet, on the other hand, has streaks of gray in her long red hair, and there are faint lines around her mouth and at the corners of her eyes. Lines I don't remember seeing when I last visited. She's still beautiful, though. If possible, the lines and hints of gray actually make her more so.

I don't make any move to get into the car, and Jet's gaze slides to the poster behind me. Her thin shoulders rise and then fall as she lets out a deep breath. "I was going to tell you."

"When?"

A woman with a stroller waves to my aunt as she walks past. As her gaze shifts to me, it fills with barely suppressed curiosity.

I debate walking away, but I don't exactly love the idea of people in town talking about my poor aunt and her difficult American niece. I've had enough people talking about me over the past few months to last a lifetime.

With a sigh, I toss my bags into the back of the Buick and then climb into the passenger seat.

Despite the heat, my aunt is wearing a sweater over a pair of burgundy-colored scrubs: her unofficial uniform as a personal care assistant at one of the local nursing homes. It's broiling inside the car, and I can feel my own clothes sticking to me in seconds, but she doesn't put the air-conditioning on. Given how old the car is, I'm not sure the air-conditioning even works.

I stare at her expectantly, waiting for an answer.

"Your father and I talked about it," she says as she signals and pulls away from the curb. "We thought it would be better to wait and see what happened before telling you."

"You mean he thought." It really shouldn't surprise me. My father doesn't like things that are unexpected or unpleasant. Things that are unexpected or unpleasant tend to distract him from his work. Which is, I suspect, one of the reasons I've been sent here for the summer.

Aunt Jet flexes her hands around the steering wheel. She's always hated confrontations. Big ones, little ones, ones that exist only in her head—they all set her on edge. Silence fills the car, heavy and awkward. "It wasn't just your father," she says finally. "There are things he'd rather I not talk to you about, but holding off on telling you about Riley was a decision we made months ago, together."

"Okay, but you've known I was coming for the past two weeks. Didn't you think I'd see the posters when I got here?"

Her cheeks flush. "We were wrong—I was wrong—and I'm sorry."

"What other things doesn't Dad want you talking to me about?" I ask as the other part of what she said sinks in.

The look Aunt Jet shoots me makes it clear she thinks I should already know the answer to that. And I do, actually. I was just curious about what she would say. "No talking about the family legacy," I say, imitating the crisp, slightly fake-sounding voice my father uses in interviews. "No filling my daughter's head with nonsense about old houses and strange gifts."

Aunt Jet shoots me a small, tight smile. "Something like that."

So, basically, the same stuff my dad has been fighting with

Aunt Jet about since I was twelve.

"The posters say Riley's been missing since March." A little of the anger creeps back into my voice; I can't help it.

Aunt Jet loosens her grip on the wheel and then reaches out to touch my hand. I pull away before she can make contact. I want to stay angry—I have a right to be angry—and people have a very hard time staying angry when my aunt touches them.

Jet places her hand back on the wheel. "They think he got lost in the woods outside of town. He went walking there a lot, apparently. There was a late snowstorm the day he went missing. It made searching hard."

"That doesn't make any sense." I shake my head, recalling how fascinated Riley had been with the forest around Montgomery Falls the summer we spent together, how much time he had spent trying to map them. "Riley knew those woods. Really well."

"You've never been out there in the winter," says Aunt Jet, not ungently. "Things look different. It gets dark early and stays dark until late, and the snow plays tricks on people. Even without getting caught in a storm, it would have been easy to get disoriented. And there aren't that many cell towers outside of town. You'd be surprised how spotty coverage gets."

I guess it's a fair point. Montgomery Falls really is a tiny speck in the middle of a whole lot of nothing. Even when Riley used to drag me out on hikes, we'd lose service if we ventured too near the logging roads or went the wrong way.

And once you're past the logging roads, well, then it's just open wilderness for hundreds of miles.

"Noah's been back since it happened," Aunt Jet says.

Noah. Riley's big brother. He's two years older, so I guess that means he was away at college. Probably the Canadian equivalent of an Ivy League school given how smart he's always been.

Jet launches into awkward small talk. I don't exactly tune her out on purpose, but my thoughts keep distracting me. All I can manage are monosyllabic responses, and after a few minutes, I can't even keep those up.

It wasn't just topography Riley was obsessed with that summer. He was fascinated by the things people lost among the trees. Discarded soda bottles. Old tires. Pennies and pocketknives. Broken axes and rusting bits of equipment near the logging roads. He almost never touched the things we found; he just recorded them in a small, black notebook.

The Book of Lost Things—that's what I called it. His parents had another name for it. He had been diagnosed with obsessive-compulsive disorder a few months before moving to Montgomery Falls, and they worried the time he spent in the woods was unhealthy, that it was tied to his OCD.

Maybe it was and maybe it wasn't.

I don't know. I don't know if Riley knew.

They fought about it sometimes, he and his parents. They fought about the amount of time we spent out there. Hours and days and weeks—if you added it all up. Lost time spent exploring lost paths and examining lost objects.

How could someone who had been so fascinated with lost things step into the woods and become lost himself?

It takes Aunt Jet pointing out a new sign—the words "Montgomery House: Vacancy" set in neat black letters against an off-white background—to pull me out of my thoughts. If she hadn't spoken, I might not have realized that we had turned off the street. I might not even have realized we were driving up the long crescent that leads to the house she and Dad grew up in.

"The historical society tried to make me take it down," she says, speaking of the sign, "but I did a head count of all the plastic flamingos in the neighborhood. And I asked one of the boys in the house to take photographs of the new basketball hoop the president of the society attached to the carriage house at the end of his driveway."

Riverside Avenue is a street that's been undergoing an identity war for decades. Back when the town was at the center of a small industrial boom, the rich built their homes here, but as industries folded and fortunes dried up, the houses sat empty. At one end of the street stand rambling Victorians that have been restored to their former glory by new owners, and at the other are houses that have been drawn and quartered into apartments, their manicured lawns paved over and their iron gates taken off the hinges. Spanning the gulf between the two factions are places like Aunt Jet's.

A year ago, Jet renovated and started renting out rooms to supplement what she makes at the nursing home. She's hardly alone. The university is one of the few industries in town that's still booming, and people have turned making money off of students into an art form. People say that half the mortgages in town are paid for by undergrads renting rooms in basements or attics. Without the university and the military base forty minutes away, Montgomery Falls would probably be a ghost town.

If Jet had been renovating almost any other building,

no one would have cared. But it was Montgomery House. Home of the founding family. One of the oldest structures in town. The historical society had not been happy with the changes my aunt had made; my father had been even less so.

Dad and Aunt Jet both left Montgomery Falls right after high school, but when their mother—my grandmother—got sick, Jet came back. She gave up her studies, a fiancé, and her whole life so that she could take care of things here. She was twenty-one.

My grandmother hung on for fourteen years. More than long enough for Jet's old life to have passed her by while my dad finished school, met my mother, and started his career. In a way, Jet giving up those fourteen years made it possible for my father to have the life he wanted, away from the town he had always been desperate to escape.

That much guilt and resentment between them makes things . . . complicated.

In the end, all Jet had was an old house and a fickle-tempered black cat named Brisby. Five years ago, Dad tried to get her to sell Montgomery House. He said it wasn't healthy, the way she clung to it. He said it was foolish not to try to get as much as they could while the waterfront property was still worth something. He was thinking of the both of them, he claimed. He wasn't being selfish. He was thinking about her.

He had been charming. He had been persuasive.

His pleas had absolutely nothing to do with the fact that he— or, I guess, we—were having money problems. Nothing at all.

Aunt Jet refused.

Montgomery House is one of the two reasons my aunt and

father have barely spoken in the past five years. I'm the other.

"Most of the university students have left for the summer, so it's quiet," says Jet as she parks in two deep ruts in the lawn. "We only have three guests until September. You'll barely notice anyone is here, and hardly anything's changed."

Living with three complete strangers doesn't sound like the kind of thing you barely notice, but I don't say so as I slide out of the car and grab my bags.

Aunt Jet heads straight for the porch, but I stay where I am for a moment, staring up at the house.

People in town say the place is haunted, and it's not hard to see why. Between its peeling gray exterior and its peaked slate roof, it's a sprawling shadow caught between the green yard and the river. By some trick of the light, the windows always look flat and black during the day—like the house has dozens of eyes that are constantly watching you.

Inside, it's filled with dark corners and hidden nooks and the smell of old leather and books. It creaks and groans at night, and you can hear the old pipes rattle in the walls at odd hours.

Maybe some people would call it creepy—Riley used to say it made his spine itch—but it's never really felt that way to me. To me, it just feels . . . *right*.

It feels right and I've missed it.

"Hello," I whisper.

The house doesn't whisper back, but I imagine there's some tiny, imperceptible shift. The shaking of a shutter in the breeze or the shifting of a shadow as I follow Aunt Jet up the porch steps.

She pauses and turns, one hand on the doorknob as she

examines me with a small, worried frown. "You didn't pack much," she says, nodding toward my bag.

She's not wrong. The duffel bag is big, but it's not that big. A week's worth of clothes, plus a couple of extra T-shirts. A mostly blank notebook, a charger for the ancient iPod I was allowed to bring, and Pengy—an uninventively named stuffed penguin that I definitely don't need but felt wrong leaving behind.

Until Dad actually put me on the bus, I was sure he was bluffing, so I hadn't exactly put a lot of effort into packing. Not that I want to get into that with Aunt Jet. As far as I know, Dad's given her only the CliffsNotes version of what happened back in New York—just enough to explain why I'm not allowed my cell phone or laptop or to call Lacey, probably—and that's fine with me. The less Aunt Jet knows, the less she'll prod me to talk about it. "The backpack is pretty full, too."

She doesn't look convinced, but she lets it drop.

Just before following Jet inside, I glance at the house next door. A tall hedge borders the property, obscuring everything but the top two floors. Despite all the time that's passed, my eyes go straight to the second floor, to the second window on the left.

Riley's window.

Aunt Jet is wrong: Montgomery House has changed in what feels like a hundred different ways. Some changes—like how the shelves in the cupboards and fridge are all labeled with people's names or how the formal parlor has been transformed into a common area with a TV and mismatched sofas—would be impossible to miss; others—like the absence of a particular antique or painting—are so small that I find myself questioning my memory.

Despite all the changes, my room is still the same. Even though I've never lived in Montgomery House for more than a few months over various summers, the third bedroom on the second floor has always been mine. When Aunt Jet renovated, she left this room exactly as it was.

"You haven't changed, either," I murmur as Brisby—fat and fickle as ever—follows me inside. He nips my ankle and then promptly claims the bed.

Being in here is like being in a time warp. The bookcase is crammed full of paperbacks about magic boarding schools and faeries and little orphan girls with hair every bit as red as my own, the bedspread is the kind of pink floral monstrosity I loved when I was twelve, and my dad's antique typewriter—an old Olympia he dragged down from the attic as a teen—is still on the desk.

A mobile of the solar system hangs from the ceiling. Riley and I made it from a kit. We both wanted it, but he insisted I take it home.

He was always like that. Kind. Until the day he wasn't.

Brisby hops down and darts under the bed just as the door opens. I turn, expecting Jet, but a strange guy stands on the threshold.

Correction: a gorgeous strange guy stands on the threshold.

"Sorry," he says, "I didn't realize anyone was here." There's a soft edge to his words. An accent I can't quite place. "So, are you in need of medical supplies, or are you just into Swedish folk music?"

"Huh?" It takes me a second to realize he's talking about my shirt. I can count on one hand the number of people I know who have heard of First Aid Kit, let alone who know what country they're from.

He glances at the bags on the floor and then back at me. He's so tall that I have to look up to meet his gray gaze. "You must be the niece. Mary Catherine, right?"

He lifts his hand. For a horrible second, I think he expects me to shake it, but he just smiles and runs it through his sandy-colored hair.

"Cat," I correct. "Only my dad and aunt call me Mary Catherine."

"Cat." He says my name slowly, rolling it over his tongue like it's a flavor he's trying out. "I'm Aidan. Aidan Porter." He nods toward the desk. "I was wondering if I could borrow that."

I glance over my shoulder and then back at him. "The typewriter?"

"The typewriter."

"Why?"

"Why not?"

Other than it's not the 1970s, I don't actually have a counter-argument. Besides, it's not like I'm planning on using the thing. I walk to the desk and lift the Olympia. It's heavier than it looks, and I stumble as I turn back to him.

"Whoa." He takes two long strides into the room and lifts the typewriter from my shaking arms before I drop it. As he does, I notice that his feet are bare. *He has nice toes*, I think, which is a ridiculous thing to notice.

"Thanks." I feel a blush creep over my cheeks and down my

neck. Unlike me, Aidan has no problem holding the typewriter, even though the thing must weigh forty pounds.

He turns and heads for the door, then pauses and glances back. "I don't suppose I can borrow paper, too?" He raises one eyebrow in a manner that's either charming or arrogant—I have a feeling I would have to know him better to figure out where the two diverge or overlap—and then turns and walks down the hall, just trusting that I'll follow.

Telling myself I'm only trailing after him because I don't have anything better to do, I grab a stack of paper from the top desk drawer and then follow him to a room at the very back of the house. It's the room my dad always wrote in whenever we came to visit because it has the best view of the river.

The last time I was in this room, it was filled with sturdy antiques. Now it's host to the kind of cheap white furniture that you buy in boxes and assemble at home. There's a sleek flat-screen in the corner, but underneath it sits a huge, hulking machine and a stack of those big black tapes people used before DVD and Blu-ray. VHS tapes. I may have a room full of vinyl back home, but even my love of vintage has its limits.

Aidan sets the typewriter down next to a laptop while I hover a few steps over the threshold, clutching the paper, unsure what to do. "You know you need more than just paper, right? It takes these things called ribbons." Even though my father does most of his work on his computer, he picked up an old typewriter last year. He occasionally drags it out to the dining room table, where he'll use it for a day or two until he remembers how much he likes the ability to copy and paste.

Aidan opens one of the desk drawers and pulls out a typewriter ribbon, still in its original packaging. "Google is a marvelous thing."

"Truly boundless," I concur.

"You can find out anything. For instance, did you know this house has a Wikipedia entry?"

"I did not know that." I try to keep my voice level, but inside, I'm wondering just what Aidan would find if he googled me right now.

Oblivious to my sudden discomfort, he says, "I looked up the house before I moved in. Figured anything this old might have an entry. There's a photo of your father on the porch. I think it's from one of his books."

"The picture of him in the horrible tweed jacket with the elbow patches?"

Aidan nods.

"He loves that photo." Personally, I've always thought it makes him look like a pretentious ass—which might not be that far off the mark. I love my father, but there are times when it feels like he's trying to hit every Serious Male Author stereotype in the book.

Aidan turns and leans against the wall. "I heard he's some kind of big-shot screenwriter."

I shrug. "I guess." My dad's done well—really well by Montgomery Falls standards—but of my parents, my mom is the famous one. The one who gets spreads in *Variety*. The kind of screenwriter whose name gets mentioned almost as much as directors'. Dad almost never talks about her. Not unless he has to. I usually see her once or twice a year. She takes me out for dinner sometimes, when she's in town for meetings. She's tall and thin and elegant and very, very cold. It's always weird and uncomfortable. I always feel like she's staring at me, like she's trying to figure out if some mistake had been made at the hospital.

"I found some of your father's old drafts down in the study. Pretty cool stuff."

"You're a writer?"

Aidan laughs. "Nah. I just read everything." His hair falls across his forehead, and he brushes it back distractedly. "I kind of admire it, though. The way writers get to create worlds and people. The way they can manipulate reality. It must be like playing God."

I shake my head. "My dad's ego is big, but I don't think it's that big." Then, because I really don't want to talk about my father, I say, "You go to the university?"

"Riverview High."

My gaze slides to the laptop and then over to the Olympia. "And you're cheating on your laptop with an ancient typewriter because . . . ?"

"Don't you ever just find old things interesting?" He presses one of the keys three times. *Rat-tat-tat.* "Tell me that sound isn't cool. Besides, I flunked English and have to take classes over the summer." He flashes a self-deprecating grin that somehow manages to do the exact opposite of self-deprecate. "Turns out that in order to pass a class, they expect you to actually show up. Figured typing my papers on this would make things a little more interesting. Or at least atmospheric."

Feeling slightly more comfortable, I step farther into the room, far enough to set the stack of paper down on top of a threadbare ottoman that had to have been rescued from the depths of the house. An expensive-looking camera bag sits on the floor next to it.

"So, you're still in high school but you live here?" Normally, I wouldn't ask what feels like a very personal question of someone I've known for all of five minutes, but we are virtually living together.

A low laugh slips out of his throat. It's a good laugh. It's the kind of laugh that wraps itself around you and makes your pulse jump and skip. Pretty boys should not be able to laugh like that. There should be a limit on the number of advantages one person has. "I'm an army brat," he says. "Dad got transferred to the base outside town last summer, but after seven months, they moved him again. I didn't want to go, so I stayed here. I'm a year older than everyone else because my family moved so much when I was a kid. Since I'm eighteen, it's not like there's some big issue with me being on my own."

"What about your mom?"

An expression I can't read passes over his face. "Where he goes, she goes."

"My mother's in California," I say.

"Do you see her much?"

"No." I hardly ever talk about my mom—even to Lacey, who is slightly obsessed with all of my mother's movies—and I'm not sure what compelled me to open up to a guy I've just met. Maybe it's because I know what it's like to get left behind when you don't fit into someone else's plan. Even with Dad, a lot of the time it feels like I'm something he grudgingly works around—like I'm on his list of priorities, but maybe only third or fourth down. "I'm sorry about your parents."

Aidan shrugs. "Honestly, I seem to get along with them a lot better when they're on the other side of the ocean. Besides, this place isn't so bad. And at least now there'll be someone my own age around for the summer. Back in May, when your aunt told me you'd be spending a few months here . . ."

The surprise must show on my face because he trails off mid-sentence. I swallow. "My aunt told you about me coming in May?"

He shrugs. "Around then. End of April or the start of May."

So at least six weeks.

Dad had acted like sending me here had been a spur-of-the-moment decision, like some last straw had finally split in two, but he'd been planning to off-load me on Jet for months. And Jet? Back in the car, she hadn't bothered correcting me when I said she'd known I was coming for two weeks.

Logically, it doesn't change anything—I'm still here for the same amount of time regardless of when they told me—but my chest still feels tight with anger. "I'd better go," I say awkwardly, taking a step back. "Stuff to unpack."

Aidan crosses the room before I can turn away. "Hey," he says, leaning toward me and putting a hand on the doorframe. "I don't know if I said something wrong, but if I did, I'm sorry."

There's enough room for me to squeeze past him, but only barely. Even being careful, there would be only inches between our skin, and after what happened on the bus, I'm not exactly feeling adventurous.

His brows pull together, a small crease forming between them. "Seriously, you look upset. If I did or said anything . . ."

"It's not you. You didn't say or do anything wrong." Aidan continues to stare, that tiny line still there. "It's *really* not you," I say, overcompensating and overemphasizing.

The crease disappears like it never existed. "A bunch of my friends are watching a movie tomorrow night. Calling it a 'party' probably makes it sound a lot more interesting than it is, but why don't you come?"

"You're asking me to hang out with you and your friends?"

"Yeah."

"Why?"

"So much suspicion in one so young." He presses a hand to his chest like I've mortally wounded him. "Why wouldn't I?"

"No . . . It's just . . ." I have friends back in New York. Or at least I did. Depending on who you asked, my proximity to Lacey even makes—made—me somewhat popular. But there's no Lacey here to make me look good. I'm exhausted, I smell like I've been on a bus forever, and thanks to the unexpected bombshell that Dad and Jet had my arrival planned for ages, I probably seem like Mood-Swing Girl. "You don't know me," I say, settling on the least embarrassing and/or revelatory answer I can think of.

"So, you'll come hang out with us and I'll get to know you. Besides, we're essentially going to be living together. Chances are I'll go downstairs to get a glass of milk some night and forget to wear pants. I'd like the chance to win you over before the sight of me in Transformers boxer shorts turns you off completely."

It almost sounds like he's flirting, but I'm not the girl guys flirt with. Not often, anyway. Not with Lacey around. And, honestly, it's probably better that way. But Lacey isn't here, and Aidan is staring at me, waiting for me to respond. "They make Transformers boxers?"

"Probably not," he admits, one corner of his mouth quirking up and the other following in an uneven grin as he steps back, "but think of all the insecure guys it would give hope to."

I want to say something witty and biting, but instead, I just shake my head and turn away.

As I retreat down the hall, I think insecurity is not a problem a guy like Aidan Porter has ever needed help with.

FOUR

I WAS SUPPOSED TO CALL DAD WHEN I GOT TO MONTGOM-
ery Falls—"So I know you got in safely," he'd said as he practically
pushed me onto the bus—but I don't trust myself to talk to him
without yelling, and all yelling will do is convince him that he was
right to keep things from me as long as he had.

I can't even take my anger to Jet because, as it turns out, Montgomery House being home to a bunch of strangers translates to a
distinct lack of privacy.

Each time I try to talk to her—in the kitchen or the study or
even coming out of the bathroom—someone else wanders past. A
nursing student on her way downstairs with a basket of laundry.
The man who's staying at Montgomery House until his divorce
goes through. Aidan with his pale eyes and his sandy hair and his
crooked smile.

Eventually, I give up. I slide into bed, but despite how tired I
am, I spend hours staring at the ceiling, watching the shadowy

shape of that Styrofoam solar system as it spins in the breeze from the open window. Thoughts loop through my head on repeat. Dad. Jet. Lacey.

Riley.

Riley, who I've tried so hard not to think about over the past few years.

It feels like I drift off for only a moment or two, but when I open my eyes, the room is filled with sunlight, and the alarm clock on the nightstand says it's almost noon.

The last time I slept this late, I'd had food poisoning. Dad had been in California for a meeting, and I had been staying at Lacey's.

I always stay with the Chapmans when Dad is away. *Stayed*, I guess, given that the days of sleepovers are pretty much over.

Lacey's apartment is loud and chaotic and filled with warmth. There are boisterous family dinners where her parents—both professors—dance circles around each other as they debate everything from deforestation to pop stars to how to harness reality television as a potential agent of change. There are movie marathons and cooking lessons and epic board game nights—things Lacey takes for granted because she can have them anytime she wants.

It's so different from my own home, where Dad and I maybe eat together two or three times a week before he shuts himself up in his study to work.

The night I had gotten food poisoning, Gwen, Lacey's mom, had stayed up with me for hours as I heaved my guts out.

I didn't just lose Lacey when our friendship unraveled. I lost her parents, too.

I push myself to my feet and haul wrinkled clothes from my duffel bag. There's no point in thinking about Lacey or her mom or how I'm pretty sure I miss their apartment way more than I miss my own. Once things break, you can't just put them back together. The cracks are always there. You can't go back.

Dressing quickly, I pull on jeans and an old Go-Go's concert T-shirt—one that's a little too tight but that, according to Lacey, makes my chest look fabulous. I tell myself that I'm not choosing the shirt just to see if the boy down the hall knows anything about classic girl bands or because it emphasizes certain parts of my body. That would be ridiculous.

I give the shirt a small tug, making sure it's not clinging too much, then I shove my feet into a pair of flip-flops and head downstairs.

The nursing student—I think her name is Marie—looks up from a textbook as I step into the kitchen. "Summer classes," she says. Her accent is different than Jet's. The words are longer and softer. Acadian, I think. "Your aunt says you are still in high school?"

I nod.

"Lucky."

The girl at the table can't be more than a few years older than I am—she has to remember what high school is actually like—but I just shrug noncommittally and ask if she's seen Jet.

"Basement," says Sam, the divorcé, as he wanders in to grab something from the fridge.

I head for the small staircase tucked between the refrigerator and the pantry. On the way down, I rehearse what I plan to say to Jet. Things like how she could have—*should have*—told me the truth even if Dad didn't have the guts. About how, maybe, I wouldn't have been so resistant to the thought of coming back if I had felt like I'd had any choice in the matter and if they had just been honest with me from the start.

No matter how big of a mess I had caused back home, I still deserved to have a say.

"Aunt Jet?" My voice comes out louder than I intend it to; it bounces off the walls of the cavernous basement and probably startles the mice that nest down here no matter how many traps get set.

"Back here."

Bare bulbs hang from the ceiling at regular intervals, but they don't do much to dispel the shadows. I work my way through a maze of old furniture, boxes tied with blue twine, and steamer trunks. My aunt used to raid those trunks with me when I was little, looking for costumes and treasure.

Jet looks up as I approach. Her hair is pulled back in a loose bun, and she's wearing a pair of paint-splattered overalls. A roll of masking tape circles her wrist like a bracelet, and there's a black marker poking out from her pocket.

She's managed to clear a wide patch of floor by pushing furniture and boxes off to the side. Jonathan Montgomery—the man who founded a town and named it after himself—watches disapprovingly from a nearby oil painting, his thick, dark brows pulled down into a point. The ghosts of Montgomery House aren't crazy about being disturbed.

"What are you doing?"

"I thought it might be good to clear things out a bit. We could use the extra space." Aunt Jet barely glances at me as she tries to drag the world's biggest and ugliest antique desk off to the side. After a minute of trying to make it budge, she gives up.

I step forward and peer at the desk. A piece of masking tape on the corner reads SELL in big, black letters. In fact, almost everything around me has a strip of tape attached—all reading SELL, DONATE, KEEP, or TRASH. It's like two hundred years of family history have been reduced to those four words.

"You're selling stuff?"

She passes the back of her hand over her forehead, wiping away a bit of sweat. "Mr. Jacobs agreed to come over and look at a few pieces. He runs the antique store downtown."

I mentally work out the ratio of sell to keep. The sell pile is winning. By a significant margin. "This isn't just a few pieces."

She still doesn't quite meet my eyes. "You should head back upstairs. Have you eaten? I thought it would be best to let you sleep . . . you must have been tired . . . Aidan took the car to run an errand for me, but he should be back soon. If there's something you'd like that we don't have, we can make a trip to the grocery store. Or I could run out on my own, if you'd rather stay here."

There's a nervous, apologetic note to her voice, as though not having the right kind of cereal is some kind of affront. "I don't need you to go to the store. Aunt Jet—what's going on?"

With a sigh, she finally meets my gaze. "I'm thinking of selling the house."

"What? How can you sell Montgomery House? Where would you go?"

The words come out fast and loud, and Jet immediately glances toward the ceiling as though worried someone upstairs might have overheard. Voice notably softer than mine, she says, "I thought maybe I'd rent an apartment nearby. Someplace where I could still be close to the river. I don't really know where else I could go."

I try to picture my aunt and Brisby in a small one-bedroom a stone's throw from the house she grew up in. "But Montgomery House is your home. It's the family home." Sure, it doesn't belong to me in the way it belongs to her or even Dad, but it's always felt at least a little bit mine. I may have spent years telling myself I never wanted to come back here, but I always wanted there to be a here that I could come back to.

"Between maintenance costs and the property taxes . . . there's just not enough money to keep things going."

"What about the tenants? Aren't you getting money from them?"

"Not enough. The roof is leaking, the wiring is ancient, the whole heating system needs to be overhauled. These big old houses need a lot of attention. They need resources I just don't have. Your father tried to warn me." She bites her lip and twists the circle of masking tape around her wrist. "I'd appreciate it if you didn't tell him . . ."

"That you're clearing out the basement?"

Jet sighs and nods. "I'm sorry—I know it's putting you in an awful position." She really does look sorry. She looks downright miserable.

And, just like that, there's no way I can confront her over the fact that she and Dad waited all those weeks to tell me their

42

plans—not while she's standing in the middle of all this stuff, trying to figure out what can be off-loaded for cash. In an attempt to set my feelings aside, at least for a little while, I ask, "What can I do to help?"

Relief flashes across her face. Aunt Jet turns back to the desk. "Maybe if we both lift and pull?"

I go to her side and curl my hands around the edge of the wood. The thing really is a monster. In addition to being bigger than any desk has a right to be, the clawed legs twist and turn until they rise and form four scowling faces—one face for each corner. I can't imagine who on earth would want to buy it. It looks like the kind of desk you'd find in the home of the world's wealthiest, antique-loving serial killer.

"Where did this thing come from?"

"It belonged to Sarah Montgomery. Your great-great-aunt. She had it commissioned in New York and shipped here. She used to sit at this desk and—" Jet abruptly cuts herself off.

"And?"

She shakes her head. "I promised your father."

Right. No filling my head with nonsense. "I wouldn't actually tell him if you said anything. It's not like he would ever know."

A slight blush darkens her cheeks. "*I* would know."

"So?"

She ignores the question and tightens her grip on the desk. I'm not sure what else I was expecting: with very few exceptions, Jet does what other people want.

"Ready?" she asks.

Suppressing a frustrated sigh, I lift my corner, managing to get it at least a few inches off the ground.

"Pull!"

The two farthest legs screech against the floor and then make a sharp, cracking sound.

"Stop!" Jet begins to lower her corner, but as she does, her hand slips and brushes mine—

A battered cardboard box. My name scrawled in black. My aunt's voice. "I can't do this . . ."

Jet quickly pulls away from my touch, and the world comes rushing back. We both lose our grip on the desk, and even though we had managed to lift it only a few inches, it lands with a loud thunk and the sound of breaking glass.

Aunt Jet closes her eyes and pulls in a deep breath through her nose. Her expression is one of saintlike patience, but the lines at the corners of her mouth deepen as she says, "Guess I should have checked the drawers before we tried to move it." She shoots me a small, wan smile that is not at all convincing. "It's not your fault."

I wait for her to ask me what I saw, but she doesn't. She would have, before, I think. I guess asking now would violate my father's rules.

The phone upstairs rings.

"I'll be right back." Jet heads for the stairs but pauses to turn when she's halfway there. "I haven't told the boarders that I'm thinking of selling. I don't want to upset them before we know if we can even find a buyer. I need the money they bring in."

"I won't say anything."

"Thank you, Mary Catherine."

A faint headache blossoms along the edge of my skull as Jet

44

slips from sight. Thankfully, the contact between us had been so brief that the resulting pain isn't that bad. The meaning of what I saw seems pretty straightforward. Jet may have agreed to take me for the summer, but she's not happy about it. With that realization, the anger is back. Anger and frustration and, maybe, a little bit of hurt. If she had put her foot down—if she had just stood up to Dad—I'd be back in New York. I wouldn't be her problem. A small voice in the back of my head asks if that's what I really want. I ignore it.

Needing a distraction, I begin emptying out the desk. The top drawer is filled with old travel guides. Paris, London, Rome. I open a book with a picture of Tokyo Tower on the cover. There are notations on every page. Little exclamation marks and tiny plans in Aunt Jet's small, elegant script. A picture falls out from between the pages and lands at my feet. I pick it up. It's Aunt Jet, but younger. My age, even. Her hair is cut short and she's smiling widely. A tall, thin boy stands next to her, close but not quite touching. I've never seen the boy, and I've never seen Aunt Jet smile like that.

The other travel books are all similarly full of plans.

As far as I know, though, my aunt has never left North America.

I set the stack of books on top of an old steamer trunk that's been tagged for the keep pile and then turn back to the desk.

The second drawer is filled with leather-bound journals and ledgers, all resting under an old curved knife in a leather sheath. The knife looks like something a big-game hunter would have carried on his belt while on safari; I have a dim memory of it being on display somewhere—the study, probably—when I was a kid. I lay it on the corner of the desk and turn my attention to the journals. The first few are blank—like someone ordered a stack of journals in bulk a hundred years ago and then forgot about them. I set them aside, next to the knife, and then flip through a journal that's filled with diagrams and sketches of the old textile mill. The mill my family had owned and operated for decades.

There are notations about equipment and floor plans and even maps of the tunnels that exist underneath the main structure and the surrounding outbuildings—the ones my great-grandfather built when he had delusions of setting up a smuggling empire and wanted to move things around the grounds without being seen. According to family lore, he spent more money on the tunnels than he ever made on crime. Thirteen men had died in those tunnels in 1944 after a fire broke out in the mill. Their lungs filled with smoke and their fingertips turned raw and bloody as they tried to claw through the tunnel walls.

People in town like to say that the fire was the beginning of everything that went wrong for the Montgomerys, but Dad says things started falling apart long before that, that the money had been running out for more than a generation—hence the attempt to turn to crime—and that the mill would have closed in another year or two anyway.

But blaming the fall of the town's founding—and formerly richest—family on a tragic fire and thirteen dead men makes for a better story.

The Montgomerys hadn't exactly been beloved before that, but the fire made us downright hated. And people in small towns tend to hold on to their hate for a long, long time. Dad was born more than three decades after the fire, but he said he could still feel that hate every day as he sat in classes with kids whose grandfathers and great-uncles had died in the tunnels.

The same is true of Aunt Jet, I guess, though she seems to have made peace with it better than Dad has. I guess that probably went along with staying in Montgomery Falls.

I start to slide the journal back where I found it, but as I do, I notice a smaller book wedged against the side of the drawer. I pull it free and then haul in a sharp breath as I recognize the torn Marvel sticker on the cover.

Riley's book.

The Book of Lost Things.

A fragment of a memory fills my head.

Riley reaching out to touch me and then thinking better of it. Crouching down in front of me instead, that book in his hand. Waiting for me to look up at him. Making me look up at him. "You're amazing, Cat. You're like one of the X-Men. Like Professor X."

I trace the sticker with my fingertip.

How on earth had his book ended up down here?

Swallowing roughly, I flip to a random page, to a list of lost items, each accompanied by a description, a location, and the date we came across it. Some of them I can remember clearly—the engine from an old van, a broken hacksaw, a doll with one blue eye missing—but others are so mundane they left no impression: Doritos bag, striped sock, broken pen.

I turn the pages until I reach an entry that reads: *Saint Anthony medal. Mill. August 12.* The day he and I and Noah slipped through the fence at the mill. The day everything began to change.

47

It's the last item on the list. Had Riley started a new journal after that day, or had August twelfth and the week that followed marked the end of his obsession with lost things?

I flip to the end of the book, to the other list Riley had kept that summer—a record of each time I had lost my grip on reality. It's not there. The pages have been torn out, leaving only jagged edges behind.

Like I had never existed.

FIVE

I SPEND THE REST OF THE AFTERNOON TRYING NOT TO THINK about that small black book and the entry for that long-ago August day—with limited success. Without a laptop or phone, I eventually turn to the TV in the common room for a distraction, but Marie and Sam are binge-watching some sort of weird Canadian costume drama. Sam keeps chuckling at the wrong moments, like some strange, delayed laugh track.

I only last two episodes before I give up and head to the study to tell Aunt Jet I'm going out for a walk.

"It's only your first full day in town," she says, frowning nervously at me from her position in one of the huge, wingback armchairs. "I'm not sure that's a good idea."

"Montgomery Falls isn't exactly a sprawling metropolis," I say. "I'll be fine."

"It's just that I promised your father I would take care of you."

Brisby slips into the room, headbutts Jet's leg, and then mewls until she closes her book and scratches him under his chin. "It's not that I don't trust you, Mary Catherine; it's just that I don't want it to be another five years before you're allowed to visit again."

The study is one of my favorite spots in Montgomery House, but as I envision spending my time in Canada negotiating every outing, it feels like its book-lined walls are closing in. This one moment could set the tone for the next few weeks.

"I just don't think it's a good idea," Jet says a little more firmly, a little more decisively.

I quickly run through arguments and counterarguments in my head. Assurances about being home before it gets late. Promises to stick to the good parts of town and not talk to strangers. But one look at the way Aunt Jet is staring at me—her face sharp and owlish, her thin shoulders set in a straight line—and I suspect not a single assurance or promise will work.

Because she dislikes confrontation, it's easy to assume my aunt is a pushover. And she is—sometimes. But she stood up to Dad when he first wanted her to sell the house. And she spends each week taking care of people who can't take care of themselves anymore. That takes strength.

And the look she's giving me right now is not that of someone who's going to cave.

Footsteps sound on the stairs. Inspiration strikes as I glance over my shoulder in time to see Aidan heading down the front hall. "I'm going out with Aidan and some of his friends," I say quickly. "They're watching a movie. Aidan asked me to go."

Aunt Jet sets her book aside. "Aidan?" She waits for him to

appear in the doorway and then says, "You asked Mary Catherine to the movies?"

The smallest flicker of surprise flashes across his face, there and gone so fast that Aunt Jet doesn't catch it. Surprise and something else—something that might be amusement. "A few friends and I are hanging out and watching movies over at Chase Walker's house," he says. "Chase's dad is the principal of the elementary school. You probably know his mother—she volunteers at a bunch of places around town. I thought it might be nice for Cat—Mary Catherine, I mean—to meet some people. We get together every week. Mr. and Mrs. Walker order pizza for us and let us hang out in the rec room as long as we don't make too much noise."

He's good. Really good. It's hard to imagine I can get into much trouble at the home of the local principal and the official town do-gooder. Aidan even managed to imply there will be parents present without Aunt Jet having to ask. The only other person I know who's that good at spinning things is Lacey.

Still, Aunt Jet hesitates.

"You said you trusted me," I say. A tiny little push.

She doesn't look entirely happy or convinced, but she picks up her book and finds her place. "Be home before it gets too late, please. Remember the house rules."

Once Aidan and I are safely outside with the door closed behind us, I remark, "That is an impressive talent for bullshitting."

A faux-wounded look crosses his face. "Nothing I said was an untruth."

"Chase's mother?"

"Really is an obnoxious, insufferable humanitarian."

"And his father?"

"Has technically been fired from his position after getting caught in the copy room with the school secretary, but that is not yet common knowledge."

"Montgomery Falls' very own soap opera." I shake my head. "So what are the house rules?"

"Your aunt locks the front door at midnight. If you're not inside by then, you're out of luck."

"You've got to be kidding." Aidan is the only one of the boarders who is a teenager. Heck, Sam has to be older than my father and Aunt Jet. Isn't half the point of being a grown-up not having to deal with things like curfews?

Aidan nods toward the old porch swing with its peeling paint and rusting chain. "Let's just say that thing is not the most comfortable of beds. I spent two nights on it last month before I found an alternate way in and out of the house." He flashes me a grin and then heads down the porch steps as a Honda with scratched paint and brakes that screech in protest pulls into the driveway.

I follow Aidan as the car comes to a stop. One guy sits behind the wheel while another rides shotgun.

"Well," I say as Aidan pulls open the passenger-side rear door, "I'll see you around."

The instant the words leave my mouth, I cringe. Of course I'll see him around: he lives in the same house.

Aidan raises an eyebrow. "I thought we were going to watch a movie. You have a better transportation option? If so, can you take me with you?"

"Hey!" protests the driver. "There's nothing better than the Beast."

"Dude, any car would be better than this thing," says the guy in the passenger seat. "The taillights don't work, and it still smells like the old lady you bought it from. We're going to get rear-ended and that smell is going to follow me into the afterlife."

Aidan ignores them both. He just stands there, eyebrow still slightly raised.

"*You're* going to watch a movie," I clarify. "*I* just needed a hall pass."

"I feel so used."

"Like you wouldn't get off on that?" I don't know where the words come from. They sure as hell don't sound like me. They're fast and witty and sultry enough to earn me an appreciative hoot from the guys in the car. They might even be enough to make up for my stupid comment about seeing him around.

"Dude, she has you pegged. Pegged!" says Shotgun Boy.

I wait for Aidan to tell him to shut it or to hit me with a comment as saucy as the one I just gave. Absolutely worst-case scenario, he'll call me a five-letter word that rhymes with "witch" and we'll spend the next few weeks awkwardly passing each other in the hall on our way to the bathroom.

He doesn't do any of those things.

Instead, he adopts an expression that is earnest and angelic, laying it on so thick that it's hard not to laugh even as his wide gray eyes make things inside of me twist.

Even if I were open to relationships—which I am not for a

whole bunch of very good reasons—Aidan is not my type. Sure, he seems interesting and has an appreciation for vintage things, but he's cocky and pretty. I don't usually go for guys who are either. That's always been Lacey's thing. She always goes after the shiniest one in the room while I secretly crush on artists and geeks. Still, it's a bit hard to remember that with Aidan standing in front of me, looking at me that way.

"Please." He takes two steps toward me, invading my personal space without quite touching me, the way he did last night. I get the sudden feeling he does that a lot—steps into spaces to see how far he's allowed in. "Look . . . Normally, I'm all for duplicity, but I really need my room. If your aunt finds out that I lied for you, she'll probably kick me out."

If he knew how desperately my aunt needs the rent checks his parents send, he'd know there's no way he'd get kicked out over such a small infraction. But if Aunt Jet does put the house up for sale . . . if someone does buy it . . .

I've known Aidan for a grand total of thirty minutes—or just over a day if you're generous and count all of the actual hours since we met—but I believe him when he says he needs his spot in the house. I understand why Jet doesn't want the lodgers to know she's thinking of selling, but looking into Aidan's eyes, it suddenly doesn't seem fair to keep that information from him.

He mistakes my brief flash of guilt for hesitation. "Come on. It'll be fun. You'll meet new people. We're all harmless."

"If you weren't harmless, would you admit it?"

His lip quirks up in another lopsided grin. The girls of Montgomery Falls have probably texted their friends about the precise angles of that smile. "So suspicious. You really are a New Yorker."

The guy in the driver's seat leans on the horn. "Dude. She doesn't want to come. Stop trying to use your charm like it's a hunk of Kryptonite."

But maybe Aidan's smile is Kryptonite, because I find myself stepping past him and sliding into the back seat of the too-hot car. The air inside smells like Cheetos and lavender and hair spray. Aidan slides in beside me and pulls the door closed with a slam.

"That's Joey," he says, gesturing toward the driver, "and that's Chase." Both boys twist in their seats to get a good look at me. Joey's thick, black-rimmed glasses slide down his nose, and he pushes them up, absently. He doesn't smile; he doesn't even blink. It's unnerving. Chase, on the other hand, smiles broadly. Given his muscles, backward ball cap, and the fact that he's wearing a T-shirt with the Riverview mascot on the front, I'm guessing he's a jock.

A jock whose father, apparently, sleeps with secretaries in the copy room.

"Cat's from New York," Aidan says. "Her aunt owns the boardinghouse."

"Wicked," says Joey. He still doesn't smile, but he gives me the tiniest of nods before turning back around and throwing the car into drive.

I haul my seat belt across my chest. "New York?"

"Montgomery House. It's the fourth most-haunted place in town."

"What are spots one through three?" I ask.

"University library is three," says Chase, jumping in. "Fifth floor. A librarian hung herself up there in 1953."

"Train bridge is number two," says Joey. "On account of a rail employee who died while a train was crossing. People say he walks the bridge at night with a lantern. They say that if you see the glow, you'll be dead by morning."

He sounds so serious that it's impossible not to laugh. "Somehow, Montgomery Falls doesn't seem classy enough to have its own banshee."

Joey's eyes lock on mine in the rearview mirror. "Banshees haunt specific families."

"Here we go . . . ," mutters Aidan.

"And they're not actually ghosts," Joey continues, ignoring him. "Amateurs frequently make that mistake."

"If everyone who sees the glow from the lantern winds up dead, how does anyone know about it?" I counter. I'm pretty proud of my logic, but the look he shoots me is withering.

Chase jumps in before Joey can answer. "People tell people. Joey's grandpa told his mom he saw lights on the bridge. The next day, he had a heart attack. And Riley Fraser told Amber Preston he saw the light the day before he disappeared."

"Riley's missing, not necessarily dead," says Aidan. He rolls down the back window and drums his fingers on the edge of the door. "And Amber was drunk when she told everyone that."

"You guys know Riley?" *Of course they do*, I realize. Montgomery Falls has only two high schools—one English and one French—and neither has more than a few hundred students.

"Everyone knows Riley Fraser," says Joey darkly. "Varsity athlete. Homecoming king. Center of the universe. Too good for just about everyone and everything."

Riley? No matter how many years have passed, I can't imagine Riley as a jock or being comfortable at the center of the universe. Sure, I had thought the picture on the poster looked like it belonged to someone who could be class president or prom king, but that didn't mean I actually thought Riley had become the kind of guy who would be either of those things.

He could be so quiet and distant—even with me, and he claimed that I knew him better than anyone. Most of that was just him, I think, but some of it was the OCD. He said it was like having a sort of background noise in his head. A lot of the time he could tune it out, but sometimes it got too loud and pulled his attention inward.

That whole summer, his parents—especially his father—kept pushing him to make more friends. Friends who would still be there when school started in the fall. Friends who would help him fit in. "I don't need other friends," he kept telling them. "I have Cat."

"Other people wouldn't get it," he told me. "They wouldn't get me."

Because we were both different. Because we both had things that made us different.

It's strange to think that the first boy I ever kissed, the boy who said he didn't need anyone other than me, had turned into someone who would be a stranger.

"You haven't asked about spot number one," says Aidan, drawing my attention back to the boys in the car.

"What's spot number one?"

"The textile mill. Because of a fire."

"And the girl," interjects Chase. "Three kids found a dead girl up there five years ago."

"She knows about the girl, idiot," says Joey as he slows for a red light.

And just like that, not thinking about that last entry in Riley's book becomes impossible.

Going to the mill that day had been my idea. I had been wanting to go ever since I overheard someone talking about how chimney swifts roosted in the old buildings. You could see groups of them in town all day long—small, soot-colored birds that rose and fell on the air like puffs of smoke—but at the mill, you could supposedly see thousands of them. So many that they blocked out the sun. So many that the sound of all of those wings was like thunder.

Noah overheard us planning. He didn't rat us out and he didn't try to stop us, but he insisted on coming. "It's dangerous," he had said, like the extra years he had on us made some sort of difference.

We hiked up to the mill and slipped through the fence. Riley spotted a small, silver medal with the initials NMK engraved on the back in the weeds. He bent down to pick it up and fell behind.

NMK.

Nora Michelle Knight. A history major at the university who had wanted to get a look at the brickwork at the old mill. She hadn't known she had a heart condition. A time bomb in her chest that went off when she was alone.

I spotted her first, then Noah.

He grabbed me and spun me around as he told Riley, still behind us, not to come any closer. He pulled me to his chest and told me not to look, even though it was already too late. Her eyes had been open, and there had been something crawling on her cheek. That's what I remember—but I've never been entirely sure if those were details I actually saw or if they were things I picked up from Noah when he touched me.

Riley hadn't listened. Over Noah's shoulder, I watched as he drew closer. He drew closer, and in the distance, thousands of swifts filled the air like smoke

The light turns green and the car jumps forward.

Chase is staring at me. "Right. Montgomery. You were there. You're the girl who was with Riley and Noah Fraser."

One of the joys of small towns: find one dead body and that information will follow you around forever.

Joey pulls into a parking lot and kills the engine. To our right is the town's lone coffee shop. To our left is a row of stores crowded so closely together that they might as well be a strip mall. A pharmacy sits at one end, an old video store at the other. I shake my head, unable to quite believe video stores actually still exist.

We all climb out of the car. "So you guys are what? Like those people on TV who run around hunting ghosts?"

"Nah," says Chase. "Just horror fans. We're organizing Montgomery Falls' first horror film festival. And by 'festival,' I mean a double feature in the town square on a Tuesday night because that was all they'd give us permission for."

"I'm not just a fan," mutters Joey.

Chase rolls his eyes. "Okay. I'm just a fan. Joey is also into local hauntings and writes horror movies. He's been working on one about the town, but he won't let anyone see it."

"Performance anxiety," Aidan says to me in a stage whisper. "Hey—Cat's dad is a hotshot writer. Maybe she can give you pointers."

I open my mouth to make some excuse about how I don't really know anything about writing, but before I can get a single word out, Joey says, "Elliot Montgomery. Everyone in town knows who he is. And my screenplay is a work in progress. It's not ready to be seen."

There's a snide, arrogant tone to his voice that's grating.

"Hey," he says, "did you notice anything while you were up at the mill that day?"

"You mean aside from the dead girl?"

"Right. Any unexplained phenomena? Supernatural activity or hostility? I've been wondering if the presence of a Montgomery would trigger any of the ghosts of the men who died in the tunnels."

"You think the ghosts are angry at us?"

"Of course. Wouldn't you be pissed?"

He and Chase launch into a debate about the best angry ghost movies with Aidan interjecting. None of them notice when I fall back. They just keep walking until they reach the video store and then disappear inside.

I decide to give them a few minutes—long enough, hopefully, for Joey to forget all about the mill and his questions. Pulling in a deep breath, I run a hand through my hair. As I do, the bracelet on my wrist—just a cheap, braided cord with some beads—catches on a tangle and breaks. The cord falls to the ground at my feet, but the beads scatter.

Only then do I realize that I'm not alone.

A guy stands just to the left of the pharmacy door, a small paper bag in his hand. He must have come out just as Chase, Joey, and Aidan walked by. There's something vaguely familiar about the sweep of his dark hair over his forehead and the tense set of his shoulders and the way he holds himself. But he's older now—five years older—and it takes a moment for it to click. When it does, my stomach drops

Noah. Noah Fraser.

It feels slightly surreal, seeing him. For a moment, the two Noahs overlap—the one standing outside the drugstore and the one who exists in my memory—but then I blink and the illusion shatters.

Noah bends down and picks up one of the beads from my broken bracelet. He straightens and holds it out to me.

There are angry red marks on his knuckles. Cuts that have scabbed over. He used to play the piano, I remember suddenly as I look at his hand. On warm summer nights, the sound of his playing would drift through the Frasers' house and out into the yard. It's one of those tiny, insignificant details that lodges itself in the back of your mind, buried until something small dredges it to the surface.

I cross the space between us and then hesitate. There's no way for me to reach out and take the bead without risking skin brushing skin. Instead, I form a cup with my palms and wait for him to drop the bead inside.

As he does, I have the ridiculous urge to ask if he still plays the piano, if he can tell me the name of the song he was playing that afternoon before we went to the mill. I want to tell him about the classical music concert Lacey's mom took us to—Ludovico Einaudi—and how one of the songs felt like seeing a thousand birds in flight. How I had to get up and leave. How I locked myself in a bathroom stall until it felt like I could breathe again.

The silence between us goes from awkward to oppressive.

Eventually, it becomes too much. "I don't know if you remember me." The words come out strained and halting. The idea that he could forget me seems impossible, but five years is a long time—especially when I was in his brother's life for only a handful of months. "I used to hang around with Riley."

Noah switches the small paper bag from one hand to the other. It rattles softly with the unmistakable sound of pill bottles.

"Cat," he says finally. "Cat Montgomery. I remember you."

His voice is different. Older and deeper. It no longer breaks in the middle of sentences.

Someone calls my name. Turning toward the video store, I see Aidan and Chase standing outside. Noah glances toward the sound, then gives me a small nod and starts to walk away as the boys head toward us.

I spend most of my days trying not to accidentally touch people, but without thinking, I reach out and grab Noah's sleeve, forcing him to pause and turn back. "I'm sorry about Riley," I blurt out, knowing he must have heard those words a hundred times, but needing him to hear them from me, too. Not because they're the words you're supposed to say—the words everyone says—but because I really, really mean them. Despite everything that happened between Riley and me, I really do mean them. "I hope they find him."

Noah's shoulders stiffen. When he speaks, there's a sharp edge to his voice. "I don't."

This time when he turns to walk away, I don't try to stop him. I'm too stunned.

I'm still staring after him when Aidan and Chase reach me.

SIX

THE IDEA OF PHYSICALLY RENTING MOVIES SEEMS ARCHAIC.
I'm sure the video store must have been here the last time I was in town—it seems like the kind of place that's been in the same spot forever—but I don't remember it. Given how big I am on vintage stuff, you'd think I'd be in heaven as I wander the aisles, but my idea of paradise still includes streaming.

Not that I'm paying all that much attention to my surroundings; my run-in with Noah has me so thrown that I'm not sure I can pay much attention to anything.

"They just keep a handful of cult movies that haven't been released on DVD or online," says Aidan as he plucks a bulky VHS case from my hand. "The university has a surprisingly active—and discerning—film club." He sets the video back on the shelf and studies my face for a moment. "Are you all right?"

"Sure," I say quickly. "Why wouldn't I be?"

"Because whatever Noah Fraser said, it seemed to shake you."

"No shaking," I lie. "Nothing bad was said." Just past the VHS section, on the far wall, is a doorway with a red curtain. "What's through there?" I ask, trying to change the subject.

"Used to be dirty movies," says Chase, wandering over, "but the family who bought the store a few years ago is really uptight, so now it's just a staff room."

"Shut up," says Joey.

"What?" Chase spreads his hands, holding them palms out. "You complain about your family being uptight all the time."

"One of the perks of being friends with Joey," says Aidan, "is unlimited free rentals."

His words are still hanging in the air when the curtain swishes, and a small, dark figure emerges.

The clothes are different—a short, black dress that looks like something Wednesday Addams would wear—and the pigtails are in braids with strands of red ribbon woven through, but the girl from the movie theater is unmistakable.

"Dammit, Joey. Tell your girlfriend to stay out of the staff room."

I glance at the woman behind the counter. I didn't notice it when I came in, but she bears a distinct resemblance to Joey. Enough that they have to be siblings.

"I dropped something and it rolled under the curtain." The girl—Skylar—holds up a container of lip gloss as proof before tossing it into a voluminous black bag. "You know, you really should think about getting another kind of coffee machine. Those little gourmet pods you like? Totally bad for the environment. And if you're going to switch, maybe think about fair-trade coffee. Be a responsible consumer. You know?"

The woman's scowl deepens, but Skylar just cruises past her, shooting me a curious glance before launching herself forward and throwing her arms around Joey. The movement is so exuberant that when he puts his arms around her, I'm not sure if it's to return the hug or to keep them both from tumbling to the floor.

"This," says Aidan, "is the only girl without enough sense to realize she can do better than Joey."

"We've met." Skylar manages to twist in Joey's arms without breaking the embrace, though she knocks his glasses askew in the process. "I caught her tearing down some of the posters around the theater. She's totally my hero."

Given that I was ripping them down in broad daylight, in plain sight, "catching" might not be the most accurate characterization, but I have the odd, slightly inexplicable suspicion that correcting her would feel like kicking a puppy. A weird, gothy puppy who hangs out in curtained-off rooms in video stores and crusades for globally responsible coffee consumption, but a puppy nonetheless.

"Cat is staying at Montgomery House," supplies Chase. "Aidan invited her to movie night."

A cartoon-wide grin spreads across Skylar's face. "Finally! Another girl in the Monster Squad." She detaches herself from Joey and makes a grab for me. For a nerve-wracking second, I think she's going for my hand, but then she latches on to the corner of my shirt. "We'll get snacks," she says, tugging me toward the door. "You guys get a movie—NOT *Carrie*.

"They always lose it over the stupid locker-room scene," she confesses, continuing to pull me forward. "Boys are so basic."

Part of me wants to stay with Aidan, but the way he keeps looking at me makes me think he knows I'm lying about being okay. Going with Skylar provides a temporary escape from more questions.

She doesn't let go until we're outside and have reached the drugstore. My broken bracelet is still on the sidewalk; the lone rescued bead feels heavy in my pocket. I glance around for Noah, but he's long gone.

"Monster Squad?" I ask, struggling to get my bearings as I follow this tiny hurricane inside.

"Joey found this old movie from the eighties. A bunch of kids team up to hunt monsters. Frankenstein and Dracula and stuff. They call themselves the 'Monster Squad.' Turns out the movie itself is filled with the kind of jokes that make me think eighties nostalgia might be overrated. Still, I like the name. I figured we could adopt it and rehabilitate it. It's better than what everyone at school calls us. Our little group, I mean." She talks the way she moves: sentences that are small, quick steps, each split into three when one would do.

"What do they call you?" I ask, unable to keep from thinking of all of the things I've been called recently back in New York.

"Nothing good," says Skylar. She grabs two wire shopping baskets, hands one to me, and then steers us toward the snack aisle. "Well, they don't really give Chase and Aidan a hard time," she amends. "Mostly Joey and me. But I still like the name." She tosses a bag of chips into each basket and then holds up two packages of licorice—one red, one black. "What flavor do you like?"

The question takes me aback. For a while, eating in front of

Lacey had felt . . . complicated. Eat too much and I would get slightly worried looks and hints that I was loved just the way I am but that I'd better not get any bigger because there are limits to how large someone's heart can stretch. Eat too little and it would be just as bad. It didn't used to be that way—at least I don't think so. In my darker moments, I wondered if Lacey had some new ideal weight for me. Fat enough that I wasn't a threat, not so fat that I drew the wrong kind of attention. A magic number where I faded into the background just enough while still being sufficiently present to be her best friend.

"I'm more of a Whoppers girl," I say experimentally.

I wait to see if she'll react the way Lacey would, but Skylar grins, drops the licorice, and adds two boxes of Whoppers—the big kind like you get at the movies—to her basket.

"I can't believe you're staying at Montgomery House," she says with a small, wistful sigh. "I love that place. The woman who owns it is awesome. Joey and I teamed up on this local history project ages ago, and she let us take pictures inside. Aidan helped. He and Joey are in the school photography club. It was so great. Joey borrowed this old camera—a thirty-five millimeter or something—because he wanted to try shooting real film. The film was more expensive than I thought it would be, but totally worth it because Joey had so much fun. That's when we started really hanging out. Me and the guys. That project—and the house—totally brought us together."

"The woman's my aunt."

"So you're a Montgomery? *Very cool.*"

She may be the first person I've ever met who thinks being a Montgomery is a good thing. Heck, according to Joey, even the ghosts are mad at us.

Skylar reaches the end of the aisle and spins, practically doing a pirouette. "Where are you from?"

"New York."

"We should have told the guys to get something set there. I bet Joey could list ten horror movies set in New York. Just off the top of his head. He's like a walking IMDb." She says this like it's a huge selling point in his favor.

I feel like I'm falling behind as I try to keep up with the jump and skip of her words. "It doesn't matter. I'm not really a horror fan."

Skylar's eyes go wide, and she actually stumbles back a step, as though my words are literally too much for her to handle. "Don't worry. We can fix it."

"Fix what? Me not liking horror movies?"

"Yup. It's fixable. One hundred percent. We just have to find the right movie. Or movies."

"I figured horror fans were born, not made."

"Not always. I didn't start getting into them until a year ago. I found this old book at a yard sale. *The Dual Self in Horror*. It was all about how a lot of really old horror movies have all this interesting stuff to say about the human psyche. That's when I started talking to Joey. I wanted to watch all of the movies from the book, but some of them were hard to track down." She tilts her head to the side and stares at me thoughtfully. "If you were a character in a story, what kind of story would you want it to be?"

The question seems vaguely ridiculous, but the expression on her face is so earnest that I think about it seriously before answering. "The kind where the girl slays dragons and fights monsters, I guess."

She nods like this makes perfect sense. "Why?"

"Because I like the idea of not being afraid."

As the words leave my mouth, I know that's not exactly it. It isn't that the girls in those stories are unafraid—it's that they push past their fear. They push past their fear and they somehow manage to turn their weaknesses into strengths.

I envy that.

I wait for Skylar to laugh. She doesn't.

"I like the idea of not being afraid, too," she admits, and there's something deep and serious in her brown eyes. She gives her head a small shake and smiles. "People think horror movies are just about gore—and some of them are—but that's not all they have to be about." She skips backward, spins again, and disappears around the corner of the aisle.

I follow. I'm thinking about her words and not really paying attention to where I'm going, and so I walk right into her when she comes to an unexpected stop.

I don't hit her very hard, but I still manage to knock the bag from her shoulder. It falls to the ground and her lip gloss—the same lip gloss she had chased into the staff room of the video store—rolls under a nearby display rack.

Skylar doesn't make any move to retrieve it. In fact, for the first time since I've met her, she stands completely still.

Her attention is focused on two girls at the very end of the aisle. Neither is paying any attention to us. One is on her phone, the other is talking to the pharmacist at the counter.

"Skylar?" I nudge her gently with the corner of my wire basket. The contact seems to spur her into motion. Abandoning her lip gloss, she turns and retreats the way we came, walking so quickly that she's almost running.

The girl at the counter—a blonde with tortoiseshell glasses—glances up, but Skylar is already out of sight. The girl shoots me a small, curious glance as I set my basket on the floor and crouch down to retrieve the lip gloss, but quickly turns back to her conversation.

My fingers skim dust bunnies and grit before finally closing on the small container. I stand and examine the label: Raspberry S'more. I tuck it into my pocket, next to the bead from my bracelet, grab my basket, and head for the front of the store. Skylar's basket, still full, sits abandoned by the checkout.

After a few seconds' hesitation, I empty out the contents of both baskets and fish a Canadian twenty out of my back pocket as the cashier rings everything up.

Skylar is waiting for me outside. When she sees the bags in my hands, a blush darkens her cheeks. "I'll pay you back," she says softly.

"Don't worry about it." Given that both Jet and Dad are having money problems, I should probably accept the offer, but I feel weird taking Skylar's money when she looks so miserable.

I almost ask her if she wants to talk about it—the reason she bolted from the store—but then catch myself. The more personal questions you ask people, the more questions they feel like they can ask you in return. And the closer you let yourself get, the harder it is to remember how dangerous friends can be.

I learned a long time ago that it's better not to let people get too close.

Riley taught me that. I let myself forget, with Lacey, but I'm not going to forget again.

SEVEN

"EARTH TO CAT." AIDAN PAUSES ON THE TOP PORCH STEP TO look back at me.

The difference in our heights is accentuated by the fact that I'm two steps down, and as I stare up at him, I realize that I have no idea what he had just been saying, that I can't, in fact, recall anything he said during the walk home. There had been some story about a kayaking trip, I think. Or strip poker. Or strip poker while stranded on an island during a kayaking trip.

Guiltily, I pull my hand out of my pocket, away from the bead Noah had handed back to me outside the drugstore. "Were you making things up to see if I was paying attention?" I ask, suddenly suspicious.

The corner of Aidan's mouth pulls up in that uneven grin. "Might have been." He walks over to the porch swing and sits, sprawling his legs out in front of him.

Out of habit, I reach for my phone to check the time, only to remember I no longer have a phone.

"Don't worry: we've still got thirty minutes before lock out."

Slightly doubtful, I cast a glance at the door, but then cross to the swing and sit next to him. I'm careful to leave a few feet of space between us. The rusted chains groan in protest as Aidan tries to set the swing in motion. "You know," he says, "calling this thing a 'swing' might be a little optimistic."

"No kidding. I'm pretty sure it's been hanging here since the thirties." Unbidden, an image of Riley fills my head. Orange-and-blue-striped T-shirt. Messy hair. A scab on one knee. Sitting cross-legged on the swing with a checkerboard in front of him. The checkers were a compromise. Riley had tried to teach me chess, but I was a lousy player. I didn't have the patience for drawn-out strategy, and I hated sacrificing my pawns.

"Hey . . ." Aidan twists a little and leans toward me, his gray eyes darkening. "Are you all right?"

I fully intend to lie to him again, but I must hesitate a little too long because the beautiful boy in front of me does something unexpected. He inches forward—not so much that we might accidentally touch, but enough that I can tell his next words are earnest—and says, "You can tell me if you're not. I get that we don't really know each other, and maybe I'm completely wrong, but I have a feeling that you're the kind of person who's used to pretending everything is fine."

"And you think I'm not fine?"

"Name three things that happened in the movie."

"There was a lot of blood. And screaming. And loud noises."

"You do realize that just listing off horror movie tropes is cheating, right?"

"Can't blame a girl for trying."

"Admit it, you've been somewhere else pretty much all night."

I bite my lip.

"You really can talk to me, you know," Aidan says.

"I've been thinking about Noah Fraser," I admit. "Today was the first time I've seen him since I was a kid."

Aidan leans back. "Noah's a strange guy."

I ponder this. Noah is only two years older than I am, but that difference seemed bigger when we were younger. He was always so dark and serious—a shadow at the edge of the Fraser house. I remember being a little intimidated by him, but I wouldn't have called him strange. "What makes you say that?"

Aidan shrugs. "He dropped out of some university in Ontario after his brother went missing. He spends most of his time wandering around town, putting up posters. When he's not doing that, he hangs out down at the Riverbend, drinking and getting into fights."

There are three bars in Montgomery Falls. The Riverbend is the one people go to when they've been banned from the other two.

Fights would explain the marks on Noah's knuckles. The rest—dropping out of school and putting up posters and drowning your sorrows—all sounds pretty normal to me . . . or at least it would if it hadn't been for what he said outside the drugstore. Why keep putting up posters when you don't want someone to be found? Still, I say, "None of that seems that weird, all things considered."

"Small town. Lower threshold for weird." Aidan shrugs again. "Tell me something: Why are you so interested?"

I pry up a flake of peeling paint with the edge of my thumbnail. How many hours did Riley and I spend out here, on this swing, red checking black and black checking red?

"I was friends with Riley."

"Past tense?"

"Just for one summer. I haven't spoken to him in years." There's something about Aidan that makes him easy to talk to, and so, as the minutes edge closer to midnight, I tell him about Riley. About how Riley's parents moved in next door the last summer I spent at Montgomery House. About how neither of us knew anyone, so we got to know each other.

I don't tell Aidan everything, though. I don't tell him how Riley and I helped each other or how he made me feel safe.

I don't tell him about *The Book of Lost Things* or what happened after that day at the mill.

And I don't tell him how what happened with Riley left me scared to let anyone else get too close, to let anyone else know about the things I can see and do.

Still, I tell him a lot. More than I normally would. It leaves me feeling off-balance and a little exposed and something else, something I can't really put my finger on. It's like talking about Riley opens this door that I've been trying to keep shut in my head for a really long time.

It hurts a little, opening that door. Enough that I remember why I spent so long keeping it shut.

"I hung around with Riley and his friends when I first moved here with my folks," Aidan says, after I've finished, "but his mom decided I was a bad influence. She was *not* happy when I moved in next door."

"Why?"

"Honestly?" He runs a hand back through his hair. "You can't tell your aunt . . ."

I make an exaggerated show of crossing my heart. "Hope to die."

He shoots a glance toward the front door. "A bunch of us were bored one day and hopped the fence at the mill. Someone saw us and called the cops. The others got away, but Riley and I weren't fast enough. It was my idea, so I took the blame when we got caught. I had to do three months of community service."

Montgomery Falls is a small town. That Aidan thinks there's any way my aunt is renting him a room and is somehow unaware of this story is kind of baffling. "What happened to Riley?"

Aidan shrugs. "He's rich, and I had already told the cops it was my idea. Nothing."

"He just walked away?"

Aidan looks genuinely puzzled. "What else was he going to do?"

I think about Riley. About how guilty he felt anytime I ended up scraped or bruised after one of our adventures in the woods. "That doesn't seem like something he would do." Even after what happened between us, that doesn't sound like Riley.

"You were twelve the last time you saw him?"

"Yeah."

"People change."

77

I guess I should know that. "What's the deal with Skylar and the posters by the movie theater?" I ask, partly because I want to know and partly because I don't want to start thinking about all of the ways I'm different from how I used to be. "What's the deal with her and Riley?"

"Ahhh," says Aidan, drawing out the single syllable. "Skylar did mention you saw the posters, didn't she?" He seems to think about how to answer for a moment, then says, "The two of them hooked up at a party last March. Before Skylar was with Joey. Skylar thought it meant something. Riley didn't. Riley's girlfriend, Amber, definitely thought it meant something."

"What happened?"

"What happens when mean girls get meaner? Amber and her friends posted stuff online about Skylar, wrote stuff on her locker, sent pictures and dirty texts to her phone, and called her house so many times her parents had to change their number. That was just in the couple of days before Riley disappeared. After that, it got really bad. They acted like she had something to do with it. They told everyone she had been stalking him. The police even searched her house. Everyone was acting like she was capable of murder. You've met Skylar. She cries when she steps on grasshoppers."

The actual circumstances might be different, but the texts and phone calls, the posting stuff online—it all sounds horribly familiar. Maybe I hadn't originally done it for Skylar, but I'm suddenly glad I'd torn down the posters. Maybe if there had been someone to take down some of the things that had been said about me, the last few months wouldn't have been so hard.

"Anyway," says Aidan, "Joey had been spending some time with

Skylar before that—all of us had, I guess—but that was when we officially took her in."

"You make her sound like a stray."

"We're all kind of strays." The crooked grin makes a reappearance. He pulls out his phone, checks the time, and then stands. "Four minutes to midnight. I'd better get you inside."

I push myself to my feet and then cross the porch. When I reach the door, I wrap my hand around the knob, but pause to turn back to him. "Because you don't want to sleep on the porch?"

Aidan leans against the doorframe. "Because I don't want your aunt thinking I'm a bad influence. She might not want you coming out with me again."

Again? I shake my head. I'm no good at this. I've never known how to figure out if the things boys say mean what it seems like they might.

Aidan shifts his weight forward, and I have the sudden, panicked thought that he's going to try to kiss me. And I can't kiss him. I can't kiss anyone.

I fumble with the doorknob. My palms are sweaty and they slip against the metal, throwing me slightly off-balance. The door flies open and I stumble over the threshold.

I turn, face scorching.

Aidan stands on the other side of the door, looking vaguely amused. He smiles and bows slightly at the waist like he's in some sort of movie based on a Jane Austen novel. "Good night, Miss Montgomery."

Too embarrassed to come up with anything resembling a reply, I practically run for the stairs.

I swear I can hear him humming softly as I flee. I'm not certain, but it sounds like an old Velvet Underground song.

I reach my room and close the door. I'm sweating, but I'm not sure how much of that is the June heat and how much is the thought of kissing the boy who lives down the hall and who listens to the Velvet Underground and can identify international folk duos.

Making friends is a bad idea, and crushing on someone—anyone—is even worse. Especially when it's someone you've known for less than thirty-six hours. *Besides*, I think as I change into a tank top and sleep shorts, *even if I do like him and he does—for some strange, improbable reason—like me, nothing can happen.*

Nothing ever happens. I always make sure of that.

I climb into bed and pull the sheet up to my chin, but no matter how hard I try, I can't sleep. If sending me to Montgomery Falls was supposed to get me away from trouble, then it's beginning to feel like a wasted effort.

EIGHT

"CAN I ASK YOU SOMETHING?" I TIGHTEN MY GRIP ON THE bottom of the stepladder as Aunt Jet struggles to change a light bulb in the upstairs hallway.

Aidan's door is open a crack, but I know he's not inside. I overheard him tell Sam that he was going for a run.

Aidan is gorgeous. He's smart. He listens to decent music, and okay, maybe having two bands in common isn't a lot to build on, but each time he looks at me, I have the feeling that he's seeing me. *Really* seeing me. Not Lacey Chapman's best friend or Elliot Montgomery's daughter or any of the other labels I hide behind. Just me. Cat.

But what do you say to a guy who maybe—just maybe—wanted to kiss you when you know you can never kiss him back?

Even if you want to.

And there's a distinct possibility that I do want to—or, at least, that I would if circumstances were different. If *I* were different.

But I'm not different.

And so I've done the only sensible thing: I've spent the past few days avoiding him—which is not easy when you live in the same house.

Jet mumbles a curse under her breath as she struggles to twist a new, high-efficiency bulb into the socket. She has a shift in a few hours, but for now she's wearing jeans and a T-shirt and her long hair is held back by a blue bandanna. She looks younger than she did the day I arrived—younger than she'll probably look when she gets home from work. Over the past couple of days, it's been hard not to notice the fact that she looks years older after a shift; not for the first time, I wonder if maybe she's been using her own Montgomery talents to somehow help the people she looks after. As far as I know, Jet's abilities don't have the same physical impact mine do, but that doesn't mean using them is entirely without consequence.

"Do you want me to try?"

"No. I've got it." She lets out a puff of air and adjusts her hold. With one final twist, the bulb is in.

"Is it even safe to use those?" I ask. I'm all for combating the climate crisis, but I'm pretty sure most of the fixtures in Montgomery House are at least a hundred years old.

"It's fine," she says, climbing down. "Riley helped me replace the ones downstairs last fall."

"Riley helped you around the house?"

"Sometimes."

That surprises me. Given what happened the last time I saw Riley, it's hard to imagine him ever setting foot inside Montgomery

House again. *Maybe it wasn't as bad as you think*, says a small voice in the back of my head. I ignore it.

We move the ladder to the next fixture, and then I backtrack to get the package of new bulbs as Jet climbs back up. "What was it you wanted to ask me?" she says.

"Do you ever find it hard? Being a Montgomery and, you know . . . being around other people?"

"I think being around others can be challenging for anyone."

"Right. But, like, when you were my age . . . say you wanted to touch someone. But things happened when you did. What would you do about that?" My face flushes so red that I'm kind of amazed the hallway doesn't fill with smoke. This was a bad idea. A stupid idea.

Aunt Jet abandons the light fixture and steps down. "Is that what happened in New York?" she asks hesitantly.

The expression on her face looks perilously close to pity. Which does not make this conversation easier. I don't want anyone pitying me. "This doesn't have anything to do with New York. I was just curious."

Aunt Jet opens her mouth. Closes it. Frowns.

Dad and his stupid rules, I think. It's impossible to keep the bitterness out of my voice. I don't even try. "You know what, never mind."

"Mary Catherine . . ."

Before she can say anything else, I'm gone.

I'm not the first Montgomery to be different.

Jonathan Montgomery left a tiny island with a suitcase of

silver—stolen from a shipwreck, according to what Jet told me when I was little—and a new bride: Eleanor Morgan Montgomery. He built Montgomery House for her. He built it before Riverside Avenue had a name. Before the town was anything more than a glorified logging camp on unceded Wolastoqiyik territory. Some people say Montgomery Falls exists only because Eleanor Morgan Montgomery wanted to live in a town and Jonathan Montgomery wanted to make her happy.

Strange things are said about Morgan women from Mercy Island, and strange things were said about Eleanor. While her husband had brought a suitcase full of silver, she had brought a deck of cards wrapped in silk and tied with a blue ribbon. She used the cards to tell the future and see into the past—at least that's how the story goes.

For all Eleanor's supposed ability to see the future, though, she hadn't seen the influenza outbreak that would take two of her children or the fire that would burn Montgomery House to the ground with her inside a year later. She's buried in the old cemetery on the edge of town. Local kids dare each other to walk over her grave at midnight.

The second Montgomery House—this Montgomery House—wasn't built until a decade later when Jonathan and Eleanor's oldest son returned to Montgomery Falls to establish a textile mill. He had three children: a boy who was stillborn and twin daughters who claimed to be able to speak with the dead, but only on alternating days.

Ask my father about any of this and a pained expression will cross his face. According to Dad, there were no suitcases filled with silver or cards tied with ribbon. There were no psychics and no one ever talked to the dead.

You would think someone who makes his living conjuring worlds out of thin air would have a little more imagination—especially since his own mother had a way of knowing things she didn't have any earthly right to know and his twin sister can calm people with the touch of her skin. But for Dad, all of that stuff is just superstitious nonsense. One of the reasons people in town treated him differently.

Still, even though he thinks it's all nonsense, you would think he might have noticed what started happening to me a few months before my twelfth birthday. You would think he would have noticed when I stopped hugging people or when I started wearing long sleeves no matter how hot it got outside. When I started flinching whenever anyone got too close.

Things like that, after all, can be signs of all kinds of different trouble.

Me? I thought I was losing my mind.

Imagine you're eleven years old. You know there's something wrong with you. Really, really wrong. You know you're seeing and hearing things that aren't there. But it's not all the time. It only happens when you touch someone else. Only ever as long as you touch someone else.

You're not sure what's happening. You don't know what to do. You think maybe you should tell someone, but you don't know how to explain what's going on.

You stop touching people—just to be safe. You stay away from your friends until they're not really your friends anymore. You find excuses to skip school. Maybe you start praying, even though you've never really prayed before.

It was Aunt Jet who figured out what was happening. She noticed how withdrawn I was when Dad and I arrived that summer. How quiet and scared.

"Moodiness"—that's what Dad told her when she asked him about it. "Typical preteen stuff."

Unlike Dad, Aunt Jet has never been in denial about what can happen when you're a Montgomery. Unlike Dad, she paid attention and asked the right questions. She tried to help me—at least until Dad found out and accused her of putting foolish, dangerous ideas in my head. "Delusional"—that's what Dad called her, even though she was one of only two people who had paid enough attention that summer to know that I needed help.

Riley was the other. Riley, who didn't have any sort of second sight but who still seemed to see everything.

The memory of his voice drifts through my head. I tell it to go away, but it's stubborn.

What if we start recording it when it happens? We know you see things when people touch you, but we don't know what or why. If we start writing it down, we could find a pattern. We could crack it like a code.

I don't want to crack it, Riley.

It'll be better if we figure it out. I promise.

"Mary Catherine?"

I jump. After retreating to the study, I'd curled up in one of the chairs with a book, but I've been staring at the same page for the past hour.

Aunt Jet stands in the doorway. She's dressed for work: burgundy scrubs, sturdy white shoes, hair pulled back in a neat bun.

"I'm sorry," she says. "About earlier."

"It's okay," I say, even though it's really not. Jet is the only person I know who might have some idea of what it's like to be me, but because she's too interested in reestablishing peace with my father, I can't talk to her about it.

Sometimes I think I might hate my father. Just a little bit.

"I was wondering," she says hesitantly, "if you could do me a favor." She crosses the room and hands me a white envelope with CONFIDENTIAL stamped across the front in angry red letters. "Would you mind running this next door? The mailman delivered it here by mistake. I'd take it over, but I have to be at work in fifteen minutes and I don't think it should wait until tomorrow. It looks important."

I glance down at the envelope. It's addressed to Riley's mother.

I haven't set foot in Riley's house since I was twelve, and given what happened with Noah a few days ago, I'm not exactly keen on changing that. "I don't think a day will make a difference," I say, trying to hand the envelope back.

Jet doesn't take it. "It might be nice for Noah to see a friendly face. It might be good for the two of you to get reacquainted."

"Trust me, Noah Fraser does not want to see me." *Or possibly anyone*, I add silently.

Aunt Jet fixes me with a heavy, disappointed look. "He's had a hard time, Mary Catherine. The whole family has."

My aunt may be a pushover, but she is surprisingly good at laying on the guilt.

Reluctantly, I stand and set my book on the edge of the chair. According to Aidan, Noah spends most of his time skulking around town and hanging out at dive bars. He's probably not even home.

Aunt Jet nods approvingly. "Don't just leave it in the mailbox," she says as I follow her outside.

Right. Of course. That would be too easy.

I wait until she climbs into the Buick and drives away, then I cut across the lawn, heading for the tall hedge that separates the Montgomery and Fraser properties. The shortcut Riley and I had used all that summer—a narrow space created by a weird bend in the trunks and helped along by hundreds of crossings—is still here, though it's a tighter squeeze than it used to be.

I pluck a twig from my hair as I step out the other side and into grass so high that it hits me midcalf. All of the flower beds are filled with the shriveled remains of dead tiger lilies and hungry weeds. The yard was like this when they first moved in. It was wild and neglected—until Riley's mother brought in a team of landscapers who left it looking neat and trim and just a little bit fake.

As I climb the front steps, I think about ignoring Aunt Jet's instructions and shoving the envelope into the mailbox, but having committed myself, I might as well see things through thoroughly.

I reach out and ring the bell. No one answers. I wait and try again. Just as I'm thinking I'll have to leave the envelope in the mailbox after all, the door opens a crack.

Riley's mother stares out at me through a four-inch gap.

I swallow. "Hi, Mrs. Fraser. My aunt asked me to bring this

over." I lift the envelope a little, holding it out in front of me. "It got delivered to us by mistake."

The one sky-blue eye I can see watches me unblinkingly.

I shift my weight from one foot to the other. Thinking maybe she just doesn't recognize me, I say, "I'm here visiting Jet for the summer. I'm Mary Catherine. Her niece? Elliot's daughter?"

She watches me for a moment more, then opens the door fully before heading down the hall.

Unsure of what to do, I step over the threshold and follow her toward the back of the house. Outside, it's early evening, the sun still bright and full, but inside, all of the curtains have been drawn. The Frasers have a housekeeper—or at least they used to—but even in the dim light, a layer of dust is visible on the half-moon tables that dot the hallway like stepping stones. There are pictures on the tables, but each frame has been turned facedown. I lift one of the pictures as Mrs. Fraser disappears through the kitchen door at the end of the hall. Riley stares up at me. Younger than he was when they moved in. Maybe only seven or eight. There's a gap in his smile where one of his front teeth should be. Gingerly, I set him back down, just the way he was, and then head for the kitchen.

I remember the kitchen, like almost everything else in the Fraser house, being immaculate. Now the island in the center of the room is covered in take-out containers and the dishwasher door hangs open. Mrs. Fraser sits at the table as a kettle on the stove begins to screech. She draws her thin, pale pink robe tightly around herself.

Even like this—no makeup, not dressed, hair loose and a little wild, and acting like one of the living dead—she is startlingly beautiful. "Too beautiful for her husband"—that's what people in town used to say. "Too weak to stand up to his crap"—I remember Noah muttering that once, when he didn't know his brother and I were listening.

"Mrs. Fraser?"

She blinks, slowly, and seems to realize I'm here for the first time. "Hello, Mary Catherine."

"Hi." I fold the envelope and shove it into my back pocket. I don't know what it contains, but I'm pretty sure it isn't something Riley's mom can deal with. Not today, anyway.

The kettle on the stove continues to wail. As I cross the room to turn off the burner, I realize all four are on. It's lucky she hasn't burned down the house. I switch them off and then look for a clean mug and a tea bag. Not finding either, I settle for pouring her a glass of water from the tap.

I set the glass in front of her. There's a small, white paper bag on the table—one that looks identical to the bag I saw Noah carrying the other day.

Mrs. Fraser wraps her fingers around the glass, but doesn't drink.

"Is Noah home? Or the housekeeper?"

"Ruth doesn't come anymore," she says.

"Oh."

"Have you come to play with Riley?"

Before I can answer, before I realize what she's about to do, she sets the glass on the edge of the table and reaches for my hand.

I have a single moment of clarity—a moment when I try to

pull away as her nails dig into my skin—and then a roaring sound overwhelms me, filling my ears and my head as I'm thrown back.

The kitchen ceiling becomes a slate-gray sky as a gaping hole, six feet deep, opens up in the floor below me.

Dirt pours into my mouth as I try to cry out. It floods my throat and nose and slips into the space between my eyelids and my eyes. I can't breathe. I can't see. I can't—

Suddenly, air comes rushing in, and the kitchen slams back into place.

I gasp as tears blur my vision and roll down my cheeks. Noah is there, pulling his mother away. She doesn't look at him. Her eyes are locked on me as she says, "I hear him. At night. He comes home to sleep in his bed. He wants to be here."

Taking a step back, I accidentally knock over a chair and send it crashing to the ground.

Noah glances at me. He opens his mouth as though to say something, but then gives his head a sharp shake and guides his mother from the room.

I will myself to move, to get out of the house. My mouth and throat feel bone-dry. I swear, I can still taste grit; the remembered sensation is so strong that if I were to spit, I think I'd spit mud.

I manage to take a step toward the back door, then another. I slip outside and across the screened-in porch and then around the house. By the time I'm through the gap in the hedge, I feel a little bit steadier. Still shaken, but steadier.

It's not the first time I've been buried alive, but it's the first time in a long while.

"Cat!"

I don't turn around. I keep going until I reach Montgomery House.

Noah calls my name a second time, closer now, and adds "please" at the end. It's the "please" that does it. The way he sort of trips over the consonants.

I turn at the bottom of the porch steps, putting the house at my back.

My eyes keep watering. I scrub at them, annoyed; I know it probably looks like I'm crying when, really, it's just the memory of all that dirt. The second my feet stop moving, I become aware of the headache. It pulses in bursts of three—faintest, fainter, faint.

Noah catches up and then stops just in front of me. Red marks run down his cheek. Scratches, I realize. My hand tingles in response. When I glance down, I notice three red crescents in my palm. "Is she always like this?"

Noah follows my gaze and mutters something under his breath. He reaches for my hand and flinches when I pull away.

There's something wary and a little wounded in the way he looks at me. The wariness isn't new: he had it years ago, always looking slightly startled whenever someone spoke to him, more comfortable with books than people. But the wounded edge? The wounded edge is definitely new.

"It's not you," I say, surprising myself. "I just don't like to be touched." I reach into my back pocket and pull out the envelope. "This got delivered to our place by mistake. I was supposed to give it to your mom, but . . ." My voice trails off as a particularly strong burst of pain flashes through my head.

Noah takes a deep breath as he reaches for the letter. His eyes are darker than I remember. A brown so dark they look almost black. "Thanks."

I stand there, torn and confused. It doesn't make sense. Why wouldn't Noah want Riley to be found? How can someone who is capable of such a horrible thought get that hurt look in his eyes? On impulse, I hand Noah the letter and then touch his wrist.

I touch his wrist, and as I get sucked down, I try to control what I see. I'm not really sure what I'm doing; I've only ever tried to do this once before. The pain in my head flares brilliant and bright and—

A windswept hill. A slab of granite with Riley's name chiseled above two dates. A sky that's the exact same shade of blue as the bike Riley used to ride. Warm sun on my face and a soft breeze over my skin.

Peace. It's peaceful here . . .

And then it all disappears. It rushes away with a popping sound, leaving me swaying slightly on my feet.

Both of them think he's dead, I realize. *Both of them think Riley's really gone.*

"What did you do?" says Noah. There's no way he could have felt anything—as far as I've ever been able to tell, no one but Jet has ever felt anything when I touched them—but he's staring at me with the strangest expression on his face.

"You want him to be found. You don't want Riley to stay missing." Without giving Noah a chance to reply, I turn and climb the steps. I don't look back, but I can swear I feel him watching me as I disappear into the safety of Montgomery House.

NINE

I MANAGE TO MAKE IT UP THE STAIRS AND TO MY ROOM,
but the idea of crossing the extra few feet to the bathroom—even
if it's the only way to get to the pills in my backpack—is laughable.
I get as far as my bed, and then my legs stop cooperating.

The pain hasn't been this bad since the night everything in
New York blew up. Before that, it had been years.

I close my eyes and try to lie absolutely still, desperately hoping
that if I'm quiet and motionless, the pain will abate.

After a while, someone knocks on my bedroom door. I start to
glance at the alarm clock on the nightstand, but then think better
of it: I can't see the numbers without turning my head, and turning my head feels like a very bad idea. Turning my head would
anger the microscopic armies that seem to be waging a very large
war between my temples and behind my eyes.

The door opens.

Noah.

I simultaneously try to push myself up and shove Pengy out of sight. The little warring armies are not happy, but at least Noah won't see me cuddling a stuffed penguin. *Don't throw up. Don't throw up. Don't throw up.* I cling to the three-word mantra and concentrate on breathing deeply through my nose as I somehow manage to raise myself to a sitting position. I turn on the bedside lamp and wince.

The wince doesn't go unnoticed. Noah closes the door partway, leaving it open a few inches so that it still lets in some light from the hallway. Then he crosses the room and turns off the lamp. "Better?"

"Yeah," I admit, studying his face in the dim light. He looks more or less like he did out in the yard, but the way I see him has changed.

The images I get are tricky. Sometimes they're undeniable—like what I saw when Mrs. Fraser grabbed me. Her greatest fear is that her son is dead. That he is buried somewhere, abandoned in the dirt. That he is turning to dirt himself.

More often than not, though, their meaning isn't straightforward. It's like reading tarot cards or staring at those paintings of inkblots. A tombstone can be fear, but it can also be desire. Someone who wants to hurt themselves. Someone who wants to hurt someone else. Someone who is watching someone else suffer and who just wants the pain to end.

Noah told me he didn't want Riley to be found, so when I touched him, I tried to see desire.

I had been prepared to see something awful, but it was peaceful, up on that hill. It didn't feel like a bad place.

Noah reaches into his pocket and pulls out a prescription bottle. "I brought you these."

"You expect me to take strange pills from a guy I don't know?"

That slightly wounded look slips back into his eyes; really, though, what does he expect?

"That's why I brought the bottle. So that you can see what they are. The doctor prescribed them for my mom's migraines."

"How do you know I have a migraine?"

"You used to get sick sometimes, if someone touched you. I didn't remember that until Mom grabbed you—until I saw your face in the kitchen." He hesitates, then adds, "Riley used to say you saw things. That you were some kind of psychic."

"I have no idea what you're talking about." It's stupid to feel betrayed, but I do. Even after everything that happened, I expected Riley to keep my secrets. Just like I had kept his.

As long as Noah's here, I guess I might as well take advantage of him. "I have pills. They're in my backpack. In the bathroom."

He disappears into the Jack and Jill bathroom I share with Aunt Jet. He comes back with the pill bottle and a little paper cup filled with water, both of which he sets on the nightstand.

As I down two pills, Noah sits—not next to me on the bed the way I imagine Aidan would, but on the floor, making sure not to invade my space more than he has to.

"Don't be angry at Riley for telling me," he says. "He worried about you." Silence stretches out between us, and then he adds, "I worried about you, too. You were so little and scrawny, and sometimes you'd have these fits where you just sort of keeled over."

"Oh, yeah," I say, crumpling the cup and returning it to the nightstand. "I was an adorable child." It's hard to imagine I ever met Noah's description, but there are pictures to prove it. If my life were a Judy Blume novel, getting my period would have heralded the start of a magical time. Instead, I gained psychic powers and thirty pounds, and I had to start using my allowance to buy tampons and acne facial washes—you know, things I shouldn't have been embarrassed to ask my dad to buy but somehow was . . . probably because of the patriarchy or something. I twist the edge of the comforter between my fingers. "You noticed me?"

"You were at our house practically every day. Hard not to notice."

"I don't know why Riley told you I was psychic. It was probably a joke or something. He was probably just messing with you."

"So you didn't see anything when you touched me?"

"Why did you tell me you don't want Riley to be found?" I counter.

He glances at my hand as though checking for a trace of those red marks. "You saw my mother. She thinks she can still hear him. That he's out there. That he comes to the house at night. Her doctor says she'll get over it, but the thought that he might be alive is the only thing holding her together. Once they find him, once she realizes he's dead, I won't be able to stop her from completely breaking. I put up posters because she keeps asking me to, and I pretend he's still out there, and I wait for the day it all falls apart."

"You don't know that he's . . ." I can't quite bring myself to say the word "dead," but I don't need to: Noah knows what I mean.

"It's been three months. Some people say maybe he ran away, but he wouldn't have done that to Mom. He wouldn't have put her through that. And he sure as hell didn't get lost in those woods."

I stare at him. "What are you saying?"

I think maybe I know, but the idea is so big and horrible that it hovers just out of reach.

Instead of answering, Noah pushes himself to his feet and walks over to the window. He doesn't say anything for a long minute. "You can see his room from here."

I swallow. It feels like there's a lump in my throat. "Yeah."

He turns back to me. "If you were psychic, would you tell me?"

"Psychics aren't real."

"Then why did you just look away?"

I force myself to meet his gaze. "I wouldn't have pegged you for the kind of guy who believes in stuff like that."

"I wasn't."

"What changed?"

"Desperation." The expression on his face is so intense that it feels like I might burn up under the heat of it.

"Why would it matter? Even if I was psychic, which I'm not because they don't exist, why would it matter to you?"

"Two years ago, a kid was murdered in Charlotte County. There was a local woman—a psychic. She helped police find the body."

I sit up a little straighter as something twists in my stomach. "Murdered? You don't think . . ." One look at his face, though, and it's clear that's exactly what he does think. "But who would do that? Who would want to hurt Riley that badly?"

There is a fierceness in Noah's eyes that makes me shiver. "I don't know, but I'm hoping you can help me. I can't find Riley without it destroying my mother, but I can find whoever hurt him. Because someone did. There's no way he ran away or got lost. I don't care what anyone says. Someone out there hurt him—either on purpose or by accident—and then covered it up. It's the only thing that makes any sense. I'm going to find them."

"And then what?"

"I'm going to make sure they can't hurt anyone else."

It's the kind of line you expect to hear in a bad movie. The kind of line that should be delivered by a burly action star. It should sound ridiculous coming from Noah Fraser. But when he says it, it doesn't sound ridiculous. It doesn't sound like a line at all.

"I need your help, Cat. You were Riley's best friend."

"Five years ago." I push myself unsteadily to my feet. "And, anyway, I'm not psychic." A sharp, stabbing pain drives through my temples. Too much movement before the pills have had a chance to really kick in. I squeeze my eyes shut, and because they are shut, I don't see Noah cross the room and reach for my arm in an attempt to steady me. I don't see him, and I don't try to move away.

Noah touches me, and I'm pulled back into his head.

A short time ago, his greatest desire—a desire he probably can't admit to himself because it contradicts what he thinks he wants—was for Riley to have a final resting place.

But that was then.

This time when I get dragged into Noah Fraser's head, I see something darker. Violence and blood and the things he wants to do to whoever hurt his brother.

I wrench myself away, and as I do, my arm hits the lamp on the nightstand. It crashes to the floor and breaks, sending shards of broken porcelain sliding across the hardwood.

The bedroom door opens. "Cat?"

Aidan stands in the doorway, hair wet from the shower, a plain black T-shirt clinging to his chest. He glances from me to the broken lamp to Noah. "Are you all right?"

"She's fine," says Noah.

"How about you let her answer?"

I'm okay, I say—or at least I try to. My head is still full of blood and violence, and the pain is so intense that it makes my vision go black at the edges. Somehow, I manage to find my voice. "I think you should go," I say. I can't bring myself to look at Noah. Not after what I saw.

"Will you think about what I said?"

"I don't have to. I can't help you." Even if he's right, even if someone out there hurt Riley, there isn't anything I can do to help.

He stares at me for a long, painful moment. "Won't and can't aren't the same thing," he says before turning and leaving. His footsteps fade down the hall. A moment later, the heavy front door slams closed.

It feels like the whole house lets out a sigh of relief.

Aidan turns to me, face serious. "What was that all about?"

"Nothing," I lie.

I'm not psychic. I'm not psychic, and I can't help Noah Fraser.

TEN

AT LEAST ONE GOOD THING COMES OUT OF MY BIZARRO confrontation with Noah: it seems to clear the air between Aidan and me. The thought of the maybe-kiss still lurks in the background, but what happened with Noah is big enough and strange enough that it gives us something else to talk about the next day. Not that I tell Aidan what really happened. Feeling only slightly guilty, I play the nighttime visit off as just another example of Riley's older brother being, well, kind of weird before asking Aidan if I can borrow his laptop for a few hours after dinner.

Maybe it's a shitty thing to do, but I'm not blowing my carefully cultivated cover of normalcy because of Noah Fraser—no matter how sorry I feel for him.

And I do feel sorry for him. *Really, really sorry*, I think as I stare down at his face on the screen. Someone set up a prayer page for Riley, and it's filled with pictures from the vigils and search parties. Noah is in some of them, looking uncomfortable and angry in the background.

In addition to pictures, there are comments. Hundreds spanning the past three months. I spend an hour reading them and barely make a dent. All of them seem normal. Supportive. None hint at the idea that someone out there might not have liked Riley, let alone have wanted to hurt him.

The news stories I find aren't any more help. Despite Noah's insistence that someone out there had harmed—maybe even killed—Riley, none of the stories indicate the police have ever suspected foul play. *Police have no clues. Public asked for help. No new leads.* The same clusters of words appear over and over. The same people, too. Teachers and friends, but also people who didn't seem to know Riley well but who obviously liked talking to reporters.

The fact that I finally get on a computer and am looking up stuff about Riley instead of checking what's happening back in New York is not lost on me. It doesn't mean that I'm taking Noah's request seriously, though. I'm not helping him. Definitely not.

Even if I wanted to help, what on earth could I do?

Noah's voice echoes through my head. *You were his best friend.*

A shout from Sam drifts up from the kitchen, mercifully cutting into my thoughts. "Mary Catherine! Phone!"

I shove the laptop under a pillow and push myself to my feet. Technically, Jet hasn't told me not to borrow any of the computers in the house, but given that she's been keeping her own laptop out of sight, I can't imagine she'd be happy to catch me online.

I pass Sam in the downstairs hall on my way to the kitchen. "Is it my father?" I spoke to my dad a few days ago, an uncomfortable call that kept cutting in and out because he was on his way to a writers' retreat upstate before flying out to California for meetings.

Sam shrugs. "It's some girl."

Lacey. My heart skips and then races. She must have gotten the number from Dad or found it online.

Part of me wants to run for the phone; another part of me wants to head back upstairs and pretend I'm not home. It's tempting to believe Lacey has had enough time to think and calm down—maybe even enough time to be sorry—but there's this tiny voice in my head that says things can't possibly be that easy.

I force myself to walk into the kitchen. Taking a deep breath, I wipe my palms on my jeans and then lift the receiver. "Hello?"

"Way to keep a girl waiting."

It's not Lacey; the call isn't even really for me. Relief and disappointment wash over me. I'm not sure which is stronger, so I try to tell myself that I don't really feel anything.

"Hang on, Skylar. I'll get Aidan."

"Wait! I'm calling for you. Sorry. I didn't know your cell number. I wanted to know if you felt like going to a movie? Tonight? With Joey, Chase, and me? I have the night off from work." Before I can ask, she adds, "Aidan can't come. He has an essay due for English Lit Rewind."

I hesitate. The idea of getting out of the house for a few hours is appealing, but I have a feeling that the more time I spend with Skylar, the more I'll have to remind myself that friends aren't something I want—or need—in my life.

"Please? I know you don't like horror movies, but this one is supposed to be really, really good. Like, seriously great. And it's only five bucks to get in 'cause it's cheap night. I'll pay. I'm paying for Joey anyway."

There's something sad and hopeful in her voice. That puppy-dog factor that makes me feel like I'll be kicking her, somehow, if I say no. "You don't have to pay for me."

"You're coming?" She lets out an actual squeal. "Chase and I will be there in twenty minutes. Joey's going to meet us downtown."

Any chance to change my mind is cut off with the click of the receiver.

"That was amazing!" Joey lets out a wallop for emphasis as the four of us spill into the alley between the theater and a bridal shop. "AFUCKINGMAZING." He throws his half-empty popcorn bag into the air.

It may be the first time I've actually seen him smile.

"Hey!" objects Skylar as we're peppered by kernels.

"Sorry, Sky." He tugs her close, gently spins her around, and then carefully finger-combs the debris from her hair.

Chase glances at me and rolls his eyes.

I try to smile, but it feels tight around the edges. I tell myself that I am not missing out, that I am fine with the way things are, but there's this tiny weight in the center of my chest as Joey frees the last bit of popcorn from Skylar's hair. His fingertips skate along her temple, like touching her is the most natural thing in the world.

I imagine what it would be like to touch someone—and be touched—without having to worry about what you'll see inside their head. No matter how many times I have the thought, it almost always makes something inside my chest feel tight.

Skylar turns toward me as Joey steps away. "Hey—are you okay?"

"Yeah. Of course." Without consciously thinking about it, I had raised a hand to my own temple. "Headache," I lie. "It'll go away in a minute."

The guys pull ahead of us.

"I'm sorry about the movie," she says. "I thought it would be better. Too many gags and jump scares and not enough depth."

"How would you change it?" I ask. It's a question my father asks me every time I bail on a TV show or complain about a book.

She bites her lip as she considers the question.

Chase waits for us at the mouth of the alley. "You guys look serious."

"We're trying to figure out how to fix the movie," says Skylar, rocking up on her toes a little bit with each step.

"What?" Joey stops in the middle of the sidewalk and turns. His glasses slide down to the tip of his nose; he pushes them up, absently. "You can't fix something that's perfect."

Chase snorts. "You think every low-budget, supposedly found-footage movie is perfect."

"I've never said that."

"No? Do you even remember your list of suggestions for the first, inaugural Montgomery Falls Horror Fest?"

"Inaugural means first, idiot."

Chase glances at Skylar for confirmation. She nods, and his gaze turns beseechingly to me. "Sorry," I say, shrugging. "Inaugural does, indeed, mean first."

Joey laughs, and the sound seems to trip and stumble. His laugh is as awkward as the rest of him. Even Skylar seems to cringe a little.

"When is the horror festival?" I ask.

"Last week in August," says Chase.

"I still say we should have timed it for Halloween." Joey shakes his head. "Imagine watching *Halloween* on Halloween."

"Right," says Skylar, "because sitting in the middle of the town square in October for five hours wouldn't be cold at all."

Joey drapes an arm over her shoulder and tries to raise his eyebrows in a way that I can only guess is meant to be flirtatious. "You don't think I could keep you warm?"

Skylar blushes.

Glancing up at the darkening sky, he says, "I have to get home. My old man's been giving me grief about taking the car out. He thinks the cops are going to pull me over for the taillights, and he doesn't want to get stuck with the ticket." He glances at Chase. "You and your cousin can still take a look at it tomorrow, right?"

Chase nods. "Yeah. Just bring it by around noon."

Skylar pouts, but she doesn't try to convince Joey to stay; she just gives him a kiss and sends him on his way, slapping his butt as he turns. She watches until he rounds the corner, then spins back to Chase and me. "Where to now?"

No one has any ideas—Skylar and Chase because they've already been everywhere about a million times and me because I haven't been anywhere—so we end up going to McDonald's, where Chase tries to set a new record for number of hamburgers consumed by a single varsity athlete in sixty minutes. Skylar buys me a Happy Meal, claiming I need sustenance and a toy. "Since Joey bailed, you're my date," she says.

I try to give her the toy—a blue plastic bear from some kids' movie that matches the pink one she got with her own meal—later, as we stand to leave. She hesitates, but her eyes light up. "Really?"

I shrug. "Sure."

She beams and takes the toy from my tray. "Don't tell anyone, but I really love this movie," she confides. "I've seen it four times."

None of us really feel like going home yet, so we end up wandering and finally reach the old train bridge.

Years ago, trains passed through Montgomery Falls every day. They stopped after the last mill closed. The tracks are still here, though, slicing the town in half, and the bridge is still standing. It spans the whole river—almost a mile—its iron beams slowly turning to rust.

I guess pulling up the tracks and tearing down the bridge would be like admitting all those jobs and all that money are never coming back.

I glance up at the bridge. Even though it's no longer in use, light bulbs hang down from the overhead crossbeams at semi-regular intervals. "Didn't you say Riley saw a light up there before he disappeared?" I ask Chase, momentarily forgetting the things Aidan told me about Riley and Skylar and that maybe I shouldn't mention him around her.

"So?"

"So, if the bridge is lighted anyway . . ."

"Huh. I never thought of that." Chase frowns and then

brightens. "The ghost light would be moving. It would stand out. And it's probably blue."

"Why blue?"

"Blue is more ghostly. Ghostlier."

"You think the ghost is worried about its street cred?"

Chase laughs. Unlike Joey's laughter, there's nothing awkward about the sound. It's easy and good-natured. He pulls his ball cap out of his back pocket and slips it onto my head, not noticing how I tense up. "Why are you so interested in the light? Scared you'll see something if we go up there?"

"No."

"Good." He grins and starts up the slope to the tracks.

Skylar and I follow.

"Ghostly glows aside, why bother lighting the bridge if there aren't any trains?" The incline is steeper than it looks, and my voice comes out a little on the breathless side. "I don't remember there being lights the last time I was here."

"The lights haven't been up that long," explains Skylar. "People thought they would be pretty."

"And they thought they'd be a good idea after Riley crashed his dad's boat into the bridge," says Chase as he reaches the top.

"Seriously?" I remember the week his father had bought that boat. A "pleasure craft"—that's what he called it. Big enough to carry twelve, with a little cabin underneath the deck.

Riley took a bunch of people out on the boat after the Riverview Lions won a game back in November. Amber. The guys from the team. A few people from school. They were having a great time until Riley hit the bridge. The cops arrested Riley for—" He turns back to Skylar. "What was it, Sky?"

"Property damage—though they weren't exactly thrilled about all the drinking on the boat."

"He was drunk?" No matter how much Riley might have changed over the past few years, I can't imagine him being stupid enough to drink and get behind the wheel of anything.

"Nah," says Chase. "Everyone else was, but Riley practically never drank."

"You weren't there? Aren't you on the team, too?"

Skylar pokes him as she reaches his side. "Chase was in the supply closet with an adoring Lions fan."

"It wasn't a supply closet. Don't make it sound so cheap."

As I reach the top, I lose my balance. Chase grabs my arm to steady me. Thankfully, I had pulled on a long-sleeved shirt before heading out. "Pretty sure Aidan will kick my ass if I let you tumble to your death." He plucks his hat from my head. "And this one is my favorite. I don't want to lose it."

I swallow. The drop isn't that bad, but the idea that Aidan might be upset if I fell makes my heart speed up just a little, and as I follow Chase and Skylar to the wooden barrier that stretches across the mouth of the bridge, I can't help but think of that night on the porch and the way Aidan had leaned down toward me.

I tell myself that Chase is exaggerating, that Aidan wouldn't really care. I remind myself that nothing could happen even if he did. Still, there's a part of me that holds on to Chase's words, wrapping them up and tucking them away to examine later.

Even though it's dark, the moon and the glow from the street-lights on the avenue below are enough to illuminate big black letters that spell out NO TRESPASSING and DANGER. There's a gap underneath the words where someone has kicked in the bottom two boards of the makeshift wall.

With his long legs and muscular arms, Chase just clambers over the barricade, but Skylar and I have to wriggle underneath.

Even though the bridge is lighted, the bulbs are so few and far between that there are thick pools of shadows separating each small circle of light. Chase starts across, fearless, but I stay in place, staring down at the gaps between rail ties while I try to run a mental structural analysis on a bridge that's been neglected for decades.

If it was built to handle freight trains, surely it can hold three teenagers—even if one of them is on the chubby side.

"Don't worry," says Skylar, picking up on my hesitation. She digs in her oversized purse and then hands me a large wrench, a ring holding about fifty keys, and a pack of wax crayons. "Hold these," she commands, then shoves her hand deep into the bag. She comes up with her phone and turns on the flashlight function.

"Do I even want to know what else you have in there?" I ask, gingerly slipping the wrench, keys, and crayons back into her bag.

"I used to be a Girl Scout. I excelled at the whole always-being-prepared thing. Got a merit badge and everything." She shines the beam from her phone over the spaces not covered by the small pools of light that dot the bridge. "Come on, Dorothy," she says, catching the bottom hem of my shirt and giving it one quick tug. "Step onto the Yellow Brick Road."

What the hell, I think. *What's the worst that can happen?*

It's cooler up here. The wind skims the water and then swoops up to wrap itself around us as we make our way across the bridge.

Once we've covered almost two-thirds of the distance, I turn and glance back. Reduced to pinpricks of light, Montgomery Falls looks even smaller than it does during the day.

If Riley told someone he saw the ghost light, does that mean he was up here the night before he disappeared, or would he have just seen it from below?

Not that I actually believe in the ghost light.

Chase walks to the edge of the bridge, to a gap between two support beams. At first, I think he just wants a better view of the water, but then he crouches down like he's going to try to hang off the side.

"What are you doing?"

Skylar is looking in the other direction. At the sharp note in my voice, she turns and then curses.

Chase just laughs. "Don't think I can hang off the edge?"

And here I thought Joey was the asshole of the group.

Skylar passes me her phone, slapping it into my hand so hard that my palm stings. As she does—

My back collides with a wall, hard enough to bruise. Hands slip under my skirt as I tug at someone's shirt. A mouth against mine that tastes like beer and caramel. Someone I want. Someone I need. The body pulls back and I see a familiar face. Riley. And in the background, laughter and cruel words like the ones on the poster. They rise up like a tidal wave . . .

The bridge comes rushing back. Somehow, I manage to keep my balance. Somehow, I manage not to drop the phone between the ties as Skylar grabs Chase's arm and pulls him away from the edge.

She hits his shoulder with her tiny fists. "You. Are. Not. Funny."

I think Chase grins. I think he says something, but I turn away too quickly to catch it. A wave of heat rushes across my face. Things inside tighten at the remembered sensation of a body against mine. It feels wrong. Not just because I saw something that should be private, but because of the taunts that followed. Because I didn't just see Skylar's desire: I saw her fear.

I clench my left hand.

I *hate* this.

Keeping my back to Skylar and Chase, I stare out over the water, waiting for the stolen heat inside of me to fade. *No wonder Lacey hates me*, I think. *No wonder Riley was scared of me.*

"Cat?" Skylar steps up next to me. "Chase was just being an asshole. He's sorry. We're sorry."

A faint headache blossoms at my temples. I know I should tell her that's not it, that they didn't do anything, but it's easier to let her think that I'm mad at them than it is to try to explain what's wrong. It's safer.

"It's okay," I say, taking the coward's path as I run a hand over my face. I start to turn to Skylar, but the moon slips out from behind the clouds, and something at the edge of the water catches my eye. I try to shine the light from the phone toward it, but we're too far from shore. The beam travels out over the water for a few feet and then scatters into the darkness.

The phone beeps: a warning that the battery is low.

"Skylar . . ." I bite my lip and then point to the northern bank. "Is that someone in the water?"

Chase steps up beside us and squints into the dark. "Probably just driftwood."

But he doesn't sound sure. Without discussing it, we all start walking toward the north end of the bridge. We're still several yards away when the glow from the moon shines enough light on the riverbank to see that the dark shape at the water's edge definitely isn't driftwood.

I don't know which of us starts running first.

With his long legs, Chase beats us to the north barricade. This time, there isn't any hole for Skylar and I to slip through. He laces his fingers, forming a step with his hands. He boosts us up, first Skylar, then me. My knee collides painfully with the top boards as I go over, and I almost fall as I come down on the other side.

Chase hits the ground a few seconds after me. He pulls out his own phone and shines it toward the water. The riverbank on this side is muddy and choked with crabgrass and the roots of dead trees. Chase passes the light over the water's edge, and I see it: a dark shape only half on shore.

"It's just garbage," he says. He lets out a relieved laugh that cracks a little in the middle.

I wait for the tightness inside my chest to unclench. It doesn't. In my hand, Skylar's phone beeps again. I start down the muddy slope, struggling to keep my balance. The beam of light flickers and then goes out as the phone dies.

"Cat?" Skylar calls my name from the top of the bank. "It's nothing, just leave it."

But the closer I get, the less like nothing it seems, until I'm close enough that even without the light from the phone, I can pick out a red shirt and a pair of high-tops.

ELEVEN

I STUMBLE THE REST OF THE WAY DOWN THE BANK ONLY TO
lose my balance at the bottom and hit the ground hard. Chase is
right behind me. In the glow from his phone, I catch a glimpse of
a pale face and dark hair. A girl.

It's not Riley. Relief floods me as I push myself unsteadily to
my feet.

Skylar starts crying. Huge, panicked sounds.

"Holy shit." The beam from Chase's phone shakes almost as
badly as his voice. "Holyshitholyshitholyshit. It's Rachel. Rachel
Larsen."

For a split second, I see someone else. Another girl lying dead
in the dirt. The girl Riley and Noah and I found up by the textile
mill.

Pushing the image aside, I step around Skylar and edge forward. Chase grabs the back of my shirt. "Wait. We can't touch
her."

He hands Skylar his phone. She can't seem to stop crying, but she shines the light over the girl, over soaked clothes and tangled hair. There's no telling how long the girl—*the body*—has been here or how long she was in the water before washing up on the riverbank. There are dark splotches on her face—bruises or dirt, maybe—but it's her arms that make me gasp. Her skin is covered in thin, precise cuts. Dozens of lines that form either crosses or Xs, depending on the angle.

Chase grabs a stick of driftwood and approaches the body. He prods it gently, and it lets out a small, gasping noise and moves ever so slightly.

Cursing, Chase jumps back.

It takes me a few seconds to comprehend what's happening, to realize that the girl—Rachel—is still alive.

Skylar grabs my arm.

"Shitshitshitshit." Chase repeats the word over and over as he drops the driftwood and pulls Rachel out of the water. Too late, it occurs to me that maybe we shouldn't move her, that she might have internal injuries.

"Rachel?" Chase crouches in the mud. "Can you hear me?"

She doesn't answer.

Skylar pulls in great gulps of air like she's on the edge of hysterics as she grips my arm. I take Chase's phone from her and dial 911 as Chase presses two fingers against Rachel's neck, checking for a pulse. When he finds one, his whole body seems to sag in relief.

I try to tell the 911 operator what happened. She's skeptical—even more so when I can't tell her where we are. After a minute, I give up and hand the phone to Chase.

He stands and starts pacing. "We're on the north side of the river. Near the old bridge. Through the trees just before Miller Field, if you're on the highway. We found Rachel Larsen. She's a student at Riverview. She's in really bad shape. She was in the water. She's barely breathing." He's quiet for a minute, listening to something the operator is saying. "Just a second."

He hits mute on the phone. "She wants one of us to stay on the line and walk to the highway so the police can find us. It's not far. Maybe ten minutes through the trees. Longer in the dark. But someone should stay here. With her."

Skylar is still crying. Chase whirls on her. "Jesus, Sky—would you stop it for five seconds?"

She cries harder.

"Don't yell at her," I snap, my own voice practically a shout.

Instantly, I regret it. Chase looks like he's on the verge of tears, too. "I'm sorry." He turns to Skylar and folds her into a hug. "I'm sorry, Sky. I didn't mean it."

He looks at me imploringly over her shoulder. "Someone needs to go to the road. Someone needs to stay here." From the tone in his voice, I know he doesn't want to be the one to decide. I know he's asking me to make the choice.

I swallow. The last thing I want is to be left here on my own, but Chase at least has an idea of how to get to the highway. And Skylar can't stay here. Not like this.

"I'll stay," I say, wishing my voice didn't shake. "You and Skylar go to the highway. I'll stay here."

Relief and guilt flash across Chase's face as he pulls away from

Skylar. "You have your phone, right? So you can call us if anything happens. What's the number?"

I shake my head. "I don't have a phone."

His voice gets loud again. "How can you not have a phone?"

I shrug, thinking that if I die out here, my dad will at least spend the rest of his life second-guessing his choice to cut my technology privileges. Oddly, the thought isn't all that satisfying.

"Sky, where's your phone?"

"Shit . . . ," I say, briefly glancing back the way we came. "I dropped it when I fell." Not that it would do much good with the battery dead. "It's okay, Chase. I'll be all right."

"None of this is okay. We can't just leave you here."

"You have to. I'll be fine." At the look on his face, I add, "Okay, not *fine* fine, but fine enough."

He lets out a frustrated string of curses, shakes his head, and then turns toward the trees. As he walks away, he unmutes his phone and tells the operator that he's heading to the road.

Skylar hesitates. Before I can guess what she's about to do, she throws her arms around me. For someone so tiny, she has the brute strength of a tank. Thankfully, the closest she comes to touching skin is the tickle of her hair against my neck.

"Be careful," she says. She squeezes me a little tighter, almost like she's trying to keep me from falling. "You're okay," she says just before she lets me go.

You're okay. Not you *will* be okay. The phrasing tugs at some memory, some half-forgotten thing, but I can't catch it.

She turns and heads after Chase.

I watch the glow from his phone for a minute, and then, not knowing what else to do, I lower myself to the ground next to Rachel Larsen.

I don't know if she can hear me, but I talk to her anyway. I tell her that Chase and Skylar are getting help, that she just has to hang on a little longer. And then I lie. I tell her that she's all right and that she's safe, even as every noise around us makes me jump.

Rachel makes a small sound. So small that I'm not sure if it's real or if I imagined it. I lean closer just as her eyes flutter open. She reaches toward me. There's a long leather cord twisted around her fingers. I don't want to touch her, but I force myself to take her hand.

I don't see anything. It's like that time I accidentally touched Lacey one night when she fell asleep during a movie: there's just nothing.

Something cool and smooth presses against my palm. I turn her hand over, revealing a small, silver circle. The glow from the moon is just enough for me to make out the design etched on the front.

Saint Anthony. The patron saint of lost things.

My breath catches in my throat.

I turn it over. Three letters are engraved on the back: NMK.

Nora Michelle Knight.

The last time I saw that medal was the day Riley Fraser began to hate me. The last time I saw that medal was the day Riley Fraser realized I'm a monster.

TWELVE

EACH TIME I CLOSE MY EYES, I SEE RACHEL LARSEN. I SEE HER hair billowing in the water and the cuts on her arms. I see her flinch as the paramedics touch her. I almost never dream, but I'm scared of what I'll see if I sleep.

Most of all, though, when I close my eyes, I see the Saint Anthony medal clasped in her hand.

So I stop closing my eyes. I lie awake, every lamp in the room lit, one arm around Pengy, my own hand wrapped around the blue plastic toy from the kids' meal.

Skylar had given it back to me as we sat wedged in a patrol car with Chase, the three of us wrapped in orange blankets as blue and red lights swept the night outside. I wasn't cold, but I couldn't stop shaking. She slipped the bear into my hand. "For bravery," she said, voice low and solemn, like the bear was some sort of prize for a job well done.

I hadn't been brave. All I had done was stay behind. But I took

119

the bear. It's stupid to think that something so small could make me feel better in the face of something so big, but it had—sort of. With my hand wrapped around that silly lump of plastic, it was a little harder to remember how clammy Rachel's skin had been or how that small silver disc had felt in my hand.

I ended up holding the bear on the ride home and while a police officer explained to Aunt Jet what had happened. Later, I had brought the bear into the bathroom, setting it on the edge of the vanity so that I could see it while I took a shower and tried to scrub the smell of the riverbank off of my skin.

I hold on to it now as I slip out of bed and creep down the hall. All of the other bedroom doors are closed, and the house is quiet save for the soft sound of the television in Sam's room. He sleeps with it on all night; he says that he's still not used to sleeping alone and that the noise helps.

Sidestepping loose floorboards, the ones that groan and squeak and always ratted me out on nights I snuck out to see Riley, I make my way downstairs, then slip on my flip-flops and head outside.

The sky is still dark, but there's a tiny hint of mauve on the horizon. In another hour, the birds will sing themselves hoarse and the sun will rise like it's any other day.

I make my way to the hedge and then push through to the Frasers' yard.

A light is burning up in Noah's room. Feeling like the boy in some old teen movie, I grab a handful of pebbles from the nearest flower bed and begin tossing them at his window. Unlike the boy in a teen movie, my aim sucks. I must throw ten rocks before one finally hits its target.

Noah pushes open his bedroom window and leans out. He stares down at me for a second and then disappears.

A minute later, I hear the screen door creak open. I head back through the hedge, trusting Noah to follow as I make my way to Aunt Jet's porch. It's not until I lower myself to the old swing that I think about the fact that I'm still in my pajamas.

Noah doesn't seem to notice. I'm probably not a girl to him—not like that, not really. Just some old friend of his kid brother.

There's plenty of room on the swing, but he doesn't sit. Instead, he leans against the porch railing. He shoots a glance at my little plastic bear, still tightly gripped in my hand. "New friend?"

Two nights ago, I'd been embarrassed at the thought of Noah catching me with a stuffed animal. Now, I don't care. The bear is the one thing I'm not even going to try to explain.

"Something happened." I struggle to figure out where to begin. "I was on the train bridge with some people from Riley's school. We found a girl on the riverbank. She was barely breathing."

"Who was it?"

"Rachel Larsen. Do you know her?"

Noah shakes his head. "I don't think so."

Montgomery Falls is small, but he's older than Skylar and Chase. Even if his path had crossed Rachel's, he might not know her by name. His eyes narrow as a second question occurs to him. "Was it an accident?"

I pull in a deep breath. "I don't think so. It looked like someone had tried to hurt her . . . and . . . ." I falter. I don't know how to say it, so I just blurt it out. "She had something of Riley's."

Noah pushes himself away from the railing, the gesture so hard and sudden that the old wood makes a sharp, cracking sound at the force of it. "What do you mean?" He takes a step toward me, then stops. His whole body practically radiates tension.

The look on his face is so raw, so intense, that it's hard to find my voice; somehow, I do. "That day up by the mill, when we went to see the chimney swifts, Riley found this medal on the ground. A saint's medal like the ones they sell in the Catholic bookstore. After everything was over, after they identified her, we realized it was hers. Nora Knight's. Her initials were engraved on the back."

There's a beetle on the porch floor. Small and black with a tan stripe across its back. It makes its way toward my foot, each tiny step slow and deliberate.

"I remember," says Noah. "The police asked if we had noticed anything that might help identify her. Riley told them about the medal, told them about the initials on the back, but said he had lost it."

"He didn't lose it. He lied. To them. To you. To me. You know how he was always keeping a record of lost things? The maps and notes. How obsessed he got. I think maybe that's why he kept it. I looked it up online once: Saint Anthony was the patron saint of lost things. I think Riley thought the medal was meant for him." The beetle hits the edge of my flip-flop and veers right. "I found out about it. We argued. I told him it was wrong to keep it and that he'd get in trouble. He got defensive. Upset. I don't know: maybe he thought I was going to tell on him. I wouldn't have, but maybe he didn't know that." I can't look at Noah. I just keep staring at the beetle as it makes its way back across the porch. There's no reason to tell him what, exactly, Riley had said to me or what I had done in return.

"I knew something happened between the two of you, but he wouldn't tell me what." Noah finally crosses the porch and sits next to me on the swing. It feels like a long time before he speaks again. "He was different after that summer. After we found her and you left. He stopped going into the woods for a while. Stopped keeping those lists and journals. At first, my parents thought that meant he was getting better. They thought it meant that the doctors were wrong and that he didn't have OCD after all. That it was something he just grew out of."

"Was it something he grew out of?"

Noah lets out a small, derisive sound—one that I'm pretty sure isn't directed at me or Riley. "No. He just got better at managing it. Last year, he went on medication. That seemed to help, too, but it's not just something he grew out of." He leans back and pinches the bridge of his nose. Just for a second. "When I asked him why he didn't talk to you anymore, he told me there was something bad inside of him and that you had seen it. He wouldn't tell me anything else."

A cold, tight sensation starts in my chest and radiates outward. Is that what he really thought? That I saw something bad inside of him? If that's true . . . I shake my head. "All I saw was that stupid medal. That's all I ever saw. I never thought he was bad. Ever."

"What do you mean, that's all you ever saw?"

I stare at the porch floor as my eyes start to burn. How can I tell him? How can I tell anyone after what happened with Riley? With Lacey?

"Cat . . ." Noah slides off the swing to crouch in front of me, forcing me to meet his gaze. "Whatever happened between you and my brother—I don't think it was your fault. The maps . . . the lists . . . the fear that you saw something bad inside of him . . . He latched on to things. Ideas. Stuff would get lodged in his head and he couldn't get it out. He got better at hiding it, and he got better at figuring out which thoughts made sense and which ones didn't, but if you were around him enough and you knew him well enough, you could still tell that something was going on."

Part of me wants to believe Noah. So, so badly. I want to believe that there's another explanation for what happened that day, for the way Riley looked at me and the things he said. An explanation that doesn't boil down to him believing I was dangerous. But if that's true, what does that mean for all of those walls I've built ever since to keep people at a distance? Have they all been for nothing?

It's a disturbing thought—but then I remember Lacey.

The one exception I'd made—mostly because Lacey had decided we were going to be friends and she's always been relentless when she wants something—had ended disastrously. If I had been better at keeping those walls up, the past few months never would have happened.

"What do you mean, that's all you ever saw?" Noah asks again.

The smart thing to do would be to go back inside. Keep the walls up. Keep myself safe.

But I'm not sure I can do that. Not when I keep seeing Rachel when I close my eyes. Not when I'm here, in Montgomery Falls, where memories of Riley seem to lurk around every corner.

"Cat . . ."

I'm teetering on the edge. The soft, pleading note in Noah's voice pushes me over. "I lied to you when you asked me for help. Sort of, anyway. I'm not psychic—I'm really not—but I do see things." It takes every bit of willpower I possess to keep meeting his gaze.

"That's how you knew Riley kept the medal?"

I nod. "What do you think it means, that girl having it?"

"You said it looked like someone had tried to hurt her?"

"Yeah."

"Then I think whoever killed my brother is linked to that girl." Noah's eyes flash as he pushes himself to his feet. He looks hard and a little bit dangerous.

I think about that tiny sound Rachel had made and the feeling of her hand in mine. I had lied. I told her she was safe and all right, but she hadn't been all right and she hadn't been safe, and whoever hurt her is still out there.

Noah is certain that his brother is dead. I don't want to believe that, but either way, I have to know. I have to know what happened to Riley, and if there's any way I can help stop what happened to Rachel from happening to anyone else, I have to try.

I pull in a deep breath and then let it out in a rush. "I changed my mind. I'll help. I'll help you find out what happened to Riley."

THIRTEEN

I SLIP BACK INTO MONTGOMERY HOUSE JUST AFTER SUN-
rise. I don't want to; I want to stay out on the porch with Noah,
but I figure I've scared Aunt Jet enough for one night without her
waking up and finding my bed empty.

Thankfully, the house is quiet and all of the other bedroom
doors are still closed as I make my way to my room.

I set Skylar's plastic bear on the nightstand, then grab my iPod
and slide in my earbuds before stretching out on my bed. When I
close my eyes, I see Noah's face. Hard. Dangerous. Determined.

He's so sure I can help.

I want to, but it's not like I've ever been able to do anything
useful with the things I see. I've certainly never been able to use
them to help anyone—myself included.

At some point, he's going to realize that I was right the first
time. He's going to realize that there's nothing I can do.

I'm going to let him down . . . There isn't anything I can really do . . . I told Rachel she was safe . . .

It's warm in the room, but I tug the sheet up, wrapping it around me. I'm still scared to go to sleep, but I'm so, so tired.

Weight on my chest and shoulders, pinning me down.

I can't move. I can't see. I can't cry out. Rough, whispered words fall around me—"perfect, so perfect"—and then shatter as something bites into my skin over and over.

I try to lash out, but I'm not strong enough. I . . .

"Cat."

This time when I strike out, my fists connect with something soft and yielding. Something warm.

My eyes fly open. Aidan stands next to the bed, hands up, palms out.

"You were having a nightmare," he says, low and cautious, like he's worried I might try to hit him again.

I push myself to a sitting position. My heart feels like it's trying to claw its way out of my chest. My earbuds are tangled around my neck, but the iPod is nowhere to be seen—probably lodged between the bed and the wall. The clock on the nightstand reads 10:04 a.m.

"I knocked and called your name."

"Thanks for waking me," I say, voice hoarse and filled with the grit of sleep. I mean it. Normally, my sleep is empty. A flat, gray nothingness broken only by dreams on rare occasions, but of course I would have nightmares after what had happened last night. Who wouldn't? I swing my legs over the bed, frowning as another thought occurs to me. "What are you doing in here?"

"Your aunt asked me to get you." Aidan shoves his hands into his pockets as he rocks back on his heels. His hair is still sleep-mussed, but he's dressed, wearing faded jeans and a gray T-shirt.

The fact that he's more or less fully clothed makes me self-conscious about my own outfit, and I cross my arms over my chest in a futile attempt to cover up. For the second time in a handful of hours, a boy—a good-looking boy—has seen me in my pajamas. It's the kind of thing I wish I could tell Lacey.

As I stand and head for the bathroom, Aidan adds, "There's a police cruiser in the driveway. What's going on?"

I trip on the hem of my pajama pants as I whirl. "What?"

"Police cruiser. Driveway."

"Have you talked to Chase or Skylar today?"

"Why? Why are the cops here?"

I want to shake him. "Have you talked to them? Have either of them texted you?" I grab a pair of jeans from the back of the desk chair and haul them on over my pajamas.

"I haven't talked to either of them since yesterday," he says with a small shrug.

Aunt Jet was supposed to take me into the station this after-noon to give a formal statement. What could be so bad that it couldn't wait a few hours? What could be so bad that the police would come to the house?

I dart past Aidan and race down the hall. He calls out after me, but I ignore him. In my haste, I almost trip over Brisby on the stairs, but I manage to keep my balance and follow Aunt Jet's voice to the study.

Inside, she's talking to a man in a tan uniform. They both stare as I stumble to a stop just over the threshold.

The officer's gaze travels from my bare feet to the rat's nest of my hair as he takes in my appearance. Too late, I realize that the earbuds are still dangling around my neck.

"Mary Catherine," says Aunt Jet, her voice weirdly stiff and formal, "this is Chief Jensen. Given everything you went through last night, he thought it might be best if he took your statement here."

"Absolutely," he says. "No need dragging you kids out to the station."

Jensen doesn't look old enough to be a chief of police—not even in a town as small as Montgomery Falls. When I think of police chiefs, I imagine gray hair and gravitas from years of experience on the force. Chief Jensen does not have gray hair, and it's hard to imagine he has all that many years of experience. He can't be more than thirty, and he looks better suited to appearing in ads for cologne—chiseled jaw, rugged five-o'clock shadow, broad shoulders—than policing a town that's 40 percent rowdy college students.

But gravitas? Gravitas, he has.

He nods toward one of the chairs. "Why don't you sit." He makes no move to do the same. Aunt Jet, too, stays standing. Despite the heat, she's wearing an oversized sweater that hangs down past her hips.

I perch on the edge of the nearest wingback, toes pointed forward, back ramrod straight. As an afterthought, I pull the earbuds from around my neck and stuff them behind an embroidered cushion.

It's not until I'm sitting that I realize that maybe I should have closed the study door. Noises from the rest of the house drift in: the blender in the kitchen, the pipes thumping as the washing machine runs, a creak on the stairs.

Jensen pulls a small black notebook and a little yellow pencil from his shirt pocket. "I've already spoken with Skylar and Chase. They gave similar accounts of what happened last night, but I'd like your version as well."

Haltingly, I tell him about going to the movie and for food and to the bridge. I don't look at Aunt Jet as I rush through the part about crawling under the barricade. I describe how we spotted Rachel in the water. How we weren't even sure what we were seeing until we got closer. How I stayed behind while Chase and Skylar went to the highway to get help. As I talk, Jensen scribbles notes, his large hand dwarfing the pencil.

"Do you know Rachel Larsen?"

"No."

"Ever seen her before?"

"Not before last night."

"Never?"

I shake my head.

"But Chase and Skylar knew her?"

"They seemed to. Chase told the emergency operator that she went to Riverview."

"You volunteered to stay behind?"

I try to remember. It's all a bit jumbled—almost like what happened was too much for my brain to hold on to. "I think so," I say slowly, "but I'm not sure."

"You must have been scared. Why would a girl volunteer to stay there, at the edge of the river, alone?"

There's nothing wrong with what he says, but something about the way he says it makes me nervous. I glance at Aunt Jet. She gives a small nod of encouragement, but her lips are pressed into a hard, thin line.

"We couldn't leave her on her own, and Chase said someone had to go to the highway."

"So why not ask Skylar to stay behind?"

"She was scared."

"And you weren't?"

"No—I was . . . I just . . ." It almost feels like he's testing me, but I can't figure out why. "Chase knew the way to the highway, and Skylar was so scared that she was better off going with him."

Aunt Jet moves next to me and rests her hand on the back of the chair.

"Is she going to be all right?" I ask. "Rachel Larsen?"

Instead of answering my question, Jensen reaches into his pocket and pulls out a small plastic bag. As he steps forward, I recognize the Saint Anthony medal. "You told one of my officers that this belonged to Riley Fraser."

I feel a small twinge of relief. I wasn't entirely sure the officer had believed me when I said it was important. "Rachel had it in her hand. Are you going to dust it for prints?"

Jensen's mouth twists a little around the edges. Almost like a scowl, but not quite. "The girl was found in the water. I can tell you right now whose prints we'll find. Hers. Yours. The officer you gave it to." He shakes his head. "What makes you think this belonged to Riley Fraser or that it needed to be dusted for prints?"

"I've seen it before. At Riley's."

It's not a lie. Not exactly.

He flips to a page somewhere near the middle of his little book. "You told Officer Theriault that you arrived in town last week."

"She's visiting for the summer," says Aunt Jet.

Jensen ignores her. "You also told Officer Theriault that the last time you were in Montgomery Falls was five years ago."

I nod, not sure what that has to do with anything.

"So, you haven't seen Riley Fraser or this medal for five years."

"No."

"What makes you think it's the same one?"

"The initials on the back are the same." As I speak, it occurs to me that there is one thing that's different about the medal: When Riley found it all those years ago, it had been hanging on a thin silver chain. Not a leather cord like the one that had been tangled around Rachel's fingers.

I open my mouth to tell him, but Jensen cuts me off. "Even if you're right, how do you know it isn't just something Riley Fraser gave the Larsen girl? It's not unheard of. Guy sees a girl, likes her, gives her something of his."

"The medal was special. Riley wouldn't have just given it away."

"How can you be sure?"

"I just am." Because he was ashamed of it. Because even just the idea of me knowing he had it was enough to make him hate me. But I can't say any of that without going into the story of how Riley found and kept the medal in the first place. Telling Noah was one thing. Jensen isn't Noah.

Almost as though he can read my thoughts, Jensen says, "Have you told anyone else that you believe the medal you found belongs to Riley Fraser?"

I nod and then shake my head.

"Which is it?" He stares at me so hard that I have to fight not to squirm.

I have no idea what I did wrong, but I could swear he's angry.

In that split second, I decide not to tell him about Noah. "I told that woman at the river—the police officer. That's it. Just her." Jensen doesn't say anything for a long moment; he just continues to stand there and stare. "Is Rachel going to be okay?" I ask again, when I can't take the silence any longer.

"Depends on how long she was in the water and how long she was lost in the woods before that."

"Lost?"

"We found her car, abandoned with a flat, north of the river. We think she tried to take a shortcut back to town. Once she comes to, once she's well enough for questions, we'll be able to ask her."

I stare at him in disbelief. "But the marks on her arms . . . the cuts . . ."

"Could have just been scratches."

I think about the small lines etched in her skin. How precise they had seemed. How there had been dozens of them. "Those weren't scratches."

"You're a doctor? Premed student?"

"Even if they were just scratches," I say, trying to ignore the heat that fills my face, "even if she just got lost in the woods, she had Riley's medal. Doesn't that . . ." I root around in my brain for every cop show or mystery novel that has ever crossed my path, trying to find anything that will help me not sound like an idiot kid. "Doesn't that indicate some sort of connection?"

"Connection to what?"

I stare at him uncomprehendingly. "To Riley's disappearance."

"No reason to think anything is connected," he says.

"You can't be serious." My voice rises; I can't help it.

"We looked into Riley Fraser's disappearance for months. There isn't anything to suggest he didn't just get lost or run away. It happens all the time. Kids are unhappy at home. They run east to Halifax or west to Toronto. Nothing mysterious about it. And that kid had plenty of problems."

I don't know if he's referring to the wrecked boat or to Riley getting caught up at the mill, or if there are other things I haven't heard about yet. Somehow, I don't think he'll tell me if I ask.

"As far as the girl goes," continues Jensen, "we don't know anything at the moment. In a few months, this place is going to be crawling with students. Parents will be dropping off their kids for their first year of college, and they want to leave them someplace safe. I'm not stirring up a panic just because you think you might have seen something that ties Riley Fraser to Rachel Larsen—not when we don't have any reason to believe he didn't just run."

"Riley's brother told me he wouldn't have run away."

Jensen flips his notebook closed with a snap. "Now you listen to me: I don't want you saying anything to Noah Fraser or his mother. That family has been through enough, and the last thing I need is his father coming back and throwing more reward money around and getting in everyone's way. Do you understand?"

Leather creaks under Aunt Jet's fingertips as she tightens her grip on the chair. "My niece has answered your questions. She's given you what I would think is valuable information—especially for the Fraser family—and you're treating her like she's done something wrong."

"No," he says. "I'm making sure she knows better than to go kicking over any hornet's nests."

Aunt Jet steps out from behind the chair and puts herself between us. "Would you excuse us, Mary Catherine?"

"We're not finished," says Jensen.

"Yes," says Jet, "you are." Even though her voice trembles slightly—even though she hates confrontation—there's a hint of steel underneath the words. "Mary Catherine, why don't you go get some breakfast. And close the door behind you, please."

I don't need to be told twice.

I swear I can feel Jensen's eyes bore holes into my back as I practically bolt from the room.

FOURTEEN

IN THE KITCHEN, I TAKE A JAR OF CHEEZ WHIZ AND A LOAF of white bread out of the refrigerator and grab an unopened bag of ketchup-flavored potato chips from the cupboard. Aunt Jet claims keeping bread in the fridge helps it stay fresh longer. Personally, I think the cold drains away all the taste and that there are about a hundred potential flavors of chips that I'd rank above ketchup, but when in Canada, do as Canadians do.

The floorboards in the hallway creak. *Probably Aunt Jet come to check on me*, I think, but when I glance over my shoulder, I see Aidan.

"Chief Jawline hates you."

"Jawline?" I raise an eyebrow and turn back to the task at hand, coating two slices of bread in thick layers of cheese before slapping them together.

"Don't tell me you didn't notice his rugged and manly jaw or his perfect five-o'clock shadow. I'm pretty sure he measures his stubble with a ruler to get it that precise." Aidan comes up behind me, reaches around my waist, and snatches up my sandwich.

"Hey!" I press myself against the counter, but there's no need: even while reaching around me to steal my food, Aidan manages to keep a few inches between his body and mine. Despite the fact that he keeps pushing boundaries, it's almost like he instinctively knows I need a fraction of personal space at all times and adjusts his position accordingly.

Lacey was always good about that. She thought my need for personal space was some sort of anxiety thing, and I let her think that because then she didn't push for explanations.

I wait until Aidan retreats, then quickly make another sandwich. "So, you were eavesdropping."

"There's nothing good on TV this time of day."

"Uh-huh." As I put the bread and Cheez Whiz back in the fridge, my gaze falls on two small, black canisters wedged between a carton of eggs and a stick of butter. I lift one, frowning.

"Don't open it," says Aidan.

I turn to him, canister in hand. "Why?"

"It's leftover film. Joey and Skylar were doing a photo project and forgot the unused rolls here."

Right—Skylar had mentioned something about a project. That Aidan had helped and that he and Joey were in some photography club together. "You just figured you'd keep it?"

Aidan shoots me a wry grin. "Payment for helping them with the project. I read online that keeping film in the fridge helps the quality. Something about stable temperatures."

"Fascinating." I put the canister back, then close the fridge door. I take my sandwich and the chips over to the table and sit across from him.

There are dark circles under his eyes. "You look tired," I say, without thinking.

"Thanks," he says wryly. "I was up late working on that stupid essay. Which is nothing, apparently, compared to the night you had." He takes a bite of his stolen sandwich.

"How much did you hear when you were listening in?"

He shrugs, mouth full, and then swallows. "Pretty much everything."

"Well, you're right. Jensen hates me."

"To be fair, Jensen hates everyone. I'm pretty sure the only person he's genuinely civil to is his daughter, Ellie. It's part of the whole lone-wolf image. You should have seen the strip he tore off me that time Riley and I got caught at the mill. I was almost glad when he called my father—and I am never glad when I have to deal with my father. You know I'm actually a little upset with you, right?" he asks, abruptly switching direction.

"Why?"

"You and Skylar and Chase had an adventure without me."

"It was not an adventure." I take a bite of my sandwich. It feels heavy and gross in my mouth, and swallowing it is an effort.

"Sorry," he says, sobering a bit. "You really think there's some connection between Riley and whatever happened to Rachel?"

I hesitate. Jensen's insistence that the marks on Rachel's arms could be scratches has me slightly thrown. Enough so that I can't help but second-guess myself. It was dark and I was scared; what if I didn't really see what I thought I saw? What if I'm wrong about the medal not being something Riley would just give away?

"I don't know," I say eventually. "I mean, she had something of his, but maybe that was just a coincidence. Riley knew her, right? You guys all do. Were they close?" As soon as the words leave my mouth, something inside of me twists. Riley *knew*, not Riley knows. *Were*, not are. Like I've started thinking of him in the past tense.

"Rachel and Riley are friends with a lot of the same people, but I don't think I've ever seen them alone together." Aidan regards me intently for a moment and then says, "The police department tweeted about Rachel this morning. They said a girl was found in the river but that there was no indication of foul play."

"You're joking?" As he shakes his head, all the frustration I've been trying to keep penned up for the past thirty minutes rushes to the surface. "How can they say that? They haven't even talked to her yet."

"You heard him: he doesn't want to risk a panic. The university is one of the few things that keeps Montgomery Falls afloat. If people are scared to send their kids here, the town takes a hit."

"So you're saying Jensen is basically the mayor in *Jaws*?"

A small, appreciative look flashes across Aidan's face. "That reference would score you major points with Joey. He's already all over what happened. He texted me after he saw the tweets. I guess Skylar hasn't had a chance to talk to him yet."

I'm suddenly very glad Joey wasn't with us when we found Rachel. He'd probably have treated the whole thing like a scene from one of his stupid horror movies. I open my mouth to say so, but other voices suddenly boom down the hall.

"Fault . . . Mary . . . abuse . . ."

"Investigation . . . troublemaker . . . just like . . ."

I'm only able to catch every third word, but it sounds like my aunt and Jensen are on the verge of coming to blows. The voices rise to a crescendo. A moment later, the front door slams.

Calmly, as though everything is totally normal, Aidan opens the bag of chips.

Aunt Jet strides into the kitchen. The sleeves of her sweater have been rolled up to her elbows—almost like she actually was on the edge of a physical altercation. "Insufferable, jealous, entitled man." She spits out the words the way other people spit out curses, but when her eyes land on Aidan and me, she hauls in a deep breath and makes a visible effort to pull herself together. She walks to the table, grabs a handful of chips from the bag, and pops a stack of them in her mouth. If one can chew angrily, she's chewing angrily.

"Am I in trouble?" I ask.

My aunt swallows and brushes the crumbs from the front of her sweater. "Don't be ridiculous. You didn't do anything wrong. If anything, I'm proud of you for pushing against his nonsense. This isn't about you. His mother was a Morgan. Second cousin. He's always thought he had a claim to the house, and he's upset . . ." Jet trails off. She glances at Aidan and then quickly looks away.

There are only so many things Jensen could be upset about that Aunt Jet wouldn't want to speak of in front of Aidan. He must suspect she's thinking of selling Montgomery House. Maybe he even knows that she called that antique dealer. It's a small town and people talk.

Jet is wearing an old opal ring that once belonged to my grand-mother. She slips it from one finger to another and then back. "Since we don't have to go to the station, I think I'm going to go upstairs and lie down. Will you be okay? *Are* you okay?" Worry flashes across her face. She reaches out and touches my shoulder carefully. The touch lasts only a second, but it's oddly comforting.

"I'm fine, Aunt Jet." The idea of actually *being* fine after every-thing that's happened in the past twelve hours is a little ludicrous, but it's not like there's anything my aunt can do to make any of it better.

"One of us should call your father and tell him what happened."

"I'll do it," I say, even though I have absolutely no intention of following through. It was Dad's choice to banish me for the summer; I'm not going to spend an hour on the phone reassuring him that I'm safe and that he made the right decision. I just fig-ure letting Aunt Jet think I'll call—or have called—will delay the prospect of talking to him.

Aidan watches me, shrewdly, as Jet leaves the room, then reaches, again, for the bag of chips. "Are you actually going to call your father?"

"Next question."

"Okay: What's a Morgan?"

"It's kind of stupid."

He stares at me expectantly.

"You know Mercy Island?"

The fact that he has to think about it reminds me that he's not from here, either. "Island off the coast, right?" he says. "Got cut off last winter when the ferry couldn't make it across."

"That's the one. There were two Morgan sisters. One who stayed on the island and kept the lighthouse and another who married Jonathan Montgomery and came here. So, technically, every Montgomery in Montgomery Falls is descended from a Morgan."

"Sounds very *Dark Shadows*."

"*Dark Shadows*?"

"This old gothic soap opera. Joey managed to find about a hundred episodes online. I think I made it through all of three, and that was under duress."

I shake my head. "Ever think of getting new friends?"

"You like Skylar."

"I can't argue with that." Besides, given my own tendency to gravitate toward old bands and vintage stuff, maybe I should cut Joey a little slack for liking an old TV show.

"So you and Jensen are related."

"Apparently." It's not really a pleasant thought.

"And he doesn't seem to like you."

"Doesn't seem to."

Aidan's eyes sparkle as the corner of his mouth twitches in a grin. He lifts a potato chip, holding it aloft as though raising a glass for a toast. "In town less than two weeks and you're already on the bad side of the chief of police. It's nice not being the only troublemaker in the house."

FIFTEEN

THE IDEA THAT NOAH DRIVES A BLUE CONVERTIBLE BMW doesn't really compute. Not because he can't afford it—the Frasers have always had tons of money—but because he doesn't strike me as caring about that sort of stuff.

"What?" he asks, picking up on the fact that I'm staring at him as the river flashes by below.

"Don't take this the wrong way, but you don't exactly match the car." And he doesn't. His jeans are worn through in places, and his T-shirt is so faded that I can't make sense of the design on the front. He looks like he'd have trouble scraping up fifty dollars, never mind enough for a luxury car.

"It was one of my father's," he admits. "He gave it to Riley just before he moved out."

"Was this before or after Riley crashed his boat?"

Noah takes his eyes off the road long enough to glance at me. "You heard about that?"

"I definitely heard about that."

Noah shifts gears and turns off the bridge. "The car was before the divorce. The boat was after. And as you've brilliantly deduced, I'm not really a BMW kind of guy. My Jeep's back in Ottawa. I would have driven it here, but I didn't realize I'd be staying this long."

"Couldn't you go back and get it?"

"It would take a few days to fly out and then drive back."

"And you don't want to leave your mom alone?"

He nods once, gruffly.

I pull open the glove compartment. Other than the registration, which is indeed in Riley's name, the small space is empty. I tell myself that there's no reason to be disappointed: if there had been anything interesting in the car, surely Noah would already have found it.

I push the glove compartment closed and then twist around to grab a doughnut from the open bag on the back seat. I take a bite, managing to sprinkle toasted coconut crumbs all over the place in the process. This morning, I hadn't been able to finish a sandwich, but when Noah showed up with coffee and doughnuts, my appetite returned with a vengeance. Even telling him about Jensen hadn't been enough to kill it.

After what happened last night, it feels somehow wrong to be enjoying food while the sun shines on a summer day. It does not, however, feel wrong enough to stop me.

Noah may not look like he belongs in the BMW, but he handles it effortlessly, pushing the speed limit and hugging turns like he's used to driving fast cars. I study his knuckles as his hand moves between the gearshift and the wheel, looking for a sign of those marks I had noticed that first day outside the drugstore. They're almost gone. "Can I ask you something?"

"Sure."

"Do you really get into fights down at the Riverbend?" This, like the car, is something that doesn't quite fit. Noah can be stand-offish, even surly, but he seems too smart to be hanging out in that kind of place and getting into that kind of trouble.

He winces very slightly. "Who told you that?"

"Just something I heard around."

"Twice. Once after I got back and once a couple of days before I saw you."

"Why?"

"My father has pissed off a lot of people over the years. Some of them think Riley disappearing is just my family getting what it deserves."

"And Riley?"

"What about him?"

"What did people think of him?"

Noah shrugs. "Everyone liked him. Everything seemed to roll off him. Even the whole boat thing seemed to be fine in the end."

"But you were away at school, right," I prod. "So you wouldn't necessarily have gotten the whole picture . . ."

"I guess."

I want to ask him if he knows anything about what happened between Riley and Skylar, but doing so feels like it would be talking about Skylar behind her back. It's one thing to have asked Aidan about it—Aidan is Skylar's friend; asking Noah is different.

The trees crowd the road closely on either side. After a few minutes, they thin out—just for a moment—and I catch a glimpse of the train bridge through the break. "It's up here. Just around the bend, I think."

Noah slows the car. As we round the curve, the trees open up entirely, giving way to a muddy field.

"Here."

Ignoring a No Trespassing sign on an old fence post, Noah pulls off the road, taking the BMW over ruts and through puddles like he's driving his Jeep instead of a sleek German car. We finally come to a stop at the edge of the field.

"Are you sure this is it?" he asks as we climb out.

"Yeah." I glance down at the tire tracks; dozens crisscross the mud. "They had to leave the police cars here. The ambulance, too. They put Rachel on a stretcher and carried her through the trees." I start making my way along a footpath, trusting Noah to follow.

After a few minutes—five, maybe ten—the trees begin to change as lush greenery shifts to dead, barren branches. Soon, the river comes into view. Bright and blue with white clouds reflected on its surface.

Tall grass and low bushes crowd between the trees as the ground slopes down to the water. Even from here, you can see signs of last night's activity. Footprints in the mud. Styrofoam coffee cups. Crumpled bits of paper.

I glance at Noah. There's a tightness around his eyes and mouth that wasn't there moments ago.

"What is it?"

"No police tape."

He's right. There's nothing to indicate a half-dead girl was found here. Nothing to warn people off.

I guess that's one way not to start a panic.

"Come on." Noah begins to reach for my hand to help me over the uneven ground but then catches himself—either because he remembers that my headaches are connected to touch or because he's actually gotten the whole memo about women kicking ass.

I head toward an oblong imprint in the mud. *The stretcher*, I realize. I glance toward the bridge. It's close, but not that close. If the moon hadn't been full, if it hadn't slid out from behind the clouds at the exact right moment, if I hadn't been standing at the exact right spot looking in the exact right direction, would I even have seen her? I imagine lying out here all night. Dying out here. Able to see lights across the river but unable to get to them. It's a lonely thought in a lonely place.

I crouch down and press my palms to the mud, to the spot where Rachel had lain. "She was here," I say. There's a smaller imprint next to the one left by the stretcher. I touch it, shivering as my body remembers the damp and the cold. "And I was here. I took her hand, and that's when I noticed the medal."

I feel, rather than see, Noah stare down at me for a long moment. When I glance up, I can't read his expression.

He walks to the water's edge. "This is where you pulled her out?"

"Chase did. A few feet over."

I stand and join him at a spot where the shoreline curves like a question mark. The bend forms a sort of natural trap for things taken by the river. Driftwood and bits of garbage have washed up here—but so have other things. A child's plastic ring. A kayak paddle. An old blue bottle that glints in the sun. "Riley would have liked it here," I say. "At least twelve-year-old Riley would have."

It takes a moment for Noah to get it. When he does speak, his voice is oddly thick. "All these lost and forgotten things."

"Noah . . ." I move a little closer to him, thinking that I should tell him I have Riley's journal, that I found it down in Aunt Jet's basement. I don't know if having it will help him or hurt him— maybe it doesn't matter either way—but he should still know about it. Before I can say anything, though, there's a rustle at the top of the hill.

Noah and I both go still as a man starts down the slope.

He's older than Aunt Jet. In his fifties, maybe. He's tall and angular with thinning brown hair over a sunburnt scalp and bushy brown eyebrows that stand out even at a distance. It's like his body had decided to focus most of its hair-growing energy on cultivating those two patches.

He's so intent on his footing that he's almost to the bottom of the hill before he notices us.

"You kids shouldn't be here." A camera rests on his hip, its black strap slung over his shoulder. He tugs on it, the gesture oddly stiff and awkward.

Noah takes a small step forward. "We were just hiking along the river, Mr. Harding." As the words leave his mouth, Noah changes. His face opens up, his shoulders straighten, and there's a lightness in his voice that I don't recognize. He hooks his thumbs through the belt loops of his jeans in a gesture that reminds me of Aidan.

The man scowls, looking like a disgruntled owl. "You go to Riverview?"

"Graduated a few years ago." Noah gestures at the man's camera. "Great day for taking photographs. You're here to get shots of the river? I saw that one you took last summer. The one that won that big contest."

Everything about him is charming, affable, likeable. *If he can act like this*, I think, *why does he skulk around so much?*

The man hesitates, then nods, opening up just a bit under Noah's flattery. "That one was part of a series. Got published in a travel magazine. You're right: would be a good day to photograph the river, but the police asked me to shoot some pictures of the shore."

Noah frowns. Not his real frown, but a paler, less biting version. "They say why?"

"Something about a girl they found on the bank." He slides the camera from his shoulder and twists the lens cap. "Have you kids heard anything?"

"Not a thing," says Noah.

The man nods again, the gesture small and slight. "You'd better get going. Don't want to catch you in any of the photographs."

"We were just heading back up to our car anyway. Nice day for a walk, but it's going to be a scorcher."

Harding mumbles something noncommittal as we walk past. As his gaze slides to me, his eyes narrow. Something about the look sends a small shiver down my spine.

I glance back as we hit the top of the hill. Harding is standing a foot away from where we found Rachel, camera pointed down at the spot where she laid in the mud, but his eyes are on Noah and me.

I wait until we're back in the car before speaking. "Who was that?"

"A photographer. Kind of weird."

I roll my eyes. "Figured that part out, thanks."

Noah glances at me, weighing the sarcasm in my tone. It's a tiny reminder that we don't really know each other. "He used to own a one-hour photo place on Main Street—at least that's what I've heard. It went under when everyone went digital. Now he photographs weddings and portraits and stuff. The school hires him to take the yearbook pictures."

"And he freelances for the police. Busy guy." Given the size of the Montgomery Falls Police Department and the fact that the town normally has a low crime rate, I guess it makes sense that they would outsource some things. Still . . . "If Jensen really thinks Rachel just got lost, why bother getting photos?"

"Covering his butt, I guess," says Noah. "This way, if it turns out later that he's wrong, he can at least say he did something." He starts the car and pulls out of the field, but instead of turning left and retracing our route back to Riverside Avenue, he turns right.

"We're not going home?"

"I'm starving."

I twist in my seat and snag the bag of doughnuts.

"I need real food," he says, shaking his head.

Ten minutes later, we pull into a diner on the wrong side of the town limit—a long tin can that's meant to look like one of those '50s setups with lots of neon and atmosphere.

Part of me can't help hoping the real 1950s didn't look quite this sad or shabby as I follow Noah inside and to a back booth. Everything—the floor, the tables, even the menus—seems to be coated in a thin layer of grease, and though it's just a little past noon, the place is practically deserted. Only one other booth is taken, and most of the stools at the counter are empty.

"It's busier at night," Noah says. "Mostly truckers." He hesitates for a moment and then asks, "Do you feel anything?"

"You mean like the draft from the air conditioner?"

A waitress comes over for our order. Noah asks for a cheeseburger and fries. They serve an all-day breakfast, so I order two eggs, sunny-side up—unlike my mood—and bacon. We both get Cokes.

After she walks away, Noah leans forward. "Rachel works here."

"You told me you didn't know who Rachel Larsen was."

His eyes flash at the hard, suspicious note in my voice, and I instantly want to retract the words.

"I made a few calls before I picked you up."

"Sorry," I say softly.

"It's okay," he says, but he doesn't quite meet my eyes when he says it. "Do you feel anything?"

"Like what?"

"Like . . . psychic stuff?"

"I'm not a psychic. I've told you that."

"But you see things when you touch people. I wasn't sure if it's just people, or if it works with objects, too." He glances around the diner, probably thinking that Rachel has touched every saltshaker and tabletop. If I could pick up things just from objects, it would have been a great place to bring me. Of course, if I could pick up things just from objects, I'd probably never leave the house.

"I'm not psychic. Not like that, anyway. I can't read people's thoughts or feelings just by looking at them, and I can't pick up something someone touched and tell you anything. I don't see the future or the past, and I wouldn't have the first clue what to do with a crystal ball or a deck of tarot cards." For some reason—maybe because I've spent the past few years reminding myself that it's not safe to tell anyone the truth—I find it hard to look at him while I talk. "When I touch people, though, I do see things. Either something that they really want or that really scares them. Desire or fear."

It took a while to figure out. That whole summer with Riley, I wasn't sure why, exactly, I saw certain things and not others. Eventually, though, I realized everything always fell into one of those two categories.

I sneak a glance at Noah. He looks serious. Thoughtful. "What's it like? The things you see?"

There's a butter knife on the table. I pick it up and turn it over, catching the reflection of the spinning fans that dot the ceiling, trying to gather and parse my thoughts. How do you explain something that feels so inexplicable? "There was a woman on the bus on my way here. Old. Friendly. She looked like someone's grandmother and she smelled like vanilla. Like she had just baked cookies. She sat down in the seat next to me, and I wasn't careful enough. She touched me. All of a sudden, I was drowning. I couldn't breathe and I couldn't break free."

"She was scared of drowning?"

"No . . . I didn't see fear when I touched her. It was a desire. She was holding me down, holding me underwater. But it wasn't really me." I struggle to put it into words that will make sense. "Sometimes, when I get sucked in, it's like I'm forced to act out a part. I'm not myself. When she touched me, I became the person she wanted to hurt, but I just as easily could have seen the whole thing from her eyes. It's a crapshoot. I can't control it."

I scoot forward in the booth. My knees brush Noah's. Out of habit, I flinch, but then I remember that we're both wearing jeans. I should still move away, but there's something comforting about the contact. Even though it's slight. Even though he probably doesn't even realize we're touching.

His face darkens as he thinks through what I've just said. "So, she wanted to kill someone?"

"Maybe. Probably not, though. She probably just wanted revenge, and that was the form the image took. Think about how many times in your life you've thought you were mad enough to kill someone."

The way he looks at me makes me wonder if he's thinking about that night in my bedroom, if he's worried about what was running through his mind when he touched me. "Everyone thinks that sometimes," he says carefully.

"Exactly. Everyone thinks that sometimes. The things I see aren't literal. The same image from two different people can mean two completely different things. Sometimes," I add, thinking about what happened with Skylar on the bridge, "what people fear and what they desire are tangled together. And sometimes people fear the things they want or want the things they fear."

Noah is quiet for a moment, turning over what I've said. "What happened on the bus? After you saw what you did?"

"I changed seats at the next stop."

The ghost of a smile breaks through the seriousness on his face. Something inside of me unknots. I had done it: I told someone. I told someone, and the world didn't end.

"Can you control it—whether you see desire or fear?"

"I don't know," I admit. "I've only ever tried a couple of times. And it's not like I've had a lot of chances to practice: I don't make a habit of touching people." I shrug, the gesture stiff and awkward, the aches in my body reminding me that I haven't slept enough in the past twenty-four hours.

"And when you touched Riley, you saw the medal because . . ."

"That's what he was most scared of that day. He was scared he'd get in trouble for keeping it."

I've thought about it sometimes, those times when I've let myself think about him at all: What would have happened if I had seen desire that day instead of fear?

"Did you ever touch Riley before that?" asks Noah. "Did you ever see anything else?"

I hesitate. Fears and desires are personal. Maybe the truest reflection of who someone is. Sharing them seems wrong.

But then Noah leans forward. Anxious. Attentive. In that moment, he reminds me so much of his brother that it makes my chest constrict. On the surface, they don't look alike. But sitting here in the booth, eager for any scraps I can give him about Riley, Noah's face gives up some of its harsh, guarded look. That's when I see it. The similarities that are subtle. The ones that have to be searched out. The angle of his jaw and the way his eyebrows pull together when he's thinking. The way he leans forward, one elbow resting on the edge of the table. Something about those small similarities—those tiny things that remind me of Riley—loosen the words and quell the thought that they might be some form of betrayal.

"I try not to touch people, but it was all still new to me that summer. And it was hard around Riley. It was easy to forget to be careful. It didn't happen a lot, me touching him. Maybe a handful of times. He was scared of the forest at night. I never quite understood that—how he could want to spend so much time in a place that scared him on some level."

"That's it? Just the forest?"

"He was worried your dad was going to leave."

The waitress returns and sets our food on the table. I wait until she's out of earshot before speaking again. "Most of his desires were normal kid stuff. He wanted to be an executive at Disney so that he'd get free passes to Comic-Con and could control what Marvel stuff got made. And he wanted to be strong enough to beat up some of the kids at his old school."

I nod toward Noah's burger. "It's going to get cold." I lift my knife and fork and dig into my own food. The eggs are overcooked and the bacon is practically black around the edges, but eating gives me an excuse to stop talking.

Riley was so certain that what was happening to me could be

155

managed with practice. We'd sit on his bed, door open a crack because his mom insisted, and go over and over the things I had seen. "What about this one?" he'd ask, leaning in and pointing to a line in the list he'd made, not noticing the way my breath would catch or how I'd trip over my words a little when I responded. Not noticing the way I'd watch him sometimes.

And I'd try to help him, too. When I could. When the thoughts in his head got so loud he needed someone to tell him it was okay.

After a few bites, Noah sets the remainder of his burger down. "Did you try to control what you saw when you touched me?"

"Yes."

"Why?"

"I hadn't seen you in five years, and practically the first thing you said to me was that you didn't want Riley to be found. It didn't make any sense."

"What did you look for?"

"Desire."

"And what did you see?"

"That you didn't mean it. That you want someone to find him."

"And the other time?"

"What other time?"

"When I touched you in your room."

I tug at my sleeves, making sure they cover my wrists. First one and then the other. On some level, I think I've been actively trying not to think about it. Not because I don't understand the desire for revenge, but because I don't want those images in my head. "I don't remember," I lie. "Anyway, I don't understand how my little messed-up ability can help—even though I want to."

"You said you saw the medal because Riley was scared of getting caught. Odds are, whoever hurt Riley and Rachel has to be scared of getting caught, too. Especially since Rachel is alive. All we have to do is get you in the right place with the right person."

"Or persons," I say, to be thorough.

"Or persons," Noah agrees.

He makes it all sound so reasonable, so easy. But it's not. Not at all. The thought of what Noah's proposing simultaneously makes my skin crawl and my stomach drop. "You're banking on the fact that I can control it. That I can choose to see each person's fear. I can't. Even if I could, it's not like I can just walk up to every person in town and try to see what they're afraid of on the off chance it's connected to Riley or Rachel."

"Why not?"

"There are probably laws against touching random people on the street. This is Canada. You're all ridiculously considerate and reserved."

Noah does not laugh.

"Fine." I sigh. "For one thing, I've only tried to control it twice and I have no way of knowing if either time worked. Maybe I saw exactly what I would have seen if I hadn't tried to do anything at all. For another, did you not notice how sick I was that night you came up to my room? That's what happened when I tried to control what I saw."

"But the pills help?"

"They help a little. They're not some magic cure-all." I pull in a deep breath and let it out slowly. I know I sound angry, but I'm not. Not exactly. I'm frustrated and still kind of scared at the idea of talking to anyone about this. "That first year, after it started happening, I got headaches pretty much any time I accidentally touched anyone. Bad ones. Sometimes so bad that I couldn't do anything for hours. It happened often enough that eventually my father noticed and took me to a doctor who ran a whole bunch of tests and then told him it was migraines." I want to tell Noah how hard the appointments and tests had been for me. How I had to work so hard at not flinching each time I was plunged into the head of someone who was just trying to help me get better. But I'm not sure I can describe it. Not adequately. "Over the years," I say, "it's gotten more bearable. At least some of the time. Touching someone always hurts, but I usually have to go for the pills only when someone's desire or fear is particularly strong or if I touch them for longer than a few seconds. And in those cases, the pills help. Other times, though, the pain is a lot stronger. If I touch too many people in too short a period of time, they barely make a dent. And it seems to be the same when I try to go looking for something on purpose."

An older couple comes in. For a second, I think they're going to sit near us, but then they take one of the booths near the front.

Once Noah seems sure they're too far away to overhear, he says, "If you became desensitized to some of it over time, how do you know it wouldn't eventually get easier—less painful, at least—to read people on purpose, too?" He holds out his hand, palm up, the way you would at a fortune-telling booth. When I don't reach for it, he raises one eyebrow. "Scared?"

"Of getting hit in the middle of the head with an invisible sledgehammer? You bet."

"I just think maybe it would be worth practicing. See if exposure could help—both with the pain and with being able to choose what you see. Maybe you could even control the vantage point."

"Meaning?"

"Meaning no more being the person who gets drowned." He nods down at his hand. "You've already touched me, so I'm a perfect guinea pig."

I make no move, and he eventually lowers his hand. "You can't go the rest of your life like this, Cat."

"Like what?"

"Afraid to touch anyone. Wearing long sleeves in the middle of summer to cut down on the chance. When's the last time you hugged someone? Or let someone hug you?" I don't answer, and he presses on. "When was the last time you were held? Other than my brother when you were a kid, have you ever even kissed anyone?"

"How did you—?" I shake my head. I guess it doesn't matter how he knows I kissed Riley that summer. My first, disastrous kiss.

Noah mistakes my silence for confirmation. "Don't you want that?" His eyes grow darker with the words. "Don't you want to touch someone and be touched?"

"Not everyone wants that." I try not to think about Aidan and that night on the porch or watching Joey touch Skylar or the chances I've let pass by because I've been too scared of what might happen. Because I know what will happen.

"You're right," says Noah. "Not everyone does want that, and if that's the case with you, I'll never say another word about it. If that's the case, I shouldn't have said anything." His voice is so earnest that it breaks something inside my chest. He half rises from his seat, leaning over the booth. Leaning down over me. He raises his hand and places it alongside my cheek, not touching, but so close that I can feel the heat radiating from his skin. "If I'm wrong, I promise you, I won't say another word. But if I'm right . . . you need to think about this. You need to think about what it might mean, going through the rest of your life keeping everyone at a distance."

"Do you honestly think I haven't?"

His hand is so close. It would be so, so easy to turn my head. Just a little bit. To turn into that touch. Suddenly, the diner is too small and too loud and he is far, far too close.

I slide out of the booth.

I don't run. Not while he's watching. But as soon as I'm outside? Then I run and I don't stop until I hit the very edge of the parking lot.

Noah Fraser thinks he knows everything, but he doesn't. He doesn't know anything at all.

He wants me to trust him, but I still haven't recovered from the last Fraser boy who thought he could help me.

SIXTEEN

I HEAR THE CRUNCH OF NOAH'S SHOES ON THE GRAVEL parking lot before he speaks. "Cat . . ."

I tug on the door of the BMW. Locked. I can't look at him. I have this horrible feeling that if I look at him, I'll end up yelling or crying, and neither option is all that appealing. "I want you to take me home."

"Just let me explain."

But I don't need any explanations. He's already said plenty. He thinks there's something wrong with me. That I need to be fixed, somehow. If it weren't for Dad and his stupid technology ban, I would just call Aunt Jet to pick me up. For a second, I think about going back into the diner and seeing if they have a pay phone, but then I remember that Jet is at work; she traded shifts so that she could be home with me at night. "Just take me home, Noah."

He doesn't say anything, but after a long moment, I hear the jangle of his keys as he pulls them from his pocket.

We drive back in silence, and as soon as the car comes to a stop in front of Montgomery House, I'm out the door.

"Cat—wait!" Just before I turn away, I see him reach for something between the seats.

I almost make it to the porch steps before he catches up with me. "Just take it," he says, stepping in front of me and holding out a brown file folder. "*Please*, Cat."

"What is it?"

"Everything I've been able to find out about the week Riley disappeared. Please just read it. Maybe you'll see something I missed."

Closing my eyes, I draw in a deep breath. I let it fill my lungs and then slowly let it out. *You're not doing this just for Noah*, I remind myself. *It's bigger than that.* I open my eyes and take the folder.

"Cat, I didn't mean what I said, I—"

I shake my head. "Please move." I could squeeze past him, but he's standing right in the middle of the stairs, not leaving nearly enough room for comfort.

"We need to talk about what happened."

I shake my head again. "I don't have to do anything." When he still doesn't move, I turn and walk around the side of the house, to the seldom-used kitchen entrance. I let myself inside, close and lock the door, and then lean against the frame, clutching the folder to my chest.

I'll help Noah. For Riley's sake and for Rachel. Because I held her hand down at the river and told her she was safe. I'll help Noah, but I don't have to talk to him. Not right now.

* * *

The three days that follow dawn hot and humid. Each day, Noah calls. Each time Aunt Jet answers, I beg her to make excuses. She doesn't like lying—she keeps making these low, disgruntled clucking sounds like she's some sort of chicken—but she does as I ask. Aidan's been much more chill about the whole deception thing. Not to mention creative. The one time Noah came to the door, he told him I was at a public lecture about melting Arctic ice sheets and that he could find me on the second floor of the Montgomery Falls Public Library.

The Montgomery Falls Public Library does not actually have a second floor.

Noah isn't the only one who calls. Apparently, Jet hadn't actually believed me when I said I'd call Dad, so she phoned him and told him everything. To say he's rethinking sending me here for the summer would be an understatement. Aunt Jet, too, seems worried that maybe he's made a mistake. Despite the heat, she keeps fixing me cups of hot chocolate and offering to make runs to the video store. I don't have the heart to tell her that I haven't liked hot chocolate since I was about ten, so I keep surreptitiously tipping it down the drain.

When I haven't been dodging phone calls or assuring my aunt that I really don't need her to rent *Frozen* or *Moana*—movies I admittedly did love when last I was here—I've been poring over Noah's folder and the pieces of information it contains. The names of people who saw Riley the day he disappeared. His class schedule. A reminder that he had an appointment with the guidance counselor to talk about colleges. I already knew Riley was an athlete, but I didn't know that he was on both the baseball and basketball teams or that he was on student council. As I look over his schedule, I wonder when Riley had found the time to just breathe.

Skylar, Aidan, Chase, and Joey—all of their names are in the file. So is Rachel's. It's a stark reminder of how small Montgomery Falls is. Skylar and Aidan both had bio with Riley. Chase had basketball. Rachel served with him on student council. All five of them were at a party a few days before Riley disappeared. In another place, it might seem significant, but in a town where the graduating class of each high school is fewer than sixty people, it would be strange if their names *didn't* show up.

The folder also paints a picture of what things were like in the weeks after Riley disappeared. Printouts of newspaper articles, lists of the people who signed up for search parties and the maps they used, tips called into a hotline Riley's dad had set up for the reward—it's all here. Even bits of what looks like the police file on the case. I have no idea how Noah managed to get his hands on all of it.

Both Chase and Aidan volunteered with the search parties, which makes sense. It also makes sense that Skylar wouldn't have volunteered, given what I saw on the posters when I arrived in town and what Aidan told me.

There's a note in the folder about some of the things Riley's girlfriend and her friends have said about Skylar—things that make it look like Skylar cornered Riley and practically assaulted him. Things that make it look like she was obsessed and one step away from building a shrine to Riley in her bedroom. The police interviewed her about it. More than once.

From what I saw when I'd accidentally touched Skylar on the bridge, Riley had kissed her back just as fiercely, but you'd never guess that if all you did was read the folder.

Given what was happening to Skylar, it makes sense Joey wouldn't have volunteered to help the search parties. I want to hold it against him, but as far as I can tell, loyalty to Skylar might be his one big redeeming quality.

There are also clues about Riley himself in the folder, if you read between the lines—the classes he took, the people he hung out with, the things he was seen doing in the days leading up to his disappearance. I try to assemble a picture from these bits and pieces, but none of the configurations seem right. None of the pictures match the boy in my memories.

The more I try to make things fit, the more I think about the Riley I knew. And the more I think about the Riley I knew, the more it feels like there's this weight inside my chest.

By 8:00 a.m. on Sunday, the temperature has already crept up past scorching, and it's hot enough that I'm wearing one of my two pairs of shorts and a tank top. Even with the ancient metal fan I lugged up to my room from the basement, my bare legs stick to the hardwood floor every time I shift position.

I force myself to focus on the papers in front of me.

The police department organized three search parties in the two months following Riley's disappearance. The second one— the one they held after the snow had gone down enough to make searching the woods truly possible—focused on a strip of forest that's bordered by the textile mill on the east and town on the north. Keep going past the mill, and eventually you'll hit the old logging roads. Cross those, and it's just you and open wilderness for hundreds of miles.

I lift one of the crude, hand-drawn maps the searchers had used. It's not nearly as good as the maps Riley used to make. It shows a few of the main paths, but none of the smaller ones that crisscross the woods.

It does, however, show the creek.

The creek isn't big enough to have a name. Not really. Riley called it the Rio Tiny because it seemed to wind its way through the whole of the woods, shrinking to a trickle in some places, but never completely drying up.

He had spent an entire week mapping it, plotting the curves and slopes. He wanted to be a cartographer when he grew up, even though Noah told him that cartography was a profession that died out centuries ago.

"Do you actually like doing this?" I'd asked one day. I had been following Riley along the creek for what felt like hours, occasionally pausing to overturn a rock with the edge of my shoe or to examine webs spun by spiders in hollow places. We were at the top of a steep slope. A place where the creek turned rushing and wild as it plunged down. The falls part of Montgomery Falls.

He glanced back over his shoulder. His hair stuck up in a dozen different directions in the heat, and there was a sunburn on the back of his neck. Angry and red and peeling around the edges. "Hanging out in the woods?"

"Mapping them." It had seemed kind of fun at the start of summer. Like a project. But the longer we did it, the more intense

Riley became. Maps that he had spent weeks on—maps that I thought were better than anything you'd find in a book—were no longer good enough. Angles that were close enough before weren't close enough now. Details that seemed important had been replaced with details I didn't understand. A broken Coke bottle, an old piece of machinery dragged into the trees from the textile mill, a crumpled wrapper—each of these became a number on one of his maps.

"Do you want to stop?" A worried expression crossed his face.

"No!" I said, a little too quickly. "This is fun, this is great." Because, when you got right down to it, I'd do just about anything he wanted if it meant getting more time with him. As it was, I was painfully aware of how few hours there were in the summer and how much it was going to hurt when it came time to leave. Riley was the only one besides Aunt Jet who had any idea what was going on with me. "Honest," I said, because Riley was still looking at me with a worried expression on his face, "I'm having fun."

I was paying more attention to convincing him than to where I was stepping, and my foot came down on a loose patch of ground.

I started to fall, but Riley was faster than gravity. He caught my arm, keeping me from plunging down to broken limbs—or something worse.

And as he touched me, I saw what he was scared of. He wasn't scared we would get in trouble for being in the woods or that I would be mad at him. He wasn't even scared I would get hurt—not exactly. He was scared of something bigger. He was scared the forest was going to take me, the way it took other lost things. He was scared it would take me and he wouldn't be able to find me.

"You're okay," he had said as he glanced past me to the spot where the ground dropped away. "You're okay."

Pain started to blossom across my temples as he touched my skin, but I didn't want to pull away. I wanted to stay there, close to him, even if it hurt.

The memory hits me hard. Hard enough that my anger at Noah suddenly seems small. Maybe even a little irrational. Because every moment I stay angry at Noah is a moment I'm not really doing everything I can to figure out what happened to the boy who was scared he would lose me to the woods and not be able to find me.

Of course, it's not until I'm through the hedge, ready to make peace and standing in the empty driveway, that I remember the last message Noah left with Aunt Jet yesterday, the one about how he was taking his mother out to their cottage on the lake and would be gone for two nights.

Aunt Jet's eyes had been extra reproachful when she relayed that particular message. I think Noah reminds her of what she gave up when she came back to Montgomery Falls.

Given the state Noah's mom was in the last time I saw her, I can't imagine a few days of fresh air and water will help, but at least he's trying.

I run my fingertips over my arm, over the spot where Riley's hand had clamped around me all those years ago as he kept me from falling.

"You're okay," he had said. The same two words Skylar said to me at the riverbank as she hugged me tight enough to bruise. That's why it had felt familiar.

And there, again, is another part of the puzzle that doesn't quite fit. The idea that Riley could be with someone as great as Skylar—even for just a few hours at a party—and let her go. I know people change, but that boy in the woods? I think he would have liked Skylar. I know he would have.

My gaze drifts up to Riley's window as an idea starts to take shape in the back of my mind.

I don't let myself think about whether what I'm about to do is right or wrong as I walk around the side of the Fraser house and head for the back porch. The spare key is still there, still tucked in a small gap underneath the third step. Keeping a spare key in the same hiding spot for five years doesn't seem like the best idea, security-wise, but since I'm the one benefiting, I probably shouldn't complain.

The first thing I notice when I step into the kitchen is that it's clean. The take-out containers are gone, the pile of dishes reduced to a single plate. Even the floor looks like it's been washed; it squeaks underneath my shoes as I cross the room.

Now that I'm inside, it's a little harder not to feel like I'm doing something I shouldn't, but I don't turn around and leave. I just make my way up to the second floor and push open Riley's bedroom door.

I expect it to stick—it always stuck when they first moved in—but it doesn't.

It's far from the only thing that's different.

The room I remember had been weird and geeky—like Riley himself. Even though his parents had more money than anyone in Montgomery Falls. Even though his dad made him get up early every Saturday morning for golf lessons at the country club. With his skinned knees and his homemade maps and his lists of forgotten things, Riley had been weird and wonderful, and his room had been a reflection of that.

But gone are the maps and the Marvel posters and the models of rockets and airplanes. The Star Wars sheets have been replaced with a plain blue duvet, and the walls are dotted with posters of depressingly generic bands and swimsuit models in bikinis.

I stare at one of the women on the wall. Long blond hair. Toned stomach. Perfect breasts covered by small triangles of red fabric.

If that's what he wants to wake up to, what's the chance he would ever even glance at someone like me?

It's a stupid, stupid thought. I don't know why I think it. I don't know why it would even matter. Any guy with a room like this wouldn't be my type, either.

I pull my eyes away from the poster and force myself to focus on the rest of the room.

Riley's laptop sits closed on his desk next to a stack of college brochures and applications. I've barely even thought about what I might do after high school, but it looks like Riley already has a whole plan of attack. Lacey is the same way. She's been stockpiling college brochures since freshman year. Up until a few months ago, every time she got a new one for herself, she made sure to get an extra one for me. She'd even mark off things that she thought might interest me. Little pink and blue Post-its—pink for things like dorms and campus activities, blue for academics.

I push the thought from my mind.

Being in here is hard enough without thinking about Lacey on top of everything else.

I open Riley's laptop and hit the power button. After so many months, I expect the battery to be dead, but the screen flickers to life. I take a few shots at the password. None of them work. I guess that would have been too easy.

I slide open the top desk drawer, and my breath catches. I'm not sure what I was expecting—more brochures and applications, maybe—but instead I find a pad of graph paper and the beginnings of a map.

A strange, sharp ache fills me as I pick up the pad and flip through it. More maps and diagrams. The room may have changed—Riley may have changed—but some things had stayed the same.

I turn back to the topmost page. The lines aren't long enough to be streets, but they don't seem to curve the way the paths in the forest do. Unlike most of the other maps, there aren't any notations on this one. No clues as to what Riley was mapping. On impulse, I pull the sheet free, fold it, and slip it into my pocket. Noah must have gone through all of this stuff already, but there can't be any harm in checking the map against the ones used by the search parties or against the area where Rachel was found.

It's a stretch, but it's not like I have any other ideas.

As I place the pad back in the desk, I notice a small bottle of pills wedged in the corner.

It rattles as I lift it out. Half full. Riley's name is on the label, along with the name of the prescription and the dosage. A small orange warning sticker says not to consume alcohol while taking.

I think about what Chase told me about how everyone but Riley had been drinking the night of the boat crash and try to reconcile that with the taste of alcohol I remember from touching Skylar. I can't.

I turn the small plastic cylinder over in my hands. Noah said the pills had helped. Jensen claimed there was nothing to say Riley hadn't just run away; but if he had, wouldn't he have taken the pills with him? If I were running, my own pills would be one of the first things I'd grab.

Heart heavy, I put the bottle back in the drawer and then go sit on the edge of Riley's bed. It's getting harder to believe that Noah might be wrong, that Riley might still be out there. The duvet is slightly wrinkled, and I imagine Noah or Mrs. Fraser coming in here to just sit and think about everything they've lost. Again, I feel like I'm doing something wrong by being here, but I don't leave.

I smooth out one of the wrinkles with the flat of my hand as my gaze drifts to a framed photo on the nightstand. The frame doesn't match the rest of the room. Pewter daisies and hearts with the word *Always* in script along the bottom. Definitely something that looks like it was picked out by a girl. Probably the same girl Riley has his arms wrapped around in the photo. I lift it and turn it over. *To Riley, Love Amber* is written in metallic Sharpie on the back and encircled with a heart.

I flip the frame back over. I recognize Amber as one of the girls from the drugstore that day I was with Skylar. The one who had been at the counter. The blonde with the tortoiseshell glasses who'd shot me the small, curious look.

She looks sweet and innocent in the photo. All big blue eyes and bright white teeth and apple cheeks. All glossy smile and shiny hair. She looks happy. Like everything in her world is exactly as it should be.

But Riley isn't smiling. His arms are wrapped loosely around her, but he looks stiff and uncomfortable. Awkward and out of place and more like the boy I used to know than he does on any of the posters around town.

"Where did you go?" I whisper to the boy in the photo. The house around me is silent.

SEVENTEEN

WHEN I GET BACK, AUNT JET ASKS IF I WANT TO GO WITH her to church. It might make me feel better, she tells me. I doubt it—Dad's a hard-core atheist, and while I'm still on the fence about the whole religion thing, I'm probably edging that way—but the alternative is staying here, waiting for Noah, feeling like I should be doing . . . *something*.

So I tell her I'll go.

I head up to my room, where I slip on a pair of black jeans and a black T-shirt. It feels too casual, but when I meet Aunt Jet in the hallway downstairs, she tells me I look fine.

"I'm glad you're coming with me," she confesses as she pulls a scarf from the hall closet and wraps it loosely around her neck. The strip of fabric is long and silky and covered with small, delicate flowers. The house is filled with things just like it. Scarves and gloves and fur coats wrapped in tissue paper. "Trappings," my father calls them. Reminders that the Montgomerys once had money. Though the scarf looks nice around Aunt Jet's neck, there's something a little sad and faded about it.

As I climb into the car, I think about the tenants in the rooms and the sell pile in the basement and the fact that there's old money and new money and then there's money that's just lost.

It's hard to imagine Chief Jensen would care about any claim he thinks he has to the Montgomery estate if he knew how little is actually left.

Aunt Jet slides behind the wheel, sighs, and then struggles to move the seat up. As we pull away from the house, she adjusts the rearview mirror. "I wasn't able to change my shift tonight," she says, a worried, apologetic note in her voice. "I have to go in at six. I'm going to talk to Marie and see if she can look in on you."

"I don't need a babysitter."

"I know you don't." Aunt Jet says the words so quickly that it's obvious she doesn't know that at all. "It's just that with everything going on, with what happened the other night, I'd feel better if I knew you weren't on your own."

As we pass the downtown strip, I catch sight of one of Riley's missing posters. To be honest, I don't exactly relish the idea of being alone. Though I'd never admit it, it's been kind of nice having Aunt Jet hover over me. Dad's never really hovered much— even those times when someone really should have been hovering.

It makes me wonder what the past few years would have been like if I had fought Dad about pulling away from Jet and this place. At the time, I thought I was happy to have an excuse not to come back here because, if I did, sooner or later I would see Riley again. But maybe that had been a mistake. Maybe I wouldn't have felt so bad about myself if there had still been one person in my life I wasn't hiding parts of myself from. If there had been one person who hovered.

But even though I want Aunt Jet to stay home tonight, I know I can't be selfish. Her job is hard enough without worrying about me during her shift. "It's okay. Really. I know you need to work."

In response, she shoots me a small, relieved smile as she pulls into the church lot.

The service doesn't start for another twenty minutes, but there are so many cars that Aunt Jet has trouble finding a parking spot.

"Are there always this many people here?" I ask as we make our way toward the church steps.

"People have been upset since Riley went missing. Coming here can be comforting. And after what happened a few nights ago . . ."

"People need comfort."

She nods.

I half hold my breath as I step inside. The last time I came close to any religion was Lacey's second cousin's bat mitzvah three years ago—between that and the fact I'm a walking abomination out of a scary story, it feels like God and I might not exactly be simpatico.

While I don't burst into flames, it doesn't take me long to feel like I've made a mistake. The crowd is so closely packed that not touching anyone is an effort. And if that isn't bad enough, everyone seems to be whispering about Rachel Larsen and how she was found. They whisper about me, Skylar, and Chase.

Two men hand out programs. One is young and in a suit the color of a robin's egg, the other older and wearing a faded pinstripe. They flank a set of polished interior doors that lead to rapidly filling pews.

As Jet and I join the line, I realize the older man is familiar. Thinning hair, sunburnt scalp, bushy eyebrows—the photographer from the riverbank.

He doesn't so much hand out programs as thrust them forward. The movement is almost as awkward and jerky as the sparse pleasantries he strings together for each person who greets him.

Noah believes I might be able to control my weird little skill set—and that it might get less painful—with practice. I'm not convinced, but if I'm serious about using what I can do to help find out what happened to Riley and Rachel, there are probably worse places to start than with the photographer who freelances for the police.

As the line inches forward, I reposition myself so that I'm standing to Aunt Jet's left. As she greets the younger man, I turn to Harding.

If he recognizes me from the riverbank, he doesn't show it. He thrusts a program toward me. I try to remember what I did when I touched Noah, but there's no time. Harding's hand brushes mine, and I have just a fraction of a second to register the image on the front of the folded sheet of paper—Jesus cradling a toddler as a lamb kneels at his sandal-shod feet—and then . . .

Ropelike flames shoot up my arms and wrap around my wrists.

177

They pull me down.

Down into heat so strong that my skin peels from my bones as my nostrils fill with the scent of burning flesh. All around me, I can hear people screaming. How can I hear people screaming when I'm burning, burning, burning—

The church comes rushing back. The program falls to the ground, and Jesus smiles up at me from the floor. I pull in a deep breath. My chest still feels like it's on fire.

When I look up, it's to find Harding staring at me, his bushy brows pulling toward each other like two caterpillars about to duke it out.

"Mary Catherine?" Aunt Jet turns to me, concern flashing across her face.

"I forgot something in the car," I lie, the words coming out high and uneven. "You go in. I'll be right back."

Turning away before she can examine me too closely or ask any questions, I squeeze through the crowd, desperately trying to avoid coming into contact with anyone else.

It's not until I'm outside and halfway across the parking lot that I stop thinking I can smell the scent of burning bodies.

A low granite wall separates the church grounds from a neighboring park. I find a spot under an oak tree and perch on the stone. The faint strains of an organ drift on the air, and the pain in my head pulsates and builds between the notes. It's my own fault: I should have thought about what desires and fears a church might bring to the surface. All images require some interpretation, but it doesn't take a genius to figure out that what Harding fears isn't ordinary fire—something plenty of people are terrified of—but fire in the biblical sense.

I wish Noah were here. Not because I need to tell him what I saw—what I saw probably doesn't mean anything—but because I want someone to tell me that I'm okay. I want someone to tell me that seeing monstrous things does not make me monstrous myself.

"Cat?"

I glance up. Skylar is standing next to me, on the church side of the wall. It takes me a second to recognize her. Gone are her usual clothes, replaced by a long, floral-print dress and a beige cardigan. Her black hair is tied back in a simple ponytail. When I glance down, I see pantyhose-enclosed legs ending in a pair of low, practical pumps.

"Why do you look like a Sunday school teacher?" I ask, not even trying to keep the confusion from my voice.

"Because I am. Sort of. I help out with the Sunday school classes. I should be in there now, but I saw you." She tugs on the edge of her sweater. "You looked upset."

"I'm okay," I lie. In my head, I still see fire.

Skylar does not seem convinced.

"Really. I'm just not big on church. I'm waiting for my aunt, but you should go back inside." It's hard to make my voice all that emphatic with the growing pain in my head, and I'm oddly distracted by a bright yellow sticker stuck to the bottom of Skylar's cardigan. A smiling sun encircled by the words *Jesus Loves You*.

It's hard not to stare at that sticker. It's like Skylar is some kind of Jekyll and Hyde . . . if Jekyll were an adorable goth and Hyde were a cardigan-wearing Sunday school teacher.

Okay, maybe not my best analogy.

Instead of leaving, Skylar slips off her shoes and claims a spot next to me on the wall. "I don't really want to," she admits. "Everyone in there is talking about Rachel."

"Do you know if she's awake yet? If the police have talked to her?"

"One of my mother's friends works at the hospital. She said Rachel woke up yesterday but isn't well enough to be released. No idea if anyone other than the doctors have spoken with her." She runs a hand over her ponytail. "I wanted to call you."

"Me, too," I say. And it's true: I had wanted to call. I had even gotten her number from Aidan.

"It's just weird, right? Like, what do you say? 'Thanks for hanging out—sorry about the whole finding-an-almost-dead-person thing. I promise we'll have more fun next time.'"

I laugh before I can stop myself. The pounding in my head is not impressed. For a second, I feel like I might throw up, and the sensation is so strong that I lean over and put my head between my knees.

Why didn't I think to bring my pills? Well, that one's easy: it's not like I had planned on deliberately diving into anyone's head. My only saving grace is that the contact had been so brief. The pain isn't what I'd rate low-to-moderate, but I can already tell that it's not going to build to the level it hit the night I went snooping in Noah's head.

"You really do look awful."

"Thanks." Then, because I know she wasn't trying to be

critical, I add, "I get migraines." Not the truth, but better than an outright lie.

"Do you want me to take you home? I have my car. My mom's staying for Bible study after the service, and she always gets a ride with one of her friends, so I don't have to wait for her."

"What about Sunday school?"

"There are five of us and only thirty kids. Pretty sure they can cope. Besides, I've gotten volunteer of the month six times in a row. I'm, like, one of only two volunteers under sixty they trust with a set of keys to the building—supposedly because I've earned the privilege, but really because I'm the only one who always comes in early to set up. That's got to be worth a little grace." She stops, suddenly, and blushes. "Sorry. That's probably way more information than you wanted. Or needed."

I gesture at her clothes and the church. "Is all this for your parents?"

She thinks it over, then shrugs. "Maybe, I guess. It's hard. You know? Figuring out how much of anything is you. How much is for somebody else."

I do know. "And the horror movies?" I ask.

"What about them?"

"Are they a form of rebellion?" I realize that in the span of just a few minutes, I've pretty much abandoned my earlier intention not to ask her any personal questions.

Skylar shakes her head. "No. That would be sad and cliché." She pushes herself off the wall. "Come on. We'll text your aunt. Tell her you weren't feeling well."

"I don't have a phone," I remind her.

"You can use mine. Incidentally, you did me a total favor dropping my old one by the river. Perfect excuse to ask my parents for a new one."

"You know, there are easier ways to get a new phone."

"Not in my house, there aren't."

She grins. Despite the pain in my head, I find myself grinning back.

EIGHTEEN

SKYLAR MAY BE DRESSED LIKE A SUNDAY SCHOOL TEACHER, but she drives like a demon. While the air from the open passenger-side window makes the pain in my head recede a bit, the speed at which she takes turns and the abruptness with which she breaks at stop signs make my stomach both flip and flop.

"Sorry!" she says as I brace myself against the dash.

By the time we reach Riverside Avenue, I'm seriously wondering just how hard it is to get a driver's license in this country.

As Skylar slows for the turnoff to Montgomery House, I crane my neck to get a look at the driveway next door. The front gate is closed, but I can see clearly through the gaps between the wrought-iron slats. The BMW isn't there. Even though I know Noah isn't supposed to be back until tomorrow, I still feel a small pang of disappointment.

"She really is beautiful, isn't she?" says Skylar as she eases the car down to a crawl.

"Who?"

"The house."

I stare up at Montgomery House, trying to see it through different eyes as we come to a complete stop. I've always loved it, but I've never really thought of it as beautiful. I guess it is, though—in a neglected sort of way.

"Do you want to come in?" The words feel stiff and awkward. Other than Lacey, it's been years since I've really invited anyone over. I'm not entirely sure why I'm doing it now. I try to tell myself that it's just because Skylar went to the trouble of driving me home, but I don't think that's the only reason.

"Really?" Skylar grins like an invitation to my aunt's run-down boardinghouse is the best thing that's happened to her in ages. Given the events of the past week, I guess that might actually be a possibility.

I know getting close to her—getting close to anyone—is a bad idea, but I like her. I can't help it.

Still beaming, Skylar climbs out of the car and bounces on the toes of her tiny pumps. Her heels make a click-click sound against the pavement as she waits for me to join her. "Joey texted me before church. We were going to hang out this afternoon, but he had some flash of inspiration and wanted to work on his script instead."

"You don't mind?"

"No. Yes. Maybe." Her brow furrows as we walk up the stairs and across the porch. "Should I?"

I shrug. Honestly, I don't know. It's not like I've ever been in a relationship.

It's not the first time Skylar has been in Montgomery House, but she still stares at everything like she's trying to soak it all in as she follows me through the door and into the front hall. Brisby winds around her ankles, and she reaches down to scratch him behind the ears. "You remember me, don't you?" she says softly. To me, she says, "Did you know a pair of ghost hunters spent a week here in 1991?"

I do know. It's a story Dad likes to tell—how this couple who claimed to have investigated haunted houses all over the world spent a week in Montgomery Falls, poking around the grounds of the old textile mill by day and sleeping at Montgomery House at night. How every time they felt a draft, they claimed it was a spirit trying to communicate from beyond. On their way out the door, they'd been caught with a suitcase full of old knickknacks and moth-eaten strips of cloth. Things they claimed were soaked in psychic energy.

"You know the house isn't really haunted, right?" I'm not opposed to the idea of ghosts, but surely if there were any here, I would have seen them by now.

Skylar straightens and then raises her shoulders in a tiny shrug. "All things are haunted—at least to somebody."

She walks to the staircase, lowers herself to the bottom step, and coaxes Brisby over. When he complies, she pulls him onto her lap. I expect him to hiss or squirm away—any affection Brisby bestows is always strictly on his own terms—but he purrs and settles in.

"I'll be right back," I say as Skylar fishes a bag of cat treats from her bottomless purse.

I head up to my room and duck into the bathroom. After popping two pills, I splash some water on my face. *Skylar wasn't wrong*, I think, leaning toward the mirror to study the dark circles under my eyes, *I really do look kind of awful.*

When I step back into my bedroom, it's to find Skylar has followed me upstairs. There's a piece of paper in her hands—one of the newspaper articles Noah had printed out—and a puzzled expression on her face. When I glance down, I realize the contents of Noah's folder are still spread out over the floor. "Sorry," I mutter, rushing forward to sweep up the mess.

She lifts another piece of paper: the mystery map I had found in Riley's desk. "What is all this stuff?"

I say a small prayer of thanks that the notes about her supposed obsession with Riley are on the very bottom of the pile.

"I don't suppose you know where that is?" I ask, nodding toward the piece of paper in her hand.

"I don't think so." She studies the lines for a moment and then shakes her head and looks up. "No. I don't recognize it. Cat, *why* do you have all of this? *Where* did you get all of this?"

I hesitate. I don't want to tell her that Noah gave me the folder. To me, keeping the folder is an understandable act in a situation that is anything but understandable. But people might twist it somehow. I think about the way Noah tried to protect me up at the mill all those years ago, how he pulled me to his chest and told me not to look; I don't want to give anyone another reason to say he's strange—no matter how angry I've been at him over the past few days.

I take the papers from Skylar and slip them back into the

folder. "I know it seems stupid—like some sort of Nancy Drew complex—but after we found Rachel, I started thinking maybe there was some sort of connection."

"Between what happened to her and Riley disappearing?"

"Yeah." I walk over to the desk and slide the folder into the top drawer. Leaving it out was beyond careless. Aunt Jet is already on edge about the whole Rachel thing. What would happen if she walked into my room and found all that stuff spread out on the floor?

"What's a Go-Go?"

I turn. Skylar is holding my Go-Go's shirt up to her chest. It's obviously way too big for her, but she nods approvingly at her reflection.

I shake my head. "Girl group from the eighties. My friend Lacey and I—" I cut myself off. I had been about to tell Skylar how I got the shirt, how Lacey found out the band was in New York for some sort of charity concert and insisted we stake out their hotel. Lacey didn't even like their music—she just thought it would be fun for me. Because she knew I liked them. We couldn't get tickets to the show, but Lacey managed to find the room number of the girl who managed the merch table.

For the past few months—ever since the night things fell apart—I've been careful to think of Lacey in certain ways. It's like if I focus only on the bad stuff, I won't miss her as much and I won't be as hurt by the things she has—and hasn't—done.

It's the same thing I did with Riley, I realize. On the rare occasions I allowed myself to think of him, I only let myself think about how much he had hurt me. It seemed safer that way.

Skylar stares at me expectantly, waiting for me to finish my sentence. "My friend Lacey and I got matching shirts," I say. The words are awkward and anticlimactic.

"It must be hard: being away from everyone for the summer."

I shrug, uncomfortable. "It's not that bad." Given that Lacey and pretty much everyone we know had stopped talking to me long before I got on that bus, being here shouldn't feel all that different. But it does, somehow.

"Hey—Joey and I are going to Saint John sometime this week. Tomorrow, maybe, or the day after. You should come." Skylar's voice is casual, like the invite is an afterthought. She rushes on. "They have this great old record store down there—at least, I think it's supposed to be great, I don't know much about records—and all of these neat secondhand shops." Her words come out so fast that I have to replay them back in my head.

She twists one of the buttons on her cardigan around and around until it's in danger of popping off

She's nervous. The realization takes me aback. I think about the first time I talked to her, how she told a total stranger that the word scrawled on a poster referred to her, how she had stood there, head held high like it didn't matter what I thought.

Skylar stares at me, waiting for my answer.

Given that Aunt Jet was talking about finding me a babysitter as recently as an hour ago, I can't see her letting me take a road trip. "My aunt's kind of paranoid with everything that's happened. I don't think she'd let me go."

Disappointment flashes across her face, though she tries to hide it quickly. "Makes sense. Totally understandable."

"Do you want to sleep over?" I blurt the words out on impulse, without thinking them through. On some level, I suspect this is a horrible idea, but I hate the thought that I might have hurt her feelings. And I really don't want to spend the evening by myself. "I know you probably have other stuff to do, but I thought—"

"Yes!" The single word comes out so loud that Skylar presses her fingertips to her lips as though she's startled herself. "Yes," she says again, at a normal volume.

"Your parents won't mind? After what happened with Rachel, I mean."

A little bit of the brightness leaves her face. "Honestly, I think they'll be happy at the idea of me spending time with a girl. They don't exactly like the fact that all of my friends are guys."

"Why?"

"They think boys lead to trouble."

I want to ask about what happened between her and Riley— about the posters and the girls and that flash of images I got when I touched her on the bridge—but I don't know how. Despite my determination not to get attached to anyone, I like Skylar—I really like her—and I'm scared that if I ask her about Riley, she won't want to stay.

So instead, I tell her something that I haven't told anyone. Not Aidan. Not even Noah. "My dad sent me here because I got into trouble in New York. Not over a boy—not exactly—but it was pretty bad. My best friend doesn't even talk to me anymore. No one really does." I think about the online groups and the hashtags about how I'm a lying freak. Maybe Lacey wasn't responsible for the posts, but she had liked them. The night I trashed my phone,

I had seen her name in a long list of people who thought I was getting exactly what I deserved.

A series of expressions crosses Skylar's face, too quick and complex to make sense of. I wait for her to say something, but instead, she pulls out her phone.

I can feel my face grow hot as I stand in the center of my room, watching her fingers dart over the screen.

Stupid, I think. It was stupid to tell her that I don't have any friends. Maybe she's looking up my name online. Maybe she's found the posts—the ones the school didn't force people to take down because it turns out that their zero-tolerance policy only covers what happens on school grounds. My heart hammers in my chest as my stomach ties itself into knots. I don't know what to do, so I just stand in place. Waiting.

Skylar nods to herself and then slips her phone back into her bag. "There. That's sorted."

"What's sorted?"

"I texted Joey. He and Chase are coming over. We're having a movie day. We can kick them out later—except, I guess, for Aidan because he lives here."

"I thought Joey wanted to work on his script?"

"He docs, but he said he can work on it later. He's going to pick up Chase, and they're going to hit the video store."

"I don't really know if I feel like watching a bunch of horror movies," I say tentatively.

"Me neither," says Skylar. "I mean, I love the genre, but after the other night . . ." It's warm in the room, but she shivers. "Joey has very strict instructions. No horror movies. Nothing heavy.

Nothing scary." A thought flashes across her face, and she hauls out her phone a second time. "Maybe I should tell Chase, too." Her thumbs skate across the screen. She texts like she drives: very fast and very furious. "Should I text Aidan?"

I open my mouth to point out that Aidan lives down the hall and then jump when a masculine voice says, "Text Aidan what?" from just behind me.

I curse under my breath. "You make less noise than the cat."

Aidan leans against the doorframe. He's holding a ball of blue twine—like the stuff Aunt Jet has been using down in the basement—and he tosses it lightly from hand to hand as a cocky grin spreads across his face. "Want me to start wearing a little bell?"

"Oh!" Skylar takes a step forward. "I have a collar you could put it on!"

Because of course she does.

"Joey and Chase are on their way over," she tells him. "We're having a movie day. And then a sleepover."

"Great. It's been forever since I've seen your boyfriend in footie pajamas."

Skylar crosses the room, not so much walking as skipping. She plucks the ball of twine from Aidan's hands. "I will be sleeping over. With Cat. The rest of you can do what you want."

"Touché." He hits the bottom of her hand, sending the twine bouncing up in the air. He catches it, easily, and then turns his back on us and heads down the hall.

I call out after him. "Where are you going?"

"Gonna order a pizza. If I do it now, they can pick it up on the way over." A second later, his bedroom door clicks shut.

When I glance at Skylar, she's watching me with a curious expression on her face. "He doesn't have a girlfriend," she says.

"Who?"

"Aidan."

"Why would I care if Aidan has a girlfriend?"

She smiles and shakes her head. "No reason."

NINETEEN

JOEY AND CHASE SHOW UP WITH THREE SUPERHERO FLICKS,
one buddy comedy, and some thirty-year-old Japanese cartoon about a reincarnated princess who fights monsters by night and is a normal high school student by day. I can't figure out what logic possibly went into that choice—until I see the expression on Skylar's face.

"I love old anime," she says, taking a seat on Aidan's bed and settling in. "It's literally the best."

Joey doesn't comment, but I'm pretty sure I see him smile—once, quickly—as he gets the first movie ready. It really is kind of hard to dislike him when I see him around Skylar. Maybe he doesn't mean to come off as arrogant and dismissive. Maybe he's just kind of awkward.

Somewhere between the end of the anime and the start of the second superhero flick, Jet sticks her head in and asks if we want her to order Chinese for dinner before she leaves for work.

Everyone's still full of pizza, but no one says no.

I duck out of Aidan's room and trail her down to the kitchen. "Are you sure?" I ask. "You don't have to order us food. You don't have to spend the money."

Jet stands on her tiptoes to retrieve a take-out menu from the top of the fridge. "I'm glad you're making friends," she says. "What do you think? A couple of different combo plates and maybe an extra container of rice?"

"They're not really my friends," I say, leaning against the counter.

"Maybe not yet," says Jet. "And even if that turns out never to be the case, I still think it's good for you to spend time around other people. I know coming here wasn't what you wanted, but I would like this summer to be good for you. I like having you here."

"I kind of like being here," I say, surprising myself. I reach for the menu. "Maybe combo A and B?"

Aunt Jet smiles, and I slip back upstairs.

I flop down next to Skylar on the bed as, on screen, two extremely bulky men duke it out—destroying what looks like an entire city in the process. "Which one is the good guy?"

"I think they're both bad," says Skylar sleepily. She's curled up on her side, and she's using her cardigan for a pillow. She perks up, though, when Aunt Jet delivers the food.

We keep up a running commentary through the rest of the movie and improvise our own dialogue for the dramatic scenes.

By some sort of unspoken agreement, no one says anything about what happened that night by the bridge, and for the first time in days, I start to feel almost normal—or at least as normal as I ever do.

As the credits roll, Aidan claims the last egg roll. "You know," he says, grinning at Skylar and me, "I've heard tales of boys who manage to get two girls in their bed."

Skylar rolls her eyes. "Cat and I are not *in* your bed. We are merely *on* your bed." She grabs her cardigan and throws it at his head, but he just pushes himself back, the wheels of his desk chair carrying him out of range.

"Joey, your girlfriend attacked me."

Joey shrugs and gets up to examine the contents of Aidan's bookshelves. "Given what an asshole you can be, I'm amazed more people don't give throwing things at you a try."

"*Je ne m'excuse pas pour ce que je suis.*"

"Your accent sucks."

Chase lifts the cardigan and peels the Jesus Loves Me sticker from the bottom. He presses it to his shirt, right over his heart. He gives the sticker one last pat and then glances at Skylar. "What did your parents say? You know—after." Everyone seems to go still. "I know we're all acting like nothing happened, but . . ."

"They were really freaked," says Skylar. "And mad about the whole trespassing thing. My father yelled for almost two hours. I timed it. I'm pretty sure the only reason I'm not grounded is that the officer who drove me home after it all happened told them we were heroes and that Rachel would probably have died if it hadn't been for us."

"No one told me I was a hero," says Chase. "Jensen just showed up the next morning and asked me a ton of questions."

I sit up a little straighter. "Like what?

Looking slightly uncomfortable, Chase says, "Like how well do I know Rachel and was it my idea to cross the bridge. Oh—and why I left you behind and went to the highway. He acted like I had some sort of choice, like the 911 operator wasn't the one who told us that someone had to go meet the police and the paramedics." He shakes his head. "What did he ask you?"

"A lot of the same stuff," I say. Which is more or less true. "He wanted to know if I had volunteered to stay behind with Rachel. He thought that was weird. That's about it, really."

Aidan raises one eyebrow a fraction of an inch but stays quiet.

Part of my silence is down to fear of Jensen. He was so adamant that I not tell anyone about the medal, and he probably has the power to make my time in Montgomery Falls a living hell if he were to find out I blabbed. Maybe he'd even take things out on Aunt Jet—a possibility that doesn't seem all that far-fetched given how they'd been yelling at each other.

But that's not the only reason I don't say anything. I like Skylar and Chase—and even Joey might actually start to grow on me given enough time—but I don't know them. Not really. If I tell them about the medal, it'll just invite a ton of questions. Questions about how I know it was Riley's and why I'm so sure he wouldn't have just given it to anyone.

"I really didn't want to leave you behind, you know," says Chase.

"It's okay," I say, "someone had to stay."

He shakes his head. "Whoever attacked Rachel could have still been out there. They could have gone for you."

Skylar pushes herself to the edge of the bed. "So none of us are buying the lost-in-the-woods story?"

"No way," says Chase. "Even if Rachel had gotten lost, that wouldn't explain how she ended up in the river. And it doesn't explain all those cuts."

"I don't remember any cuts," says Skylar slowly. "Maybe they were scratches or something?"

I shake my head. "That's what Jensen tried to tell me, but they looked too perfect. Too neat. When I told him that, though, he got pissed."

"You told the chief of police he was wrong about something?" Joey whistles thinly through his teeth. "Bet that went over well." He stares at me curiously. "What did you think the cuts looked like?"

"Like small crosses, maybe. Like something . . . deliberate or . . ."

"Ritualistic?" supplies Aidan.

"I was just going to say 'planned,' but sure: let's go straight to the ultracreepy."

Skylar shivers. "This whole thing is so weird."

"Yeah," agrees Chase. "Everyone's still trying to get used to the Riley thing, and now this."

"Don't forget about the pets," interjects Joey distractedly as he pulls a book from the shelves.

"Pets?" I ask.

"A bunch of dogs and cats went missing in December. They found a few of them near the school. They'd been disemboweled."

My stomach does a slow flip. Suddenly, all the takeout seems like it might not have been a great idea.

"There were articles in the paper," explains Skylar for my bene-fit. "We started keeping Baxter—my basset hound—inside except for bathroom breaks. He was not happy."

"If the cuts you saw on Rachel Larsen really did look ritual-istic," says Joey, "then the police should take another look at the pets."

"You think it's connected?" I ask.

"I think it's a pattern. Three months between the pets and Riley Fraser." Joey counts the time on his fingers. "Three months between Riley going missing and Rachel turning up in the river. I think something is using Montgomery Falls as a hunting ground."

"You mean someone," corrects Chase.

"No. Some*thing*."

"Like an animal?"

"Worse." Four pairs of eyes stare at Joey blankly. "What if something came across the border?"

"Like an American?" asks Chase uncertainly, like it's a joke he hasn't quite worked out. He glances at me.

"Not an American, idiot. A monster."

For a very long minute, the only sound in the room is a slight whirring noise from Aidan's DVD player as the movie spins, for-gotten, inside. The longer the silence goes on, the more awkward it gets. I wait for someone to laugh, but no one does.

Skylar breaks the silence just before it hits a truly unbearable level. "You think monsters are queuing up at the border stations to cross into Canada?" she asks, using the kind of gentle, measured tones reserved for people on the verge of losing it.

Joey rolls his eyes. "Using the border stations would be ridiculous. And a complete waste of time when everyone knows sneaking across is a joke. My cousin did it last month."

"Your cousin tried to float across the Saint John River on an air mattress," corrects Aidan. "And he had to be rescued by the Americans when he got caught up in the current."

"My point stands. Jesus, guys. Do you not realize that Derry is only a few hours from here? A few hours is nothing." He holds up the book he had taken from Aidan's shelf so we can see the cover. Stephen King's *It*.

"Derry doesn't exist," says Aidan calmly. "And before you say it, there's no Castle Rock, either. There is a pet cemetery out near the trailer park, but I'm relatively certain nothing has ever come back to life after being buried there."

Joey ignores the *Pet Sematary* crack. "Maybe Derry and Castle Rock don't exist as literal towns, but do you think all that shit just comes out of one man's head? He gets those ideas from somewhere."

I suddenly want to steer the conversation elsewhere. Because Stephen King doesn't just write about zombie pets and monsters lurking in sewers. Sometimes he writes about girls who seem a lot like me. I force my voice to sound light, teasing. "And you're saying what? That the monsters are real and have made the trek here of all places?"

The words aren't any worse than anything Aidan said, but if a look could strip skin, the one Joey levels at me would flay me alive. Skylar stands and walks over to him. She puts a hand on his arm. "Joey . . ."

He ignores her. "Do you have any idea how many horror movies I've watched? How many books I've studied?"

"You know the definition of 'fiction,' right?"

"And you know all stories originate somewhere, don't you? Or didn't your hotshot writer father ever tell you that?"

"Whoa . . ." Aidan stands, holding his hands up, playing peacemaker. "It's not a contest."

"No? Maybe it should be. Maybe someone who doesn't know anything about monsters shouldn't be here. And maybe you shouldn't be so quick to jump to her defense just because you've suddenly got a thing for chubby Americans."

"Joey . . . ," says Skylar again, at the exact moment Chase says, "Too far, dude."

My face flushes. On the one hand, it's the second time one of Aidan's friends has implied he might be into me. Despite my determination to keep people at bay, the idea that a guy like Aidan might be interested in me is kind of nice—not to mention flattering. On the other hand, the way Joey's voice twisted around the word "chubby" makes it pretty obvious that he's the kind of guy who thinks it's an insult.

I'm not insulted—not by the word "chubby," at least—but that doesn't mean I'm not angry. *Someone who doesn't know anything about monsters*, huh? If I told Joey half the things I've seen—the things that have been done to me when I've been pulled into other people's wants and fears—he'd probably piss himself. "Let me guess: You think you're going to be the big man who swoops in and saves the town with his extensive knowledge of movie plots?" I snap. "This isn't your stupid screenplay. Even if there was a monster, how would you find it?"

It's not a serious question, but Joey takes it seriously. "We talk to Rachel. Find out what she saw."

"And I'm sure she'll be thrilled to answer your not-at-all-crazy questions."

"Have you even read a single horror novel? It starts with the pets and Riley and Rachel. It doesn't end there. We have to talk to her." Joey's voice is getting steadily, disproportionately louder.

"Joey . . . Rachel wouldn't talk to us. She hates me, and she thinks you're a freak." Skylar tries to slip her hand into his, but he brushes her off. "I'm sorry. But she does."

Joey turns to Chase, who promptly says, "Can't be me, dude. I hooked up with her last year."

"Cat?" We've all been so focused on the mini-standoff that not one of us heard the bedroom door open. Noah stands in the hall, looking uncomfortable and out of place. "The guy who answered the door downstairs said you were up here."

His hair is tussled, and there are dark circles under his eyes. He looks like he hasn't slept since the last time I saw him. His expression is distant and guarded as it sweeps across the room, making him look more like the boy I saw outside the drugstore than the one who sat across from me those first few minutes at the diner. For some reason, the change makes me sad.

I stand and take a few steps from the bed, then pause, uncertainly.

Skylar's gaze darts from Noah to me and then back. People in town have made Skylar's life miserable over what happened with Riley. Given that, it's possible I should have told her I knew the

Frasers. Then again, it's not like there's been a natural opportunity. It's not like Skylar herself has ever told me just what happened.

Chase pushes himself to his feet and crosses the room. Noah is still standing in the hall, but Chase extends his hand over the threshold. "I'm sorry about Riley. We were on the basketball team together."

"Thanks." Noah shakes Chase's hand. As he does, his guarded expression slips—just a little bit. He glances at me. "I wanted to talk to you. I didn't realize you weren't on your own."

Skylar grabs her heels from the floor next to Aidan's bed and slips them on. "Joey was just going."

This is clearly news to Joey, who scowls. "I wasn't done talking."

"Yes," says Skylar, grabbing his arm and pulling him toward the door as Noah stands aside to let them pass, "you were." She shoots me a confused, slightly hurt glance before they both disappear down the hall.

I'm guessing the sleepover is off. I try to tell myself that it's for the best, that I don't really want to get too close to Skylar or anyone in the squad, but I still feel a pang of disappointment.

Chase sighs. "Joey's my ride, so guess that means I'm out, too."

He follows them, leaving Noah, Aidan, and me alone.

Part of me feels like I should apologize to Noah for avoiding him, but I'm not entirely sure I have anything to be sorry for. "I thought you were away until tomorrow."

He glances at Aidan. "Plans changed. I can come back, if it's not a good time." His voice is carefully blank. Polite but detached. Given that I've been dodging all of his calls, I guess I can't blame him for keeping his guard up.

Aidan grabs his copy of *It* and then heads for the now-vacant bed. "It's my room, so I hope you're not expecting me to leave." His tone is light verging on playful as he stretches out and kicks off his sneakers.

I ignore him. "Now's good," I tell Noah, struggling to match his careful tone. "Why don't we go outside?"

Aidan keeps his gaze on his book, but as I head for the door, he says, "Let me know if you need rescuing." He adds something low and in French, the words too quick for me to catch. Unlike Joey, I think his accent is just fine.

God save me from flirtatious boys who speak French and who may or may not like chubby girls, I think as I follow Noah down the hall.

TWENTY

I KNEW WE'D SPENT MOST OF THE DAY WATCHING MOVIES, but it's still surprising to see the sun sinking toward the horizon as I step outside and follow Noah across the backyard.

"How was the lake?"

"Depressing. I thought getting my mom out of the house for a few nights might help, but all she did was beg to come back. She wanted to be here in case Riley came home. She's still convinced she hears him at night. I'm driving her down to Saint John later this week. There's a psychiatrist there who specializes in grief and trauma. Her doctor thinks it might help." Noah shakes his head. "When we got back to the house, she said someone had been inside. She said it must have been Riley."

Warmth creeps across my cheeks. Even in the fading light, he catches the blush.

"It was you?" he says slowly. "You broke into the house?"

"I didn't break in. Not exactly. I just remembered where the spare key was." Maybe I should apologize, but I don't. I kick off my shoes and then step out onto one of the large rocks at the river's edge. I sit and slip my feet into the water. It's cool, but not unpleasantly so. "I just wanted to see his room."

"Why?"

"I don't know."

I glance over my shoulder. Noah is watching me. "I really don't know," I say. Even I can hear the defensive note in my voice.

As long as we're careful, there's enough space on my rock for Noah to sit without running the risk of touching me, but he rolls up the bottoms of his jeans and wades into the river, coming to stand next to me instead. We both look out over the water, at the reflected glow of the setting sun.

"Yes," he says. "You do. I don't think you're the kind of person who ever does anything without having a reason."

I'm not sure why I don't want to tell him. Maybe because I'm not sure I can wrap my head around my feelings about Riley. They're messy and complicated, and I don't know how to sort through them. "I don't really know Riley. It's like there's two of him. There's the Riley I remember from when we were kids, and there's this other Riley who everyone else knows. The one who crashes boats and plays basketball and dates blond girls named Amber."

"Everyone's like that, Cat. Everyone shows different sides of themselves to different people at different times. I'd think you, of all people, would know that."

"It feels like more than that. The difference is just so huge. I thought, maybe, if I saw his room, it would help."

He's quiet for a minute. Like he was choosing his words carefully. "I don't think the difference is as huge as it looks on the surface. A lot of it was an act for our father. Riley thought that if he could be perfect, Dad might stick around. He tried to make himself into what he believed our parents wanted. He always had trouble accepting that our father is just an asshole."

"What about you?"

"I've always been a disappointment, and I've never had any illusions about who my dad is." Noah's voice is so matter-of-fact. Like he's telling me he has brown eyes or dark hair.

"Can I ask you something?"

"Sure."

"Jensen told me that Riley had problems. Did people in town know about the OCD?"

"Some people suspected, I think. If they were around him enough. But he was good at hiding what was going on. He worked at hiding it. Because of Dad, I think he worried other people might think less of him if they knew. I'm not sure he gave people enough credit. I think they would have understood. Much more than he thought they would."

"How did he hide it?"

"He had tricks."

"Like?"

"Like if he felt like he had to write something down or say something to himself, he'd haul out his phone and text. Pretend like he was texting someone else when it was really just himself. If he had to count something, he'd tap it out like he was just tapping out the beats to some song stuck in his head." Noah shrugs. "I don't remember them all. We didn't really talk that much after I left for school."

"Why not?"

"I don't know. I was busy with stuff there and he was busy with things here." He pulls in a deep breath. "I was majoring in psychology. Did I tell you that?"

I shake my head.

"I had it all planned out. Undergrad. Grad school."

"Did you pick psychology because of Riley?"

"No." He glances at me, maybe to make sure I'm really interested and not just being polite. "I took an intro class, and one of the assignments was to find five research papers and summarize them. All I had to do was pick papers at random, but I spent hours checking out different titles and ideas. It was the only class where I wasn't reading things just because I had to. I figured that had to be some kind of sign. I think it was maybe the first time I ever thought I could be really passionate about anything."

"I'm sorry."

"For what?"

Everything, I think. For Riley and his mom and the fact that he had to give up school to come back here. "Does your dad know? Does he know what's going on with your mother?"

"Yeah." So much heaviness is in that one word. Noah draws his arm back and then flicks his wrist, like he's skipping an invisible stone across the water.

"Is he going to come back?"

"Would you want to come back to this?"

I don't know what to say to that, so I don't say anything. I'd like to think that I'd step up and do the right thing, but I guess it's easy to say that when you don't have to back it up.

I slide off the rock and into the water. It's colder than I thought it would be, but I wade out until it's up to my waist. When I'm far enough, I let myself fall so that I can float on my back. We used to do this when we were kids sometimes. We used to float.

Noah wades farther out. He dunks his whole body under and then comes up next to me. The water along this stretch of the river is calm and slow, but even so, we gradually drift from Aunt Jet's property line over to the Frasers'. The water is deeper here. Too deep to touch the bottom with my toes.

"I'm sorry, too," he says.

"For what?"

"All that stuff I said at the diner. For acting like I knew what I was talking about. I didn't have any right to act that way."

"No, you didn't." I'm grateful for the growing dark around us. Some things are easier to say in the dark. Sometimes, darkness can make you brave. "You weren't entirely wrong, though. I told you not everyone wants to touch and be touched—and that's true—but I'm not sure it's true of me. You asked if Riley was the only person I've ever kissed. He's not."

"Do you want to talk about it?"

"Not really."

"Okay."

"It's not anything really traumatic or anything." And it really wasn't. There was a guy. There was a party. There was a moment when I allowed myself to think that maybe things could be different, that maybe I could be different. There was the press of lips and fumbling hands and a tiny, tiny moment when something inside of me flared to life. And then I saw what he wanted. Who he wanted. And it wasn't me. But I'm not going to tell Noah that. It's sad and humiliating, and I'm worried it would change how he looks at me. "I just thought I should tell you that you weren't wrong."

"I still shouldn't have pushed you. Not the way I did. I thought I knew what was best for you. It was stupid."

"And arrogant. Don't forget arrogant."

"That, too."

It's strange, floating out here in the dark. It's quiet and peaceful, but eerie. In the distance, I can see the lights from the train bridge reflected on the water's surface. Unbidden, an image of Rachel pops into my head. Her tangled hair. Her wet clothes. The marks on her arms. I shiver. The movement makes me sink, just for a second.

I come up sputtering. Noah tries to reach for me, tries to help me, but that just makes it worse. I go under again as I try to avoid his touch. When I come back up, I swim for shore.

"What is it?" He's right beside me, matching my strokes. He follows me up out of the water.

"I'm sorry, I just . . . One second I was in the river with you, the next, I was seeing Rachel. The way she looked when we found her." I'm still shivering. I can't stop.

"Just a sec," Noah says softly. He jogs across the yard and disappears into his house.

I sink down to the ground as he reappears and makes his way back to me. He's carrying an old plaid blanket. He drapes it over my shoulders and then settles beside me.

"Thanks," I murmur, tugging the blanket more tightly around myself.

He studies me for a moment, then tilts his head back and looks up at the night sky. "After that day at the mill, I'd see things. Her. Nora Knight. When I was dreaming, of course, but I'd see her lots of times when I was awake, too. I could be walking down the street or the hallway at school, and all of a sudden, I'd glance down and there she'd be, on the ground."

"It's different."

"Not that different."

"Rachel wasn't dead."

"No, she wasn't." He turns his gaze back to me. "I'm not sure that makes finding her any less traumatic."

"We have to find out what happened to her, Noah." Haltingly, I fill him in on how I had tried to do as he'd asked and what happened when I touched Harding. "I don't think I can control it. It definitely didn't feel like I had any control."

"Do you think what you saw means anything?"

"No. I'm not religious, but it seems like fire and brimstone might be a logical fear to have inside a church."

"What about the people you were with back at the house?"

"What about them?"

"Did you try to touch any of them?"

"Why would I?"

"Because we should be looking at everyone. We should consider every possibility."

"I told you: if I try to touch everyone in town, my head will

210

explode. Besides, Skylar and Chase were with me when I found Rachel, and Aidan and Joey were both at home. None of them could have been involved."

Noah looks like he wants to argue, but he just says, "So then what were you all fighting about? I could hear the guy with the glasses all the way downstairs."

"That was Joey. Joey—who has read many fine horror novels and watched hundreds of horror films—thinks a monster is behind Riley's disappearance and what happened to Rachel. Like, an actual monster. Possibly from Maine."

"Why Maine?"

"Because that is where Stephen King lives. Stephen King, according to Joey, is not so much crafting fiction as he is telling it like it is. Keeping it real, if you will."

"You're joking." Noah stares at me, waiting for me to laugh. I don't. "That's ludicrous."

"Says the guy who asked for my help because he thought I was psychic."

"Completely different. For all intents and purposes, you might as . . . well— Wait, you don't honestly think he has a point?"

"No. I think he's being really, really ridiculous. Possibly delusional. I'm just pointing out that there actually is weird, inexplicable shit in the universe." Somewhere in the distance, one of the neighborhood dogs starts to bark, reminding me of something else Joey said. "Did you know people's pets started going missing in December? That people were told to keep them inside because someone was hurting them?"

"I was away at school."

"Riley didn't mention it? Or your mom?"

"No reason they would. Not like we have a dog or a cat. What else did Joey say?"

"That he wants to talk to Rachel Larsen."

Noah leans forward, plucks a blade of grass and rubs it between his fingers. "I've been thinking about that, too. About how we should talk to her once she's home."

"Do you think we can afford to wait until then? If Joey goes up to the hospital and starts asking her about monsters . . . if he gets to her first . . ."

"You think he'll make her so uncomfortable that she might not talk to anyone else?"

I nod. "We should go before they send her home. Tomorrow, maybe." Another thought occurs to me. "And I think we should ask Aidan to come with us."

"The guy who rents a room from your aunt? The one who looks like a walking ad for hair products and is somehow under the impression that you might need rescuing?"

My lips quirk a little at that. Aidan really does have ridiculously good hair for a boy. "You don't like him?"

"I don't care enough not to like him. I'm just not sure why you want to bring him along."

"Because Rachel probably isn't going to remember me. If she does, the memories aren't going to be great."

"And I'm just Riley Fraser's freak older brother." The words are flat, said without any emotion. That doesn't mean they're emotionless.

I remember how Skylar touched Joey up in Aidan's room.

212

Light, comforting touches that are taken for granted. I wish, suddenly, that I could touch Noah. I could chance it, I could touch him somewhere safe, but touching people at all is a dangerous habit—one I can't afford to fall into. "Rachel doesn't know you," I say gently, "and she doesn't know me. I think having someone with us who she does know might help."

Noah sighs and climbs to his feet. "All right. We can ask your boyfriend to come along."

"He's not my boyfriend," I say as I stand. There's a weird, defensive note in my voice. When Joey and Chase imply Aidan might be into me, it's exhilarating and a little confusing—though not in a bad way. With Noah, it feels different.

And I have no idea why.

He follows me to the hedge. When I reach the gap, I turn and shrug off the blanket. "Thanks," I say, handing it back.

"Cat?"

"Yeah."

"I knew the library didn't have a second floor."

I smile a little at that. "Good."

He hesitates for a second, like he wants to say something else, then gives his head the tiniest of shakes. "Good night, Mary Catherine."

As I squeeze through the hedge, I feel a small, puzzling flash of disappointment. When I get to the top of the porch steps, I glance back. I think I see a shadow—Noah, watching to make sure I get inside—but it might just be my imagination.

TWENTY-ONE

WHEN I GET BACK INSIDE, I FIND AIDAN SITTING ON THE bottom of the staircase, dressed for a run and lacing up his shoes. His gaze travels over me, slowly, and he lets out a low, appreciative whistle. "Did Fraser try to drown you? Did I drop the ball on the whole 'rescuing' thing?"

I stand there, self-conscious and dripping on the hardwood floor. I am very, very glad my T-shirt is black. "Impromptu swim."

"Little late in the day."

"Says the guy going out for a night run?"

He slips a hand into his pocket and pulls out a phone. "Joey forgot it. Figured you wouldn't feel like seeing him again tonight, so thought I'd go for a run and swing by his place." The phone disappears back into his pocket. "And I need a break from Skylar. She's convinced you're mad at her. There are only so many ways a guy can say 'wait and talk to Cat' without losing his mind. I swear, if they could find some way to convert her angst into fuel, it would solve the energy crisis."

I feel like I'm two steps behind. "Skylar is here?" I glance back at the small window next to the door. Sure enough, her car is still in the driveway. I'd been so preoccupied that I had walked right past it without noticing.

"She's in your room. I thought you guys were having a sleepover?"

"Well, yeah, but after the thing with Joey, I just figured she left with him."

"You thought she bailed on you to chase after her boyfriend *after* her boyfriend was rude to you?"

"Well, yeah."

"That is some stellar forward-thinking feminism."

"You are not seriously going to sit there and try to mansplain feminism to me."

"No. Now, if I were Joey . . ."

"Why are you even friends with him? Seriously, though."

Aidan stands and shrugs. "Decent entertainment value. Plus, as previously noted, all the free video rentals I can watch."

"You know you can just stream things now, right?"

"Streaming lacks poetry. Also, if you haven't noticed, your aunt's Wi-Fi really sucks." He grins, but then his expression slides into something uncharacteristically serious. "On the off chance you actually are mad at Skylar, do me a favor and go easy on her? She really does feel bad—both for what Joey said and for not pushing back against him more. Joey will be sorry, too. Once he calms down. He does this sort of thing sometimes. He acts like everything is part of a plot from a movie. I'm pretty sure it's some

215

sort of coping mechanism. He's been feeling massively guilty that he didn't stay with Skylar the night you guys found Rachel, and so he's acting like this."

I'm still fairly certain Joey being there would have made the situation exponentially worse, but I don't point that out. "I need to ask you a favor," I say instead.

"Sounds serious." Aidan makes a fist with his left hand and gently presses it to the bottom of the banister.

"Noah and I are going to go talk to Rachel Larsen. Tomorrow. About what happened. And I'm kind of hoping you'll come with us."

"You didn't seem thrilled with the idea of talking to Rachel when Joey mentioned it."

"That's different. Joey wants to accost her and interrogate her about things from Stephen King's backlist. Things that don't actually exist."

"And you want to . . . ?"

"I want to ask her about the medal she was holding when we found her."

"The one you think was Riley's?"

"The one I *know* was Riley's."

Aidan stares at me thoughtfully. Stares so long that I have to resist the urge to squirm. "Why do you want me to come if Noah Fraser is already going with you?"

"Because you know Rachel. You'll be a friendly face."

"My face *is* ridiculously friendly. They should use it on tourism ads." The words are joking, but his gray eyes are dark.

"So you'll do it? You'll come?"

"I don't know, Cat. She's in the hospital. She's probably not going to want to see anyone."

"Just think about it, please? Maybe sleep on it before making up your mind?"

"Will you be upset if the answer is no?"

"No," I say.

"You're a horrible liar, Cat Montgomery." He walks past me and heads for the door. Just before stepping outside, he says, "I'll think about it. Just go easy on Skylar, okay?"

He doesn't wait for my response; he doesn't even bother closing the door. He just crosses the porch, descends the steps, and then takes off into the night at an easy, loping pace. I watch as he jogs past Skylar's car, and then I shut the door.

I'm not mad at Skylar—if anything, I just feel guilty for not making an effort to be up front about knowing the Frasers.

Instead of heading directly to my room to talk to her right away, though, I swing through Aunt Jet's bedroom and use it to access the bathroom. I know I'm going to have to explain my connection to Noah—and to Riley—but I really don't feel like explaining the state of my clothes. Nor do I want to stay in said clothes for a minute longer than absolutely necessary. A deep, deep chill feels like it has settled into my bones, and the water from the river kind of smells like wet dog.

I peel the fabric from my clammy skin and then grab last night's pajamas from the hook on the back of the bathroom door. Not wanting to take the time to blow-dry my still-damp hair, I run a brush through the tangles and then pull it up into a ponytail.

"Cute," says Skylar when I open the bathroom door. She nods

toward the tiny little record albums that dot my pajama bottoms. She's sitting on a sleeping bag on the floor. The bag must be Aidan's. Even though Skylar's purse seems to defy all laws of physical space, there's no way she could get camping gear in there.

"Is that my shirt?" I ask. The fabric hangs in folds on her small frame, making it hard to see the design on the front.

"And Aidan's shorts," she says, pushing herself to her feet. "Is that okay? If it's not, I can go . . ." She takes a step toward the door and then stops, looking lost and uncertain.

"I didn't think you'd still be here," I say. A crestfallen look sweeps across her face, and I realize how the words must sound. "I thought you'd be too mad at me to want to stay," I say quickly. "Because of what happened with Joey. And because I didn't tell you about knowing the Frasers. I mean, you never really told me why those posters by the theater were marked up, but it's not exactly rocket science to figure out I should have told you I knew Riley and Noah. The shirt is okay. Totally and utterly okay."

Skylar's shoulders sag, and she lets out a deep breath. "Joey was being kind of a jerk. And Aidan filled me in about Noah and Riley; he said you knew them when you were a kid." She hesitates and bites her lip, then says, "That's why you have that folder, isn't it? It's not just some Nancy Drew complex; it's because you knew Riley."

I nod. "We were friends."

"It must have been hard—finding out he was missing."

I sit on the edge of the bed. I open my mouth to say it's fine, but Skylar is watching me with a look of such naked concern on her face that I can't do it. I can't lie. For years, I've told myself that

I didn't care about Riley, that I wasn't supposed to care about him, that I would be an idiot to care. But I did. I do.

My gaze falls on that stupid Styrofoam mobile, and the room gets blurry around the edges.

Skylar disappears into the bathroom. She comes back, a moment later, with a wad of toilet paper in hand. "I couldn't find any Kleenex," she says apologetically as she sits next to me on the bed and passes me the makeshift tissue.

I blow my nose, embarrassed, and then wipe my eyes roughly with the back of my hand.

"Do you want to talk about it?"

It's strange. Noah asked me the same thing just a little while ago. I don't remember the last time anyone asked me that when I was upset. Lacey had to have asked, at some point over some thing, but it feels like it must have been a long time ago. And Dad? Well, my father has never been a fan of talking.

I shake my head: I've done enough emotional disclosure for one day.

"Okay." Skylar is quiet for a minute, then says, "I'm really, really sorry about Joey."

"It's not your fault." And it isn't. "I'm glad you stayed." The words are a little stiff and awkward, but I mean them.

She smiles. "Me, too."

Later, when the room is dark, I turn over on my side. I can just barely make out Skylar in the borrowed sleeping bag, but I don't think she's asleep. "Can I ask you something?"

"Sure."

"What happened between you and Riley?" I'm not asking

because I think there will be some clue hidden inside her answer. I'm asking because I genuinely want to know. I want to understand, and right now, I don't. I can't imagine Skylar slipping off to make out with someone else's boyfriend, and I definitely don't understand how she can still want Riley the way she does and be with Joey. And some part of her does want Riley. Even though he's gone. Even after everything that happened. I saw it that night on the bridge. I felt it.

The sleeping bag rustles as she turns over to face me. "I used to do volunteer work. Before I started working at the theater. Before I started hanging out with Joey and Chase and Aidan. I didn't have a lot of friends, and my parents thought volunteering would be good for me. That's how I met Riley. He got assigned to some of the groups I volunteered with. For his community service after the whole thing with the boat. I mean, I'd had classes with him, but I had never really talked to him that much."

"Why not?"

"I don't know. He was popular. I'm not. It seemed like that mattered somehow." Skylar sighs. A small, tiny sound. "He used to try to make me laugh. He said I had a really great laugh. That my laugh was almost—*almost*—worth the community service. I started looking forward to his stupid jokes even though they weren't really all that funny. But the more time we spent together, the fewer jokes he made. Until he almost never made jokes at all. He would tell me about stuff at home. About his dad and his parents' divorce and how it felt like everyone had all these expectations of him. I started feeling like everyone else saw him one way and I got to see him another. Does that sound stupid?"

"No," I say softly. "That doesn't sound stupid at all."

"I started thinking about him. All of the time. There was this party. I didn't want to go, but Joey wanted to check it out. We weren't dating," she says adamantly. "We just went as friends. Riley was there. He was drinking—which was weird because Riley never drank. We ended up in a room. Talking. He and his girlfriend had split up, and he was really upset. I think maybe that was why . . . with the alcohol. He told me that he hadn't been the one to crash the boat. That it had been Amber. His ex."

"So he took the blame?"

"I guess? He said it was his fault. Because he had gone below deck. Because he hadn't been paying attention. And he said he deserved to get in trouble, that it was his turn. I think he actually used the word 'payback,' though I never figured out what he meant by that."

Aidan. Maybe Riley felt guilty over what happened the day they snuck into the mill. "What else did he say?"

"Nothing. He started kissing me, and I started kissing him back. I knew it was wrong. I knew he was upset about Amber, but I thought maybe, just maybe, he liked me a little bit, too."

The memory of what I saw on the bridge comes rushing back. The feeling of my back colliding with a wall, a hand slipping under my skirt—Riley's hand slipping under my skirt. I feel myself flush in the dark. It hadn't just been kissing. "What happened? After, I mean?"

"One of Amber's friends walked in on us. She had her phone. There was a picture. I'm pretty sure everyone in school saw it. Riley told me the two of them had broken up, but Amber told everyone it was a misunderstanding, that it wasn't true. Amber is popular and really, really well liked. No one believed me."

I swallow. I know what can happen when you cross someone really popular.

"Is that why you said Rachel hates you? Was it something to do with Amber?"

"She's one of Amber's best friends. They all said stuff. They all did stuff. Joey took care of me after. Or at least he tried to. And Chase. They both tried to be buffers."

"Is that why you're with Joey? Because he tried to take care of you?"

"No. It's a point in his favor, but it's not the reason."

"What about Riley? Did he stick up for you afterward?" *Please say yes*, I think. Because if she says no, I don't think there's any way of ever reconciling the boy who was my friend with the person Riley became.

"I don't know." Skylar's voice is so soft that I have to strain to hear it in the dark. "He disappeared a few days later."

TWENTY-TWO

LIKE THE REST OF MONTGOMERY FALLS, THE HOSPITAL IS not what you would call large; it is, however, big enough to have a gift shop. "Do you think we should get something?" I ask, pausing in front of a dusty window display. "Like flowers or balloons, maybe?" Even though I've never officially met Rachel, showing up empty-handed feels weird.

"No idea," says Noah.

Aidan isn't any more help. He just shrugs and scans the hospital lobby. He's barely said two words since Noah picked us up. I keep thinking about what Skylar told me last night and wondering what Aidan would think if he knew Riley took the blame for what happened with the boat out of guilt. If it were me, I think I'd want to know. But it's not me, and it's not really my secret to tell.

"You know," I say, "if you really don't want to be here, it's okay." It's not like visiting a probably-traumatized girl and asking her about what has to be the most horrible night of her life is on my list of top ten ways to spend an afternoon. To be honest, I was kind of surprised that Aidan agreed to come—especially given how reluctant he had been about the idea.

He turns his gaze to me and gives his head a small, sharp shake. For the first time since leaving the house, it feels like he's actually paying attention. "Sorry. I kind of have a thing about hospitals."

"You honestly don't have to come with us," I say, a little more gently. "We can talk to her on our own."

"No. You were right when you said Rachel will probably be more comfortable talking if you're with someone she knows. She hates the rest of the squad. And your friend"—his lip quirks up just the tiniest fraction of an inch as his gaze darts to Noah—"glowers. Glowerers make people nervous." He turns toward the gift shop. "Get her a stuffed animal. She'd like that more than flowers or balloons, I think."

We pick out a teddy bear with a red heart on its fluffy white chest. Noah insists on paying. Bear in tow, we head to reception, where they don't hesitate to give us Rachel's room number but do warn us that visiting hours end in fifteen minutes.

We round the corner of the pediatric ward, and all three of us come to a sudden stop.

There's a cop sitting outside Rachel's room.

He glances up from a magazine. He can't be more than a year or two older than Noah; he's so young that I wonder if he's really a cop or if he just rented the costume—an impression not helped by his bright red hair and the spray of freckles across his face. Seriously, his hair is even redder than mine.

"Who are you here for?" he asks.

"Rachel Larsen." I clutch the bear against my stomach as Aidan slips his hands into his pockets.

"No visitors." The cop starts to turn his attention back to his magazine but pauses as he catches sight of the figure behind me. "Noah?" He stands.

"Buddy." Noah steps forward to shake the other man's hand.

Buddy? Red hair and freckles and his name is *Buddy?*

"What are you doing here, man?"

Noah gestures toward me. "This is Cat. She was friends with my brother."

Buddy's grin shifts into something more solemn. He's still shaking Noah's hand, though the movement becomes considerably slower. "I'm sorry about your brother. Everyone is. Riley was a good guy. *Is,*" he corrects, maybe figuring Noah might still be holding on to some shred of hope. "Riley *is* a good guy."

"Thanks." Noah extricates himself from the other man's grip. "Listen, Buddy, Cat's the one who found Rachel down at the river. She wanted to see her, to tell her how glad she is that she's okay."

A look crosses the other man's face that seems genuinely apologetic. "Can't let you guys in. The chief said she isn't supposed to have visitors."

That doesn't make any sense. Jensen had been so adamant that Rachel had just gotten lost in the woods. Why would he make someone guard her hospital room? Then again, maybe it's like sending Harding out to photograph the riverbank: a way to cover his butt. "Did something happen?" I ask.

Buddy shrugs. "A reporter showed up the day after she was brought in. Her parents were fit to be tied. They threatened to sue the hospital and the city and the police department—pretty much anyone they could think of. I guess that's why I'm here. To make it look like the chief is taking their complaints seriously."

"You guess?" says Noah. "You didn't ask?"

"Oh, I asked. The chief just isn't big on answers."

Still hugging the teddy bear, I try to look young and harmless. "I promise: I'm not a reporter."

Buddy hesitates, and Noah says, "Come on, man. We won't tell anyone you let her in." There's a weight behind the words. Noah looks older suddenly, standing in that hallway. Way older than me. Older than the man in front of us.

Officer Buddy hesitates for a second longer but then nods. "Go on—they're sending her home in the morning anyway." His gaze drops to the bear. "Good luck finding a place to set that down. Flowers have been getting dropped off at reception for days. Lucky girl."

"Yeah," Aidan drawls, pulling out the word and making it spin sharply at the end. "Winding up half dead and fished out of the river is probably worth it if it means getting a bunch of crap from a hospital gift shop."

I catch the edge of his shirt and pull him into Rachel's room, leaving Noah to smooth things over outside. I open my mouth to snap at Aidan—the guy is doing us a favor, after all—but I'm distracted by the riot of color that suddenly surrounds us.

Flowers spill over tables and onto the floor. At least a dozen balloons hover in the air, and there are enough stuffed animals for the mother of all teddy bear picnics. There are so many shapes and colors that it takes me a minute to focus on the slight figure sitting up in the hospital bed.

Rachel Larsen stares at us. Her bandaged arms hold a stuffed animal: a rabbit with one torn ear and fur that probably started out white but is now dishwater gray. Her face is pale and drawn, but her eyes are sharp. They're blue, I realize, a light blue the color of thin sea ice. I couldn't tell that in the dark. And her hair, which I had assumed was brown, is actually a dye job. One of those blacks that has a blue sheen when you see it under the right light.

Rachel sits up a little straighter as her eyes sweep over us.

Aidan's distaste of hospitals still seems to have him a little off-balance, but mocking the officer in the hall must have helped because he sounds more like himself when he says, "Hey, Rach."

She bites her lip. "Aidan?" She says his name like a question, like she's wondering what he's doing here.

"Cat wanted to meet you." I step forward as Aidan adds, "Cat Montgomery, she's—"

"The one who stayed with me." Rachel's voice is deep and husky. The kind of voice you hear femmes fatales use in old movies. It doesn't seem to match the rest of her.

"You remember?"

She shakes her head. "The police told me. They said you stayed with me while Chase Walker went to get help. He's a good guy, Chase."

I make a mental note to tell Chase that his trek to the highway that night has apparently canceled out his other transgressions. I want to be fair to Skylar and say that she was there, too, that she went with Chase so that the police and the paramedics could find us, but I hold back.

Bringing up people Rachel dislikes doesn't seem like the best way to get her to talk to me—even if leaving out the part Skylar played feels disloyal.

I set the teddy bear on the floor next to a crowd of others and then walk to a green chair that someone has pulled next to the bed. I hesitate, uncertain, but Rachel nods. "Sit. Please."

There isn't a second chair in the room, so Aidan slips around the bed and perches on the windowsill.

Rachel fidgets. She touches the stuffed animal on her lap, the blanket, her hair—it's like she can't quite stay still. "They said you held my hand? They said I spoke to you?"

"You didn't say anything. Your eyes opened once, but it didn't seem like you were really conscious." I think about how I didn't see a thing when I touched her hand. No desire. No fear. Nothing. "You were in really bad shape."

"Tell me about it," she says with a small, bitter laugh as she runs her fingers over the bandages on her arm.

"Do you remember anything? How you ended up in the water or what you were doing that day?"

She shakes her head. "Just little flashes. The doctors say it's stress or trauma or something. That my brain is trying to protect me. That I might remember as more time passes."

Aidan leans forward. "But you don't remember now?"

Her gaze darts to him, and a tiny crease forms between her

brows. "Not really. I remember going to work and punching out with Amber, but nothing concrete after that."

"Amber as in Riley Fraser's girlfriend?" I ask.

Rachel nods. "We work the same shift sometimes. I usually give her a ride home, but she had her parents' car. I remember walking across the parking lot and telling her how much nicer it is working the early shift because there's still a few hours of daylight left when you get out."

"So it was early?"

"Four thirty—maybe five, I think." Her voice gets quieter. "The police said I got a flat on the way home."

"But you don't remember? You don't remember the flat?"

Before Rachel can answer, a nurse sticks her head in the doorway. "Visiting hours are over." She hovers, waiting to make sure we leave.

I stand, awkward and unsure of what to say or do. It's strange: knowing you were there on the worst night of someone's life but not having them remember.

I move closer to the bed. "You were holding something." I keep my voice low because I'm not sure how much the officer in the hallway can hear, and I don't want what I'm about to say to get back to the chief. "When I took your hand, you were clutching a Saint Anthony medal attached to a string of leather."

"I don't . . . ? I'm not sure what that is?"

I hold my thumb and forefinger about an inch and a half apart. "About this big. Silver. A man on the front."

That small crease appears between her brows again. "I don't . . . I don't remember that."

"It's not yours? Not something that you found or that someone gave you?"

"I don't think so . . ." A bit of the color drains from her face.

"You need to leave now," says the nurse, her shoes squeaking against the tile floor as she comes farther into the room.

On impulse, I reach forward and touch the back of Rachel's hand. I touch Rachel's hand, and as I get pulled in, I try to control what I see, I—

Sensations and images that are almost too quick to catch. A too-small space. Not enough air. Darkness. Flashes of red. Red rectangles. Taillights pulsing in the dark like a heartbeat. A single thought in a voice that isn't mine: "No one is ever going to find me . . ."

I sway a little on my feet as I step back.

"Sorry," I mumble as the nurse says, again, that we have to leave.

"C'mon, Cat." Aidan places a hand on my shoulder, gently, guiding me from the room. I stumble as pain explodes behind my temple, and he shifts his touch to my arm to steady me.

Normally, I'd be worried about his hand and whether my shirt covered enough skin to make the contact safe, but my head is filled with what I saw in Rachel's head and those eight words: *No one is ever going to find me.*

TWENTY-THREE

RACHEL LARSEN HAD BEEN TAKEN. THE SENSATION OF BEING in a too-small space. The taillights in the dark. Her fear that no one would find her. I'm sure of it. Her memories are locked under the surface, but her fear is still there.

Unfortunately, knowing that hasn't exactly been a huge help.

"Ugh." I collapse back on Noah's bed and stare up at the ceiling. "Are you sure we shouldn't try to tell Jensen what I saw?"

It's something we've talked through over and over in the three days since the hospital.

"How would you explain it?" Noah says patiently, for the hundredth time.

I don't understand how he can sound so calm.

"I still feel like maybe I should try." I close my eyes, just for a few seconds, and Rachel's voice fills my head. *No one is ever going to find me.* Knowing she had been taken and not being able to do anything about it—not being able to tell anyone other than

Noah—is almost worse than not knowing what had happened to her at all. Almost.

Noah crosses the room. "Move over."

I sit up and scoot toward the wall. The mattress dips as he sits on the edge.

"It's so useless, what I can do. We know someone grabbed Rachel, but we don't know who. We don't know if they let her go or if she got away. We don't even know how she ended up with the medal, and that's the only thing we have that *might* connect what happened to her to whatever happened to Riley. For all we know, they're not connected at all. Maybe Riley dropped the medal in the woods and Rachel found it by some one-in-a-million chance. Even the things we're sure about—the taillights, the trunk—aren't things we can explain to anyone. I mean, Rachel doesn't even remember them. Not really. It's useless." *I'm useless*, I think.

"Cat . . ." I ignore Noah, and he says my name a second time, a little more forcefully. When I give in and glance up, he says, "If it weren't for you, we wouldn't have any idea what happened to her that night."

"So?"

"So, you're amazing, Mary Catherine Montgomery."

You're amazing, Cat. You're like one of the X-Men. Like Professor X.

I hadn't been amazing then, and I don't feel amazing now.

"I mean it," says Noah.

"Shut up," I mumble. My fingers twitch with the unfamiliar urge to push him or hit him. Not in earnest. Just in the way I've seen other girls act. How Lacey occasionally acts when flirting with someone she likes. "Another thing has been bothering me . . ." I say, partly because something really has been bothering me and partly to redirect the conversation.

There's a snow globe on the nightstand. Palm trees and a sandy beach. Noah does not strike me as a palm-trees-on-the-beach kind of guy. I pick it up and turn it end over end, causing a mini-blizzard. "Why would Jensen make that guy—make Buddy—stand watch outside Rachel's room? I mean, I know he said it was because of reporters, and sure, maybe one got through that first day, but it's not like Rachel's disappearance made national news. How many reporters could realistically have been staking out the hospital, waiting for a chance to get close to her?"

"Buddy did say he thought Jensen was just trying to save face, that he wanted to make it look like he was taking the complaints from Rachel's parents seriously."

"Maybe . . ." Jensen hadn't struck me as the kind of man who cares about saving face or dealing with complaints, but I could be wrong. I set the snow globe back on the nightstand. As I do, my gaze falls on a backpack next to the bedroom door. "I wish you didn't have to go to Saint John tomorrow," I admit. All we've done over the past few days is go round in circles, but there's been something comforting about spending so much time together. There's been something comforting about not carrying what happened to Rachel by myself.

"I have to."

There's a note in Noah's voice that makes me realize how selfish it is to want him here when I know the reason he's going. "They'll be able to help her," I say, my voice sounding sure even though I'm not sure at all.

There's a loose thread on the comforter. Noah catches it and pulls, ripping out the stiches. "Can I tell you something?"

I nod even though he's not looking at me.

"Part of me just wants it to be over. Part of me hopes that we'll go down there and they'll tell me that she's too sick to bring home." He gives the thread a sharp tug, breaking it.

"That's normal. That's human."

"It doesn't feel very normal. Or very human." The Adam's apple in his throat rises and falls as he swallows roughly. "You know what's even worse? There are times when I think I hate him a little bit. Riley. I hate that I had to give everything up and come back here. School, my friends, Jenn—"

He cuts himself off.

A girlfriend, I realize. He left a girl to come back here.

I wonder what's she like. What they're like together. I imagine Noah touching her the way Riley touched Skylar, and a small spark flares in my chest. If I didn't know better, I'd almost say it was jealousy, but I can't be jealous. It wouldn't make any sense.

Noah stretches out on the bed. He's too tall and lying the wrong way: his feet hang out over the edge.

After a second's hesitation, I stretch out beside him, careful to leave space between us. I inhale deeply. He's so close that I can smell the soap off his skin.

"You didn't tell me you had a girlfriend."

"*Had* being the operative word. Figured it didn't matter."

I want to ask if he misses her, if he wishes they were still together, but there's this tiny voice in the back of my head that tells me to leave it alone. That leaving it alone is somehow safer.

Noah rolls onto his side and studies my face. "You'll be careful, right? While I'm gone." This close, I can see tiny flecks of color—golds and greens—in his brown eyes. "Whoever hurt Rachel and Riley is still out there."

My hair falls over my face as I shake my head. "I'll be fine."

Noah reaches out, catches a strand of my hair, and pushes it back. If I were to move my head just a fraction of an inch, his fingers would brush my skin. "Just be careful."

The expression on his face is so earnest that it makes something inside of my chest twist. I remind myself that he wants me to be careful because he needs me. I'm Noah's ticket to figuring out what happened to his brother, that's all.

It would be stupid to confuse that need for anything else. It would be stupid to ever really let him in.

"I think maybe I was too hasty in sending you there for the summer." Those are the first words out of my father's mouth when he calls the next morning. No buildup. No hello or how are you. Just a complete readiness to uproot me again without asking what I want.

I cradle the phone between my shoulder and ear as I stretch the cord to the max, trying to reach the counter and the bowl of cereal I had been in the middle of pouring. "I thought you were in California."

"I am."

"So, I'd just be going home to an empty apartment?"

"Certainly not. I thought you could come out here. You can

hang by the pool while I'm in meetings. We can go to Disneyland. You can even see your mother—if you want to."

My father hates amusement parks and he loathes my mother. He must really be worried.

"I'm fine. Nothing's wrong."

"Finding a girl in the river is not 'nothing,' Mary Catherine."

"Dad, I told you: she was just some girl who got lost in the woods. It was a fluke." I may not believe the official police story of what happened to Rachel, but I'm not above using it. And I can't let my father pull me out of Montgomery Falls. Not right now. I can't do that to Noah. I need to be here for Riley and for Rachel. To find out what happened to them. But even as I have that thought, my mind goes to Skylar and Aunt Jet and even Aidan—to other reasons to stay. The realization that I would miss them takes me by surprise and throws me off-balance.

"I don't think being there is healthy for you."

"Yeah, well, you didn't think staying in New York was healthy, either." I carry my cereal to the table and sit. "Remember how you cut me off from everything and then shipped me to Canada?"

"You're reframing the narrative, Mary Catherine. I haven't been keeping you away from social media to punish you. It wasn't healthy, you reading those comments from those kids and getting those messages. In time, I hoped you would understand that."

Slowly and softly, I beat my head against the kitchen table three times, making the spoon clink against my bowl. "How are the meetings going?" I ask once I've finished.

"We're not talking about me, Mary Catherine. Do not change the subject."

"Why not? Your work is important. It affects me, too."

Usually, feigning flattery and interest is a surefire way to deflect my dad's attention. This time, however, it doesn't work. "I'm just worried about you, pumpkin."

Pumpkin? The last time my father called me pumpkin, I was probably about six. For a split second, I think he must be really worried and feeling extra paternal; then I hear the faint voice of a woman in the background and wonder if the endearment is just for show. My father hasn't always been above using my existence to signal to women that he's caring and sensitive and responsible— something I've only realized as I've gotten older. I don't think he ever does it on purpose. He's just really charismatic, and really charismatic people sometimes manipulate on instinct.

"Maybe you're right," I say, trying a different tactic. "Maybe I should fly out there. I mean, you'll only be in meetings a few hours a day. We'd get to spend tons of time together. We could go to Universal Studios and the beach. We could check out the Hollywood Walk of Fame and Grauman's Chinese Theatre."

Dad doesn't answer right away. Thirty seconds go by and then a minute, and then I realize something: he hadn't thought it through. He feels like he should tell me to leave Montgomery Falls, but he doesn't actually want me to come to California. He confirms it by saying, "We don't have to make a decision right this instant."

"Okay." I should be relieved—I'm getting what I want—so why do I feel like I'm being rejected somehow?

"I love you, kiddo."

"I know." And the thing is, I do. My dad's not perfect, but I've always known he loves me. At least in the ways he's capable of.

Aidan walks through the back door just as I'm setting the receiver in the cradle.

"You all right?" he asks.

"Been better." I glance up. Whatever else I might have said vanishes into the ether at the sight of toned muscles and glistening skin.

"What?" Aidan makes a show of sniffing himself as he tosses his T-shirt over the back of an empty chair. "Do I reek?" He pours himself a tall glass of chocolate milk from the fridge and then leans against the counter. A pair of black shorts hangs ridiculously low on his hips, and sweat-damp curls cling to his forehead. He's like a walking PSA on the benefits of calcium or exercise. I resist the urge to tug at my own shirt, to make sure it's not clinging too tightly to the pudge around my stomach and hips.

He pulls a chair out from the table, spins it around, and then straddles it so that he's sitting with the chairback pressed against his chest. I can still see plenty of skin, but it's a tad less distracting.

Imagine doing Jell-O shots off those muscles. That's what Lacey would say. She'd peer at him over the top of her fighter-pilot shades—the pair with the little rhinestone heart in the corner of the right lens—and lick her lips.

Aidan takes a long swig of milk, then raises his eyebrows. "What?"

I give my head a shake. "Sorry. Just imagining what my friend Lacey would say if she saw you walking around like that."

"She'd disapprove?"

"Pretty much the opposite, actually."

He grins and flexes a bicep, the gesture more goofy than sexy, particularly given that he has a milk mustache. "She sounds like she has excellent taste. You must miss her."

"I guess."

"Well, not that I don't fully endorse this whole 'rattle around a giant house looking like someone kicked you in the shin and stole your puppy' thing, but I ran into some people while I was out jogging. There's a party tonight. I think you should come—unless you have plans with Tall, Dark, and Mopey."

If I didn't know better, I'd almost think he was jealous. I'm not sure how to feel about that. For one thing, it's hard to believe. No guy has ever been jealous when it comes to me—at least not that I'm aware of. Why would they? I've never let anyone get that close. "Noah is not mopey. Besides, he's out of town."

"Great. You can come with me to Amber's."

"Amber Preston?"

Aidan nods.

Given that Amber was Riley's girlfriend and saw Rachel the day she disappeared, she'd be a logical person to try to read, and going to the party might be a perfect opportunity. The idea of going without Noah, however, feels strange.

Apparently, I take too long to answer because a look of mock exasperation flashes across Aidan's face. "Amber's parties are not a fate worse than death. You might even have fun. Come with me. We'll have a good time."

We'll have a good time? Wait—is he asking me as some sort of date?

"Just you and me?" I ask, because I'm not sure how else to figure things out.

"Chase is coming with. Given what happened between Skylar and Riley . . ."

"She and Joey aren't going."

"Right."

I don't exactly love the thought of going to a party where Skylar wouldn't be welcome, but it's probably too good of an opportunity to get close to Amber—not to mention to other people who would have known Riley—to pass up.

Aidan's phone chirps in his pocket. He ignores it. "Come with me."

"You don't think having a chubby tagalong will put a dent in your style?" As soon as the words are out of my mouth, I want to take them back. I don't know why I said it. It's not like I'm pointing out anything that he doesn't already know. He has eyes; he knows I'm not skinny. And he has Joey to point it out if he ever forgets.

Aidan stares at me, a slightly bemused expression on his face. He shakes his head. "You, Cat Montgomery, could never dent anyone's style."

And, just like that, I guess I'm going to a party.

TWENTY-FOUR

AMBER PRESTON LIVES ON THE EDGE OF TOWN ON A CUL-DE-
sac that cuts into the forest. Her family's split-level ranch house is
distinguishable from the neighboring split-level ranch houses only
by the color of the front door and the fleet of cars out front.

"Okay," I say as Chase parks his mom's Malibu on the street,
"is it just me or is it not weird that Amber would plan a party
when one of her best friends was recently hauled out of the river
and is barely out of the hospital?"

Aidan chuckles. "Amber's parties are more opportunistic than
planned."

"In other words," says Chase as we climb out of the car, "they
happen whenever her parents go out of town regardless of whatever else is going on." As we head up the driveway, he shoots me a
smile that's bright enough to light up the block. "This is your first
Canadian party, right?"

"Let me guess? Flannel shirts and maple syrup shots will be out in full force."

"Smartasssssssssss." Chase pulls out the word, winks at me, and then ambles toward a group of guys who are all wearing varsity jackets even though the night is plenty warm. They slap him on the back and let out exuberant whoops.

I shake my head. "I don't get it."

"Get what?" Aidan asks.

"Chase is obviously popular."

"Yes."

"But he spends all of his time hanging out with Joey."

"Yes."

"Why?" I mean, I can sort of see Skylar being drawn to Joey because they're both so different and I can see Aidan falling in with them because he's always been the new kid, but Chase just makes no sense.

Aidan shrugs. "Never underestimate the value of childhood loyalty." He steers me down a concrete walkway and into a sprawling backyard that leads right up to the edge of the trees. A few people call out greetings to Aidan. More than a few stare at me.

A girl detaches herself from a group and slips a hand into the crook of Aidan's arm. "You came." She curls up against him like she's been there before. She's curvy and pretty with jet-black hair and wide brown eyes. Even though I still can't figure out if this is some sort of date in Aidan's mind, I don't like seeing her at his side. I don't like how easily she leans into him, how effortlessly close she is.

How she can touch him.

"Who's your friend?" the girl asks.

"Cat meet Tanya."

Tanya flashes me a small smile that looks genuine before turning her attention back to Aidan. "How's summer school? I can't believe you're stuck here instead of in France."

I stare at Aidan, surprised. "You were supposed to go to France?"

"I was supposed to visit my folks," he says to me. To Tanya, he says, "I thought you were spending the summer with your grandmother."

"I am. I'm just down for the week." In an effort to include me, she says, "My grandmother lives up in Listuguj."

"Listuguj Mi'gmaq First Nation," Aidan supplies, for my benefit. "It's four or five hours from here."

Tanya tries to press herself even closer to his side, but he gently disentangles himself. "Let's get something to drink," he says, looking straight at me.

"She's pretty," I say, once we're out of earshot.

"I guess," he says.

We reach the house and cross a wide wooden deck. "It must be hard: being stuck here instead of spending the summer abroad."

Aidan makes a noise that's half snort, half chuckle. "Honestly? I flunked on purpose. Summer school is way easier than dealing with my drill sergeant father. Besides," he says as we reach the door and he holds it open, "there are more interesting things here."

It's stupid, but as I squeeze past him, I'm glad he can't see me smile.

It takes only a second, though, for the smile to fade.

The kitchen is a riot of noise and bodies that makes me instantly regret stepping inside. I've never liked parties—too many people, too many chances for accidental contact—though I usually tolerated them for Lacey.

"Where do you think Amber is?" I ask, trying to ignore the way my nerves seem to tingle beneath my skin.

"Why?"

Even though I've already dragged Aidan to the hospital to talk to Rachel, I don't want him to know that I have an ulterior motive in being here. I like the idea that Aidan is separate—or at least mostly separate—from all the stuff with Riley. That, unlike Noah, he wants to be around me for who I am and not what I can do. That he thinks I'm normal. And because I like the idea of being a normal girl at a normal party for normal reasons—and because I like the idea of being here with him—I don't tell him the truth. "Just curious," I say with a small shrug.

Taking my words at face value, Aidan pulls a guy aside to ask if he's seen the hostess.

"She's upstairs with Troy. Go ahead and interrupt them, if you don't mind getting your ass kicked."

Aidan runs a hand through his hair and shrugs. "There you have it," he tells me with a rueful smile. He grabs two bottles of beer from the ice-filled kitchen sink and leads me back outside. Several people beckon him over as we make our way across the yard, but he ignores them and heads for an old oak tree.

A tire swing hangs from one of the branches.

"Hop on."

I oblige, a little uncertainly.

Aidan pops the cap off one of the bottles and hands it to me.

I take it, careful to keep my fingers far away from his. Not that I have any intention of drinking. I need a clear head, and after what happened the last time I drank at a party . . .

Aidan opens his own bottle, takes a swig, then sets it down in the grass.

Clumsily, I try to keep a hold on both the bottle and the swing as I take a small, experimental push. The tire spins in a slow, wobbly circle.

"Not many tire swings in New York?"

"Not in my neighborhood."

"A tire swing virgin."

"Not all of us can be worldly army brats, a tire swing in every town."

Chuckling softly, Aidan steps behind me. He catches the swing, then pulls it back and lets go. I tense as he starts to push me, but he keeps his hands on the tire, not brushing me at all.

"Why do you really want to talk to Amber?"

"I told you: I'm curious."

"And this has nothing to do with the fact that she was Riley's girlfriend or that she saw Rachel the day Rachel ended up in the river? I'm not stupid, Cat. I know you and Noah Fraser have a whole Hardy Boy–Nancy Drew thing going on." He doesn't sound angry; if anything, he sounds vaguely amused.

"All right, fine. We're trying to find out what happened to Riley."

"The whole town searched for Riley for months. Most people are starting to say he just ran away. What makes you think he didn't?"

"Noah. And that medal."

"You told Jensen Riley wouldn't give that medal away, but you wouldn't tell him why." Silence stretches out between us. Aidan catches the swing and spins it around. "And you're not going to tell me, either, are you?"

There doesn't seem to be any reproach behind the words. In fact, when I shake my head, Aidan actually smiles. "Like I told you: never underestimate the value of childhood loyalty."

He steps away so that he can grab his beer. "I wouldn't ask Amber about Riley. She's still really messed up about it." He drains the last of the bottle, tosses it toward a nearby cluster of bushes, then steps back to the swing. This time, instead of pushing me, he corkscrews the tire, turning it around and around so that the rope twists tightly up, lifting me until my toes barely scrape the ground.

"I have a proposal," he says, gripping the edge of the tire tightly.

"Yes?"

"I'm not going to ask you to stop playing Nancy Drew, but I suggest you spend the next hour just having fun."

"Fun?"

"Strange concept, I know. But pretend you came here because you like me and that you didn't have a nefarious purpose. Just for an hour."

"I didn't come here just for nefarious purposes." And it's true. I do like Aidan. I like spending time with him. I like how light he makes everything seem. I like the idea that maybe he wants me. Even though that would open a whole host of problems and complications. Even though I've spent years trying to convince myself that I don't really want anyone—at least not enough to ever risk acting on it. "One hour of fun?"

"And then it's back to solving mysteries."

I tell myself that one hour won't make a difference. That Noah is in Saint John and doesn't even know I'm here, so there's no reason to feel like I'm somehow betraying him—or Rachel or Riley—by giving in to Aidan. Or by liking the way Aidan is looking at me.

Noah doesn't see me that way.

I'm sure he doesn't.

And Aidan is here. Right now.

"One hour of fun . . . ," I agree, infusing the words with more enthusiasm than I feel.

In response, Aidan lets go of the tire swing and the world spins.

The party keeps spinning after we leave the swing. Everyone seems to know and like Aidan. They keep trying to pull him into conversations while I hang slightly back. He's pretty good at extracting himself—until he gets hauled off by a trio of guys who swear they need him to settle a bet.

Then he disappears, and I'm left to wander on my own.

Occasionally, I see Chase. He's always in a group. Maybe not at the center, but near it. Each time he spots me, he tries to wave me over. Each time, I smile and shake my head. It's the first party I've been to since what happened back home. Keeping at least a little distance from the masses just feels safer.

If Lacey were here, she'd be with him. Always in the big groups while I hung out somewhere off to the side. Watching. Waiting until she decided it was time to leave.

At the time, I had never really questioned it. At the time, the arrangement had suited me just fine. But after a few months apart? After a few months apart, I'm less sure.

A girl crashes into me, jolting me from my thoughts. "Watch it," she slurs. She squints at me through red-rimmed eyes. "I don't know you."

Amber.

In the photograph with Riley, she looked perfect. Now, she's a mess. Her shirt—which I'm pretty sure is designer—is ripped at the shoulder and stained with what I hope is just beer, and there are bits of grass and mud clinging to her black skirt. Her boots—also designer, I think—have too much heel for the grass: they sink in like golf tees, causing her to wobble and then go over. She crumples to the ground, ass hitting grass, and lets out a long sigh that morphs into an alcoholic burp. I glance around, looking for her friends, but this corner of the yard is virtually empty.

"Do you like my party?" she asks, looking up at me with wide, watery eyes.

"It's great." My tone couldn't be less convincing, but it's not like she's actually listening to me. She probably won't even remember this tomorrow.

"I thought it would make me feel better. I thought maybe I wouldn't miss him if everybody else was here." She tries to crane her neck. "Everybody is here, right?"

She's so sad and pitiful that trying to question her about anything feels a little monstrous. Still, I find myself asking, "Who are you trying not to miss?"

It's not that I don't already know the answer. It just seems like an easy way to get her talking about Riley.

The squint is back. Her eyes narrow until I'm not sure how she sees anything but her own lashes. "You're not from here."

I guess the five seconds when she glanced at me in the drug-store were not memorable. "I'm visiting. I'm here with Aidan."

Her eyes open a little bit at that. "Aidan. Aidan is awesome. Aidan understands. Everyone else wants me to just forget about Riley. You know what my mom said?" She doesn't wait for me to answer. "She said Riley probably ran away—that he left me, so why care about where he is now? It's not like I can just . . ." Amber's eyes go wide as she loses the trail of her thoughts. "I think I'm gonna be sick."

She tries to climb to her feet, can't make it, and falls back on her ass. *Oh, hell,* I think, *it's not like I probably wasn't going to do this anyway.* I reach down with both hands and grip her around the forearms. As I start to pull her up, as I start to get sucked down, I try to find her fear on the off chance it connects to Riley or Rachel—

Strong arms around me. A warm body at my back. Skin against skin. "It's okay . . . Everything will be okay." A deep voice, soft against my ear. "You're safe."

The arms tighten around me.

"I'm going to take care of everything. You're safe."

Safe . . .

I blink, dazed, as the night comes rushing back.

Riley.

It's the first time I've heard his voice in five years, but I know

249

it's him. Just like I know the shape of his arms and the weight of his body against mine.

I know these things because Amber knows them.

An ache spreads through my chest. I feel lost. Lost and empty.

Amber stumbles away from me. She makes it to the nearest bush and hurls.

This couldn't have been what Aidan had in mind when he said I needed to have fun.

I wait for the pounding in my head to come. When it does, it's slow and light, practically just a background hum. Maybe it's proof of Noah's desensitization theory, or maybe it's something to do with the caliber of Amber's desire.

And I must have seen desire. I must have done something wrong.

Wearily, I help Amber up again. This time, I'm careful not to let skin touch skin. She's so off-balance that it takes us forever to make our way to the house.

Not one person offers to help as I steer her through the kitchen and up the stairs. Not one person asks if she's okay, and more than a few people snap photos of her on their phones. The fear of accidentally touching anyone isn't the only reason I hate parties.

"Bed," Amber mutters as she teeters toward a door on the right and lurches into a room that looks like it belongs to a six-year-old princess on a sugar high. All soft pastels and stuffed animals and an actual tiara on the dresser. It's a room for someone much younger, and I find myself double-checking the sparkly name plaque on the door.

I guide Amber to the bed and make sure she lands on the

mattress instead of the floor when her legs stop cooperating. She mumbles something completely unintelligible and rolls onto her side.

At least she won't choke on her own vomit, I think, turning away.

There's a jacket draped over a chair in the corner. Blue and white, like the ones the guys outside were wearing. Riley's last name is stitched on the sleeve. I lift it, gently. It's way too big for Amber. Big enough that I could easily wrap it around myself. I slip my hand into first one pocket and then the other, but all I find is a stick of gum and a crumpled movie ticket.

Feeling like a creeper, I press Riley's jacket to my chest, just for a second. My head still isn't hurting as much as it should. Maybe it's stupid, but part of me wants to believe that maybe a desire like that—a desire tied to a memory of Riley—can't hurt me.

I carry the jacket back to the bed and drape it over Amber. She doesn't open her eyes, but she pulls the jacket close, like she knows what it is even in her sleep.

I think about what Skylar told me about Riley and the boat. About how he had lied to protect the girl in front of me. About how Noah said the difference between the boy I knew and the person he became isn't as big as I might think.

I hear his voice in my head. *It's okay . . . Everything will be okay.*

As I slip out of the room, I pretend the words were meant for me.

TWENTY-FIVE

ANY COMFORT I GET FROM THE MEMORY OF RILEY'S WORDS is short-lived. Between the thumping bass of the living room stereo and the press of people in the kitchen, the memory is just too hard to hold on to. I spot Chase, still surrounded by his friends, but there's no sign of Aidan.

I slip outside.

The party seems evenly split between the house and the yard, but the deck is curiously vacant. A wooden bench runs along the railing, encircling the entire space. I take a seat in the corner where the shadows are deepest. That way, I can spot Aidan coming or going from the house while being alone with my thoughts until he turns up.

Tonight was a mistake, I think. What had I really expected to get out of coming here? That I'd have a chance to talk—really talk—to Amber about Riley? That I'd get a look inside her head and somehow find a clue as to who could have wanted to hurt her boyfriend or her best friend?

It all seems so stupid now.

The door opens, sending a triangle of light over the deck. I look up, hoping for Aidan, but it's just a couple of girls. One of them is Tanya. She trails the other girl across the deck, tugging on her sleeve. "Just one more hour."

Even in the shadows of the deck, I can make out enough of the other girl's expression to know she isn't happy. "You said that an hour ago."

"You're being such a killjoy. Why did you even come if you didn't want to be here?" Without waiting for a response, Tanya turns on her heel and heads back into the house.

Even though she was outside for only a moment, a series of cheers greets her return.

The other girl stays where she is, uncertain. Maybe she doesn't really want to leave as badly as she thought she did, or maybe she just doesn't want to leave Tanya alone. She starts to walk away and then stops and turns back to the house. She stands there, in the middle of the deck, undecided.

I don't need to watch the scene play out to know what she's going to do. As one reluctant killjoy to another, I know what she'll decide.

She'll go back in. Because her friend wants her to stay. Because she thinks maybe—just maybe—she might be needed.

The last time I thought I was needed like that had been at Lacey's. A Friday night when her parents were out of town at a conference. "Please," she had said. "I need you there. Consider it a birthday present."

Her birthday was already three days past and I had gotten her a present, but she was looking at me with big puppy-dog eyes and I caved. Because I thought someone should keep an eye on her. Because over the past couple of months, it had increasingly felt like maybe Lacey was needing me just a little bit less.

"Okay," I'd said, thinking maybe it wouldn't be so bad.

And it wasn't. Not at first.

After a little while, I'd even started to have fun. I talked to people. I drank. I let my guard down. Not all the way, but a little bit.

And because my guard was down, I wasn't prepared. I wasn't fast enough when someone grabbed me from behind and lifted me off the ground.

Nick Ames was a senior who supposedly went to public school because it helped his father's image as a down-to-earth man of the people when he was running for reelection. He was handsome, popular, and Harvard-bound. He was at the center of the sphere Lacey wanted to move into.

He was also an asshole.

"Just stay still," he said, trying to lift me over his head as a bunch of his drunken friends cheered. Nearby, other boys grabbed other girls, all trying to do the same thing.

Nick lifted me, kicking and screaming, and as he did, my T-shirt rucked up almost to my neck.

"Nice chest!" someone yelled.

Panicked, I elbowed Nick in the collarbone as hard as I could. Hard enough that he momentarily lost his grip. Hard enough that he hadn't even tried to keep me from hitting the ground. I'd ended up on the floor, in a heap, while all around me, people laughed.

Tears sprang to my eyes. Not because of the laughter—or at least that's what I told myself—but because it had really, really hurt. I pushed myself to my feet, looking for Lacey. I caught a glimpse of her through the kitchen doorway. She was in the center of a big group of people, flirting with a girl from our chem class while Matt, her ex, glared from across the room.

And I realized something: Lacey hadn't talked to me once since the party had started. She said she needed me to come, but she'd been too busy to notice when I had needed her. Anger and hurt flared in my chest along with something else. She was always comfortable in groups. Always surrounded by other people. Always at the center while I was on the outside. It wasn't fair. It was never fair.

Limping a little, I'd started toward the door, but Nick grabbed me again. He was still laughing. "Come on, it was just a joke. We were just having fun."

His fingers were wrapped around my wrist, around a slice of skin my sleeve didn't cover.

For a moment, I lost myself. I was in his head, seeing what he was afraid of while he laughed at me. And then I did something I hadn't done in five years: I said something about what I saw. I blurted out Nick Ames's biggest fear in a room full of people.

Given that his biggest fear was that people would find out his parents had paid someone to take his SATs and write his college admission essays, this was not a small deal.

He shoved me. Shoved me hard enough to send me crashing into a nearby group of people. I was grabbed and I was pushed. Again and again. Someone asked me if what I had said about Nick was true. Someone else asked how I had known. At least one person called me a liar.

I couldn't answer. I could barely think. My head was full. Full of people's fears, but also their desires. Mouths and bodies. Kisses and skin.

The drinks I'd had earlier sloshed in my stomach as pain exploded behind my temples.

And then someone else grabbed me. Hard. Around my arm, but not touching skin. Lacey yanked me through the crowd, down the front hall, and into the half bath. She pushed me inside, and I had to catch myself on the edge of the vanity in order to stay on my feet.

I tried to focus my gaze. It was harder than it should have been, and I couldn't tell if the pain rising to a crescendo in my head was from the drinking or from what I had seen. I gripped the counter a little more tightly, fighting the urge to throw up. I hadn't drunk that much. Not nearly enough to feel like this. I picked something small to focus on in an effort to make the room stop spinning. A small pink rose. I blinked. "Did you put out fancy guest soap?"

In the mirror, I could see Lacey cross her arms over her chest. "It's nice," she said, a defensive note in her voice.

"It's stupid." Whatever was causing all the pain in my head had also made me lose complete control of my tongue. I turned, putting the counter at my back. "Lacey, in another hour, they'll be trashing the apartment. None of them are going to notice that you've put out fancy soap."

"What did you say to Nick?"

The abrupt shift in topic cut through some of the pain. "Nothing."

"Nothing? He just stormed out of here, telling anyone who'd listen that you're a crazy, lying bitch."

"So? Who cares what he says?" I tried to sound flippant, unconcerned, but a thread of fear wormed its way through my stomach and worked its way up to my chest. An awful lot of people cared what Nick Ames thought and said. Including, lately, Lacey.

She just stared at me. I could hear the noise of the party through the closed bathroom door, but the silence between us was thick and awkward. I found myself babbling to fill it. "I can't believe he called me a liar. Do you know what he did? Do you know how he got those amazing SAT scores or why he got into Harvard?"

"Stop." Lacey's eyes flashed. "Do you have any idea who his parents are? Or how much people listen to him? You can't just go around saying stuff like that." Her eyes narrowed as another thought occurred to her. "Wait—did you call him out in front of everyone? Is that why he's so angry?"

My cheeks grew hot.

"Jesus, Cat. How do you even know he did anything?"

I let out a long, deep breath and just looked at her. I was tired suddenly, so tired of always hiding. "I just know."

Lacey swallowed. For just the tiniest of seconds, she looked more uncomfortable than angry, and I wondered: *How much has she figured out?* Because she had to suspect something, after four years. She had to suspect something even though she never, ever asked.

She exhaled, and the sound seemed to fill the room. Her lower lip trembled and a muscle tensed in her jaw, like she was trying not to cry. "God. Why did you even come if you were just going to ruin everything?"

"Because you asked me to." Four years of listening to her had made me a good mimic. In a voice that almost anyone would mistake for hers, I said, "'You have to come. You can't just stay home. I need you.'"

Except Lacey's voice wasn't quite that insipid.

Hurt flashed across her face. "I didn't need you to do this," she said, stepping toward the door and reaching for the knob.

"What are you doing?"

"I'm going back out there, and you're going home."

Without thinking, I reached for her hand—just to stop her, I think, though I've never entirely been sure. Maybe I only meant to stop her, but just before my skin touched hers, I wondered what Lacey was afraid of—not the fears she shared with me, but the ones she kept to herself. I tried to actually see what she was afraid of, certain it would help explain why she was acting this way, why she was choosing the people out there over me—

Red hair, wide hips, freckles. I saw myself. Not my reflection or a picture, but the way Lacey saw me.

And as I looked at myself, I felt like there was a massive weight pulling me down. Down, down, down . . .

The bathroom came rushing back as Lacey yanked her hand away.

As far as fears went, it was practically a walk in the park. Just a pretty girl who wanted to transition from popular to really popular and who was worried that her friend was going to hold her back.

I rubbed at my eyes angrily with the back of my hand. "So that's it, right? You think I'm some kind of liability."

"I never said that."

"You don't have to. God, Lacey. You're acting like I want to be here. Just admit it: You wanted me here so that you could feel better about yourself. You make me go places so that you have someone looking out for you. Someone to take care of you if you drink too much or someone comes on too strong or you lose your phone or your purse. And you pick me because I'm safe and because you can look at me and feel better about yourself. Your self-esteem is that low. You're that pathetic. You use me."

"And you don't use me?" Lacey's own voice rose until it almost drowned out the background noise of the party. "You put up all these stupid walls so no one else can get close to you and then you hold me up to everyone to prove that you're not alone. You need me to be in the middle of things because then no one looks directly at you. I'm not even sure you like me half the time." Her voice began to tremble, and her eyes filled with tears. "I tell you everything, and you never trust me enough to tell me what's going on with you."

"Lacey . . ."

"You use me every bit as much as I use you. Maybe more. Just . . ." She pulled in a deep, shaky breath. "Stay in here and sober up and then go."

"Lace . . ."

"I mean it, Cat. Lock the door. Stay in here until you can walk down the stairs without falling and then get out. I don't want you here."

"They mean that much to you? Nick and all his stupid friends?"

She shook her head, and I realized the truth: It wasn't that Nick and his friends were that important—although she desperately wanted them to like her so that she could be more popular. It was that I wasn't important enough.

Two days after the party, Nick's parents hired a lawyer. Words were tossed around. Things like "defamation of character" and "libel."

Oddly enough, those words didn't seem to help me when the first posts started going up. Posts that called me a liar. Posts that called me crazy. Posts that got dozens and then hundreds of likes.

I give my head a sharp shake, pulling myself back to the present. In the distance, I hear sirens.

The girl on the deck, the killjoy, finally notices me.

"What are you looking at?" she asks, defensive and a little mean. She doesn't wait for a response. She just stomps toward the house.

I wonder if anyone notices her return.

The sirens sound like they're getting closer. Really, really close. A few people drift outside to see what's going on. As I push myself to my feet, red and blue lights sweep the lawn and a harsh, amplified voice yells for everyone to stay where they are.

People begin pouring out of the house, and I make a run for the yard just to keep from getting trampled.

Cans and bottles hit the ground. Couples break apart. Someone rams into me from behind, sending me stumbling over the uneven ground. I try to get free of the crowd, but it's like being caught in a giant pinball machine. Most of the contact lands on my shoulders and back—safe zones—but every few paces, skin hits skin, so fast and furious that I can't make sense of the barrage of images in my head.

A hand seizes mine. I try to pull away and—

A crowd of people, all running. A girl with wide green eyes and disheveled red hair and a faint constellation of freckles . . .

I'm on my hands and knees at the edge of the yard.

It takes me a second to realize where I am, to realize I must have stumbled and fallen when I got pulled into someone's head.

Not someone's. Aidan's.

He grabs me—under my arms, where my shirt covers skin—and pulls me to my feet. "Come on, Cat. Run."

People hurtle past us, dozens of them. As he steps away, his hand grazes my wrist. The contact lasts less than a second and I don't get pulled all the way under, but again, I see myself. Just the briefest of flashes.

I force my body into motion, running clumsily with Aidan into the trees.

We're not alone. All around us, the woods are full of the sounds of stumbling partygoers, fear of police and parents outweighing fear of the woods at night.

"Are you okay?" Aidan asks, pausing after a few minutes to study my face in the darkness. "Can you keep going?"

Pain is blossoming along the edge of my skull, and my stomach rolls like I'm going to be sick. Too many people. Amber and then the crowd and then Aidan. I want to tell him no, that I can't, but harsh, adult voices yell out for people to stop.

I nod. I don't have much choice.

261

Aidan lets out a relieved breath.

We duck under branches and clamber over fallen trees until we reach a trail. It's darker, this far in. So dark that it's pure luck we find the trail at all.

Aidan pulls out his phone, thumbs on the flashlight app, and then turns in a slow circle, studying the path. A shout echoes nearby. I'm pretty sure it's someone from the party, not the police, but Aidan still turns off the light and shoves his phone into his pocket.

"I think this path heads up to the trailer park and then branches," he says, once it seems safe to breathe again. "We should be able to follow it back down to Riverside Avenue."

"What about Chase?"

"The cops probably won't bust the jocks over just a party. Us, on the other hand . . ."

I bite my lip. I can only imagine what Jensen will tell Aunt Jet if the cops pick me up or what Dad will say when he finds out. "What happens if they catch us and call your father?" I ask.

Aidan's shrug in response is tight and awkward, so unlike his normal, relaxed body language. "The worst he can do to me from across the ocean is yell."

Light flashes in the distance, cutting in and out between the trees. It's far off, but still too close for comfort.

"Come on," Aidan whispers.

We manage to stay on the trail, but it's slow going in the dark.

"Did you find Amber?" Aidan asks after a while.

"Yeah, but she was pretty out of it."

The path begins to slope steeply upward. Before long, my

calves are burning, and by the time we reach the top of the hill, my breathing is ragged and my chest feels like someone has taken a jackhammer to it. "Running up and down the woods was a lot easier before I got fat."

Aidan turns to study me in the dark. "You're not fat."

I don't know how to respond to that. What do you say when every magazine and TV show says the opposite? When there are only a handful of stores where you can shop? When you want to love yourself but there are a hundred promoted posts in your social media feeds designed to make you feel weak and inadequate?

But it's not like I can explain that to the beautiful boy in front of me. And, if I'm being honest, I'm not sure I really want to—not if he doesn't see me the way so many people seem to want me to see myself.

Aidan steps toward me. "Cat . . ."

Whatever he was going to say is interrupted by the crackle of a police radio.

"Shit." The word slips out before I can stop it.

By unspoken agreement, we leave the path and start pushing our way through the undergrowth, but the noise from the radio keeps getting closer. At one point, I'm sure I hear Chief Jensen's deep baritone, and the sound makes me stumble.

We take twists and turns through the trees until the trail is just a distant memory and I lose all sense of direction. As bad as the pain in my head had seemed after Aidan pulled me from the yard, it abates quickly. Still present, but bearable.

A dark shape hurtles toward us, and I let out a yelp as I jump out of the way.

A doe crashes past, seemingly just as scared of me as I am of it.

"This way," I whisper, veering right, hoping that the deer makes enough noise to pull the police in the opposite direction.

After a few minutes, we reach a narrow clearing. In its center sits an old, rusting trailer. The kind of mobile home that truly is mobile. A tin can you can hitch up and haul across the country.

Even in the dark, I can tell the trailer is a wreck, but it's something we can hide behind. At least until the cops get tired of trying to round everyone up.

Judging from the height of the surrounding brush, the trailer has been here for a few years. No more than four, though. As disoriented as I am, I'm positive we haven't left the area Riley and I covered that summer. And an abandoned trailer in a clearing is definitely something we would have noticed.

Riley would have been all over it.

The door hangs off its hinges, leaving the trailer completely open.

I step forward to peek inside, but Aidan's voice stops me.

"What would your dad do?" he asks.

It takes me a minute to realize that he's picking up the thread from our earlier conversation. "I don't know," I say honestly. Lacey hauled me in and out of trouble for years, but it's not like we were ever picked up by the cops. Things have been different, though, since everything that happened with Nick.

"Would he make you leave?"

"I honestly don't know."

"That," says Aidan, "would not be acceptable."

I bite my lip. I swear his eyes drift down to that spot, just for a second. "Why wouldn't it be acceptable?"

Instead of answering, Aidan leans down.

I have a choice; I can pull away. I don't. I'm tired of letting chances pass me by just because I'm too scared of what might happen. I want to kiss him. I want to know what it feels like to touch his skin and feel him against me.

I know it will hurt, but I'm not sure I care.

Heart thundering in my chest, I raise myself up on the tips of my toes and press my lips to his.

The first time I kissed a boy, I saw his fear. Sharp and blinding, it ended everything.

The second time I kissed a boy, I saw who he really wanted, and that person wasn't me.

When Aidan's lips brush mine, I see myself. Only me.

Somehow, seeing my own image keeps me anchored. It keeps me from losing myself.

Things inside me tighten as the kiss deepens. The difference in our heights is big enough that I have to strain to reach. Aidan's hands skim my arms and my shoulders and my collarbones. He pushes me back gently, and my spine hits the trailer.

I shiver even though everything inside of me feels hot.

So this is kissing, I think.

When he finally pulls away, he smiles in a way that should make my heart skip.

I stare at him, a little dazed, and I wait. My heart is still racing, but I wait for the skip. I wait for the skip and for the pain in my head to come roaring back.

The pain comes, but the skip? The skip is strangely absent.

I don't get it. My body wants him—it really, really wants him—but although my heart is racing, it's a purely physical response. I'm so confused it feels like I might cry.

"I've been wanting to do that for ages," Aidan murmurs. There's heat in his gaze. The kind of heat that I'm not at all used to seeing directed at me. He reaches out and catches one of my curls, giving it a tiny tug and twisting it briefly around his finger.

The gesture reminds me of Noah. Of Noah brushing the hair back from my face and asking me to be careful.

The memory makes the urge to cry that much stronger, but Aidan, thankfully, doesn't seem to notice.

Kissing Aidan was everything the first kiss should have been. And the second.

So why am I thinking of someone else?

"I've only been in town for a little while," I say, trying to cover my confusion. "You couldn't have wanted to do that for ages."

A beam of light slashes through the trees past Aidan's shoulder. I hold a finger to my lips and point toward the glow. Then, catching the hem of Aidan's shirt between my fingers, I tug him toward the open trailer door.

We clamber inside and kneel on the floor. I can feel grit under my palms, and a damp, musky smell floods my nostrils when I inhale. We watch through the open door as the light sweeps toward us and then swings back in the other direction.

We don't move for a long while.

Finally, when the light is no longer visible, Aidan climbs to his feet and pulls out his phone.

"Think it's safe?" he asks.

I have no idea, but being in an unknown enclosed space in the dark is starting to freak me out. "Yeah."

Aidan thumbs on the light, and I wince as my eyes struggle to adjust.

The trailer is tiny—not much bigger than a good walk-in closet. A low bed at the end of the single room takes up almost half the space.

I climb to my feet as Aidan turns in a slow circle. He illuminates each wall in turn. All four have been covered in photographs. Dozens, probably hundreds, of photographs.

"Holy shit," he says.

Me? I can't find my voice at all.

Rachel Larsen stares at me. Over and over. There are yearbook photos and snapshots and pictures that have been blown up so large that they're the size of small posters. There are pictures of other girls, too. Girls around my age. Lots and lots of them—although three or four faces are repeated over and over.

There are also pictures of other women. Half-naked figures ripped from magazines, their eyes scratched out with a ballpoint pen. Paintings that I recognize from art class and school trips to the Met. Etchings of angels and demons. A reproduction of Michelangelo's *The Last Judgment*.

And then there are the monsters. The Wolfman. Bela Lugosi as Dracula. Frankenstein with bolts in his neck and stitches across his temples. The classic monsters Skylar wears on the pins on her uniform, but newer monsters, too.

Aidan turns toward the corner where a small desk sits piled high with papers. "Cat . . ."

I rip myself away from the spectacle on the walls. There, on the desk, on top of hundreds of sheets of loose paper, is a bundle of pages that have been hole-punched and woven together with red ribbon. A ribbon that's the same shade of red as the one Skylar was wearing in her hair the first time I hung out with Aidan and his friends.

The first page has just a title, all in caps: NIGHT OF THE SHADOW STALKER.

"That's the name of the script Joey's been working on." Aidan hands me his phone and lifts the booklet. He opens it to a random page and reads, "'They found the girl at the river's edge. A game of tic-tac-toe was carved on her arm.'"

"Rachel." Hands shaking, I set the phone down and take the script from Aidan. "Have you read this?"

Aidan laughs. Not his real laugh. The kind of laugh you give when what you're thinking is so horrible that it makes you light-headed. "No. He never lets anyone see it. Not me or Chase. Not even Skylar. Maybe he wrote this afterward? Maybe the whole Rachel thing gave him the idea and he changed the script?"

I flip to the beginning, looking for any mention of Riley. Halfway down page five, I spot it: a line about a boy in a varsity jacket. The rest of the page is missing. Ripped out. The three pages that follow are also gone. "We have to get Jensen. Jensen has to see this."

"You can't be serious." Aidan takes the script from my hands and sets it back down on the desk. He wipes his palms against his jeans. "Joey is one of my best friends. Whatever this looks like . . . it's not."

"Well, that's a relief because I was just about to say it looks like one of your best friends is a serial killer."

"You don't know that." But there's a distinct lack of fight to the words; it's like Aidan is trying to convince himself more than me.

Something underneath the desk catches my eye, and I crouch down. My stomach does slow flips at the sight of thick strands of rope. Yards and yards of rope, all twisted and knotted.

A black leather square is caught in the middle of the tangle.

I tug it free, thinking too late about fingerprints and evidence, and open it. Riley's face stares up at me from his driver's license. Across from the license is one of those slots people slide credit cards into. It should be a flat rectangle, but there's a raised circle in the middle. A circle about the size of the Saint Anthony medal, as though Riley kept it there for a long, long time. Enough time for the leather to mold itself around the shape.

Aidan. I try to say his name, but my voice doesn't want to work. Around me, the trailer goes dark at the edges, and I have to use my other hand to steady myself against the filthy floor.

"Cat . . . You have to see this."

I shake my head. Whatever he's found can't be as important as what I have in my hand, but I still can't seem to find my voice.

Aidan tugs me to my feet. I sway, almost falling. I'm still holding the wallet. I can't let it go.

"Cat, look." He turns me to face a section of wall that I had missed and shines the light over another collage of photographs.

With a jolt, I see my own face. I'm at the end of the driveway at Montgomery House, hauling the trash barrels out to the curb. "That was last week."

My eyes drift down to another photograph.

A night shot taken near the river's edge. Two shapes are barely discernible in the picture, but I know one of them is me and one of them is Rachel. I don't know how I know; I just do.

The picture was taken from somewhere in the trees. After Chase and Skylar left to get help but before the police and paramedics arrived.

But as terrifying as that photo is, it's the ones underneath that make it impossible to breathe.

Four photos.

Each taken through my bedroom window.

Each taken when I thought I was alone and safe.

TWENTY-SIX

THERE'S THIS THING THAT HAPPENS IN BOOKS—I THINK there's a word for it, but I can't remember what it is—when the weather mirrors a character's internal state. *It was a dark and stormy night* type stuff.

There have been maybe three days in my life when I've truly felt like I've earned a dark and stormy sky to reflect my mood, and the day after finding out that a teenage serial killer wannabe has some sort of sick and twisted fixation on me is definitely on that list.

The universe, however, does not seem to agree: when I push myself out of bed and peek past the edge of the curtains, the day outside is all sunshine and blue sky.

I let the fabric fall back into place. Even with the window covered, though, I feel exposed. My eyes fall on the plastic bear—Skylar's plastic bear—on the nightstand. For a minute, I think throwing up might be a solid way to start the day.

Ten hours ago, I kissed the boy down the hall and found myself standing in a rusted trailer that looked like an illustration from the official *Serial Killer Training Guide*.

Seven hours ago, the police burst into Joey's house. Joey was nowhere to be found.

Five hours ago, I passed Skylar in the hallway of the Montgomery Falls Police Department. She wouldn't even look at me.

I dress in the windowless bathroom, rushing through the act with my back to the door.

Only after I've stepped out into the hall do I realize my T-shirt is on inside out and my socks don't match. It's not like it matters. Aunt Jet has put me on house arrest for the remainder of my time in Montgomery Falls—which won't be long. Dad is wrapping up his meetings and getting things in order as quickly as he can. He'll be here in three days, tops, to take me away. He wanted Jet to drive me down to Saint John and put me on the first plane out, but I'm not allowed to leave town for a few days.

I'm a witness in a major criminal investigation.

Yeah: throwing up definitely feels like an option.

Aidan's bedroom door is closed. I knock, softly in case he's sleeping, but there's no answer.

The police questioned us both last night—separately, in different interview rooms, like we were two suspects who might conspire to make our stories sync up. Because Aidan is over eighteen, it turns out they didn't have to call his parents.

He was quiet on the ride back to the house, barely speaking.

I wasn't exactly talkative, either.

As I head down to the main floor, I glance out one of the windows that overlooks the street.

A patrol car sits at the far end of the driveway. Jensen told Aunt Jet that it will be there twenty-four hours a day, watching the house, making sure Joey doesn't get anywhere near me.

Morbidly, I wonder if this is the best plan. Wouldn't an unmarked car be better? Wouldn't they want Joey to try to get close to me so they can grab him?

Maybe I've just watched too many movies.

Jet's voice drifts down the hallway as I make my way to the kitchen. "Surely I've got vacation days left. Or sick days. Or someone could trade shifts." She's sitting at the table, a cup of coffee and the remains of a piece of toast next to her elbow. Her shoulders are hunched inside a voluminous black sweater. She listens for a moment, then stands and hangs up the phone.

"Is everything okay?"

"No." She wraps her sweater more tightly around herself. "I have to go into work."

I have zero appetite, but I grab an orange from the fruit bowl on the counter. I pass it from palm to palm, using it to keep my hands occupied in a futile attempt to calm my nerves. "I'll be fine," I say, voice filled with way more confidence than I feel. "I saw the patrol car out front. The cops will keep an eye on the house, and it's not like I'll be alone. Noah is coming back today. Besides, Sam and Marie are here. Aidan's here."

Aunt Jet carries her dishes to the sink. She throws out the remainder of the toast and then rinses out her coffee mug. "Aidan's staying with Chase for a few days."

Stung, I mentally race through everything that happened last night. Maybe he thinks I'm too dangerous to be around after seeing those photos in the trailer. Or maybe the kiss was so bad that he doesn't want to deal with the awkwardness of being in the same house. It was only my third kiss, and I'm not sure the first two really count. It stands to reason that I might have been bad. That I might even have been awful. *Oh, God. What if it was the worst kiss he's ever had?*

On some level, I suspect the fact that I'm worried about my kissing skills—or lack thereof—at this precise moment in time is deeply messed up.

Aunt Jet sets the now-clean mug in the drying rack and turns to face me. "I thought it would be best if he wasn't here for a little while—at least until I figure out what to do."

"What to do about what?"

"About whether or not to let him keep renting a room. Joey Paquet is one of Aidan's friends. You never would have met him if it hadn't been for Aidan."

"*Was*," I say, voice sharp. "Joey Paquet *was* one of Aidan's friends. It's not like Aidan knew."

"He took you to that party. You were alone with him in the woods. Do you think I wasn't your age once? Do you think I don't know what kids do?"

I open my mouth to tell her that I wasn't having sex with Aidan out in the woods, that I haven't had sex with anyone, but catch myself. Even if something had happened, I wouldn't have anything to apologize for or explain. "Aidan pays rent. You can't just kick him out. You're not being fair."

"Being a parent isn't always about being fair, Mary Catherine."

"You're not my parent." I know it's a low blow the second the words leave my mouth, but it's too late to take them back.

"You're right, but I'm trying." Looking even more tired than when I first arrived, Jet walks past me and heads upstairs.

I feel like I'm upset at everyone. Me for being too hard on Jet. Jet for being too hard on Aidan. Aidan for not saying goodbye when he left, and Noah for being in Saint John—though I know that one's not fair given the circumstances.

As soon as I hear Jet turn on the shower to get ready for work, I swipe her cell phone to check her contacts. I'm leaving anyway: At this point, what's the worst that can happen if she catches me? Her passcode is embarrassingly easy to crack: 1149—the street address of Montgomery House. She has all of the tenants' cell phone numbers saved. When I call Aidan, though, I go straight to voice mail. I google Chase and get his parents' number just as I hear the shower turn off.

I try calling Chase after Jet leaves. Apparently, they don't have call-waiting in Canada because each time I phone, the line is busy. Maybe it's a good thing that I can't get through. Maybe it's some sort of cosmic sign that the conversation I need to have with Aidan—about the kiss, about the trailer, about the fact that he's basically homeless because of me—is better face-to-face.

As far as I know, the order to stay inside for the remainder of my time in town comes from Jet and not the police, but just to be on the safe side, I use the back door and cut through the hedge to the Frasers' yard. If Jet were a parent, she'd know better than to leave and trust me to stay inside. Then again, what normal person in my position would want to go out?

The sight of Noah's empty house gives me a small pang, but I remind myself that he'll be home today. Unlike the stuff going on with Aidan, I didn't have to wonder whether or not it was better to wait and tell him about the trailer in person. Besides, I know he has to be there for his mom. If I had called him, he'd have been torn between staying with her and rushing back. I couldn't be the one to put him in that position.

I think about the wallet and those missing screenplay pages and shiver. No: it's definitely better to wait and tell Noah in person.

Given that every cop in town is out looking for Joey, I don't think he's stupid enough to come near me in broad daylight, but my stomach twists up into the mother of all knots as I step out onto the street.

Riverside Avenue is never exactly bustling, but it's downright dead this morning. No cars. No people sipping coffee on massive porches or kids riding their bikes. I tell myself it's my imagination, but the quiet makes me angsty and jittery as I walk down the block.

Because it's so quiet, I have no trouble hearing a car roll up behind me. I tense and turn, but it's just the police cruiser from the driveway.

Buddy—he of the red hair and hospital duty—pulls even with me and then leans out the driver-side window. "Are you trying to get me suspended?"

I guess maybe Aunt Jet and the police are on the same page

regarding restriction of my movement after all.

Across the street, a woman lets her dog out and then keeps the door open, watching us with interest.

"Am I under house arrest?"

"Nope."

"So just not allowed out on my own?"

"Right."

I glance across the street. The dog finishes its business, but the woman continues to stare. *Doesn't anyone just watch TV anymore?* I think. Sighing, I walk around the car and climb into the passenger side.

Three pine tree–shaped air fresheners hang from the rearview mirror, filling the car with the sickeningly overpowering scent of a fake forest.

Buddy looks at me, confused. "What do you think you're doing?"

"I have to go somewhere. You're going to follow me anyway, right?"

He nods.

I reach out and flick one of the air fresheners with my thumb and index finger. It crashes against the others. Trying to channel the easy confidence that Aidan seems to wear so well, I say, "Well then, you might as well drive me. It'll save time."

TWENTY-SEVEN

SAYING CHASE'S MOM DOES NOT LOOK HAPPY TO SEE ME IS
an understatement. The last time I was over, she smiled at me
warmly and offered me a freshly baked cookie. This time when
she opens the door, her chin seems to shift several inches to the
right with an audible pop as her gaze travels from my face to the
police cruiser parked in her driveway.

"This is not a good time," she says, moving to close the door
before I can get a single word out.

"Who is it?" Chase's voice comes from somewhere in the depths
of the house.

"No one," says his mother at the exact same moment I say, "It's
Cat."

Chase appears behind her in the hallway. "Let her in, Mom."

"Chase, honey," she says, a pleading, desperate note in her
voice, "think about the neighbors. Think about what they'll say."

"I want to talk to Cat." His tone is respectful but firm.

"Honey . . ."

"Mom, I'm going to talk to my friend. If you won't let her in, we'll just go somewhere else."

She hesitates, trying to gauge how serious he is, then sighs and retreats.

Chase opens the door wide and glances at the police car. "They following you everywhere?"

I nod.

"They were here this morning. They searched the whole house. They thought maybe I was hiding him." *Him*, not Joey. "That's part of what's got her so wound up: that the neighbors saw the cops tearing the house apart. She doesn't want them thinking the police are back."

He waits for me to cross the threshold and then closes the door. His eyes are bloodshot and his clothes are wrinkled; I'm not positive, but I'm pretty sure they're the same clothes he was wearing last night.

A trio of bags—duffel, laptop, camera—rests against the wall a few feet from the door. I touch the duffel bag with the toe of my sneaker.

"Aidan dumped his stuff and left," says Chase. "Ask me how happy my mom is to have him here."

"Sorry." I follow him downstairs to the rec room. "My aunt is being . . . I don't actually know what she's being, but I can't believe she kicked him out."

"Everyone is losing it. Myself included." Chase sits down, hard, in the middle of the sofa. A video game is paused on the flat screen. He picks up the controller and sets it back into motion.

I perch on the arm of the couch while, on-screen, a tiny version of Chase shoots at a bunch of what I can only assume are space aliens. Either he's horrible at this particular game or he's too upset to do much damage. "Where'd Aidan go?"

Chase grunts. "He wanted to talk to Skylar."

Skylar . . .

Thinking about her makes everything seem even more impossibly awful. "I saw her at the police station—just for a second. I don't know if I should try to call her."

"And say what? 'Sorry I told the police your boyfriend might be a serial killer'?"

I flinch. Chase catches the movement. "It's not like you guys had a choice. I'm just saying she's upset. She might not want to see you or Aidan right now. Not that Aidan listened when I tried to tell him this."

"Have you talked to her?"

On the screen, the tiny pixel version of Chase is getting his ass thoroughly kicked. "I texted her this morning. After the cops were here. I'm not allowed to go over there. Mom's never really liked Skylar all that much. Now she thinks Skylar knew."

I think about those pictures of classic movie monsters on the trailer walls. Some of them were the same monsters Skylar likes to wear on pins. And the ribbon holding the screenplay pages together looked so much like the ribbon I've seen her wear in her hair. But just as soon as those thoughts fill my head, others come rushing in. The way Skylar didn't laugh when I told her I wanted to be the kind of person who could fight monsters. Her voice in the dark as we whispered secrets. How kind and concerned she is.

That girl wouldn't knowingly be with someone capable of such monstrous things. "She didn't know," I say. "There's no way she knew."

"That's what I said. But given that I didn't know my best friend was a monster, I'm thinking I might not be the greatest judge of character."

"Aidan didn't know, either."

Chase grunts. "Aidan's only been here a year. Joey's been my best friend since before first grade." He tosses the controller. It hits the carpet with a muffled thump. "He used to be bigger than me. Did you know that?"

I shake my head.

"All through elementary school. I got picked on because I was small and my dad was the principal. Joey looked out for me. And now . . ." He runs a hand roughly over his face. "Aidan told me what you guys found. None of it makes any sense. You heard him up in Aidan's room. Why feed us all that bullshit about monsters and needing to talk to Rachel if he was the one who did that to her in the first place?"

I've been thinking about that, too. I've been wondering if we aren't all just characters in Joey's shitty movie script. Pieces for him to manipulate and move around. What was it Aidan said to me the day we met? Something about writers being like gods . . . It's like Joey took that idea literally.

"You know what really freaks me out?" says Chase.

"Everything?"

He continues as if I hadn't spoken. "They impounded his car. It's a crime scene. When the cops were here, I overheard them say they found one of Rachel's earrings in the trunk. Just sitting there. They think it snagged on something and broke free. Up until that point, I kept thinking there must have been some kind of mistake. When I heard that, though, I realized I was just an idiot."

I stare at him, not following.

"I was in his car the day after Rachel disappeared. We were trying to fix the taillights. If I had been paying more attention, if I hadn't been so stupid, if I had just noticed the earring, then maybe none of this would be happening."

"Chase . . . That was after the fact. It wouldn't have stopped anything. It wouldn't have helped Rachel."

"You think so?" he asks, and his voice sounds more like a scared little kid than a seventeen-year-old varsity athlete. He looks young and frightened. He looks the way he did that night on the riverbank.

"I know so."

And I do.

There had been a moment, that night we all watched the movie down here, when Joey and I had reached for the same can of Coke. I don't think he even noticed, but I had. Because I notice every small movement in relation to my position. Because I constantly make adjustments. Dozens, sometimes hundreds a day, to avoid coming into contact with other people.

What if I hadn't tried so hard that night? What if I had made a grab for the can and skimmed Joey's hand? Would I have seen anything useful?

Chase couldn't have stopped what happened—I truly believe that. But me? Me, I'm a lot less certain about.

* * *

Officer Buddy is not in a good mood by the time I slip out of Chase's house. I guess having to babysit me while the rest of the force is out on a manhunt must kind of suck. When I try to quiz him about the earring and whether or not the police found anything else in Joey's car, he asks what he ever did to make me hate him.

After that, the rest of the drive is silent.

As we approach Montgomery House, a figure detaches itself from the shadows on the porch and bounds down the steps.

Buddy tenses. His left hand curls more tightly around the steering wheel while he reaches down toward the seat with his right.

It takes me a second to realize that he's reaching for his holster.

"It's Noah," I say, forcing my voice to stay steady even though I'm suddenly shaking. I want to yell, but yelling at a skittish, twenty-something cop who is reaching for his gun seems like a very bad idea. "It's Noah Fraser. It's not Joey."

I can visibly see the tension drain out of Buddy's shoulders as he lets out a long breath and hits the brakes.

Gruffly, not meeting my gaze, he tells me to get out of the car and go inside. "Do me a favor and don't even try to sneak out again."

I nod weakly and climb out of the car. I'm still shaking as I slam the passenger door.

I take one step and then two, and then Noah is there.

"Cat . . ." He starts to reach for me but catches himself.

I'm not that strong. I close the distance between us and press my face to his shirt. I don't know what to do with my arms, so I

283

leave them at my sides. Gently, carefully, he puts his hands on my shoulders, keeping the contact to where it's safe.

It's not a real hug, but it's close, and I allow myself to sink in.

It's like the day Noah hugged me at the mill to try to protect me. It's like the day Riley kept me from falling and the memory of hearing him say "safe" inside Amber's head.

"Cat, what happened? What's going on?"

I don't answer Noah right away. I don't care that Buddy is probably watching or that being this close to someone is dangerous. I just want to feel safe. Just for a little while.

TWENTY-EIGHT

AFTER WHAT FEELS LIKE SEVERAL MINUTES BUT PROBABLY isn't really that long, I force myself to step away from Noah's embrace. After years of never letting myself be held, the loss of the sensation feels a little like some sort of blow. "Come on," I say, throat oddly tight. "I'll tell you inside."

Once we're in my room with the door tightly closed behind us, I tell him almost everything.

There are only three things I leave out:

What, exactly, I saw in Amber's head, because some things shouldn't be shared.

That I kissed Aidan.

That I'm leaving in a few days.

I don't know why I can't seem to tell him that last one. Maybe because I promised to help him and leaving feels like letting him—not to mention Riley and Rachel—down. Maybe it's just that I haven't yet resigned myself to the idea of going, and telling

Noah will make it feel real.

He's quiet for a long time after I finish.

"What are you thinking?" I ask finally. We're both sitting on my narrow bed, our backs against the wall.

"About the wallet. About how it means I was right and Riley's really gone. Everyone's going to have to accept it now. Someone is going to have to tell my mother. *I'm* going to have to tell my mother." He clenches and unclenches his left hand.

"It might not mean . . . *that*," I say gently. "I know you believe he's gone, and I understand why, but we don't really know what the trailer does—and doesn't—prove. We don't even know if Riley was in the script. I never saw his name, and there were pages missing."

"Come on, Cat . . ."

"What?"

"Even if you didn't see Riley's name, who else could Joey have been writing about?"

"It's Joey. I can see him hating a lot of guys in varsity jackets. Chase aside."

"Yeah, and how many of those guys hooked up with a girl he brought to a party—a girl he ended up dating? Even if you take the screenplay out of the equation," Noah continues, "there's still the wallet."

"Joey could have stolen it before Riley went missing or found it afterward. Maybe he just thought it would be some kind of twisted joke, finding the medal and then leaving it with Rachel . . ." I think about the wallet. Something about the wallet bothers me, but it takes me a moment to put my finger on it. That raised circle on the leather had to be from the medal, but . . . the medal had been on a long cord. That's how Rachel had held on to it in the water: the cord had been tangled around her fingers. That cord was way too long to squeeze into that tiny slot in the wallet. Even the silver chain the medal had hung from when Riley first found it probably wouldn't have fit.

Noah runs a hand over his face roughly, then pushes himself to his feet. He walks over to the Styrofoam model of the solar system and taps Mars lightly, sending it spinning. "I remember you guys making this. You ran out of red paint. Riley wouldn't shut up about it until Mom went out and got you more."

I don't remember the paint or Noah being there. I just remember carrying the mobile home, taking the long way around so that it wouldn't get caught on the hedge, trying to keep the strings from tangling.

Tangled strings: that's what it feels like everything is now. Bits and pieces that should form straight lines, but the threads are all too twisted for anything to make sense.

As my gaze travels over the mobile, I try to slap a label on each Styrofoam shape, imagining each one as a piece of information.

Riley's disappearance. Finding Rachel. The marks on Rachel's arms and the medal. The things I saw when I touched her at the hospital. My eyes fall back on Mars, on the spinning red sphere.

Red . . .

"When I touched Rachel, I saw taillights. Red taillights in the dark."

Noah turns to me. "So?"

"The taillights in Joey's car don't work. They haven't worked

287

the whole time I've been in Montgomery Falls. It couldn't have been his car I saw in Rachel's head."

"Then how do you explain the earring the police found in his trunk?"

"Maybe it got there after? Maybe he kept it—like a souvenir or something." That's what serial killers do, right? They take souvenirs. That's what happens in all of the movies. "And there's something else: Rachel said it was early when she left work, but the scenes I saw in her head were definitely at night. Joey went with Skylar, Chase, and me to the movies that evening, and it wasn't full dark when we left the theater. He would have had to grab Rachel before the movie and stash her somewhere."

"He could have just left her in the trunk."

"Not his trunk. If it had been his trunk, she wouldn't have seen the taillights later. Besides, he couldn't have left her downtown for all that time. There's too big a chance that someone would have heard her." I shiver and push myself to the edge of the bed. The idea that Joey sat through an entire movie with Skylar, Chase, and me after taking Rachel is beyond creepy and messed up.

"You're saying he used someone else's car to transport Rachel after it got dark . . . Maybe even to grab her in the first place . . . You're saying finding the earring was just luck."

"Does that sound totally ridiculous?"

"No, but then whose car was it?"

"And did they know what he was using it for?"

Noah walks back toward the bed. "You said there were things in the trailer that reminded you of Skylar. We know she had reasons to hate Rachel—and my brother—and she has a car."

"She never told me she hated Riley," I say quickly.

Noah shoots me an exasperated look, one that says I'm being obtuse. "Whose car did you guys take to the movies that night?"

"Chase's. Chase and Skylar picked me up in his mom's car. Joey met us downtown."

"And you're sure Joey drove his own car?"

"He said he did. He said he had to get home before it got too late because of the taillights."

"But you didn't actually see the car?"

I try to think back to that night. The movie theater in Montgomery Falls doesn't have a parking lot. Chase had parked a few blocks away. We ran into Joey on the walk over, but I don't remember what direction he had been coming from. "No," I concede. "I didn't see his car."

"So it's possible Skylar let him use her car and that's why she asked Chase to drive."

"No."

"Cat . . ."

I cross my arms tightly over my chest. I know I'm not being reasonable, but I can't help it. "She's my friend." Maybe I hadn't meant for it to happen, but it had.

"We have to at least consider—"

"Not yet. Not until we're out of possibilities. Not unless we have to."

Noah stares at me for a long moment and then gives a small, tired nod. "All right. Is there anything else you remember about the trailer? Any sign that someone other than Joey could have been there?"

I push myself to my feet and retrieve the folder from the desk.

After separating me from Aidan, the police had dumped me in an interview room. Someone had left a pen on the table. I'd scrounged a take-out bag from the trash and written down every detail I could remember about the trailer, desperately trying to get it all out because my brain was already attempting to put as much distance between me and that small space as possible.

I hand the list to Noah. "This is everything I could remember. Somehow, I didn't think that they'd let us go back for a second look or that Jensen would show us the crime scene photos."

Noah shoots me an appreciative, approving look and then scans the list. "You didn't tell me about the pictures with the scratched-out eyes. Harding is going to have nightmares photographing this stuff."

"Not Harding," I say. "There was already someone on the way to take photos when we left. Some photographer on loan from the police department in Saint John. One of the officers was complaining about having to wait for her before they could start going through things."

"I guess using Harding was a one-off. Were there really this many photos of Rachel?"

I nod.

"And four of you?"

"I think so." I glance at the window, making sure the curtains are still shut. A thin strip of sunlight falls through a small gap. I have to fight the urge to get up, to readjust, to secure. Noah is here. The cops are here—or at least Buddy is here. I'm safe. "I'm going to get a Coke. Do you want one?" I'm not really thirsty; I just need to do something before I break down and duct-tape cardboard over the window.

"Sure," says Noah absently, still focused on the list. "Hey, what do you mean 'big'?"

I pause at the door and turn back. "What?"

He crosses the room, paper in hand, and then points to spots where I've jotted *big* next to some of the descriptions of photos. I shrug and hold my hands apart. "Not poster-sized, but close."

"So he blew up pictures of both you and Rachel?"

"And some of the other girls," I say. I head down the hall, grateful for a small break, as Noah goes back to the list.

I don't know why, but the fact that some of the photos had been enlarged makes the whole thing even more disturbing somehow. It's like a regular picture wasn't creepy enough. Wasn't *intimate* enough. I mean, where do you even get something like that done?

Downstairs, Marie is making a tuna sandwich while Brisby winds himself around her ankles, begging for a taste.

"How long do you think the cops will be here?" she asks as I head to the fridge.

I shrug.

"It's kind of unnerving, having them just sit outside. When I moved in, your aunt promised a quiet, safe building. This isn't what I signed on for."

I want to say something sharp and sarcastic—because, really, she can't honestly think any of us have any control over this—but if Jet does kick Aidan out, she'll need Marie's rent checks that much more. With effort, I ignore her and pull open the fridge.

As I reach for two cans of Coke, my eyes drift to the inside of the door, to two small canisters of film.

Aidan was in a photography club with Joey . . .

Abandoning the drinks, I head for the phone.

I pull Chase's number out of my pocket and pray his mom doesn't answer as I dial. Chase picks up on the fifth ring. When he hears my voice, he hands Aidan the phone without being asked.

"You were in a photography club with Joey, right?"

"Hello to you, too." There's an undercurrent of what sounds like exhaustion and annoyance beneath Aidan's usual charm.

I guess I can't blame him for being tired and upset. "I'm sorry about Aunt Jet," I say. "She's not being fair."

"I did introduce you to a serial killer, take you to a party where there was underage drinking, and compromise your virtue. I can sort of understand why she's pissed."

Despite the situation, I blush. Stupidly, I'm glad Noah is upstairs. "Pretty sure the compromising was fifty-fifty."

"Let it never be said that I don't find strong women incredibly attractive."

Maybe the kiss wasn't so horrible after all.

I can hear Chase in the background, asking how Aidan can flirt at a time like this. Aidan tells him to be quiet and then focuses back on me. "What were you saying about the photo club?"

"You were in it with Joey, right?"

"Yeah."

"The pictures in the trailer—the really big ones—where would you get them printed? How would you get them printed?"

"The copy center could do it. Or someone with a big enough printer."

"But not a regular printer?"

"Nah. The paper is too big. Someone with access to a darkroom could do it, too, I guess. They'd need an enlarger and the right supplies. And they'd have to know what they were doing."

I start to pace. Four steps forward—as far as the phone cord allows. Four steps back. Repeat. "Does Joey have one of those special printers?"

"No. They'd be expensive."

"And Joey doesn't have the money?"

"Cat . . . Joey's parents run a video rental store in the age of streaming."

"What about a darkroom? Could he use a darkroom?"

"Maybe, I guess. The guy who runs the photo club used to give Joey private lessons. He has this whole darkroom setup in his house. He told Joey he was wasting his talent by wanting to write. He even tried to talk to Joey's parents about it, but they thought there was something weird about the whole thing. Like he was taking too much of an interest in Joey or something. Joey crashed at Chase's for a week after that."

A weight settles in my stomach. "The photographer—is his name Harding?"

"Yeah, how'd you know?"

Instead of answering, I ask, "Does he ever let Joey use his darkroom?"

Aidan is quiet for a minute. "I don't think so," he says finally.

"Where else could Joey go?"

"The high school has an old darkroom, but the equipment is crap and it's locked up for the summer. The university might have one."

"So that's it? The copy place or Harding's house or maybe the university? Those are the only three places Joey could have gotten photos like that printed?"

Aidan lets out a long sigh. Sounding a little exasperated, he says, "I don't know, Cat. I mean, he could have gone down to Saint John. There are probably a bunch of places down there that could do it—hell, I'm pretty sure Saint John has a Walmart and maybe even a Costco. I think both of those places might let you upload photos and pick up prints. They might let you do oversized ones, for all I know."

"Does Joey go to Saint John a lot?"

"He and Skylar take road trips sometimes. They took one a few days ago."

Right. Skylar had asked me to go.

"What makes you think any of this is important?" Aidan asks.

"I don't know. Maybe it's not." I stop pacing and twist the phone cord around my finger. "Chase said you went to talk to Skylar. Is she okay?"

"She's in complete denial. Guess I can't blame her." A relieved note creeps into his voice at the slight shift in topic. I think about how miserable Chase looked when I saw him. Joey is Aidan's friend, too. I can't imagine how hard this whole thing is for him.

A floorboard squeaks. I glance up. Noah is standing in the doorway, folder in hand. "Aidan, I gotta go. I'll work on Aunt Jet, okay?"

He starts to say something else, but whatever it is comes too late as I hang up and turn to Noah.

"What did Aidan want?"

"Nothing. I called him." There's a small, bluish circle around my index finger from wrapping the phone cord too tightly. "I was thinking about those photos. The big ones. Aidan was in a photography club with Joey. I called to ask him where Joey could have had them printed."

"And?"

"The copy shop or a darkroom if he got them done around here. But Aidan also said Joey could have had them printed in Saint John. Joey was there with Skylar a few days ago."

I try to remember the exact images of myself in the trailer. What I was wearing. Where I was standing. I think all of them must have been taken at least a week ago, but I'm not certain. "There's something else . . . . maybe nothing . . ."

I sit at the table. Marie had slipped out of the kitchen while I was on the phone, but she'd left her dirty plate behind.

Noah sits across from me. "What is it?"

"Aidan said Harding took Joey on as a sort of protégé, that he gave him private photo lessons. He said that Joey's parents thought there was something strange about it. And he said Harding has a darkroom in his house. I keep thinking it's weird that the police department would use him to photograph the spot where we found Rachel and then use someone from Saint John to photograph the trailer." I swallow. "What if Harding wasn't at the riverbank because the police sent him? What if he was there because he knew what had happened the night before? Because

295

Joey told him or because he's some sort of creepy serial killer mentor . . . What if I was wrong about the hellfire stuff I saw not meaning anything?"

Noah swears under his breath. He opens the folder, pulls out a sheet of paper, and slides it across the table. "Third line down."

Paul Harding. My breath catches in my throat. I've looked at this sheet of paper before, but for some reason, Harding's name never stood out to me. And yet there it is. He took photos of the basketball team the afternoon of March 19.

Paul Harding was one of the last people to see Riley on the day he disappeared.

TWENTY-NINE

DITCHING OFFICER BUDDY IS A LOT EASIER IN THE BMW.
"You know you're going to get in trouble for this, right?" I ask, bracing myself with one hand against the dash as Noah takes a corner too sharply.

"Technically, I'm not running from the police: you are."

"Fair point."

We had called the copy place out by the industrial park. They did prints that size all the time, but the guy we spoke to couldn't remember any pictures of girls taken through bedroom windows. "Don't take this the wrong way," he had said, "but I wouldn't go around taking photos like that. It sounds like a good way to get your ass kicked."

The print shops in Saint John were a lot more difficult. We found six places that could do it, but citing customer privacy, each and every one refused to either confirm or deny that they had printed photos matching our descriptions.

While their loyalty to their customers was admirable, it was also really, really inconvenient. After that, Noah called the police station and chatted up the woman covering the front desk. He told her he was a criminology student at the university with a background in photography and asked if they ever used independent photographers. She told him they always used a photographer from Saint John and then asked for his website because she was looking for someone to take her engagement photos.

Noah turns onto a stretch of road that leads out of town. The houses are spaced farther apart out here and eventually give way to undeveloped countryside. "I still don't feel good about this," I say.

"I know," he says. "But it'll be all right."

Easy for him to say. I wanted to go straight to Harding's and stake out his house while we came up with some sort of plan—to do what, I wasn't sure—but Noah convinced me we should find and talk to Skylar first.

I slump a little farther down in the passenger seat.

"Cat . . ." He takes his eyes off the road, just for a second, and meets my anxious gaze with one that is uncannily calm and steady. "It will be okay. I promise. She doesn't hate you."

I swallow. "How did you know that's what I'm afraid of?"

"Because for someone who spends so much time trying to keep everyone at a distance, you do get attached to people."

"And how would you know that?"

"You have a remarkably bad poker face."

Noah slows the car as we approach a sleek, angular house surrounded by acres of empty land and a tall wrought-iron fence.

"I didn't know that's who lived here," he says, pulling up to an intercom.

I'm not sure what I was expecting, but a building that looks like it could grace the cover of *Architectural Digest* definitely wasn't it. Nothing about Skylar suggests she comes from this kind of money. Not her clothes or her car—nice but lower end—or the fact that she works at the movie theater.

Noah leans out the window and presses a button on the intercom.

"Yes?" A sharp, masculine voice comes through with a crackle of static.

"Is Skylar home?"

"Who is asking?" There's a hint of an accent around the words.

I unbuckle my seat belt and lean across Noah. I'm careful, but he still presses himself against the seat to minimize the chance of skin touching skin. *It's not personal*, I tell myself, *he's just being considerate*. For some reason, though, maybe because of how close we'd been just a few hours ago, the caution hurts. "My name is Cat—Cat Montgomery. I'm friends with Skylar."

"My daughter isn't here."

"Do you know where she is or when she'll be back?"

"Ms. Montgomery, Skylar snuck out an hour ago. She did not tell us where she was going. She did not ask permission."

He doesn't sound worried. He sounds angry.

Before I can even come up with a reply, the intercom disconnects with a click.

I settle back in my seat.

"Seems like a nice guy," says Noah. "He didn't even ask us to call him if we find her. Do you think he's telling the truth?"

"I don't know." I climb out of the car and follow the fence until it meets a ravine with sides so steep you'd need a grappling hook and a rope to make your way down. Slices of the house are visible through the fence. Sharp, hard angles and tinted windows. Even if Skylar's father is lying, there isn't any way to get close enough to the house to prove it.

I try to imagine Skylar living inside. Skylar with her boundless energy and the way she practically skips when she walks. It does not look like the kind of place where anyone ever skips. A heavy weight settles over me as I turn my back on the house.

"Okay," says Noah once I'm back in the car, "you've just found out your boyfriend is a serial killer on the run. Where do you go?"

It occurs to me that everyone's been throwing that phrase around. Serial killer. Even I've been doing it. But you can't be a serial killer unless you've killed. Does that mean, on some level, I've accepted that Riley is really, really gone? I know there have been moments when I've felt close to accepting it—when I thought maybe I even had accepted it—but I'm not sure I ever truly let myself believe it.

"Cat?"

I swallow and rub my eyes with the edge of my sleeve. I force myself to focus, but it's a minute before I trust myself to speak. "If you're Skylar, you don't think Joey did it. So I guess you try to find proof."

Noah throws the car into reverse and pulls out of the driveway. "Let's start with the riverbank."

* * *

We do not find Skylar at the riverbank. Or at the trailer in the woods—now roped off with police tape—or at the diner where Rachel works. With each stop, it feels more and more like we're just chasing our tails.

Even if we do find her, I have no idea what we'll say. If Aidan couldn't get through to her, what are the chances she'll listen to Noah and me?

"Where would she go if she was upset?" Noah asks as he steers us toward downtown.

"I have no idea." The fact that I don't have a clue bothers me. I feel useless.

Noah hangs a left, taking us past Aunt Jet's church.

"Wait!"

He slams on the brakes. The driver behind us blares his horn and pulls around us, shouting obscenities, but Noah is too focused on scanning the street to respond. "Joey?"

"Skylar. She has keys to the church. She uses them to get in and set up for the Sunday school classes."

"You're joking."

I shake my head. Noah checks to make sure there isn't another car behind us and then pulls a U-turn into the parking lot.

The main door is locked, but a side door is open.

"Maybe you should wait out here?" I suggest. "If Skylar is in there, she might be more likely to talk if it's just me."

"And if Joey is in there?"

My stomach twists at the thought. "Good point."

We slip inside and make our way down a carpeted hallway that smells like old hymnbooks and, slightly more improbably, day-old macaroni and cheese. The lights are off; the only illumination comes from frosted-glass windows as we pass empty offices and classrooms.

I'm starting to wonder if the church didn't just happen to get left unlocked, if this isn't just another dead end, when we reach the chapel. There, seven rows from the back, sitting in the middle of a pew, is Skylar. Her eyes are closed and her lips are moving; she has a pair of earbuds in her ears. There's no sign of anyone else. Just Skylar and the stained-glass saints.

"Wait here?" I say softly. "Please?"

Noah opens his mouth to object, then lets out a weary sigh. Even he can see Skylar is alone in the chapel. He takes two steps back—just far enough that he won't be seen. "If anything seems off, scream."

"And you'll come running to my rescue?"

"Given that I haven't done a very good job of keeping you safe so far, it's the least I can do." He doesn't look like he's joking. He looks sad and serious.

I know it's a bad idea, but on impulse, I rise up on tiptoe and brush my lips against his cheek. It's been a day or two since he's shaved, and the stubble is surprisingly rough. I don't try to control what happens, and the contact is so brief that I catch only the barest hint of images and none last long enough for me to make any sense of them.

But while I can't make sense of what I see, I know I don't see myself. The realization falls into my stomach like a stone and sinks heavily to the bottom.

"What was that for?" he asks. Surprise gives way to concern as he studies my face. "What's wrong? What did you see?"

"Nothing," I say, which is the truth. It's stupid, but until this moment—until the moment I didn't see myself—I didn't really understand just how much the way I feel about Noah has been changing.

I didn't *let* myself understand.

Because he's Riley's brother.

Because I don't let myself feel that way about anyone.

Because it's big and scary and dangerous. For some reason, far, far scarier than the idea that Aidan might be into me.

A small headache builds, but the pain is nothing compared to what else I'm feeling.

I'm a little horrified to realize that Noah's face is blurry.

"It's nothing," I say again, wiping my eyes roughly with the heel of my hand. And that's what it has to be right now. Nothing. "Stay here."

I don't give him a chance to ask any more questions; I just slip into the chapel and head down the aisle.

Skylar's music is so loud that I can hear it while I'm still several feet away, but despite the deafening blare, she somehow senses my presence. Her eyes fly open and she lets out a small, startled gasp as her mouth forms a perfect O. She pushes herself a few inches down the bench, but doesn't bolt.

That's something, at least, I tell myself.

She fumbles with her phone, pausing her music. "You're wasting your time. My parents and the police and Chase already tried to get me to tell them where Joey is."

"Do you actually know?"

A blush creeps over her cheeks. The fact that she doesn't answer is an answer in and of itself. "I wouldn't take it personally. He's probably trying to keep you from getting dragged into things." Taking a chance that she won't run, I slip into the pew and sit. I'm careful to leave a few feet of space between us—enough space, hopefully, that she feels like she has breathing room.

Her brows pull together as though she's looking for some sort of lie in the words, but there isn't one. Joey might be a monster, but he's not an idiot. Keeping Skylar in the dark eliminates the chance the police can use her against him.

"I don't know where he is."

"Okay."

She plays with a button on her jacket: the Bela Lugosi pin that had been on her uniform the first time we met. "You believe me?"

I shrug. "Sure."

"Why are you here?"

"There were photos in the trailer. I was hoping you could tell me where Joey got them developed."

"The police already asked me. There's no proof Joey took them or that he was ever at that place."

"You saw the pictures?"

Skylar is wearing a loose flannel shirt over a dark gray dress. Even though it's warm in the church, she wraps the shirt a little more tightly around herself, clinging to the fabric with her fingertips. "They showed me the photos when they came to search the house. Some from the trailer and some they said they found in Joey's room."

"They found photos in Joey's room?" That's news.

"They weren't his. I don't know how they ended up there, but they weren't his." Skylar's voice rises several octaves. I glance toward the door and catch the briefest glimpse of Noah as he sticks his head into the chapel to make sure I'm still okay.

I wave him off. "Why are you so sure Joey didn't take the photos?"

Saying each word slowly and fiercely, eyes flashing, Skylar says, "Because I know Joey. He was one of the only people who was decent to me after what happened with Riley."

I shake my head. "Skylar . . . that doesn't prove anything— other than maybe he had a reason to hate Riley and Rachel."

"The police said that, too. Maybe he had a reason to hate them, but that doesn't mean he would have hurt them. He wouldn't hurt anybody."

I decide to try something else. "Do you know anything about Paul Harding?"

Confusion flashes across her face. "The guy who takes the yearbook photos?"

I nod.

"Joey took lessons from him last year. He's supposed to help him teach a workshop tonight." Her breath hitches a little bit and her eyes fill with tears. "Was supposed to," she corrects. "He was supposed to help him tonight. At the rec center."

I reach into my pocket and pull out a crumpled Kleenex. I hold it out to her, but she makes no move to reach for it.

The suspicion on her face hurts, even though I tell myself that it's understandable.

"Take it," I say gently.

305

After a long moment, she seems to realize that I'm prepared to hold my arm out forever. She takes the tissue, blows her nose, and then inhales deeply. Her posture becomes the tiniest bit less rigid as the walls lower at least a few inches. "He didn't do it, Cat. I don't care what everyone thinks. Joey didn't hurt Rachel or Riley."

She's so sure—naively sure—that I want to shake her. I want to shake her and I want to protect her because I'm scared that if she doesn't come to her senses, she'll end up hurt.

"How do you explain the things in the trailer? Forget the photos," I say, when she opens her mouth to protest. "What about the screenplay? Or Riley's wallet? Or the earring they found in Joey's trunk?"

"I know it looks bad, but there has to be some other explanation. I told you: Joey would never hurt anyone. I don't care what anybody says. Everyone is looking for him because they think he did something awful, but no one is worried that he hasn't been heard from in almost two days. Even Chase doesn't care, and Chase is supposed to be his best friend."

"Can you blame him?"

Instantly, the walls go back up. Skylar pushes herself to her feet and turns to walk away.

I don't think; I just act.

Before she can get more than a step or two, I'm on my feet. I grab her arm, pushing her sleeve up so that I can touch as much skin as possible, trying, as best as I can, to see her fear. I have to. I have to find Joey—not just for Noah or Riley and Rachel, but because if I don't, Skylar is going to get hurt.

Around me, stained-glass saints shatter into a million pieces

306

and reknit themselves into new patterns—

"We are the monsters." The letters rise above me, oddly familiar. The phrase tugs at me. Like I've read it in a book or heard it in a movie. Before I can place it, the letters fall away, replaced by darkness.

Darkness and the sensation of weight. Above me, around me, pressing in.

Dripping water and dank, dark smells.

"Where are you?" Skylar's voice, my voice, echoes in the dark. Around me, the weight comes crashing down, it comes crashing down and . . .

Skylar whirls, breaking the contact, and I slam back into reality.

She stares at me, eyes wide and scared. When I glance at her arm, I see bruises. For a horrible second, I think I caused them, but then I realize that there are too many marks, like someone grabbed her over and over and pressed their fingers into her skin. Someone much stronger than I am.

I reach out and tug up her other sleeve, revealing a similar pattern of bruises.

"Did Joey do this?" My voice shakes. I'm so angry that I might fly into pieces. "Why are you protecting him? Skylar, someone who loves you could never do this."

"You don't know the first thing about anything." Tears fill her eyes again. They catch the light coming through the stained-glass windows but don't fall. She turns and runs, not past Noah, but out a side door, one that leads directly outside.

I don't chase her.

I'm not sure I can.

My head feels like it's going to split in two. My legs tremble, and I don't so much sit back down as fall, heavily, onto the pew. All around me, the saints watch, but not one offers any advice or help.

Too late, I realize that I forgot to ask her about the car—if she ever loaned it to Joey or if he knows where she keeps her keys.

THIRTY

ON THE WEST SIDE OF TOWN, PERCHED ON TOP OF A RIDIC- ulously steep hill, sits an old subdivision of identical, pocket-sized houses. War homes, Dad told me once. Houses that had been built for soldiers coming back from World War II so that they could settle down.

I try to imagine the neighborhood filled with families; I can't. A third of the houses have been razed to the ground. Half of the ones that remain have For Rent signs in their windows, trying to lure university students even though it's summer and there are nicer places to rent near campus.

Harding lives on the very last street. Behind his house is an abandoned baseball diamond that's so overgrown there are trees in the outfield. It's creepy and mosquito-filled, but it provides both cover and an excellent vantage point from which to stake out the photographer's house while we wait for him to leave.

I swat at the back of my neck as a mosquito tries to make me its dinner.

It hadn't been hard to get details about the workshop Skylar mentioned. From nine thirty to eleven, Harding will be teaching the basics of night shots and digital cameras at the rec center and the adjoining park.

Leaving his house empty—assuming Joey isn't inside.

I lift a pair of military-grade binoculars. "Are you going to tell me why you have these?" I ask Noah.

"Bird-watching," he deadpans.

"Fine. Don't tell me. I probably don't want to know anyway."

I raise the binoculars to eye level and scan the windows. All of the rooms look empty—except for the kitchen where Harding sits eating, by himself, at the table.

During the past two hours, we've also seen him read by himself, watch TV by himself, and shower by himself. I had looked away as quickly as possible when that happened—though not quite quickly enough. If Harding turns out to be a decent, innocent person, then I feel like we should leave a note in his mailbox warning him that people can see into his bathroom and suggesting he invest in blinds.

At this point, I think it's safe to assume he's not hiding Joey Paquet, but that doesn't mean he hasn't helped him. That doesn't mean the house might not hold some clue as to where Joey is or what he might be planning.

"Are you sure you're all right?" Noah asks.

It's been hours since the church. Enough time for the pain to fade, but he keeps watching me like he's expecting me to keel over.

"I told you: I'm okay." My voice comes out sharper than I intend. Ever since that moment in the church hallway—ever since the moment I kissed Noah's cheek—being around him has felt . . . really complicated.

We don't have time for complicated, so I'm trying to fake normal as best I can.

Unfortunately, as Noah so recently pointed out, I don't have a good poker face.

I set the binoculars down and shift positions. I've lost count of how many times my legs have fallen asleep. "Remind me of our cunning plan again?" I say, just because I have this theory that the more times I hear the words, the less scary they'll be.

I'm pretty sure Noah figured out what I was doing the third or fourth time I asked, but he still humors me. "We go in through the basement, look for the darkroom, search for any sign that Harding helped or has been in contact with Joey, and then get out before he comes back."

As far as plans go, it's shoddy at best. Maybe a three on a ten-point scale of cunning—if you graded on a curve. Unfortunately, neither one of us was able to come up with anything better.

"The binoculars were a gag gift from Riley," Noah says. "I got really stressed my first few months away at school. He got me the binoculars and a book on bird-watching and all these pamphlets for bird-watching festivals and tours in Ontario's cottage country. He said I needed a hobby that would help me chill."

"Did you go to any of the festivals?"

"Let's just say that the town of Petawawa's annual woodpecker festival is surprisingly pleasant."

In the distance, a door opens and then slams shut. A moment later, a car engine starts.

"There he goes," says Noah.

My nerves, already frayed, get just a little bit worse.

We stay where we are until full dark falls, and then we make our way across the field and to the house.

"Noah?"

"Yeah?"

"What if we go in and Joey's inside?"

"We've been watching for hours; I really don't think—"

"I know he's probably not," I say, cutting him off. "I was just wondering what happens if we're wrong and he is in there. Will we call the police? Will we call Jensen?"

"Sure," says Noah, "we'll call the cops." But he waits too long before saying it, and something in his eyes reminds me of what I saw that night he touched me in my room. The things he wanted to do to whoever hurt Riley. Images I've tried not to think about come rushing back, and a knot of fear forms in my chest—not fear of Noah, but fear for him.

It's too late to have second thoughts, I tell myself. *Besides, Joey's not even in there. There'd have been some sign.*

Oblivious to what I'm thinking, Noah walks the length of the house, pausing at each tiny basement window. "I guess it would be too easy if one of them was unlocked." He glances at me. "Did you find gloves?"

I nod and pull a pair of black leather gloves from my back pocket. They're two sizes too big and pool around my fingertips and wrists, but they're better than nothing.

Noah slides his backpack from his shoulder and crouches next to the house. His eyes dart from the small window to me and then back again. My cheeks grow hot as I realize he's trying to figure out if I can physically fit through the frame.

Lacey wouldn't have a problem. Or Skylar or Amber. Hell, any girl Noah has ever gone out with—including the one he left back in Ottawa—could probably fit through those windows with inches to spare. But me? I'll be a tight squeeze—if I can fit at all.

Something behind my eyes pricks and burns. Of all the things to get upset about, the possibility that I might be too big to commit felony breaking and entering has got to be one of the most ridiculous, but knowing that doesn't make me feel any better.

From the depths of his backpack, Noah produces a brick and a thick bundle of fabric. He slips on his own pair of gloves and then winds the fabric around the brick. "Ready?"

Not even a little, I think as I nod.

Even wrapped in fabric, the sound the brick makes as it shatters the glass is far too loud. I hold my breath, waiting. When nothing happens, I slowly exhale.

Noah knocks the jagged glass out from around the window and then lowers himself through. There's a moment when his shoulders seem to get stuck, but then he disappears down into the hidden depths of the basement.

I drop to my hands and knees and then crawl backward. Except for the brief moment when he got stuck, Noah made it look easy, but I'm awkward and clumsy and manage to cut myself three times before I'm halfway through. Noah puts his hands on my hips to try to steady me as I push my way back, and it's a sign

313

of how scared I am that my first thought isn't that his hands are just inches from my butt.

There's a moment when my shirt bunches up and his fingers graze the roll above my jeans, but because he's wearing gloves, I don't see a thing.

"Sorry," he says as soon as I'm safely inside. "I should have been more careful."

"It's not like there's really anywhere safe to grab."

"Safe?"

"You know . . . free of chub . . ." I trail off awkwardly, realizing he's just so used to trying not to touch me for fear of triggering a vision that he forgot the gloves would make it safe.

Noah pulls a flashlight from his bag and twists the bottom. "You shouldn't do that," he says softly, turning his back to me and shining the light over the basement.

We're in a small room that seems to be half laundry room, half workshop. A pile of dirty clothes lies on the floor next to an ancient washer while a corkboard spans the wall on the left. Wrenches, hammers, and a crowbar hang crookedly from hooks. "Do what?"

"Assume your size is a problem."

Unlike Aidan, Noah doesn't tell me I'm not fat. I'm not sure if that's better or worse.

He reaches into his bag again and hauls out a second flashlight. He tosses it to me, and I catch it clumsily. "I'll go left, you go right. We check down here, then upstairs."

Splitting up feels wrong, but the quicker we search, the sooner we get out of here and the less chance we get caught.

The laundry room/toolshed lets out into a claustrophobically narrow hallway. Noah heads one way and I head the other.

The first door I try is a closet—empty save for a water heater and an old picnic cooler.

I try the next one. The knob slips under my gloved hand, but I grip it a little more tightly and it turns.

Bingo. A long table holds plastic trays. Above it, strings criss-cross the room at eye level, loaded down with photographs held in place with clothespins. I shine my flashlight over the pictures. An old, rotting barn, a lighthouse, a pile of rusting machinery. Artsy, but depressingly normal.

My heart sinks.

What was I expecting? Evidence Joey had used the darkroom lying out in plain sight? Pictures of me and Rachel hanging up to dry? Some irrefutable proof that Harding was involved in whatever Joey's done—knowingly or unknowingly—or a clue that pointed to where Joey is hiding?

Even if we find something that can lead us to Joey, what then? How do we get him to tell us what—if anything—he's done to Riley? I haven't thought through that part. Not really. Not enough, anyway.

But I think Noah has. I think he's given it a lot of thought. What if, instead of helping him, I'm pushing him closer to doing something horrible?

"Cat . . ."

Noah's voice is just loud enough to carry across the basement. I exit the room, closing the door behind me.

"Found the darkroom." My own voice is just a touch louder

than the slap of my sneakers against the bare concrete floor. "There's nothing in it."

The hallway leads to a long, narrow space that seems to run the width of the house.

Noah is standing in front of the only piece of furniture in it: an old floral couch with a high back that's been shoved up against the unfinished concrete wall.

He pushes it out of the way.

"What are you doing?" I ask, but then I see it: the wall isn't concrete—it's just painted to look that way. Set in the center of the space is a padlocked door painted the same flat gray as the wall. If you didn't look closely, you might miss that it was here.

"Why would you padlock something in your own house?" I ask, confused. The lock is big and heavy, like the ones you see on the gates at construction sites.

"To keep any visitors from getting in, I guess," says Noah, lifting the lock to examine it more closely.

A lump rises in my throat. There had been that gap . . . hours between when Rachel left the diner and when she had been found. "Or to keep someone from getting out."

A sharp, stricken look flashes across Noah's face. He drops the lock and heads down the hall at a run. Seconds later, he's back, a crowbar in hand.

He sets his flashlight on the back of the sofa, angling it so that the beam falls on the padlock. He swings, and even though I know it's only in my head, I swear I feel the reverberation of the impact in my legs.

Again and again, Noah swings, each impact harder than the last.

"Noah!" I yell his name, but he doesn't slow, he just keeps swinging.

I lose count of the hits long before he finally stops. His shoulders shake and his arms tremble. The padlock is still intact, but the latch is starting to give.

"Maybe we should call Jensen?"

"And say what?" Noah's voice is ragged and desperate. "That we broke into a house and found a locked room? I'm sure he'll come running right over." He swings again, but the lock holds. "Goddammit!" he yells, hurling the crowbar across the basement.

Noah's shoulders start to shake harder. His breath comes out in funny little gasps. It's so unexpected that it takes me a minute to realize he's crying.

"Noah . . ."

His back is to me. He doesn't turn.

I set my flashlight next to his on the sofa.

I don't know what to do, so I do the one thing I would want to do if I were normal. If I were just like everyone else. I close the distance between us, and I wrap my arms around him, hugging him from behind.

He stiffens and then trembles against me.

"It's okay," I whisper, holding him as tightly as I can, even though I know it's not okay. It's not okay at all.

This whole time, he's acted like what happened to Riley is a foregone conclusion, but as I slip off one glove and press a finger lightly to his wrist, I see what he's most afraid of. He's afraid of the basement. Of the locked door. Of the possibility that Riley is in that room, wrapped in plastic and rotting, not looking like Riley anymore.

I gasp, and he pulls away. He looks down at my hand, and I quickly pull my glove back into place.

"What did you do?" A confused, almost wounded look flashes across his face, and there's a hard, suspicious note in his voice.

I retrieve the crowbar.

"Cat . . ."

Noah reaches for me, but I sidestep him. I face off against the door and swing at the lock with all my strength. The impact sends shock waves up my arm and the noise echoes through my head, but I swing a second and then a third time. Again and again, I hit the lock. Physically, I'm not as strong as Noah, but that doesn't matter: the cumulative force of all those blows adds up. I don't need to hit it hard enough to obliterate it; I just need to hit it hard enough to finish the job.

The latch breaks free, leaving splintered wood in its wake.

Both Noah and I stare at the door.

I'm scared to move, scared to push it open, but when Noah takes a step forward, I know I have to stop him. I can't let him go in there. Not until I know what's inside.

With one hand, I push him back; with the other, I grab my flashlight. Screwing up every last ounce of courage I have, I step toward the door just as a floorboard groans above our heads.

THIRTY-ONE

I GRAB NOAH'S HAND AND PULL HIM THROUGH THE BASE-
ment. Past the sofa, down the hallway, into the room with the
washing machine and the wall of tools. He crouches next to the
window and laces his fingers, forming a step so that I can reach
the frame and haul myself through.

I turn back to the house as the slam of car doors cuts through
the night.

"Noah." My voice is a strangled cry as I realize he's not following.

He shakes his head. "I can't. Not until I know. Just go."

"I'm not leaving without you."

Conflicting emotions sweep across his face. He swears, half
turns away, turns back, swears again, and then scrambles up. He
slices his cheek on a stray shard of glass but doesn't cry out.

I pull him to his feet. Gloved hand in gloved hand, we race
for the safety of the field and the abandoned baseball diamond. A

spotlight floods the yard behind us as a voice yells, "Stop!"

"Go." Noah shoves me toward a tangle of bushes just past the property line. I trip and stumble forward several paces and then end up in a crouch in the shadows. Too late, I realize he hasn't followed. Instead, he's walking back the way we came, hands held up.

"Stop!" yells the voice again.

This time, Noah listens. He should look small, surrounded by all that light, but he doesn't.

"On your knees," says the voice, and Noah complies, kneeling in the grass as two officers approach him. One has a gun drawn, and the sight makes my thundering pulse swell until it seems to drown out all other sound.

I watch them twist Noah's arms roughly behind his back. They cuff him and then haul him to his feet as Jensen strides across the yard. The chief gets right in Noah's face, yelling words I can't make out over the pounding in my head.

Paul Harding hovers in the background. Pale and nervous. Ghoul-like in the light.

Noah says something to Jensen. Whatever it is, it's enough to make Jensen stop yelling. It's enough to make him turn and look at Harding.

Their voices come rushing in as some of the pressure behind my ears pops.

"—just a kid," Harding is saying. "You can't take anything he says seriously."

Jensen tells one of the officers to go down to the basement. "Look for a gray door with a broken latch," he says.

"You can't search without a warrant." Harding's voice rises in pitch; it's almost a wail.

"You called to report an intruder in your house," snaps Jensen. "This one could have an accomplice. They could still be inside. We wouldn't be doing our job if we didn't go down and check."

Harding takes a step back, his mouth opening and closing like a fish stranded on land. "I was wrong. He wasn't inside. No one was inside."

But no one listens.

As the officer walks toward the house, Jensen tells Harding not to follow, that he'll throw him in handcuffs if he sets so much as a pinky inside before they finish their search. "For intruders," he adds, voice heavy with sarcasm.

Jensen leaves Harding sputtering and Noah standing in the middle of all that light and walks toward the very edge of the yard.

"You just going to let Noah Fraser take the fall?" he asks, coming to a stop on the property line. I'm deep in the shadows, there's no way he can see me, but I stand anyway. Noah may have wanted to throw himself on his sword for me, but that doesn't mean I have to let him.

Jensen nods approvingly. "Good girl."

Bad girls don't go to New York. They end up handcuffed and alone in an empty police interrogation room in Canada.

I guess that stupid T-shirt of Lacey's really did get it wrong.

I try to figure out how long I've been here, but with no clocks and no windows, seconds feel like minutes and minutes feel like hours. By the time the door finally opens, I'm practically crawling out of my skin, and even the sight of an angry Chief Jensen can't stop me from leaping to my feet. "What was in the basement? Was it Riley? Did you find him?"

Jensen strides across the room, all roiling energy. He tosses a folder onto the table and crosses his arms. "Sit."

I stay standing, and he says it again, the single word cracking through the air like a whip.

Grudgingly, I do what he says.

Jensen scowls down at me. The last two times I was in a staring match with the chief of police, things were different. I knew I hadn't done anything wrong. As much as Jensen seemed to dislike me—or the Montgomerys—there was nothing he could actually do to me. This time, it's different.

"Was Riley in the house?" I ask again.

A muscle in the chief's jaw twitches. Instead of answering, he says, "I've just spent the past forty minutes talking to Noah Fraser. Do you know what he told me?"

I shake my head.

"He says the two of you went to Paul Harding's place because you thought he was helping Joey Paquet. Did it ever occur to you to pick up the goddamn phone and call the police?"

"You wouldn't have believed us. You didn't believe me when I told you about the medal. You didn't think there was a connection between Riley and Rachel." I do my best not to cower under his bad-cop stare. It isn't easy. "Was Riley in the house?"

"You want to know what was in that house?" The harsh edge to his voice implies that I really don't want to know but that he's going to show me anyway. He opens the folder, then tosses a plastic-encased photo at me. Awkwardly, hands hampered by the cuffs, I lift the picture: Rachel Larsen.

The photo was taken through a window, while she was changing. It's from a different vantage point than the pictures that were taken of me; the angle is lower and the window isn't quite as far away. There are other photos in the folder. Photos of different girls taken in locker rooms and through bedroom windows. I recognize some of the girls from the trailer walls. As far as I can tell, none of the photos are of me.

And none of the pictures are of Riley.

"Hundreds of photos dating back years: that's what we found. All taken by the goddamn school photographer." Given the look on Jensen's face, I'd be terrified to be in Harding's place right now. "Harding forgot something and went back to the house. He saw your flashlights through one of the basement windows and called to report a break-in. He told dispatch that it was the third break-in this year, that someone had taken cameras and equipment a few months ago, and that someone had also broken in and used his darkroom last week."

If Joey had broken in, that would mean Harding hadn't purposefully helped him. But then why would Harding have photos of Rachel and those other girls? It doesn't make any sense. "Why wouldn't he have reported the other two break-ins right after they happened?"

The question seems to make Jensen even angrier.

"You are not part of any investigation. You are not owed explanations or updates. And after the shit you pulled tonight, I can arrest you for interference. You think that will help Riley Fraser?

What about his mother? You think she'll thank you for wasting time that could have been spent finding out what happened to her son? Do you think Rachel Larsen and her family are going to pat you on the back for what you did tonight?"

I shake my head. "I don't understand . . ."

"If you had called the police—like anyone else would have had the sense to—we could have searched the house. Quietly. We could have staked it out to see if Joey Paquet went back there or if he and Harding had any contact. Instead, anyone within a kilometer radius of that place knows we were there tonight. It'll be all over town by morning—if it isn't already."

"I didn't think . . ."

"Sure as hell right you didn't think."

The words sting. Not because I care what Jensen thinks of me, but because the last thing I ever wanted to do was keep anyone from finding the person who had hurt Riley and Rachel.

"What makes you think Harding is telling the truth about the break-ins?" I ask. I rush on before he can yell. "How do you know he isn't just trying to cover his tracks? Maybe he heard about the trailer being found and got scared. Did Noah tell you we saw Harding at the river? That he told us he was photographing it for you?" I want to tell him about the taillights, about how Rachel couldn't have been taken in Joey's car, but there's no way to explain how I know that. It's like the vision of hellfire I saw when I touched Harding. No one in their right mind would believe me—least of all someone like Jensen.

He looks at me, long and level, while seconds tick into minutes and his silence edges closer and closer to unbearable. "Noah told me he broke into the house alone," he says finally. "Claims you were only there because you were trying to stop him. That true?"

"No. It was my idea." I don't know which one of us had the idea first, and I don't care: I'm not letting Noah take all of the blame. Besides, he's over eighteen and I'm technically a minor. Assuming the Canadian system is like the one back home, I probably have a lot less to lose, legally speaking. "Probably" isn't the most comforting thought, though, and I can't quite keep my voice from trembling when I say, "It was my idea, and I'm pretty sure you can't talk to me without a guardian present."

"Oh, you're sure, are you?"

I force myself to sit up straighter and look him in the eye. Because I am sure. Talking to me without another adult present is wrong, and he knows it.

This time when I speak, my voice doesn't shake. "I want to call my aunt."

THIRTY-TWO

I SPEND THE NEXT EIGHT HOURS ALONE IN A BARREN ROOM, WON-dering what's happening to Noah and feeling like I might lose my mind.

When I am finally allowed to see my aunt, the relief is so strong that I feel like I might start crying, but Jensen whisks her away before I can get a single word out. Even through the station's thick, supposedly soundproof walls, I can hear him yelling. This time, I can't tell whether or not Aunt Jet yells back.

It's another three hours before they let me go. When they finally do, I try to tell her about Noah, but she just shushes me and signs a bunch of forms. As we step out of the station and into the bright sunlight, everything catches up with me, and the tears I've been keeping locked away come pouring out.

"It will be all right," Jet says.

That's it. Just five words. And then she climbs into the Buick and drives me home.

Eventually, my nose and eyes stop running—although it still hurts a little each time I breathe in too deeply. Aunt Jet is so deceptively calm that I don't realize how much trouble I'm in until she pulls to a stop in front of Montgomery House and says, "What were you *thinking?*"

Her voice is heavy with disappointment and anger.

Unlike yesterday, there isn't a patrol car parked in the driveway. Either Jensen doesn't have one to spare or he's so furious at me that he doesn't care if Joey turns up.

"What were you thinking?" Aunt Jet says again. Louder this time. So loud it makes me jump a little in my seat.

"I don't know."

"You and Noah Fraser had to have had a reason for breaking into that man's house. I want to know what it is."

I swallow.

"Do you have *any* idea how terrifying it was to come home and find you gone? To have no idea how long it had been since you'd left or where you were? Do you have *any* idea how worried I've been?"

"Did you call Dad? Does he know?"

"No," she snaps, "I haven't called your father. He wouldn't be able to get here any faster, and all it would do is worry him even more. And he's already angry enough at me as it is."

"Why would he be angry at you?"

"Why do you *think*, Mary Catherine?" Aunt Jet looks tired. Utterly exhausted. "Sending you here was supposed to get you away from trouble. *I* was supposed to keep you away from trouble. He's angry that I let you go to that party and that I let you spend time with Joey Paquet. I can't imagine how he's going to take the news that you've started going on crime sprees."

"It wasn't a spree. It was just one house."

As though I hadn't said anything at all, she says, "You and your father are the only real family I have left. He finally trusts me enough to let you spend another summer here, and look what happens."

"You know Dad didn't send me here because he trusted you, right? Sending me here was just the best of a bunch of bad options." At the hurt that flashes across Jet's face, I realize how the words sound. They sound cruel and mean and spiteful, and that wasn't what I intended. At all. I just don't want her to read things into my visit that aren't there. I want her to understand that Dad wasn't so much placing any great trust in her as he was using her. "Aunt Jet—"

She stares straight ahead, not looking at me. "I want to know what you and Noah were doing."

Telling the truth seems like a really bad idea, but I'm too exhausted and stressed to think of a convincing lie that won't end up making Noah and me look even worse. "We've been trying to figure out what happened to Riley. We broke into Paul Harding's house because we thought he might know something about Joey Paquet."

Aunt Jet opens her mouth. Closes it. Flexes her hands. Closes them. "Does this have something to do with what happened in New York? Are you obsessing over Riley Fraser as some sort of distraction?"

"He was my friend, Aunt Jet."

"A friend you haven't spoken to in years. You can't just use this thing with Riley to hide from your problems, Mary Catherine. Life doesn't work that way. You have to face things."

She has to be kidding, right? I stare at her and, no, she is definitely not kidding. There are times when Aunt Jet is surprisingly similar to Dad: astounding in her capacity for hypocrisy.

I push open the passenger door and climb out, then slam it so hard flakes of rust fall to the driveway.

Aunt Jet slides out of the driver's side. I stare at her over the car. "You and Dad are exactly alike. The both of you run away from everything. The only difference is that he hides in New York and you're hiding here."

"I'm not hiding, Mary Catherine. One of us had to come back here. One of us had to look after things."

"Years ago, sure. But what about now? What's keeping you here now?" I think about the stack of travel guides in the basement. All those notes and plans that were stuffed in a drawer and forgotten. I think about the picture of Aunt Jet and how different she looked. How happy. I love Montgomery House and hate the thought of not having it here to come back to, but I hate the thought of Aunt Jet being trapped even more. I walk around the car. "Do you really want to be here? Think back to when you were my age: Is this what you wanted? You're renting out rooms to strangers, you're barely keeping the place afloat, and you're emptying out the basement for cash."

She doesn't say anything. I should stop, but I don't. "Do you know what Dad says? He says this place is a mausoleum. I used to think he was being mean, but maybe he's right."

She turns away from me and walks up the porch steps and into the house.

"Please, Aunt Jet," I say, unwilling to let the subject drop as I follow her inside. "Just think about whether or not this is what you really want. You don't have to stay in the house. And if you do sell it, you don't have to stay in Montgomery Falls. You're not trapped here—not if you don't want to be."

"Where would I go, Mary Catherine?"

"Anywhere."

"And do what?"

"Anything."

She lets out a long, deep breath. "You'll understand when you're older. Things aren't as easy as they seem when you're seventeen."

I open my mouth to reply, but she cuts me off. Her voice is distant. Robotic. "You should go upstairs and change. Those clothes are filthy. I'm going to check on things here and then go next door. Someone has to tell Noah's mother what's going on."

Bringing up Noah's mother might be the one thing Jet can do to stop me from pushing. I wonder if she knows that.

"Mrs. Fraser might not . . . She's not . . ." I hesitate, thinking about how Noah's mother grabbed me the first time I went over there.

"I know, Mary Catherine," Jet says, absolving me of having to try to explain.

Not knowing what else to do, I head upstairs.

When I reach my room, the door won't open. I must have

accidentally locked it. I cut through Jet's bedroom and step into the bathroom.

She wasn't wrong: the clothes I'm wearing are filthy. The knees of my jeans are caked in mud, and there are dark smears that I'm pretty sure are dried blood on my shirt. Not to mention sweat stains from being left in an uncomfortably warm interrogation room for hours.

I shower quickly, wincing as soap gets into the shallow cuts I earned crawling through that broken window, and then haul on fresh clothes. My face in the bathroom mirror looks tired and wan. Startled. *Am I a hypocrite, too?* I wonder. I told Jet to think about whether or not this was really what she wanted from her life, but in my own way, aren't I just as trapped?

Aunt Jet shut herself up within the walls of Montgomery House, and I've built my own set of invisible walls to keep people away.

As I step into my bedroom, my gaze flickers toward the desk. Noah's folder is out in plain sight, and the pages are scattered in all directions.

My entire body goes cold. I know I put the folder back in the desk before Noah and I left yesterday. Ever since that afternoon Skylar came over, I've been careful not to leave things lying out.

Joey. My heart rate kicks up a notch as I glance toward the closet door, half expecting him to come bursting out of it like the killer in a slasher flick.

But no one comes crashing out, and after a few seconds, my heartbeat drops down to something approaching normal.

I gather up the sheets of paper, checking each one off against a mental list. It's not hard: I've studied these pages so many times that I can probably recite the contents of the entire folder from memory.

Downstairs, the phone rings. Before I can even think about going to answer it, the noise cuts off—picked up by Marie or Sam, probably.

Only one piece of paper is missing from the folder: the map I had taken from Riley's room, the one Skylar had sworn she didn't recognize.

Was she in the house? Did she take it? Does she know something I don't?

As I turn to put the folder back in its place, I realize that the curtains are open. I reach out to shut them and then freeze.

Marie is running for the gap in the hedge. She's running toward Noah's house.

THIRTY-THREE

FOR THE SECOND TIME IN A SINGLE SUMMER, I FIND MYSELF in the Montgomery Falls Hospital.

The emergency room isn't crowded. A man with a cut over his eye. A mother with a crying toddler. An elderly couple with wrinkled, paper-thin skin. No Noah.

I don't know if he's still at the station; I don't know if anyone has told him what's happened. They have to tell him, don't they? Even Jensen can't be that horrible.

Aunt Jet tries asking a nurse about Noah's mother.

"Are you family?"

She shakes her head.

"Then I can't tell you anything."

"Please," Aunt Jet says. "She would have arrived by ambulance within the last hour and a half . . . She . . ." Jet falters, apparently unsure if she should say why Mrs. Fraser had been brought in. After finding Noah's mom, Jet had called the paramedics and then

Marie, reasoning that Marie might be able to help and was closer. We wanted to follow the ambulance directly to the hospital, but a police officer had kept us at the house, asking a seemingly endless string of questions.

I pull in a deep breath. "She tried to hurt herself," I say. "My aunt found her and called the ambulance."

The nurse's detached expression becomes a little less aloof. "I really can't release patient information," she says, "but if someone self-harms, they're usually treated and then taken up to the psychiatric unit for evaluation. Fourth floor."

"Thankyou." The two syllables come out together in a rush. The nurse nods and turns her attention to a stack of paperwork.

We take the elevator up to the fourth floor and follow a line of red dots to a door with a small window—the kind that has the wire mesh inside—set at eye level. I try the handle: it's locked.

There's a sign to the left of the door—Ring for Assistance—just above a small, black button. I hesitate. The nurse downstairs wasn't supposed to tell us anything. Odds are, if we ring that bell, another nurse will just show up and tell us the exact same thing.

Aunt Jet must have the same thought. "Why don't you stay here in case Noah shows up. I forgot my phone in the car. I'll go get it, and then we can try calling the police station."

"You know they won't tell us anything, either," I say, a terrible weariness settling deep inside me as the adrenaline wears off. "If he's still there, they won't let us talk to him."

"Oh, they'll let me talk to him," she says, eyes steely. She heads for the elevators, leaving me alone.

After a few minutes, an orderly rounds the corner at the end of the hall. I lean against the wall, trying to look casual, as he approaches. He slides a key card from his pocket as he nears the ward and then presses it to a small scanner. He barely glances at me.

I try to grab the door behind him, but I'm too slow: the lock clicks softly into place just as my fingers skim the handle.

It takes only a few minutes for someone else to come through—a doctor with a thick beard and tired eyes—but he's more observant. "Are you supposed to be up here?" he asks.

I mumble something about being lost. He doesn't look convinced. For a moment, I'm sure he's going to call security, but then someone on the other side of the half-open door calls his name, pulling him away.

"Cat?"

The soles of my sneakers squeak against the tile floor as I whirl. "Noah!"

He stands at the end of the hallway, staring at me, bluish circles under his bloodshot eyes. There are dark patches on the knees of his jeans and a rip in his T-shirt. His hair sticks up in peaks, like he's spent the past few hours raking his hands through it, and the cut on his cheek is angry and red—deep enough that it might need stitches.

He looks horrible, but he is still the single best sight I have ever seen.

I launch myself across the space between us and throw my arms around him. I don't lose all self-control—I'm careful not to touch bare skin—but I squeeze him so hard that the muscles in my arms shake.

My relief is so strong that it takes me a long moment to realize he's not squeezing me back.

I step away.

His expression is cold and remote. "What are you doing here?"

The tone in his voice matches the look on his face, and I struggle to understand it. "Aunt Jet found your mom. She called the ambulance. They weren't supposed to tell us anything because we're not family, but a nurse said she was probably up here."

His eyes slide past me, to the ward beyond the locked door. "I should have made her stay at the hospital in Saint John, but all she wanted was to come back home and the doctors thought it would be okay. I should have known better . . . I've spent all this time running around, not watching her. I should have been there."

"Noah—it isn't your fault. None of this is your fault."

He lets out a sound that's a little like a laugh, but it isn't a laugh at all. "You're right." There's something in his eyes that scares me. Something that's bright and fierce and dangerous.

Just like at Harding's, though, I'm not scared of Noah; I'm scared for him and of what he might do.

And because I'm scared for him, I reach out and touch his hand.

Back at Harding's, back in that basement, I saw Noah's fear. This time, though, I try to go looking for something else. This time, I try to see desire. I try—

Blood. Thick and tacky. Sticky on my hands.

A pair of broken glasses and sightless brown eyes. Joey's eyes.

A low, ragged sound. A scream. I can't tell if it's Noah or Joey, I can't . . .

Noah yanks his hand away. "Stay out of my head, Cat," he snaps.

He moves to step around me, but I move, too, blocking his path. "Noah, even if you find Joey, you have to let the police deal with him. If you hurt him . . . They'll throw you in jail. You won't be able to do anything for your mom. You'll lose everything. Do you think Riley would want that? Do you think he'd be able to stand it?"

Noah's eyes narrow. He stares at me in a way that is painfully familiar even though he's never, ever looked at me that way before.

He stares at me the way Lacey did that night in New York. The way Riley did the last time I saw him. Like there is something fundamentally *wrong* about me. Like I'm something monstrous.

"What makes you think you have the right?" he says. "Down in that basement? Here? What makes you think you have the right to slip inside my head?"

An orderly—the same man I saw earlier—steps out of the ward and shoots us a curious glance as he walks past.

Noah makes an almost visible effort to control himself until the man is out of sight. "You had no right, Cat."

"You asked me to do it." My voice rises and breaks. I can't help it. "You asked me to help you. You didn't have any problem with me slipping into Skylar's head or Harding's. You practically asked me to touch every person in town. You even suggested I practice on you, remember? That day in the diner? 'I'm a perfect guinea pig'—that's what you told me."

"That's different!"

"How?"

"Because it was to help find Riley." He's so angry that his voice is almost a shout. "This—what you just did, what you did in that basement—is different. You didn't do it because you had to. You did it because you could."

In the distance, the elevator dings. A moment later, Aunt Jet rounds the corner. When she sees the look on my face, she stops.

The hallway blurs, and I wipe roughly at my eyes. "It's the same thing. What I did and what you asked me to do: it's the same."

Noah shakes his head. His voice becomes a little softer, but somehow, that's worse. "No. It's not. All you had to do was ask me what I was scared of in that basement or what I want now. I would have told you. It's different, and if you can't see how, then I can't explain it to you."

He steps around me. This time, I don't try to stop him.

I can't tell whether or not he does it on purpose, whether or not he does it to hurt me, but as he passes, his arm brushes mine. I can't tell, and in a way, it doesn't matter.

Noah's anger at me is so strong that I don't see anything at all when his skin touches mine. His anger is so strong that it drowns out everything else. Desire. Fear. Everything.

I don't know how long I stare at the door to the psychiatric ward after it swings shut. My head hurts—everything hurts—but it doesn't matter.

He hates me.

Just like Riley.

Just like Lacey.

Eventually, Aunt Jet places her hand on my shoulder. "He just doesn't understand. He can't."

"No. He understands." And maybe he's right. Maybe what I did was wrong. I don't know. I don't know anymore.

"Oh, Cat." Jet folds me into a hug. She's careful to keep her hands away from my skin. Somehow, that makes everything worse—the fact that Jet could calm me with a touch but that maybe she knows it would be wrong. "It's a gift, what you can do. I know it's hard to believe sometimes, but it is. You're like your grandmother. She could see so many things."

Ever since I arrived, Aunt Jet has been so careful not to admit what I am—what we are. Because she doesn't want to upset Dad. Hearing her acknowledge it now feels so strange.

It isn't until she lets me go and steps back that I realize she called me Cat and not Mary Catherine.

"Let's go home, okay?" she says, rubbing a small, careful circle on my shoulder and steering me away from that locked door.

I want to ask her if seeing things had ever done my grandmother any good, but I don't. I know she's trying to be kind.

When we get home, she says something about how the police department treated me, about how Jensen abused his power, about how she's going to get a lawyer—she seems to be blocking out the part where Noah and I actually did commit a crime. She doesn't seem to notice that I don't say anything. She doesn't even notice when I don't follow her inside.

I walk to the end of the porch and sink down onto the old swing.

I slide my hand to the underside of the bench, to a rough patch where we had carved our initials, Riley and me. I trace the letters and try to remember the way his voice had sounded on that last day.

"Have you ever kissed anyone?"

That's how it had started. Five words as we sat next to each other on the swing.

I thought about lying—just for a second. But I had never lied to Riley. "No." I waited for him to say something else, but he didn't. Each second the silence stretched out, it felt like my heart beat a little faster. "Have you?"

"No," he said quickly. "Gross."

"Gross," I agreed, even though I was pretty sure I didn't agree at all, even though the thought of what it might be like to kiss Riley had started slipping through my head when we were walking in the woods or hanging out on the porch or swimming in the river.

Silence settled around us again. Riley had an open comic book on his lap—some old issue of an *X-Men* comic we found in the basement of Montgomery House—but it was taking him a long time to turn the pages. I pretended to be deeply engrossed in a game on my phone.

"Cat?"

"Yeah?"

"I want to kiss you."

"Oh." That was the only response I could manage. My head was too full of thoughts, and my heart was beating too fast. I set the phone facedown. My hand shook. Just a little.

"Do you want to kiss me?"

I had seen Riley blush before, but never like this. His whole face was red.

"Yes," I said.

"Yes: you want to kiss me?"

"Yes, I would like to kiss you."

We twisted toward each other on the bench and then realized we were sitting too far apart. I scooted toward him. We stared at each other, neither one of us sure how to proceed. I licked my lips, and Riley watched as he leaned forward.

"Wait—what if . . . ?" I shook my head. I wanted this. I wanted this so badly, but what happened if I saw something?

"What is it?" He pulled back. The expression in his blue eyes was so concerned, so earnest, that I told myself I was being ridiculous. I had touched Riley before. More than once. Even if I did see something, it wouldn't be that bad—it was Riley.

"Nothing," I said quickly. "Everything's okay."

He leaned forward again and pressed his lips to mine.

Grape bubble gum, I thought. *He tastes like grape bubble gum.* I had just a second to wonder what I tasted like to him, if I tasted like the peanut butter and honey sandwich I'd had for lunch, and then I was sucked down—

Hands gripped my shoulders, shaking me. Shaking me so hard it felt like the inside of my head was rattling.

A smell flooded my nostrils. Sharp and sickening. "Why did you take it?" A face inches from mine. Eyes white with cobwebs. Veins turning black. The girl from the mill, but not really her, not anymore.

She pried open my hand, and a silver disc fell to the floor. I tried to pull free, I tried . . .

"Cat!" Riley's face swam above me. I was on my back on the swing, and my head was in his lap. At any other time, I'd be mortified that my face was just inches from his crotch, but right then, the thought that maybe I should be embarrassed barely registered.

I rolled away from him. Rolled off the swing. I crouched on the porch floor and gagged, but nothing came up. It felt like there was a spike being driven into my head.

Riley crouched next to me. He reached for my arm, but I flinched away. "Don't touch me. Please don't touch me."

A stricken look flashed across his face.

"You kept it," I whispered. "Why did you keep it?"

He shook his head, confused. "Kept what? What are you talking about?"

"The medal. You told the police you dropped it."

Awareness dawned in his eyes. Awareness and fear. He rocked back up on his heels and pushed himself to his feet. Riley was almost never clumsy, but he stumbled a bit, like he was having trouble finding his balance.

"Why would you keep it? Why would you want it?"

He took a step back, away from me. "I don't know what you're talking about."

He sounded scared, but that couldn't be right. He couldn't be scared of me.

I pushed myself up. The pain in my head was staggering, so strong that I had to use the swing and then the porch railing for support. "You have to tell someone. Your parents or Noah. You can't keep it, Riley."

He shook his head and took another step back. "You have no idea what you're talking about."

"Why are you lying?"

Something in his face changed. The fear became something harder. "I'm not lying. You're just a freak. You're a freak, and I'm glad you're leaving."

He turned and started to walk away.

"Wait—" I tried to go after him, tried to grab his sleeve, tried to stop him so that we could talk, but the pain in my head was getting stronger and stronger. It was always so strong back then, and it was almost like the emotions from the kiss had supercharged it. Something happened when I made a grab for his sleeve. I lost my balance. I hit him. It shouldn't have been hard enough to hurt, but he was scared. *He was scared of me.* He tried to wrench himself away, but he was standing at the top of the porch steps.

The drop wasn't far—four feet, maybe five—but he fell badly and awkwardly, and even through the pain in my head, I swore I heard a crack.

Other people were suddenly there. Aunt Jet. My father. Riley's mom.

"Broken," I heard someone say.

I turned and ran into the house, but I couldn't outrun the way Riley had looked at me.

He had stared up at me like I was something fierce and terrible. Like he was afraid of me. Like I was a monster for knowing he had taken that dead girl's medal from the mill.

We are the monsters . . .

The words I had seen in Skylar's head.

Suddenly, I know why they were familiar.

I had seen them before—with Riley and Noah. I had seen them the day we went to see the chimney swifts.

Most of the outer buildings around the mill—warehouses, cottages for the overseers, row houses for the workers—had been razed to the foundations, but a few had still been standing, and Riley had been itching to see inside them.

Noah agreed—as long as we looked in from the outside.

The first building we came to hadn't been all that large—not when you saw it in the shadow of the hulking mill, anyway. All of the windows had been smashed, letting in plenty of light. Old beer cans and cigarette butts littered the floor, and the walls were covered in graffiti. Someone had written *Here there be monsters* on the far wall in large, black spray-painted letters. Underneath, someone had scrawled *We are the monsters* in blue.

A few feet away, the top of a staircase was visible.

Riley begged to go in, to see the tunnels that everyone knew were under the mill.

I held my breath and then let it out in a relieved rush when Noah refused.

I had followed Riley faithfully all summer, but I had not wanted to follow him into that dark.

Here there be monsters.

We are the monsters.

344

Seeing that phrase in Skylar's head couldn't have been a coincidence.

Heart hammering, I head inside and down to the basement.

Aunt Jet had called the antique dealer, but he hasn't come yet. The monstrous desk is still here—along with its overstuffed drawers and the hunting knife I had left resting on its surface. I dig through the old journals and ledgers until I find the one filled with blueprints of the old textile mill.

I flip to a diagram of the tunnels. Short, angular lines—just like the lines on the map I had taken from Riley's room.

Riley had been mapping the passages beneath the mill.

Skylar is adamant that Joey is innocent. Given that, wouldn't her greatest fear be that Joey is found? And if you were Joey—if you were obsessed with Montgomery Falls and its history and its ghosts—wouldn't the tunnels be the perfect place to hide?

THIRTY-FOUR

THE FIRST TIME I SAW MONTGOMERY TEXTILES, MY FATHER and I had been hiking through the woods on a nature walk. We had just reached a break in the trees when Dad stopped and said, "There's the old dragon."

And from afar, if you squint just right, the mill really does look like some sort of hulking beast: the peaks on the roof resemble the spines on a dragon's back; the smokestacks could almost be horns; and the outbuildings and rusting machinery trail out behind the main structure like a tail. It's only as you get closer that it shifts into something else. Less dragon, more postapocalyptic ghost town.

According to Joey and Chase, this place is the most haunted spot in all of Montgomery Falls. One thing's for sure: it doesn't feel like anything good could happen here.

I leave the safety of the trees and follow the fence, looking for an opening. When I finally find one, I can't be certain that it's not the same one Riley and Noah and I found all those summers ago. It feels the same as I drop to a crouch and squeeze through the gap. The sense of déjà vu is so strong that if I look up, I'm half certain I'll see Riley holding the wire back to help me.

I come out the other side and head in what I think is the right direction. Five years is a long time, and the maps in my backpack—pages of Montgomery family history ripped from the books in Aunt Jet's basement—don't show all of the outbuildings.

I try not to think about how upset and worried Jet will be when she realizes I'm gone. Or about how it's entirely possible that I am being very, very stupid.

A rabbit darts across my path, and I yelp. "Smooth, Cat," I mutter to myself. "Really smooth." My heart is still hammering in my chest when I spot Aidan. He's standing thirty yards away, his back to me, in front of the building I had described on the phone. The late-afternoon sun catches bits of gold in his hair.

A small knot of tension eases in my chest. Aidan had been skeptical and kind of reluctant on the phone—not that I blamed him. Until this moment, I wasn't entirely sure he would show up.

Once I had made the connection to the tunnels, I hadn't known what to do. I did, however, know that I couldn't go to Noah.

I don't want to believe Noah is actually capable of killing Joey, but if I'm wrong and I were to lead him here . . . Luckily, I guess, the universe has taken things out of my hands—at least where safeguarding Noah's soul is concerned. I doubt he'd answer the phone if I called. I don't think he's ever going to speak to me again.

But I can't let myself think about that right now.

After what happened with Harding, you'd think going to

Jensen would be the smart thing to do, except . . .

Skylar.

Her parents haven't seen her since this morning—I called and talked to her mom—and she hasn't replied to a single text from Aidan or Chase. She might be down in the tunnels. Given how quickly Officer Buddy had reached for his gun yesterday—and how could that only have been yesterday?—I don't trust him, or his fellow officers, in a creepy underground labyrinth with a bunch of guns. They might shoot first and ask questions later.

They might hurt Skylar.

Unable to go to Noah or to the police, I'd gone to Aidan and Chase.

Gravel crunches too loudly under my feet as I walk forward, but Aidan is so lost in thought that he doesn't seem aware of me. It isn't until I'm a few feet away—so close I could pluck a pebble from the ground and hit him—that he turns.

He gives his head a small shake, like someone just waking from a nap. He rubs his palms against the sides of his jeans and smiles.

After the way Noah stared at me, it's nice to have someone look at me and smile. "Where's Chase?" I ask.

"His mom grabbed him as we were leaving. He said he'll meet us here."

I let out a relieved breath. Three people feels way safer than just two.

Aidan walks over to the small building and peers inside. "Let it never be said that you don't take me to the classy joints."

I go to his side. Broken glass, cigarette butts, and what looks like the remains of a campfire are all visible from the doorway. I pull out the diagrams from the Montgomery journals. "That staircase in the corner should lead down to the tunnels. I think Riley was mapping them."

"So you said on the phone. I've heard of the tunnels, but I've never been in them."

"You didn't go down that time you were here with Riley and those guys?"

"Never got the chance." Aidan shrugs. "That whole 'getting caught' thing. Joey and Chase tried to drag me out here once after that, but Jensen was pretty clear on what he'd do to me if I ever got caught on the grounds again."

"What if Jensen catches you with Chase and me?"

"Well, if you're right about Joey and Skylar being down there, Jensen will probably be too busy to care about me."

"Seriously," I say, "what'll happen if he catches you?"

"Does it matter? There's no way I'm letting you and Chase go down there alone." He frowns thoughtfully and glances back toward the mill. "Question: What makes you think Joey and Skylar would head for the tunnels when there's an entire hulking space aboveground they could hide in? Don't you think we should check the main building first?"

Even though light streams through the broken windows, some of the graffiti is in shadow. I slip the diagrams into my pocket and pull an industrial-strength flashlight from my backpack. I turn it on and sweep it over the far wall until I find the familiar letters: *We are the monsters.*

"Skylar quoted that line to me." And she did—sort of.

"All that proves is that she's been here." Aidan takes the

flashlight from my hand and shines it over the debris on the ground. "Judging from the look of things, I'd say plenty of people have been here."

I step away from the shadow of the building, out to where the sunlight can warm my skin. There's an old wooden beam in the overgrown grass; I sit on it, using it as a makeshift bench.

If I look to my left, I'll see the path Riley and Noah and I took that day. If I follow it, I'll find the exact spot—I know I'll be able to find it—where we stumbled onto that girl.

I don't look to my left.

"I can't explain how I know the words are tied to Joey," I say, forcing myself to focus on Aidan's question. "I just do."

Aidan joins me on the beam. It's the first time we've been together since the trailer. I don't really know what to say or how to act. Bringing up the kiss feels ridiculous, but not bringing it up doesn't feel right, either.

"Cat . . ." Aidan turns the flashlight over in his hands. "I know there are things you haven't told me. You can trust me. You know that, right?"

I do trust him—as much as I'm able—but it's hard. *I trusted Noah not to hurt me*, I think with a pang, *and look how that turned out.* "You thought you could trust Joey."

"That's different. Joey is an anomaly."

I shake my head. "You trust me, but for weeks, I've known that Aunt Jet has been thinking of selling Montgomery House. For weeks, I've been lying to you."

"Cat, no offense, but your aunt isn't exactly a secret agent. You would have to be completely oblivious to have lived in that house for the past few months and not realize she's been emptying it out."

"I still should have told you. Why aren't you angry at me?"

"Did Jet ask you not to tell me?"

I bite my lower lip. "She doesn't want any of the tenants to find out. Not until she knows if she's going to sell."

He spreads his hands. "I get it. I wish you had told me, but I understand why you didn't."

It doesn't seem human: how understanding he's being. I think about the kiss. How soft his lips had felt against mine and how strange it had been to touch someone and see only myself. It was perfect. He is perfect.

So why does part of me wish Noah could be the one to go down with me into the dark?

"Chimney swifts," I say suddenly and awkwardly, to hide my confusion. "See them? Those black smudges swirling like ink in water. In a few hours, there will be thousands of them. They nest in the old smokestacks."

Pointing out the chimney swifts doesn't help me not think of Noah, of course.

Aidan gives me a long, steady look, one that makes me wonder if I'm just babbling incoherently. I swallow. "How long do you think it will take Chase to get here?"

"Ten minutes. Maybe twenty."

But ten minutes pass and then twenty. Neither of us seems to feel like talking, and we're both nervous and restless: I keep checking and rechecking the contents of my backpack and Aidan can't seem to sit still for more than a few minutes at a time.

"Maybe something happened," I venture finally. "Maybe his

mom wouldn't let him leave."

Aidan hands me the flashlight and pushes himself to his feet. He hauls his cell from his pocket, tries calling Chase, and then frowns. "Voice mail." He ends the call and glances toward the sun. "There are only a few hours of daylight left. It probably doesn't matter, since we're going underground, but . . ."

"It matters," I say, standing quickly. It's not logical, but the thought of being in the tunnels after dark makes my skin crawl. Besides, I could be wrong about Joey and Skylar being underground. We might need to search the outbuildings or the mill. That, too, is something I would rather not do after the sun goes down.

What was it Joey had said that first time we met—something about how the presence of a Montgomery might make the ghosts angry? With a small shiver, I force myself to walk into the building.

Aidan follows. Glass and bits of garbage crunch under our feet as we make our way to the staircase.

"Are you sure about this?" he asks as I shine the beam from the flashlight down into the darkness below. "You don't have to go in. It's not too late to call Chief Jensen. Or Noah, if you want. Or we could start with the mill."

"I can't call Jensen. And Noah . . ." My words trail off as I pull a second flashlight from my bag and hand it to Aidan. I can't tell him what happened with Noah. "You don't have to come with me." It scares me to think about going down there by myself, but Aidan doesn't owe me anything.

He shoots me a small, tight smile. "If you go, I go." He waits for me to start down the stairs, waits for me to be sure, and then follows.

Despite the broken glass and garbage, the stairway itself seems unnervingly normal; it's like something that might lead down into an ordinary basement or a parking garage. But parking garages don't smell like damp earth and rotting things, and the farther down we go, the worse the smell gets. It wraps itself around me and slips into my lungs, and it's easy to imagine that the crunching under our feet isn't garbage, but small, delicate bones.

Eventually, we reach the bottom and an open space that must have been a storeroom.

I shine my light over the walls, over spray-painted devils and song lyrics and names linked together and surrounded by hearts. What kind of person would want to immortalize their love in a place like this?

"Jenny loves Ray. 4EVAH. Beautiful," says Aidan. The words are meant to be light and mocking, but it's hard to find anything funny down here. "You okay?"

I nod and haul out the diagrams. I'm not sure how much help they'll be. They're old and there's no way of knowing how many of the passages are still passable—even then, the pages show only a fraction of the tunnel system. I wish we had the map Riley had made. Both because it would at least be more recent and because it might be comforting to have something of his with me down in the dark.

Having something of Riley's would help me remember why I'm doing this.

The room we've found ourselves in has three archways, each

opening to a tunnel that leads to a different spot on the grounds. Judging by the diagrams, most of the other tunnels branch off these three arteries.

Somewhere down one of these passageways, thirteen men died.

"Which one?" asks Aidan.

"Right?" I hazard. It's as good a guess as any.

The walls press in uncomfortably close, and if the ceiling were any lower, Aidan would have to duck. Distantly, I can hear the sound of dripping water.

It doesn't take long for us to reach another branch, but this time, the decision is made for us: the left passage has caved in, and the opening is half hidden behind a mound of broken brick, dirt, and tree roots.

"Right again," says Aidan. He hums a little under his breath, so softly that I can't make out the melody.

Between the lack of sunlight, the stale air, and the sensation that we could be crushed at any minute, it takes everything I have to keep going, but he actually seems comfortable down here. He trails one hand lightly over the dirty old bricks that line the walls. A few small pieces break free, and I remind myself that Chase knows where we are. If we get trapped, he'll figure it out and send help.

After a few hundred yards, the tunnel widens into another room, this one so cavernous that I don't need to check the diagram to know we're underneath the mill. Old pieces of equipment— huge iron machines, the purpose of which I can only guess at—hunker together along the walls. People have partied down here, too. Crushed beer cans and discarded underwear dot the floor. There's even a paper skeleton, torn and headless.

I tilt the flashlight up toward the ceiling. It's too far above us to see whether or not the beams are black from the fire.

The place would be a perfect set for a scene in Joey's script.

I remember the way he tried to manipulate us that day up in Aidan's room. What if he wants us down here? What if he wants someone to come find him to fulfill something in his stupid movie? I tell myself that if that were the case, it's already in the script, and Jensen has the script. Ergo, if Joey wanted anyone down here, Jensen would already know and would have already searched. Because he hasn't, Joey isn't expecting us.

My reasoning is perfectly logical, which would make me feel better if it weren't for the fact that very little about the past few days has felt like it has adhered to logic.

A wide stone staircase hugs the far wall. Aidan bounds up it and tries the door at the top. "Locked."

Two tunnels branch off the room. One on each side.

"It's like one of those old Choose Your Own Adventure books," says Aidan, rejoining me. "Have you ever seen one of those? Choose right and we go to page ninety-six. Choose left and we go to page forty-three."

"I wish there were a third option," I admit.

"There is." He studies my face for a long moment. "You just put the book back on the shelf. We go home and forget we were ever down here."

It's tempting—so, so tempting. As I swing the flashlight back and forth between the two doors, though, the glow catches something on the floor.

"Aidan . . ." Worried suddenly about how far sound might carry, I try to keep my voice low. I crouch down and pluck Skylar's Bela Lugosi button from the ground. "It must have fallen from her jacket."

Something that looks almost like approval crosses Aidan's face. "Good catch."

I turn Skylar's pin over in my hand and bite my lip. Skylar is down here somewhere, and she trusts Joey. She doesn't understand how dangerous he is. He could do anything to her down here.

"We can't just leave Skylar. She's our friend." I pull in a deep breath. "Left. Let's try left."

"Why left?"

I shrug and start walking. "A hunch."

If the thinning graffiti is any indication, we're venturing farther than most people have dared. The air is staler here and probably filled with toxic mold or asbestos or God only knows what else. The walls feel like they could collapse on us at any moment. Even if we find Joey, I'm not entirely sure what the heck we can do other than club him over the head and tie him up with the rope in my backpack.

"You know," says Aidan from behind me, "some people in town say the Montgomerys are witches."

"I'm pretty sure Chief Jensen would tell you to swap that *w* for a *b*."

"Jensen is an idiot. He's the kind of guy who never actually manages to find Waldo."

I'm not so sure. It's tempting to write Jensen off as an idiot, but I think he just lets his personal feelings impair his judgment—and

356

he cares more about protecting the town's image than individual people.

That makes him a shitty cop, but it doesn't necessarily make him stupid.

Ahead of us, the tunnel branches. I shine my flashlight into each passage. Dust and dirt cover both floors, and footprints are clearly visible in each direction. I walk a few feet into the left tunnel and stop. A faint, dripping sound surrounds me. I shine my flashlight over the walls ahead. Water runs down them in thin rivulets and pools on the floor.

I turn back to ask Aidan if he thinks the other tunnel would be safer. The passage behind me is empty.

"Aidan?" I call his name softly, but the only sound is the dripping water.

I take a step back the way we came and call his name again, a little louder this time. When he still doesn't respond, my heart—already racing—starts to jackhammer in my chest.

I slide my backpack off my shoulder and root around inside. Taking a page from Skylar's book, I'd made like a Girl Scout and tried to prepare for every eventuality. My hand skims matches, granola bars, batteries, rope, and the hunting knife I'd found in the basement of Montgomery House before closing on a lead pipe that's as long as my forearm.

I pull the pipe out of the bag and take another step back the way we came.

A low, pained sound from somewhere behind me stops me in my tracks. I whirl, and the sound comes again, farther ahead, past a spot where the tunnel curves.

My finger hovers over the switch on the flashlight, but whoever is nearby would have already caught glimpses of the beam. Turning it off won't undo that.

I edge forward, flashlight in one hand, lead pipe gripped tightly in the other. I make my way around the curve. The tunnel abruptly ends, emptying into another small storeroom. A dark shape lies crumpled in the middle of the floor: Skylar.

She's on her side. Her hands have been tied behind her back, and she's curled herself into a ball, almost like she's trying to make herself disappear. Her face looks ashen in the beam from the flashlight, and her brown eyes look almost black. A smear of dried blood follows the line from her temple to her cheek, and a strip of fabric has been pulled across her mouth and tied behind her hair.

I crouch next to her and set the pipe and flashlight on the floor. Her wrists and ankles are bound with thick blue twine. The same kind of twine Aunt Jet has been using on the boxes downstairs.

I pull the hunting knife from the backpack and carefully cut through the gag. I snag her hair in the process, and she whimpers.

"Sorry! Sorry!" I hiss as I quickly move to free her hands and feet.

When I lift the flashlight to get a better look at her face, Skylar flinches. She turns her head away, but not before I realize why her eyes look black: her pupils are so huge that they practically swallow up all the brown, like maybe she has a concussion or something.

"Where is he? Is he here?" There's a raw, ragged edge to her voice.

I stand and resheath the knife, then tuck the whole thing—sheath and blade—into the waistband of my jeans at the small of my back.

"Is he here?" Skylar asks again, shivering as I pull her to her feet. Before I can answer, she loses her balance. I try to steady her, but I'm scared and not careful enough and I touch bare skin.

And then I see him. I see who Skylar is most afraid of.

THIRTY-FIVE

"WHERE IS HE?" SKYLAR'S VOICE IS A JAGGED, FRIGHTENED whisper.

Around me, the whole tunnel seems to pulse in time with the pounding in my head. It's not possible. It can't be possible. My stomach heaves and acid rushes up the back of my throat. "Can you walk?"

Skylar shakes her head and then nods. "Maybe."

Maybe is better than nothing. Maybe is definitely better than staying here.

He'll expect us to go back the way I came, back through that cavernous room underneath the mill. Instead, I pull Skylar deeper into the tunnels, trusting we'll be able to find one of the other exits. "Where's Joey?"

"I don't know," she says. She trips, and I tighten my grip on her arm to keep her from falling. "I swear, I haven't seen him since the day you guys found the trailer. No one has. Not his parents or his cousin."

"He didn't leave the bruises on your arm, did he?"

She shakes her head. "I told you: Joey would never hurt anybody."

The brick walls of the tunnel give way to solid earth. "Have you been this way?"

"No."

I guide Skylar to the wall. She leans heavily against it. When I'm sure she can stand on her own, I step away completely. I hand her the flashlight and then pull out my diagrams. This tunnel isn't on any of them.

"Do you have that map of Riley's—the one you took from my room?"

Her brow furrows. "Why would I take anything from your room?"

Of course. Of course it hadn't been Skylar. It's not like the folder would have been hard to find for anyone who had access to Montgomery House and who wanted to snoop through my things.

"Aidan is the one who left the bruises, isn't he?"

She nods. "I thought Joey might be hiding down here. I wanted to tell Chase—I thought maybe he could help me find him—but Aidan said I couldn't trust him. He said I couldn't trust anyone. We argued and he grabbed me." She runs her left hand over her right forearm and then slips her fingers under her sleeve to touch the bruises. "I wanted to tell you, but Aidan said you wouldn't believe me. Between what happened with Riley at the party and what was going on with Joey, he said no one would believe anything I said. And I was scared about what he might do if I did tell."

"And your head?"

She raises her hand to her temple. Surprise flashes across her face, almost as though she hadn't realized she'd been bleeding.

"I came looking for Joey. I didn't know Aidan was here. He followed me and shoved me into the wall. When I woke up, he was tying my wrists." Her eyes well and brim over. "I'm such an idiot."

"You're not. He fooled everyone—you, Chase, me." I try to reconcile the image I saw when I touched Skylar with the boy I kissed in the woods. How could I have stood outside that trailer with him and not have had the slightest clue?

The trailer. He must have staged the whole thing.

I think about the photos of Rachel and those other girls. Had Aidan known Harding's deep, dark secret and stolen the photos from his house, or is Harding somehow a part of this?

"Come on." I step back to Skylar and slip an arm around her. "We can talk about it later. Survival first and then self-flagellation."

The longer we're on the move, the more Skylar's strength seems to return, but our progress is still painfully slow. After what feels like an hour, we make it to another storeroom. My heart leaps and then falls as the beam from my flashlight catches an unbroken expanse of wall and the shattered remains of an old wooden staircase: there's nowhere left to go.

Even though the room is a dead end, someone has been here. Recently. An air mattress piled high with sleeping bags lies on the floor against the far wall. Next to it, a Coleman lantern glows. A handful of wooden crates are scattered around the room.

Just like in the trailer, there are pictures taped to one of the walls. But while there had been hundreds of photos in the trailer, there are only a handful here. Letting go of Skylar, I move closer. All of them are of me. Eight—no, ten—in all. An old family photo, my school picture from the third grade, a snapshot of me and Dad on the porch swing.

There are newer pictures, too. Photos that have been taken since I arrived back in Montgomery Falls. Pictures snapped inside the house. While I slept. While I helped Aunt Jet in the basement. While I curled up in the library. Each photo feels like some sort of violation: a moment in time Aidan stole from me and pinned down for his private amusement.

It doesn't make any sense. None of this makes any sense.

"The one of you sleeping is my favorite."

I whirl. Aidan stands just inside the room.

"I wondered if you would find your way here." He speaks to me, but he glances at Skylar. "You figured it out, but not because Sky told you."

I stare at him, unable to follow his meaning.

"You saw it," he says. "You saw me."

It takes a moment for it to click, for me to fully understand. Skylar didn't have to use Aidan's name. I saw his face when I touched her skin. "How do you know that?"

He crosses the room without answering.

Skylar scrambles back awkwardly.

I know I should follow, but I can't seem to make my legs work. Too late, I realize I left the lead pipe back in that other room, right next to the spot where Aidan had left Skylar bound and gagged.

Aidan closes the distance between us, but he's not looking at me. He's still looking at Skylar, a strange light in his eyes. Before I realize what he's about to do, before I can try to stop him, he grabs my hand. "Tell me what I want."

The things I see are so horrible that everything around me goes black. I think I hear Skylar call my name, once, high and frightened, but the notes are swallowed by the darkness.

THIRTY-SIX

THE FIRST THING I'M AWARE OF IS THE COLD. IT SEEPS through my clothes and into my skin, chilling me all the way through.

Skylar? I try to say her name, but my throat is dry and my tongue feels weird and big. All I can manage is a croak.

Images come back to me, flooding my senses. Instinctively, I curl up, trying to escape. I've seen the desires and fears of hundreds of people, maybe thousands, but I've never seen anything as horrible as the things Aidan wanted when he looked at Skylar.

Things that make the worst horror movie—that make anything Noah could have imagined doing to Riley's killer—look tame.

The images are so strong that just the act of recalling them seems to hit me with physical force. It feels like every muscle in my torso is contracting, like something inside of me is sharp and

365

splintered and digging in. But that's nothing compared to the pain in my head.

I roll onto my side and retch.

Aidan crouches in front of me. I try to scramble away, but he pulls me up to a sitting position. "Drink," he says, lifting a bottle of Coke to my lips. "You'll feel better."

I'm broken and shivering and there's vomit on my shirt, but I could swear that as Aidan looks at me, his eyes fill with the exact same heat they held the night he kissed me. Having him look at me that way now, when I'm like this, scares me almost as badly as what I saw in his head.

Warm liquid splashes down my face and my shirt as I pull away. I glance around. I'm still in the storeroom, still facing photos of myself, but there's no sign of Skylar. "Where is she?"

"Don't worry. I'll head after her in a minute. She won't get far."

"She's your friend." The pain in my head makes it hard to speak. "She's my friend."

"Is that why she left you? Because she's such a great friend?" Aidan stands and then reaches down in a gesture that's almost gentlemanly. I stare at his outstretched hand. How can he think I'd touch him after what just happened? He stays like that for a few heartbeats, giving me plenty of time. When he finally realizes I'm not going to accept his help, disappointment flashes across his face. He leans down. Grabbing me under my arms, he hauls me to my feet.

The gratitude I feel at not having his skin touch mine is so strong that it almost sends me back to my knees.

"I'm beyond friends. And I think you are, too—in your own way." He releases me and steps back. "On some level, you know that. It's why you were drawn to me. Why I knew we'd eventually meet."

"Why would you want to meet me?" I hadn't been anyone to him before I arrived. Nothing. This place, these pictures, his fixation—it doesn't make sense.

Aidan crosses the room and crouches before a wooden crate. When he stands, he's holding a bundle of loose pages in one hand and Riley's old journal in the other. I had been so focused on grabbing the diagrams that I hadn't noticed the book was no longer in the drawer.

"Riley told me about you once. At a party. Not right away. I had to get him pretty drunk, but once I did . . ." Aidan shakes his head. "I had other plans for him that night, but he started talking about that day we hopped the fence by the mill and how he couldn't get the tunnels out of his head. How he had started going down there. All of a sudden, he said, 'I knew a girl who could see secrets.'" He starts to read. "'July thirteenth: Cat touched cashier while buying chips. Black horse surrounded by smoke. July twenty-first: Cat touched Noah on boat. Girl in black dress. August second: Cat touched a girl at the pool . . .'"

As he continues to read, I realize the pages are the ones that had been ripped out of the journal. The charts Riley had kept in an effort to help me figure out the things that were happening to me. The pages I thought he had gotten rid of in an effort to forget I had ever existed.

He hadn't forgotten. He hadn't tried to erase me.

Aidan glances up. "There are dozens. You weren't as scared to touch people back then."

"Yes, I was." It wasn't that I touched more people that summer—as careful as I am, I touch people all the time—it's that I wasn't scared to talk to Riley about what I saw.

Aidan slips the pages back into the journal and closes the book. "Did you know he wrote you letters? Years' worth. All unsent. Actual letters written on paper. All bundled up in the back of his closet."

"You were in Riley's room . . ." I think about the photos in the trailer, the ones taken of me in my bedroom. They were shot from straight on, not from down in the yard. That was what had bothered me about the photo Jensen had shown me of Rachel. The angle was different. "You took photos of me from Riley's room. His mother said he came home at night. She said she heard him, that he slept in his bed. That was you."

"I wanted to be close to him. I wanted to understand him. It's the same reason I keep coming back here."

"Did you kill him?"

Aidan shrugs. "I told him I would help map the tunnels. The staircase collapsed under his weight, and he fell." As he talks, a light seems to fill his eyes. "He was so, so afraid. I didn't know watching someone's fear could be like that. Horror movies try to make you feel it—that rush when someone on the screen is terrified—but it's not the same thing. It's not even close."

Everything in my chest constricts.

He's never coming home.

I have to swallow twice before I can talk, and when I do, my voice shakes. "The fall killed him?"

Aidan shrugs again. "Eventually."

"You let him die." I stare at Aidan, horrified, as it sinks in. "How long?" My voice fills the space. It's shaking. I'm shaking. "How long did it take? How long did you leave him down here, dying?"

Aidan doesn't answer. He just stares at me, the glow from the lantern emphasizing that light in his gray eyes.

"You could have saved him. Everyone was looking for him, and you knew where he was the whole time." I scan the room, and my gaze lands on the pile of sleeping bags. Bile rushes up the back of my throat. Without thinking, I stumble forward. I'm terrified of what I'll find underneath, but I rip the fabric back.

Nothing. There's nothing there.

"He's not here, Cat."

"Where is he?" I picture Riley in the tunnels. Alone and dying. I picture his body lying abandoned at some dead end, like garbage. I picture all of that, and a wave of darkness rises up inside of me. I've been so worried about what Noah would do if we found the person who hurt Riley, but it never occurred to me that I would be just as dangerous. I throw myself forward, desperate to tear at Aidan, desperate to hurt him even if I hurt myself in the process.

But he deflects me easily. He shoves me back, sending me crashing into the wall of photos.

I manage to keep my feet. He moves a little to the left, positioning himself between me and the only way out as I stand there, panting.

"What about Rachel?"

"What about her?"

"It was you, right? You hurt her."

"Rachel was an opportunity. I was bored. I took your aunt's car out. I saw her walking along the side of the road. It was fate."

Aunt Jet's car. A car I've been in half a dozen times since the night Rachel disappeared. "That's all it was? A coincidence? Paul Harding didn't help you pick her?"

"You think I was working with Paul Harding?" Aidan bursts out laughing, a short bark of a sound with no humor behind it. It's indignant. Insulted. "Joey wasn't the only one he gave private lessons to. He thought I was a kindred spirit. After a while, he showed me his collection. Things he knew Joey wouldn't understand. He even let me take some of the photos home. He told me it would be our little secret."

Aidan lets out a small, derisive sound. "Rachel really was just an opportunity," he continues. "The fact that she was one of the girls Harding watched, the idea that her murder might make him sweat, that was just a bonus."

"But you didn't kill her." I try to keep the hope from my voice. If he couldn't bring himself to kill Rachel, maybe Skylar really did get away. Maybe we'll be okay.

"Rachel was tougher than I thought she'd be. I got distracted, and she made it to the river."

"And Riley's medal? Why give her that?"

"Like I said, she was tougher than I thought. I was wearing it around my neck—I wore it sometimes, to help me remember—and

370

she grabbed it. It was worth it, though, seeing the effect it had on you."

I think about the morning in the kitchen, after Aidan had eavesdropped on my conversation with Jensen. There had to have been some sign that I had missed; nobody could be that good of an actor. "And Joey? Did you kill him?"

"Don't pretend to care about Joey. You don't even like him."

"Fine. What about me? Are you going to kill me?"

Shock flashes across his face. It looks genuine, but so many things since I've met him have seemed real. "Kill you?" There's a slightly strangled, almost wounded tone to his voice. "Don't you understand?"

Before I can even think of how to reply, he rushes on. "That night at the party, when I grabbed your hand, what did you see? What did you see when we kissed? It couldn't have upset you, whatever it was. You didn't pull away. Do you really not understand how perfect you are? Riley thought you saw secrets, but the truth is so much better." He begins to pace, his steps carrying him from one side of the room to the other. "I've read everything Riley wrote about you, Cat, and I've watched you every day since you came back. You see want and fear."

As he paces, I slowly begin to inch toward the door. "Wants are easy," he says. "Anyone can guess what someone wants. But fear? Knowing what someone is afraid of? That's unlocking a door and stepping through. Imagine what you could do to someone if you knew their deepest fear. Imagine what we could do, together."

He stops suddenly and snaps his fingers. The noise seems

impossibly loud. I flinch, and as I do, something scrapes against my back. The hilt of the hunting knife. I fight to keep my face blank.

"Do you remember what I told you about your father?" he asks.

I shake my head. I can barely keep up with his madness, let alone guess where he's going to go next. All I want is for him to move just a little farther from the door. To turn his back or become distracted.

"I told you that writers get to play God. That they can manipulate reality. That's what I do. I watched Riley Fraser's life drain away. For weeks afterward, I watched the whole town search for him. It was like being a god. Standing in that trailer with you, watching as you took it all in—do you have any idea how incredible that felt? You weren't even supposed to be the one who found it, but then we ended up in the woods, and I realized it was meant to be you all along."

"Lucky me." The words slip out.

He ignores them. "But do you know what made me start to realize how much power I really have?"

"Oprah?"

The corner of his mouth quirks up in an achingly familiar smile. For a second, he looks like the boy who kissed me, the boy who walked me home after a movie night with his friends. But then the moment's gone. "It was when they searched the grounds, looking for Riley," he says. "I was in the mill. They came so close. Only one room away. And then Jensen called them back. That's when I suspected. Later, when you asked me to go with you to the hospital, that was when I knew. Rachel looked right at me and

372

nothing happened and I knew I could do anything."

That's why he had been so nervous. Not because he hates hospitals, but because he was scared Rachel would remember what he had done. A shiver crawls down my spine as I think of Rachel in that giant hospital bed, talking to the boy who had put her there.

"When you asked me to go with you," he continues, "it was a test. And I passed. It was proof."

"That you're God?" As scared as I am, I can't keep the sarcasm from my voice.

"I said it's like being a god. Not that I am God. I'm not crazy."

Right. None of this is crazy. "But why take Rachel in the first place? It couldn't have just been because you were bored or because you could or because the idea of messing with Harding was some sort of bonus."

"I wanted to get the feeling back. To see how far I could push it. Watching Riley die unlocked a door. I thought killing Rachel would open it completely."

"Why?" My voice comes out strangled. I don't understand. I don't understand any of this. "If it is a door, why would you ever want to go through it? How would you even know it was there in the first place?"

Aidan crosses the space between us and then brushes the hair back from my forehead. I jerk my head away before his skin can touch mine. "What do you want to hear, Cat? That my parents didn't hug me enough as a child or that they locked me in a small closet to punish me? How a bad man took me down to a dark basement or how I've always been secretly jealous of guys like Riley?"

"Depends. Did any of that actually happen?"

The corner of his mouth quirks up again. "I'm sure all of it happened to someone, somewhere." The smile vanishes as quickly as it appeared. "How about this: I just like it. I liked watching the whole town piss themselves over what happened to Riley. I liked watching Rachel cry and beg. I liked manipulating Skylar."

"And that's what you've been doing to me, too, right? Manipulating me? Creating clues and puzzles for me to solve. Getting off on watching me run around."

"I didn't do it to get off." He considers his words for a moment, then adds, "Well, I didn't do it *just* to get off." He inches forward, pressing into what little personal space I have left, forcing me to back up. "I did it to help you."

"Help me?" My shoulder blades hit the wall. "How could anything you've done possibly help me?"

"Skylar told me what you said to her that day in the drugstore: that you wanted to fight monsters. That you didn't want to be afraid. I knew that if I could give you a monster to fight—that if you could prove to yourself how strong you could be—you'd accept the truth."

"And what truth is that?"

He presses his body against mine and whispers in my ear. "That there are no monsters. There is no right and wrong. There are rules, and there are people who break them. You shatter so many rules just by existing. I'm not scared of that. I understand it. I understand you in ways no one else ever will. I'm the only one who will never be afraid of the things you can do."

A small, sad look flashes across his face. "It wasn't supposed to go quite like this. I wanted you to find Joey. I've been keeping him in the mill for days, waiting for the perfect chance to bring you here. I wanted you to think he killed Riley. I wanted to see what you would do—what you would ask me to do. But while I was waiting for you, I saw Skylar go down into the tunnels. I honestly didn't think she was brave enough to do that."

"Why not just steer me away from her? You could have. You didn't have to let me pick which tunnels we followed."

"I thought it was like you finding the trailer. Fate." He leans closer. His breath is hot against my skin. For a horrible moment, I think he's going to try to kiss me, but then he pulls back so he can slide his phone from his pocket. "Let me show you something," he says, unlocking the screen. "Let me show you how much I understand."

For a split second, his attention is diverted, and in that second, I reach behind my back. "You don't understand anything." And with that, I push my arm up and forward; I push the knife into Aidan.

THIRTY-SEVEN

SLIDING A KNIFE INTO A PERSON IS NOT LIKE SLIDING A KNIFE INTO anything else. Even if you catch them by surprise, their body resists.

Aidan's eyes go wide as I throw my weight behind the hilt of the blade. I lose my balance, and we both crash to the ground. I grab his phone, still unlocked, and scramble to my feet. I think he says my name, but it's difficult to hear over the pounding of my pulse.

Using the phone to light my way, I run. Through the door. Down the tunnel. My lungs burn and my legs shake, but I keep moving. I reach the storeroom where I first found Skylar; it's empty, recognizable only by the pieces of blue twine on the ground.

Skylar.

She has to be okay.

How long was I out? How far could she have gotten? I shine the light from the phone around the room, looking for the lead pipe. There's no sign of it. Frantically, I try to call 911, but there's no service.

"Cat!"

Aidan's voice echoes down the tunnel and propels me forward.

I don't know how long I run.

I try to keep track of the twists and turns, but the tunnels are all too similar. Soon, I have no idea where I am. Mice and rats scatter at my approach, but there's no sign of Skylar. It gets harder and harder to breathe, like the air is running out.

Voices ricochet through my head.

There are no monsters. There is no right and wrong.

Everyone shows different sides of themselves to different people at different times.

You're okay.

He doesn't mean it—he just doesn't understand. He can't.

You didn't do it because you had to. You did it because you could.

You use me every bit as much as I use you. Maybe more.

The voices overlap and then drown each other out until only two remain.

If you were a character in a story, what kind of story would you want it to be?

The kind where the girl slays dragons and fights monsters, I guess.

Why?

And suddenly, in that twisting maze of tunnels and dead ends, I find myself.

When I finally stumble into the cavernous room beneath the mill, Aidan is waiting.

"I'm disappointed, Cat." He walks toward me, wincing with each step. The beam from the flashlight in his hand bounces, making the shadows dance around us. I had been aiming for his stomach, but the patch of blood on his shirt is high and too far to the right. I had hurt him; just not enough to stop him.

I don't back up. I don't try to get away. What would be the point? Even bleeding, he's probably faster—he'd have to be faster to have headed me off—and he knows the tunnels. Besides, I'm tired of running. I ran away from Riley all those years ago. I ran from New York, in a way. I even ran from Noah.

Surprise fills Aidan's eyes when I don't run. Surprise and excitement.

"You really did all of that?" I ask. "You didn't make any of it up?"

"What?"

"Everything you said. You watched Riley die. You took Rachel. You framed Joey."

"I told you I did: I wasn't lying."

I resist the urge to reach for my pocket, to touch the stolen phone tucked inside to make sure it's still recording. Maybe no one will ever find the phone—maybe no one will ever find me—but at least I tried.

Slowly, like I'm some kind of animal he's worried about scaring off, Aidan reaches for me.

He told me that fear is a doorway. If that's true, maybe it can go both ways. So many of the things I see lurk under the surface: people aren't always consciously aware of them. But what if I could make him see what I see? What if, instead of fear pouring through the door into me, I pushed it back into him?

I know what Aidan wants. He wants me to help him hurt other people. He wants to be a god. But I don't know what he fears.

I take his hands in mine, and I have just a second to register the fact that he smiles. That crooked grin I thought I knew. Desire comes roaring toward me, but I somehow push it back. I try to find his most secret fear, the fear he can barely acknowledge to himself. I picture dark black threads and reach for them. Aidan's palms are tacky with blood. It sticks to me as he squeezes my hands, as I follow the threads to their source.

I don't know how I do it, but I weave the strands of his fear together and pull them to the surface. I pull them to the surface, and then I thrust them back in. Aidan's eyes go wide as he sees what I see: how utterly powerless he is compared to the world around us. How small and forgettable and inconsequential. Not a god, but an insect.

He drops the flashlight.

Pain explodes in my head. I lose my grip on Aidan's hands, and I have just a second to register the sight of him crumpling to the ground before I collapse in on myself.

The last thing I see as the shadows in the room rise up and close in is Skylar, a lead pipe in her hands, her feet planted wide. A tiny avenging angel in the dark.

THIRTY-EIGHT

FOR MONTHS AFTER THE DAY RILEY FRASER DISAPPEARED—A cold Saturday in March that seemed ordinary in every other way—people thought he would come back. More than 900 miles away, I didn't even know he was missing.

Now, of course, it's different.

People know Riley didn't get lost in the woods.

Or run away.

And while almost everyone in Montgomery Falls has gone back to believing Riley's life was every bit as charmed as it seemed from the outside, I know the truth is more complicated.

I park Aunt Jet's car on the edge of the dirt lane that winds through Hillcrest Cemetery and climb out. You can see everything from up here. The town, the river, the woods. Even the textile mill—a small, dark smudge in the distance like a constant reminder.

A breeze curls over the hill and lifts the ends of my hair but doesn't do much to ease the early August heat. I roll my sleeves up as I walk; it doesn't really help. Thankfully, it doesn't take long to find the stone. It's only been a week, after all, and the ground around it is still covered with flowers.

I pull a small silver disc from my pocket. A Saint Anthony medal. Not the one Riley found all those summers ago—that one is still wrapped in plastic in the basement of the Montgomery Falls Police Department. No, this one is new and unburdened. No initials on the back. No history. No guilt. Just a patron saint of lost things for a boy who was obsessed with lost things and became lost himself.

"Hey," I whisper, crouching down. Nothing whispers back. I don't believe Riley is really listening—if there is an afterlife, I hope he has better things to do than hang around this place—but there's still something comforting in the idea of talking to him. Even if he's not really here. Even if the person I imagine seems so different than the one everyone—the minister, his teachers, his teammates—spoke of at the funeral.

Carefully, I move a few of the flowers aside and then use the edge of the medal to dig a shallow hole. I drop the disc inside and then cover it up. "I'll come back," I say as I press the dirt back into place. "I promise."

There's something I never told Noah. Something I haven't even really let myself think about.

Last January, a few days after the start of a new year, Riley sent me a text.

Just two words: *You there?*

It had been five years, but I still recognized his number. Seeing it on my screen had made things in my chest tighten while my stomach dropped.

I didn't reply.

Because he had hurt me and I didn't want to get hurt again. Because I was angry, even after all that time. Because anger was better than guilt, and I felt so, so guilty whenever I let myself think about that day and how he had hit the ground. Because, on some level, I felt like I really was a monster.

It never occurred to me that Riley might have felt just as guilty about that day.

Now, I wonder if maybe things would have turned out differently, somehow, if I had tried to talk to him instead of running away. If I had replied to his text when I had the chance.

I know it's an impossible question without an answer, but I can't help thinking about it.

I haven't really been able to stop thinking about it since my third or fourth day in the hospital when Dad gave me a new phone. "No rules," he said.

That day, when I logged into Instagram, I saw a message from Lacey. Like the text from Riley, it contained only two words. *I'm sorry.* It had been sent three days after I left for Montgomery Falls.

I straighten and brush my palms against my jeans. As I turn, I spot a familiar figure cresting the hill.

"Your aunt said I could find you here," Noah says as he reaches me. He looks better than he did at the funeral—less tired, less ragged—but there are still shadows under his eyes, and his clothes fit loosely, as though he's lost weight. "You're still leaving today?"

I nod. It's the first time we've spoken in weeks, and it's a little hard to find my voice. "Yeah. I figured I would come by. See him without all the people around, you know?"

We stand here, awkwardly, Noah on one side, me on the other. Riley dividing us or bridging us, depending on how you look at it. Noah hasn't answered a single one of my calls or texts since I got out of the hospital. He must have gotten the messages, though, if he knows I'm leaving today.

I guess I can't blame him for not wanting to talk to me sooner. What had happened with Riley that day on the porch was something I couldn't help. It was an accident. But with Noah . . .

He wasn't wrong when he said I didn't have the right to go looking into people's heads. It's one of the reasons I want to see Lacey when I get back to New York. She isn't the only one who's sorry.

"How's your mom?" I ask finally, because one of us has to say something.

"Better." He swallows and looks away. "I think the funeral—I think actually knowing—helped."

"Good."

"You're not going to tell me I was wrong? All that time I spent convinced she couldn't handle the truth . . ." He turns his gaze back to mine.

If Noah is looking for someone to make him feel guilty, he's come to the wrong person. I know he did the best for his mom that he could. I don't see how anyone could doubt that. "I think it's hard to know just what's going on in someone's head or what they'll do."

"Except for you."

I shake my head. "It's not that much easier for me."

He doesn't seem to know what to say to that. "Your dad's already gone?"

"Yeah. He only stayed a couple of weeks. I wanted to wait until . . . well, you know." I nudge one of the wreaths with the edge of my sneaker and accidentally send it toppling over.

Noah bends down to right it. When he straightens, his cheeks are red. "I shouldn't have pushed you away that night at the hospital. You were right: I was a hypocrite."

I feel my own face flush. "Yeah, you were. But you were right, too: I shouldn't have done what I did."

My phone vibrates in my pocket. I pull it out. A text from Aunt Jet reminding me that I have to be at the station in an hour. "I have to go."

"Can I walk you to your car?" He sounds uncertain, like I might say no, like he's not the one who's been avoiding me for the past month.

Confused and a little hesitant, I nod.

I remember only bits and pieces of what happened after Skylar hit Aidan. I remember Skylar wrapping her arm around me as we made our way out of the tunnels. I remember trying to push her away, trying to warn her not to touch my skin as she told me over and over that it was okay. I remember her asking me to forgive her, telling me that she hadn't wanted to leave me behind, but that she thought maybe she could get help while Aidan was distracted. I remember the feeling of fresh air on my face as we made it to the surface. I remember sirens. Far away and then closer and then red and blue light.

Even those few memories, though, are fragmented and fuzzy around the edges.

The one crystal clear memory I have is of Noah.

Noah shoving one of the police officers who tried to hold him back, fighting to get to me. Shouting when they wouldn't let him ride in the ambulance.

I found out later, from other people, that he had followed the sirens to the mill. That he had been out, looking for me, from the moment Aunt Jet called and told him I was missing.

According to Jet, he had visited me twice in the hospital—I was just too out of it to remember.

Ever since, though, he's ignored me completely. It doesn't make any sense.

As we walk down the lane, I notice a flash of blue near the gates: Riley's BMW.

"This is a step up from your aunt's last car," Noah observes as we reach Jet's new Civic.

"Yeah. She finally discovered the joy of working air-conditioning and power windows. Her world may never be the same." Dad actually helped with the down payment. His meetings in California went well. Really, really well. Helping Aunt Jet with the car is a start, but it's not enough, and I'm going to make sure Dad knows that.

I pull open the driver-side door, but I can't seem to make myself get in. Instead, screwing up my courage, I turn. "Why have you been dodging me?"

"Dodging?"

"The phone calls. The texts. I get you not wanting to talk to me after what I did, but then why visit me in the hospital?"

For a handful of seconds, he just stares at me, and then, slowly, he says, "You think I've been avoiding you because I'm *mad* at you?"

"Well, yeah. Haven't you?"

"No." He runs a hand over the back of his neck, roughly. "Cat, it's my fault. Everything that happened to you. If I hadn't been so hard on you, if I hadn't gotten you involved in the first place, if—"

"Noah, Aidan literally lived twenty feet from my bedroom door. You did not put me on his radar. If it hadn't been for what happened in the tunnels, who knows how many other people he might have hurt?" My eyes start to water, but it's just the too-bright, noonday sun. It's just the sun, and my voice definitely doesn't shake a little around the edges as I say, "So—just to make sure we are both on the same page—you don't, actually, hate me?"

"How could you think that?"

"Why wouldn't I think that?" Seriously. Who in my position wouldn't come to that conclusion?

My phone vibrates again. I don't need to check to know it's another text from Aunt Jet. I still have to swing by Montgomery House, and I need extra time at the station to get my ticket. I hate leaving things like this, but it's not my fault Noah's spent the past few weeks avoiding me out of some weird, misplaced guilt, and I have to go. I tug my sleeves down. First one and then the other. Tentatively, giving him plenty of time to move away, I step forward and hug him. I'm careful not to touch skin or hug too tightly. I half expect Noah to stiffen or pull away, but he doesn't. He lets out a deep, deep breath, and then, before I can even guess at what he's about to do, he presses his lips to my forehead.

And I see myself. Just me.

"Don't go," he says.

But I have to. "I'll come back," I promise.

I realized, weeks ago, that I have plenty of reasons to come back to Montgomery Falls, but I think maybe—just maybe—Noah's given me one more.

"Are you sure about this? We can ask them to refund the ticket, and I can drive you down to Saint John in a few days. Flying would be so much faster and easier." Aunt Jet twists a thin, silver bangle around her wrist as we wait in line for the bus.

I switch my duffel bag from one hand to the other in order to adjust the strap of my backpack. "I like the idea of having the time to think."

In an ideal world, I'd figure out how to talk to my dad. Really, really talk to him. About why my head hurts sometimes and how he was wrong to keep me from Aunt Jet for all those years just because she wanted me to know the truth about who and what I am. About how, maybe, what happened with Riley wasn't the only reason I felt like I had to hide parts of myself away. But it's not an ideal world, and I have a feeling that's not a conversation my father is capable of having. Not right now, anyway.

I can, however, try to figure out how to make sure he doesn't try to keep me away again and how to get him to help Aunt Jet save Montgomery House—assuming that's what she decides she wants.

And then there's Lacey. I need to figure out how to talk to

her about what I saw the night I touched her and how to tell her that she was right: I had used her just as much as she'd used me. Spending more time with Skylar has helped me realize how much I kept Lacey at a distance.

None of that cancels out what happened after the party—I'm not sure anything will ever cancel that out—but I have to own up to it. Maybe what happened is too big to be fixed, but I have to try. Just like I should have tried with Riley. I used to think that once things broke, you couldn't put them back together, that the cracks would always be present and there was no point in trying. I think I'm starting to realize, though, that if all you ever do is walk away, you end up with nothing in the end.

Aunt Jet still looks doubtful.

"Really," I say, "the bus is fine."

The skepticism on her face remains unchanged, but she stops trying to talk me out of it. "You have everything?"

I hand my duffel bag over to the driver, who tosses it into the luggage bin. "Everything."

"And you'll call me when you get home?"

"As soon as I get in."

Jet hugs me, carefully, and then watches as I board the bus and find a seat. I wave to her through the window, and she waves back before turning away and heading to the car.

I settle more deeply into my seat, trying to get comfortable. More than 900 miles. Lots and lots of time to think.

I pull my journal out of my backpack. Dad had insisted I see a counselor before I had even left the hospital; it was like he was worried I'd end up irrevocably broken if I didn't talk to someone with a degree on the wall within a week of being carried away from those tunnels. It was one of the few things upon which he and Aunt Jet had agreed.

When the counselor first suggested I keep a journal, I'd balked, but then I asked Jet if I could have one of the blank, leather-bound books from the old desk downstairs.

I've caught her sneaking looks at it over the last few weeks: this black book with the yellowed pages that smells permanently like forgotten things. The sight of it seems to make her uncomfortable. Maybe it's the fact that the police found three identical journals in Aidan's room. Three journals, all taken from the basement, the first entry dated a month after he moved into Montgomery House.

I don't know what's in them—but there are rumors. Fantasies about the things Aidan wanted to do. The ways he wanted other people to hurt. Plans for attacks he hadn't carried out. Photographs and sketches.

Reporters have dubbed him the "Heartthrob Killer." Because he's over eighteen, there's no media ban on his name. Because he's over eighteen, he'll be tried as an adult.

He's not in Montgomery Falls. There's a psychiatric hospital up on the north shore—three or four hours away, depending on which roads you take—where they send people like him for evaluation before trial. He's asked to see me, a request passed from his lawyer to Aunt Jet.

Some dark part of me wants to see him, to try to understand things that can't possibly be understood. To try to figure out how much of the Aidan I thought I knew was ever really there. I keep thinking about what he did to Joey. About how he had lured Joey to the mill by tipping him off about the trailer and the police and then locked him in one of the old offices. About how Joey had been found injured and dehydrated, but otherwise unharmed.

I think a lot about the fact that he didn't kill Joey and how he let me find Skylar. Probably more than is healthy. Definitely more than I should.

Despite the things he told me, part of me wants to believe he didn't kill Joey because he couldn't bring himself to hurt his friend or because he wanted someone to stop him. That there is some spark of humanity or loyalty in him.

I'm probably just kidding myself. After all, Riley had been his friend, too, and Aidan had watched him die.

It's strange, me wanting to write in an identical book. I don't need worried looks from Aunt Jet to know this.

Aidan claimed he understood me in a way no one else ever could. That he alone would never be scared of the things I can do.

Maybe the journal is my one small way of proving him wrong. A reminder that some lines should never be crossed. I slip my makeshift bookmark out from between the pages. It's a Polaroid of Riley and me—one we took after finding an old camera in the basement. My hair is a red, frizzy cloud, and Riley's knees are scraped and bruised. I'm smiling. He's not. He's not even looking at the camera. He's staring off to the side, at something I can't see.

I wish I knew what he was thinking in that moment. I wish I could read all of those letters he supposedly wrote—letters Aidan claimed exist but that no one has been able to find.

Someone stops next to my seat. The two spots across the aisle are both free, but they flop down beside me. "So how long is it to New York, anyway?"

I look up and stare. "What are you doing here?"

Skylar shrugs, like her being here is no big deal, like she can always just be found riding around on random buses to foreign countries. "Thought you could use the company."

Despite the heat, she's wearing a pair of big, black boots over black-and-white-striped tights. She kicks the seat in front of her.

"Skylar—you can't come with me. There's no way they'll let you into the US."

"I know *that*. Little credit, please." She nods toward the window. "I'll ride with you to the border. Joey and Chase are going to follow and drive me back."

Sure enough, in the corner of the parking lot, Chase and Joey sit in Mrs. Walker's Malibu. Chase is gesturing wildly, and Joey is shaking his head.

"What are they arguing about?"

"Who will play them in the inevitable made-for-TV movie once all of this is over. Chase wants you to text your casting choices." Her expression becomes serious. "We didn't think you should go on your own. Chase wanted to drive you to New York—until he realized his passport was expired and his folks would kill him."

Something in my chest feels inexplicably tight. "You guys don't have to do this."

"Please. You're one of us. We stick together."

I grin. A big, ridiculous grin that makes my cheeks hurt.

What I had said to Skylar all those weeks ago was true: I want to be the kind of person who fights monsters and slays dragons. I want to be the kind of person who doesn't run away. But maybe it's easier if I don't try to do it on my own. If I let people in.

The way I let Riley in all those summers ago before I allowed one horrible day to undo all the good. The way I've been scared to really let anyone in since.

Montgomery Falls will always be the place where I lost Riley. But it's also the place where I found Skylar and Chase and even Joey. It's the place where I found Noah.

It's where I learned to fight monsters.

ACKNOWLEDGMENTS

Thank you to my amazing and talented agent, Emmanuelle Morgen of Stonesong. Emmanuelle, you were endlessly supportive and patient, and this book is so, so much stronger because of your feedback. On top of all that, you found it the perfect home. You are a gem and a marvel.

I cannot imagine this book without my fabulous editor, Catherine Wallace. Catherine, your insight and guidance took this book to the next level. You always seemed to know just how to coax me when I was subconsciously holding back and you made edits a joy. Thank you!

The team at HarperCollins is absolutely terrific, including Kathryn Silsand, Cindy Nixon, Christine Corcoran Cox, Lisa Lester Kelly, Chris Kwon, Meghan Pettit, Shannon Cox, and Mitchell Thorpe. Thanks, also, to the team at HarperCollins*Canada* who always take such good care of my books north of the border.

Thanks, also, to Whitney Lee of the Fielding Agency, who so

tirelessly helps my books reach countries I hope to someday visit.

Sanaa Ali-Virani read an early draft of this manuscript and her feedback was invaluable. Jodi Meadows patiently listened to early pitches and helped when I was torn between projects; as always, I am deeply grateful for her kindness. Krystal answered my questions about film without once pointing out that I really should have paid more attention in photography class—any mistakes in the subject are mine alone.

Much appreciation to the Department of English at UNB Fredericton for being incredibly supportive.

A special thank you to booksellers and librarians and to readers and bloggers. Thanks, also, to the literary festivals who have been kind enough to host me over the years.

Finally, a heartfelt thank-you to my friends and family, particularly my parents and sister who have always been unfailingly supportive.